I0710142

THE TRUTH OF A KALEIDOSCOPE MIND

PATRICK BRYCE WRIGHT

WICKED INK

PUBLISHING

Published by Wicked Ink Publishing Ltd.
www.wickedinkpublishing.com

Cover and book design © 2024 by Wicked Ink Publishing Ltd.
Editors: Raymond Griffiths & Adam Bamford

First Edition: October 2024
Printed in Canada

The National Library of Canada Cataloging -in-Publication Data is available upon request.

ISBN 978-1-998278-06-0 (paperback)
ISBN 978-1-998278-07-7 (ebook)

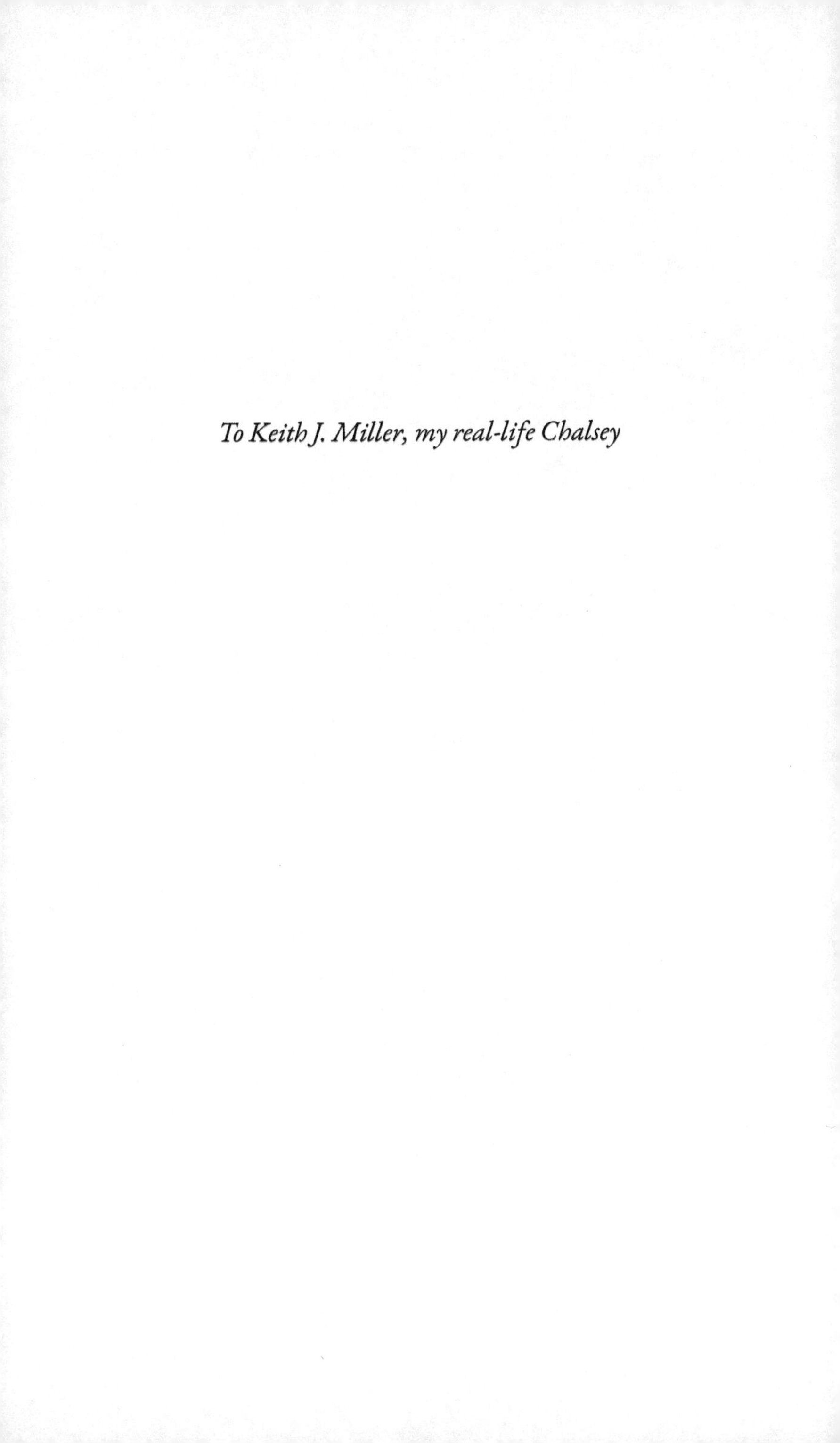

To Keith J. Miller, my real-life Chalsey

Content Warning

This novel explores the topic of adults facing childhood trauma and discusses emotional, physical, sexual, spiritual, and ritual trauma as well as previous suicide attempts. Reader discretion is advised.

THE TRUTH OF A KALEIDOSCOPE MIND

Can one man reconcile his past,
or will the shadows consume him?

Chapter 1

THE FOOL O

Michael Fredrick Anderson's car tires crunched on the gravel as he pulled into his mother's driveway. Or, rather, this red brick house and its gravel driveway had belonged to his mother. Fredrick stopped his white Toyota Camry under a towering silver maple tree and stared through his bug-splattered windshield at the Craftsman house, caught in time in the 1950s, with its porch swing, white porch columns, and old rusted TV antennae alongside a gray satellite dish.

Beside him in the passenger seat, his best friend Chalsey Montgomery leaned forward and gazed through the windshield as well. "It'll be strange to walk in and not be greeted by your mom."

Fredrick snorted. "If you weren't helping me, I'd kill myself rather than face this." He knew he shouldn't make such dark jokes, given his history, but he was in a dark mood. He turned off his car and lumbered out, his body tensing more with each step. Around him the summer blasted him with cheer, as if to slay him with toxic positivity: the golden morning sun, the circling songs of a mockingbird, and an azure sky with puffy white clouds painted onto the horizon. The grass glowed in the sunlight, and his mother's snowball bushes bloomed with stunning whiteness at each end of the porch.

Fredrick escaped all the cheer into his mother's silent living room. The unnatural stillness and lack of human energy signaled to him that his mother was, indeed, dead. Houses and other buildings had a certain tranquility, an energetic motionlessness, that only occurred when no one was present. Fredrick had entered and shattered it. Standing in the barrenness where his mother had dwelled, he wrongly filled it with his own fluctuating energy. This was not the sobbing grief of movies or TV shows, but a deep, throbbing confusion, a hurt like a lost child wandering through an amusement park long after their balloon has flown away into the sky and their ice cream has melted on their hand, searching for a parent who would never materialize.

A stack of *Southern Living* magazines teetered on the end table by the beige rocker-recliner. Even to the end, his mother had paid for a subscription and had given him her magazines once she had read them, an odd book club sentiment he had given up trying to fend off. An embarrassed ache swelled in his chest. *That stack of magazines had been intended for me.* A teal windbreaker lay over the back of the crimson sofa, and his mother's lavender purse sat on the sofa cushion. The hardwood floors shone in the sunlight pouring through the windows, revealing a stray gray hair. A live person's marks covered the room, but these items no longer had an owner. Death was the ultimate, and final, abandonment.

A sixteen-pound, orange, tabby cat scrambled out of the kitchen, claws clicking on the floor as he raced around the hard rock maple furniture populating the dining room and living room, meowing and demanding food.

"You need to lose seven pounds before I try to re-home

you." Fredrick sighed as he trudged through the house, wondering why his mother had overfed every cat she'd owned. She'd killed their first cat with diabetes and complained when her newest cat, Largo, wouldn't eat all the food she plied him with. Then Largo had gotten diabetes as well.

I've tried five brands of cat food, she'd griped. *But he still only eats half of it.*

It was easier to be angry with her than to feel any other emotion, even now. *Eat, eat, eat,* he retorted. No fight could break their relationship more than her death had. *Eat and never stop eating because you only prove you love me if you eat it all.* Fredrick's family had been a Clean Your Plate type. Everyone had been medically obese, and his mother had verbally attacked him for losing down to a healthy weight.

Chalsey trailed Fredrick and the cat into the kitchen. Towering oak cabinets reached the ceiling. White tile and white appliances offset the otherwise claustrophobic effect created by the cabinets and island. She stood at the entrance to the cellar. Even from the stairs, they could see the walls lined with boxes.

Fredrick opened cabinets until he found where his mom had kept the dry cat food. There was no container. The twenty-pound bag of food was snipped open at the top, a plastic measuring cup inside. He swallowed a groan. *Of course.* The scent of feline vitamins wafted from the opened cat food. He picked up the scoop, grimacing at the orange-brown dusting of kibble crumbs crusted to the white plastic.

"All right." He eyed Largo. "I am not feeding you an entire cup of this." He measured a quarter cup, shut the cabinet, and walked to the cat food dish at the end of the kitchen island on the floor.

"Where do you want to start?" Chalsey asked.

Fredrick paused instead of doling the scoop of food into Largo's dish and received an impatient meow for his negligence. He glanced into the cellar, uneasiness tightening his lungs. His memory of his childhood was patchy, but he recalled fearing the cellar even as a toddler.

"Might as well go through the boxes first. After all, I can't auction off stuff hiding in boxes. Also, I hate the cellar, so let's get it out of the way." He dumped the food into the dish and hated the sound of the kibbles raining down. It was like he could hear the diabetes-causing calories.

"Sure." Chalsey marched down the stairs, all confidence.

In most ways, she was the complete opposite of Fredrick: short to his tall, blonde to his brunette, bohemian to his khaki-bland. She'd gone to college in Washington state, graduating from the famous hippie but superior Evergreen State College. She'd left Kentucky as a pimple-faced, anxious teen whom boys ignored and returned radiating joy, a virtual goddess in flowing gypsy skirts, prairie shirts, and golden ringlets cascading down her back.

Fredrick had lived his entire life in Kentucky, gone to college there, and believed he'd die there, too. His too-thin, somber self moved through its days in polo or Oxford shirts and nondescript slacks, a history professor whose fire only showed when discussing slavery and human trafficking. "You're the sun, I'm the new moon," he muttered.

Chalsey had already disappeared around the corner, but she leaned backward, showing her heart-shaped face. "What?"

"Nothing." Fredrick set the measuring cup in the sink and followed her down the gray concrete stairs. He wished Chalsey's confidence could bleed into his veins like a blood transfusion of life force. *I want a new life. I want to feel strong, not descend into some mid-life crisis.*

Sunlight half-penetrated the tiny windows, leaving the cellar dim, and he yanked the chain to switch on the bare bulb overhead. A mix of cardboard boxes and plastic tubs greeted him. He spied the Christmas tree box and a stack of red and green tubs he knew held Christmas decorations. His mom had been a champion decorator, with three Christmas trees out every year so covered in gorgeous ornaments that the trees disappeared under a coating of glamor. Sleighs, reindeer, Santa figurines, angels, and teddy bears in winter clothes had congregated on every flat surface and in every corner.

In retrospect, Fredrick had seen the decline in her. She had decorated less each year for Christmas in the final five years of her life. *Last Christmas, she only had one tree out. I should have known something was wrong.*

Chalsey pointed to the corner where a dollhouse sat on the shelf along with a collection of flower-printed boxes. "Don't tell me these are all your old toys."

Fredrick's deep sigh seemed to expel his soul. He could picture the dolls, puffy stickers, and unicorns. A pink nuclear bomb could have exploded inside those boxes. "Gotta be. Figures Mom would make even the boxes girly. I thought she would disinherit me when I told her I'm a man." He shuffled over to the shelves, his sneakers squeaking. Chalsey had been his best friend in high school, while he'd still been technically intersex but medically ruled to be female. Chalsey had missed his mother's atomic explosion when he'd had gender-affirming surgery in college.

Or had it been gender-affirming?

"Despite Mom's Herculean efforts, sometimes I feel like I have no gender." Fredrick jerked the lid off a smaller box and discovered blue and red ribbons from Field Day in elementary school and a small gymnastics trophy, its brass discolored and spotted. With them was a flower-print diary, the word *diary* embossed in gold on the front.

"I didn't throw this away?" Fredrick pulled the diary out of the box and considered its tiny fake gold lock. "I bet you can't even read my handwriting. It was so bad in elementary school."

"Mine, too." Chalsey pulled the lid off another box, revealing a framed high school graduation picture: Fredrick with long ebony hair, makeup, and a girl's class ring. "It's hard to remember you looking this way."

Fredrick wrinkled his nose. "It's hard to see those pictures. I always felt so awkward as a girl." He fished through the trophy box, looking for the keys to the diary. "I might have to break this lock."

"You want to read it?" Chalsey put the lid back on her box and opened another, revealing three Barbie dolls and a rainbow-colored mass of Barbie clothes and shoes. "God, your mom really tried hard to girlify you."

"Every day. All day." Fredrick pulled on the thin piece of cardboard that held the diary shut, and it tore halfway. He yanked harder, and it ripped. Thanks to the force, the diary flew from his hands, and he snatched it back into his grasp by one corner. *My only perk: excellent reflexes.*

Chalsey picked up one Barbie. "What a classic! This is Peaches-n-Cream Barbie. This is probably worth real money."

Fredrick only half-registered her words. The diary had fallen open a third of the way in. "Jesus, my tortured, nasty handwriting. It's as bad as I remember." The letters didn't always stay between the lines, and his handwriting varied wildly, changing from blocky to bubbly or slanted to straight even inside a single sentence.

"Let's see if I have any luck reading it: 'April 5. I had a fight with Angie today.'" He snickered. "Oh, imagine that. I don't even know why we played together. We fought so much." He squinted at his handwriting. "'But I wish I'd stayed at Angie's house. Dad was home alone when I got back. He took me to my room right away.'" Fredrick felt a chill shoot through him. *Why does that scare me so much to read?* "'I always tell him how much it hurts when he touches me. But he won't stop! He never stops.'" The word *never* was in all caps, underlined three times, and took up most of the remaining page.

Fredrick tasted metal in his mouth, and his teeth ached, a feeling all too familiar. He'd been having panic attacks since he was five. His heart thudded, raced, hurt, and he clutched his chest with one hand, his entire body trembling. *That can't— that can't mean what I think it does.*

Chalsey had frozen, the Barbie wearing an apricot ball gown still in her hand. She stared at Fredrick with wide brown eyes, all the blood seeping from her already fair complexion. "'Touches?'"

"That's not—" Fredrick burst into a laugh, sharp and hysterical. "I can't mean—"

Abruptly, savagely, Fredrick began flipping through pages, spot-checking and skimming. Words and phrases jumped out at him: *tried to hide in the closet...couldn't pee for an hour...kept burning, and I cried...screamed at me...the look of victory on his face.*

Fredrick dropped to the concrete floor, sitting on his heels and rocking back and forth. The diary fell from his hands, hitting the floor and snapping shut. Fredrick rocked and rocked, his arms crossed over his chest. "It's not true. It's not true. It's not true."

But I can't remember half my childhood.

But I'm 43 and still can't bring myself to have sex with anyone.

But my therapist said I have all the symptoms and red flags of someone who's experienced sexual assault or abuse.

Chalsey knelt by him and opened her arms. Fredrick accepted the hug but kept rocking, his habitual panic response. She rocked with him.

"It's not fair." *Where did those words come from?* "It's not fair!"

"No, it's not," Chalsey whispered.

Fredrick stopped rocking as cold numbness fell upon him, an ocean's worth of shock, deep and icy and dark. The numbness was his old friend, dogging him through high school and college, flattening his days until all he imagined was a straight, gray road through a gray desert. He welcomed now what he'd hated then, his flying pulse beginning to ease and slow. He stared at the mountains of boxes and tubs around him, wondering what other horrors they would reveal.

But in the back of his mind, shining like a tiny pinprick of light, burned a single hope: *What other truths can I find? My life makes no sense, and I know it.*

Michael Fredrick Anderson, born Martha Fredrick Anderson, felt himself die on the cold cement floor and hoped his soul could claw its way back to life.

Row, row, row your boat, gently down the stream. Merrily, merrily, merrily, merrily, life is but a dream.

Fredrick sat at his mom's tiny, two-person kitchen table by the back door and stared out the window, his brain flinging childhood songs, bits of fairytales, and clips of memories at him. Chalsey had ushered him upstairs to the table and now rummaged through his mother's cabinets for herbs or herbal tea. She was a white witch, a Wiccan, a woman who walked the path of the Goddess, Gaia, with nature infusing her soul. Or so it seemed. Fredrick knew little about it. Thirty years ago, when they'd first met, Chalsey had been agnostic, Fredrick had been Southern Baptist, and neither of them had known anything about Wicca.

On the table in front of Fredrick lay the floral-print diary, its pink, lavender, and aqua flowers glaring up at him. He saw it out of the corner of his vision in all its girly wonder. Before him sprawled his mother's back deck and yard, filled with oak trees and a detached garage. A squirrel ran down the deck banister, paused, flicked its tail, and zipped out of sight.

Fredrick's mind vomited out disconnected thoughts:

There was an old woman who lived in a shoe.
She had so many children; she didn't know what to do.
She gave them some broth without any bread;
and whipped them all soundly and put them to bed.

A memory of his father's brown leather belt snapped through his mind, a mere nanosecond, but Fredrick saw it raised.

"As a psychologist, Dad was outspoken about children's well-being." Fredrick leaned his chin on the heel of his hand and discovered his face was numb. "The American Psychological Association had published studies about the damage caused by spankings. He would get red in the face just talking about it."

Whipped them all soundly and put them to bed.

"Half his clients were abused or human trafficking survivors." Fredrick's lips felt numb, too. A mockingbird landed on the deck railing, its wings spread just long enough to show him their white spots. "He had entire books about the symptoms, signs, and treatment for sexual abuse."

A flash of a memory: his dad's fingers on his own zipper. Nothing more. Just a single image.

"You know, if a person has a dissociative barrier in their brain that hides memories of abuse, that barrier will often start disintegrating when the person is in their 40s." Fredrick had double-majored in history and psychology, thinking he'd follow in his father's footsteps. But then his father had died, and he'd pursued history instead. "Is my brain getting ready to explode?"

Chalsey walked over with a cup of tea, the tea ball still

inside. "This needs to steep for ten minutes." She set the cup in front of Fredrick and settled across the table from him. "And maybe. If you read that entire diary, it's probably assured. But I'm not a psychologist, so I don't know for sure."

Fredrick peered into the cup, seeing the dark herbs trapped in the tea ball. Clearly, Chalsey had improvised. "I wish I could burn this house to the ground." Having not known he would say that, he surprised himself.

He glanced up and met Chalsey's gaze, her face lined with both worry and age. At 43, she'd survived her fair amount of pain: two divorces, a brush with alcoholism, and two career changes. But the one thing she'd suffered that Fredrick hadn't was child abuse.

Or so they'd thought.

"Every friend I made in middle school, high school, and college was molested." Fredrick picked up the teacup and inhaled the steam. "I thought I was drawing those kinds of friends because my dad was a psychologist and I was a good listener. I was always like, 'Well, Dad says that...' whatever. Dispensing advice like a little psychologist in training."

Chalsey glanced out the window and reached up, tugging on a golden ringlet. She'd once weighed 200 pounds and fought for her right to weigh what she wanted. Then she'd divorced her second husband and converted her diet to all whole natural foods with no added sugar. Now she weighed maybe 120 pounds, the smallest Fredrick had ever seen her. Food had been her way of coping with memories of her father's wandering hands. "Well, I always thought you were good at understanding me. But like you said, treating abused children was your dad's thing. So I just thought..."

A muffled thump of sixteen pounds of cat jumping down from the chair or sofa in the living room interrupted Chalsey; Frederick flinched with a rush of sadness and hilarity. Even though Largo was a cat, Frederick schooled his face and pretended he didn't hear, reacting with shame to his fatphobia. "Yeah. Guess not, huh?"

He turned his gaze upon the floral-print diary. He hadn't picked it out. In his mom's war to ensure he turned out a proper girl, she'd painted his room pink, purchased a floral-print bedspread and diary, and hung pictures of unicorns and flowers on his walls. Half of his wardrobe had been pink, half skirts, and half lace, with his mom's favorite Easter dress being a pink, lacy one. Fredrick's parents hadn't allowed him to pick out his own clothes until he was 11.

Setting down the cup, Fredrick picked up the diary instead. A sharp surge of panic hit him, making his mouth water. He tasted metal again, and his heart raced. "God. All I did was touch it, and I'm going to have a panic attack again." He dropped it and stood, walking to the oak cabinets. He wasn't hungry, but he opened and closed doors, looking at the offerings just to have something to do. Boxes of instant grits, raisins, and bonbons greeted him. "Well, I can clear up a mystery for my therapist. Why am I sexually frozen? Why do sexual abuse scenes in movies and books explode me? What is the reason behind the unrelenting anxiety and depression? Gee, I wonder."

Shifting in her chair, Chalsey leaned against the kitchen wall instead and crossed her legs. Her lavender gypsy shirt was so long it made a hill of fabric on the white tile floor. "Well, do you really have depression or anxiety? You were diagnosed with panic disorder. But is it panic disorder? Or is all of this PTSD?"

Fredrick paused, his hand halfway to a granola bar box. He snapped his fingers and turned away from the cabinet, pointing at Chalsey. "Good point. I might have been misdiagnosed." He snorted and shut the cabinet without his granola bar. "Okay, so I've been misdiagnosed a dozen times. But I'm probably *still* misdiagnosed."

A second thump sounded from the living room, followed by a third and fourth one, like someone repeatedly dropping a bowling ball. Fredrick's startle reflex caused him to glance in that direction, even though he didn't have a line of sight into the living room. *That poor, overweight cat is apparently getting some exercise.*

"You should tell Dr. Laurie immediately." Chalsey bounced her foot, her hippie-style chunky sandal threatening to fall off. "They've dragged you through how many antidepressants now? Six? Seven?"

"Nine."

"And none of them have worked. You deserve real help for the right condition."

A sharper thump, like someone stumbling into a piece of furniture, made Frederick's shoulders tighten. Then a crack and the heart-stopping horror of glass shattering ignited childhood memories of being yelled at for playing too hard in the house. "What is Largo doing?" He stalked through the second kitchen doorway, crossed the hall leading to the primary bedroom, and exited through an archway into the living room.

Glancing around at the sofa, chair, two bookcases, and entertainment center, Fredrick saw no cat. Other than the stack of magazines and the windbreaker, the room was pristine and empty, its yellow walls glowing in the sun. Frederick observed that the pictures of elephants and palm trees were paired with knickknacks of pyramids in rainbows of color, creating a vague Egyptian theme in the room.

"What the hell?" Fredrick walked through the room, scanning. When he reached the second bookcase, he discovered his mom's favorite angel figurine smashed on the hardwood floor. He glanced from the shards of white porcelain to the top shelf of the bookcase, which had been its home.

Chalsey entered through the dining room. "What is it?"

"That's impossible." Fredrick pointed to the broken angel. "That cat is too fat to jump to the top shelf, and he would have to have jumped from the floor. There's nothing close enough for him to jump from." The sofa, recliner, and entertainment center occupied positions too far away. "I've seen cats do some wild stuff—real feats of agility. But that cat could not have done this."

"You're right." Chalsey crouched by the shards and picked up a broken wing. "You know, the spirits, ancestors, and deities can send us messages in all sorts of interesting ways. It doesn't have to be a dream or a spirit visitation. The world contains a wide range of omens."

Having been an atheist since his father's death, Fredrick just shook his head. "Well, the world would be more interesting if those things were true, but you know how I feel about this stuff."

Chalsey set the wing down and stood. "I'm not asking you to be Wiccan. Just keep an open mind and track if there are any patterns. Many people report unusual phenomenon after a loved one dies. People from all different religions all over the world."

"Nothing that cool ever happens to me. But I'll keep a lookout just because it's you asking." Fredrick whisked away, heading to the utility closet for a broom and dustpan, resigning the angel to its death.

CHAPTER 2

DEATH XIII

ARMED WITH NUMBNESS AND LINGERING SHOCK, Fredrick returned to the cellar after throwing away the broken angel, Chalsey in tow.

He pulled lids off boxes, determined to resume work. *I can't let any of this stop me.* Every moment that he allowed something to delay him from what had to be done, Frederick dragged out the process of dealing with his mother's estate. His university wouldn't give him time to take care of this. They hadn't even given him a realistic amount of time off to arrange a funeral. And now more than ever, he wanted this task done. Coming back here had exploded in his face already. *I'm not letting this drag me down into a depressive episode.*

He found several black plastic tubs filled with his father's old psychology books, including the *Diagnostic and Statistical Manual of Mental Disorders III.* Fredrick flipped through it, remembering pouring over the entries for depression and anxiety when he was fourteen and checking off which symptoms he had.

In the top of the third tub, there was a box of tarot cards.

Fredrick recalled finding it as a teenager and playing with it. "Hey, this might interest you." He held up the box, showing it to Chalsey. She was bent over a box filled with old curtains, drapes, and sheets.

"Tarot?" Chalsey walked over and accepted the deck. "This is a classic Rider-Waite-Smith deck. Why would your parents have this?"

"Dad said some of his clients liked the archetypal symbols on the cards." Fredrick shrugged. "He mostly used the cards with the Roman numerals on them."

Chalsey opened the box and slid the cards out. "You mean the major arcana, the first 22 cards?" The first two cards escaped her and fell to the floor. One card was face down and one face up. "Well, that fits you right now."

Leaning over, Fredrick squinted at the card. It was bright yellow and showed a young man in old-fashioned clothes getting ready to walk off the side of a cliff. A dog ran along beside him. "I'm walking off a cliff? Well, I kinda feel like it, yeah."

Chalsey chuckled and knelt, picking up the cards. "This card is called The Fool and represents the adventurer starting off on a new journey, or if you like Joseph Campbell's discussion of the monomyth, the hero leaving on his journey." She held up the card.

"Well, I don't feel like a hero, but I guess I'm starting a new journey: a life with no parents." *A life in which I was apparently molested.* Fredrick peered closer at the card and saw the man was holding a pole with a bag tied at the end, which reminded him of old cartoons where a character left on a journey.

"Think of it as a new adventure. What else will you discover that you can use to better your life?" Chalsey flipped over the second fallen card. "Death, card XIII."

Fredrick snorted. "That fits, too." He glanced at the card as Chalsey held it up. A skeleton wearing black armor rode a horse. In the background, the sun was rising.

"But death is a new beginning." Chalsey slipped the cards back into the box. "The Death card doesn't signify that someone will die or has died physically. Usually, the death is symbolic, and the card heralds a new beginning. The old way dies and a new way begins."

Fredrick sighed and replaced the lid of the box he was on. "Well, I'd like a new way. My whole life has been panic attacks, night terrors, suicide attempts, and major depressive episodes."

"I'd say you're on a fresh path now." Chalsey set the tarot deck on the bottom step of the stairs. "If you don't want the deck, I'll take it."

"Okay. I'm not sure yet." Fredrick pulled the lid off the next tub, this one gray. "I played with those cards a bit when I was 15. Dad had brought them home. But my mom saw them and went ballistic. She told me I would summon Satan with them and that trying to tell the future was blasphemy against God."

Chalsey returned to the box of curtains and sheets. "Why? Ancient Jewish priests used divination all the time. I noticed it when I read the Old Testament for my comparative religion class. Story after story shows the priests casting lots. And what about that one story about the Israelite in Egypt?"

"Joseph?"

"Yeah. There are so many *J* names, I get them confused." Chalsey pulled a set of dusky pink curtains out of the box and wrinkled her nose at them. "He got famous for interpreting prophetic dreams, and he did divination himself. And he's, like, a Biblical hero or something."

Fredrick groaned. "Don't ask me. All the Christians I grew

up with said witchcraft isn't real and doesn't work and then said 'Don't suffer a witch to live.' Why kill someone who's practicing fake magic that doesn't work?" He pulled a scrapbook out of his box. "Wow. This is old. I've never seen this before."

Chalsey held up the pink curtains. "Don't tell me that these were your bedroom curtains when you were a kid."

"In middle school, yeah. I got rid of them shortly before I met you. Mom finally let me pick out my room color for myself when I was 13." Fredrick opened the black scrapbook and turned the faded black pages. "Wow, this belonged to Grandma Smith, my mom's mother." He fingered through the old paper report cards, newspaper clippings, and a graduation announcement with fascination. All the paper had yellowed, and a musty smell filled his nostrils, making him sneeze.

He saw an unmarked envelope and pulled a letter out of it, reading aloud.

I visited Edith MacArnold today. Supposedly, she can foresee who you will marry, and she was right about Tabitha.

He stared at his grandma's precise, perfect cursive. "Wait, seriously? My devout Southern Baptist grandma tried out divination?"

Chalsey grinned. "Weren't we just talking about that?"

Fredrick shook his head, not in denial of Chalsey but denial about all of this. He resumed reading.

I asked her about me, and she said I would marry a man who currently loves another. She said I would know when his affections turned toward me because he would bring me a bouquet of irises. I wonder if it will be Thaddeus or Hector.

He lowered the scrapbook. "Huh. I wonder who Thaddeus was."

"Was Hector your grandfather?" Chalsey pulled out lacy white curtains with tiny pink flowers on them. "Oh. These must be your bedroom curtains from elementary school."

"Yep. The girlier the better in Mom's mind." Fredrick returned the letter to the envelope. "And yeah, Hector was my grandfather. It's weird that Grandma kept her notes all this time." He flipped several more pages, found the wedding announcement for his grandparents, and flipped two more pages. He found another envelope glued to the scrapbook and pulled the letter out.

Chalsey glanced his way. "Ooooh. A letter from a lover, maybe?"

Fredrick snorted. "I doubt it." He unfolded the letter carefully. It was written on blue stationery and had yellowed corners. He read.

April 15, 1944

Dearest Lucy,
I have lost my first baby. My soul is crushed with the weight of it. I can't seem to stop weeping, but Hector tells me I shouldn't grieve so. We will try again.

He lowered the letter, shaken by the revelation. He'd never known his grandma had lost a baby.

"Hector sounds like an ass." Chalsey pulled out thick, olive green drapes and wrinkled her nose again. "Just what a grieving parent wants to hear: 'Oh, you lost a child, but that's okay. You can totally replace them with a new one. You know, like a car battery or a broken mug. It's not like your baby was a person or anything.'"

"Right? That's callous." Fredrick glanced past Chalsey, something flickering in the corner of his eye.

A young woman, perhaps only 18 years old, stood in the far corner of the cellar. She had short hair arranged in careful waves around her face and wore a white flapper dress with high-heeled Mary Janes. A long strand of pearls hung from her neck. Just like ghosts in a million movies, she was vaguely see-through. She pointed to a water-stained cardboard box beside her.

Fredrick heard words in his mind: *Death, the new beginning.*

All he could think was that if Chalsey didn't see the ghost, too, it wasn't real, and she would never believe him. "Chalsey!" he hissed, but of course, the woman faded away.

Chalsey whirled, looking where Fredrick now stared. "That entire corner of the cellar is supercharged with energy now. Did you see something?"

"I don't believe in ghosts." Fredrick's heart pounded. "I don't believe in anything. There's no God, no afterlife, no ghosts, nothing." His fingers trembled as he set the scrapbook back into its box.

He knew in a faraway sense of his body that he wasn't breathing. Chalsey had spent years coaching him to notice this. Out of sync breathing patterns contributed to panic attacks. He sucked in breaths through his teeth. His hands drained of sensation.

"It was a spirit?" Chalsey walked over to the corner.

"Don't go over there!" Fredrick flinched, but he wasn't

sure what he thought would happen. This was the same reaction he had to wasps—his worst phobia.

Chalsey waved her arm through the air. "There's nothing here now. But the air still feels supercharged. Did the spirit say anything to you?"

Fredrick felt propelled through time, remembering seeing shadows from invisible people walking back and forth across the basement wall at Chalsey's house. He'd been 17 and convinced there were no such things as ghosts. Only angels and demons. He couldn't bring himself to repeat the spirit's words. "It—it pointed at that stained box." *I'm losing my damn mind.*

"All right. Let's take it upstairs and go through it carefully." Chalsey grabbed the box and headed for the steps. "Grab the tarot cards for me, okay?"

"Sure." Fredrick picked up the tarot card box and watched his fearless friend march up the stairs. "Ghosts. No problem," he muttered to himself, following her. "Spirits? Broken angels? No problem for Chalsey Montgomery. All in a day's work, I guess." A bitter rush of envy, not unfamiliar, overtook him for a moment before he shoved it down.

Chalsey had always been this way. Whenever he was terrified, Chalsey was composed. He had to remind himself that whenever Chalsey was scared, it was about something so different that he became the cool-headed one. The reality was difficult to hang onto when he panicked.

In the sunlit kitchen, with remodeled oak cabinets that reached the 14-foot ceiling and white appliances, Fredrick tried to stay calm. Chalsey set the box on the kitchen table. Fredrick joined her, set the tarot cards on the table, and pulled the lid off the maroon cardboard box. Old, musty paper smells greeted him. On the top sat a royal blue velvet hat, squashed and flat. Fredrick lifted it out of the way and tossed it onto a chair.

Underneath lay a stack of photo albums, scrapbooks, and loose-leaf papers. Fredrick raffled through them, handing them to Chalsey, who stacked them on the gray- and white-swirled marble countertop behind them. Fredrick discovered a certificate declaring his father a Kentucky Colonel. He found his grandma's retirement certificate: 45 years of teaching in Kentucky schools. An old picture album from the 1970s came next, filled with faded photos Fredrick merely glanced at. An olive green scrapbook followed, and Fredrick recognized it as his own. He opened it and found a crayon picture of a smiling face under an oversized red sun.

"Random keepsakes, I guess." Chalsey leaned closer as Fredrick turned the pages, revealing a blue ribbon, a birthday card, and a finger-painted picture of a brown dog.

"I guess so." The spine creaked in Fredrick's hand as he clutched it. Every crayon picture and faded watercolor painting had tiny children with dogs or cats under huge, glaring suns. The adults in the pictures were always ten times larger than the other figures. "I wonder if my art says anything."

"It says you felt overwhelmed and insignificant."

Unsurprised that Chalsey had an answer, Fredrick flipped the pages faster, curious, and a booklet of notebook paper fell out, stapled in the top corner. He handed the scrapbook to Chalsey and picked it up, recognizing one of his early efforts at writing a short story. "God, more tortured, ugly handwriting." He wondered if it was the murder mystery about a girl detective or the mermaid story of the intersex merperson who fled deep into the ocean because their birth certificate claimed they were a girl, but they felt like a boy.

Big, blocky letters read *The Child Who Could See and Talk to Ghosts and Scary Spirits.*

"I don't remember this one." Fredrick read the first page, Chalsey leaning in to read as well. A picture of a child in a pink dress with an enormous bow accompanied the text.

The child was eight. Their name was Sam. The doctors said Sam was a girl, but it wasn't true. Their mom still made them wear dresses. Every night, Sam saw demons in the corner of their bedroom. The demons said they would throw the chair at Sam and hurt them.

A picture of a black face with red eyes and fangs filled the bottom of the page. Fredrick flipped the page, goosebumps flashing down his arms.

Every morning, Sam saw a ghost in the kitchen. The ghost would point at the corner. It was a woman ghost. When Sam looked, they couldn't see anything. Then Sam would go to school, and child ghosts ran everywhere. There were ghosts in the classroom and ghosts in the bathroom and ghosts in the hall. The teacher yelled at Sam for staring at the ghosts. She couldn't see the ghosts.

A stick figure of a child appeared in the middle of the page, surrounded by a dozen Pac-Man-style ghosts. Fredrick flipped another page. A huge, frowning tree filled the center of the page, the text written around it.

After school, Sam played outside. There was a ghost in the tree. The ghost said Sam should hang themself. Sam got scared and ran to the backyard. But a new ghost was by the swing set. This ghost said Sam would be O.K. if they stayed in their room and made a circle out of toys and held a cross.

So Sam went inside and made a circle of toys. They got their cross necklace and held it. No more ghosts came that day. The end.

Lowering the notebook paper, Fredrick stared out the window, not really seeing the deck. "I don't remember writing this, but it's my handwriting. I know I had to."

"You described making a sacred circle out of toys." Chalsey eased the story out of his hand. "How would you know to do that? Did you see a movie with witchcraft in it on TV?"

"Mom policed what I watched pretty hard when I was little." Fredrick watched a cardinal land on the railing, tilt its head, and chirp. Its brilliant coloring seemed like a warning: *Red. Red flag.* "She limited me to one hour of TV a day in the summers and thirty minutes during the school year. And she always stayed in the room with me, even once I reached middle school. No way would she let me watch something like that."

Chalsey set the story on the countertop. "Well, you couldn't have been older than 10 when you wrote that, and maybe you were eight since you said Sam was eight. So how did you know to protect yourself in a sacred circle?"

Fredrick left his brow crease, and he faced Chalsey. "You say that like I *am* Sam."

"Do you remember the shadow people we saw in my basement when we were in high school?"

"Shit." Fredrick looked inside the box and yanked out the next item. "Well, yeah. But that doesn't mean I saw ghosts and demons as a kid. I remember being scared of demons and stuff, but I never saw anything for real." He held up an electric blue three-ring binder. "What's this? A story about vampires visiting me in the night?" He opened the binder and discovered a typed manuscript. The title page read *The Civil War Ghost* by Marilyn Smith Anderson. "It's one of my mom's old novels. Must be really old. I don't recognize the title."

Chalsey accepted the binder. "I thought she only wrote romance."

I told you to stay out of my things! snapped Marilyn's voice inside of Fredrick's mind. The tone and intonation were so perfect, Fredrick jerked. He glanced around, but no see-through spirit of his mother appeared to glower at him.

"That's right." Fredrick pulled out the next item, a square paper folded in half. He unfolded the paper and glanced over it, discovering another letter. Or, rather, the middle of a letter with the other pages missing. The swirling, looping, perfect letters were his mother's handwriting.

> —the court said we could keep Martha. And I thought, 'Of course we will.' Of all the ridiculous nonsense! How dare anyone say Phillip and I would ever hurt our daughter. And with Phillip specializing in treating children who have experienced trauma, too! I tell you, I don't know what this world is coming to.

Fredrick lowered the page, his fingers trembling. "I don't remember ever going to court as a child."

"Court?" Chalsey snatched the letter from his numb fingers and read it. "I swear, it sounds like your parents got taken to court for a custody case."

"I don't remember *anything* like that." Fredrick glared at the floral-print diary on the corner of the kitchen table. "I wonder if I wrote anything about that in my diary."

"Hard to say." Chalsey guided Fredrick to sit in the

kitchen chair. "I think maybe we should stop working in the cellar. You're getting overwhelmed by all these shocks."

If you'd stayed out of my private affairs, then none of this would have happened, snapped his mother's voice. Fredrick could have sworn his mother sat across from him at the table. *Mind your own business.*

"You're not wrong," Fredrick said. "I think I'm losing my mind."

CHAPTER 3

THE HIGH PRIESTESS II

THAT NIGHT, FREDRICK REPORTED TO HIS OLD bedroom. Nothing else out of the ordinary had happened, and he was exhausted. That was the sole reason he would use his former room. After years, his mother had turned it into a guest bedroom and had painted the walls dark yellow. Climbing into his old bed, which was standard-sized with tall pine bedposts, felt creepy. *So my father, the supposed children's rights advocate, climbed into this bed with me to violated and assaulted me, huh?* Just what he didn't want to dwell on. But the only other bed in the house was his parents', the third bedroom having long ago been converted into an office. And the only thing creepier would be sleeping in his parents' bed. He'd left that bedroom to Chalsey, who had smudged it with sage first.

Fredrick slapped all such thoughts away. *If I ruminate on my shocking revelation, I won't sleep. Besides, none of this seems real.*

After staring at the artistic ripples in the ceiling plaster, Fredrick summoned the nerve to do his nightly prayer. Given he had long since abandoned Christianity and its silent God,

Fredrick only prayed one prayer, but he did so every night: "Divine Spirit, whoever and whatever you are, help me discover the real me. Who I am should be between only you and me, and no humans should weigh in on it." *Not concerning my mind or my body.*

Having no idea if any entity at all was intercepting these entreaties, Fredrick rolled over and tried to unclench his muscles enough to fall asleep. His stomach wanted to knot, and he breathed deeply, inhaling through his nose and exhaling through his mouth. *Even if my father abused me, he's dead now. He's been dead since I was 19. Mom's dead now. The bedroom door is locked. The front, back, and side doors are all locked. No one can get in. And Chalsey would never hurt me.*

Somewhere in the repetition of this litany, Fredrick fell asleep.

Later, he awakened from one of his usual nightmares: being chased through a house by invisible demons and unable to switch on any lights. He'd been having the same nightmare for at least 15 years now. He rolled over and glanced at the bedside clock. 3:13 AM. Only then did he realize he'd forgotten to bring a glass of water with him. *Shit. Now I have to go downstairs.*

Frederick propelled himself out of bed, steeling his resolve and creeping across the carpet. He'd never gotten over his fear of the dark, but he didn't want to hurt his eyes by turning on all the lights. *I'm a grown-ass man. I can take it.* He unlocked the door, stepping onto the cool hardwood floor, the old floorboards groaning as he made his way to the staircase. He discovered his mother had a nightlight in the hallway, as usual. *Better than nothing.*

A black silhouette stood at the top of the stairs.

Fredrick halted, his entire body frozen like a marble sculpture. His heart pounded. Goosebumps shot over his skin. *Not real. This is not real. It has to be a trick of the shadows.*

The silhouette vanished.

It's nothing. I'll turn on the hall light. It's fine. Fredrick tried to convince his body to walk two feet closer to the stairs, where the light switch waited. His heart pounded so hard it seemed to vibrate his entire body.

I told you not to tell our family secrets! shrieked a voice in his mind. His mother's voice.

The black silhouette flashed in and out of his peripheral vision.

How dare you tell that little witchy friend of yours! You promised to hold your silence!

Fredrick shot forward and flipped on the hall light. He spun in a circle, scanning the hall, but saw no black entities. "Great! Now I really *am* losing my mind." He stalked toward the stairs. *Calm down. Be reasonable. There are no such things as ghosts. There are no deities or demons, and ghosts are—*

Hands impacted Fredrick's back, and he tumbled down the stairs to the landing. Frozen and hurting, he stared up the stairs, but no one glared down at him.

Don't you go impugning our family name!

It was his mother's voice again. Internal though it was, it matched her intonation, her accent, her tone of voice.

Fredrick stood, his thigh muscles wobbling, and clutched the banister as he made his way down the second set of steps. His back throbbed from the shove, and his left hip and both legs felt bruised from the fall. *No way did I shove myself down the stairs.*

Bypassing the kitchen, Fredrick trudged down the hallway to the primary bedroom, steadying himself with one hand against the wall. He knocked on the door.

"Chalsey? I need your expertise." The tight, false calmness and the drastic understatement paired with unusual formality would be an immediate giveaway to her he was panicking.

After a pause, Chalsey's muffled voice came through the door. "What? I'm coming."

The door opened, and Fredrick and Chalsey stared at each other.

"I think my mom's haunting me. And you know I don't believe in ghosts."

Chalsey listened to his story, grabbed her sage stick and a lighter, and headed to the stairs. Fredrick limped into the kitchen and settled at the table after turning on every light he could reach along the way.

When Chalsey joined him, a frown marred her heart-shaped face, and lines creased her forehead. "I sensed malevolent energy. I didn't hear or see anything. For now, I have smudged and cleaned the stairs, hall, bathroom, and bedrooms."

Through a haze of exhaustion, Fredrick gazed at her. "God! I don't believe in any of this shit. Why is this happening to me?"

Chalsey dropped into the chair across from him. "I would need to perform a ritual to determine whether this is your mother's spirit or whether it is another class of spirit imitating your mother. I'll do that in the morning. As for why it is happening...in my experience, malevolent spirits aim to stop humans from figuring out the truth, pursuing healing, or improving their lives. You found out a truth about your childhood, you'll use it to get more help in therapy, and recovering from trauma will improve your life. That's enough to give a malevolent spirit a meltdown."

Fredrick stared at the wood grain of the table, noting dried water spots in the harsh florescent light. The wood had black flecks, and lines ran through the wood shaped like half an oval. "If a house could ever be haunted by an evil spirit, then I could believe that harming a child would attract such an entity."

"It can." Chalsey's voice was flat. "My childhood home is

exploding with them between what happened to my brother and me."

Fredrick accepted her words without argument. *What am I supposed to say? How does logic explain being pushed down a staircase by an invisible person?* "Can I sleep on your bedroom floor? I want to go for safety in numbers now."

"Sure."

Fredrick grabbed the cushions off the couch so he'd be more comfortable. He had an array of symptoms his therapist noted: excessive muscle knots, joint pain, back pain, chronic fatigue, insomnia, headaches, migraines, light sensitivity, and sound sensitivity, along with depression, anxiety, panic attacks, phobias, low self-esteem, suicidal ideation, and suicide attempts. He felt like a walking, talking medical brochure. And he certainly had too many symptoms to be sleeping on the floor in his forties.

One extra pillow and blanket later, he installed himself on the far side of his parents' old bed and listened to Chalsey's deep breathing until he fell asleep.

He awakened in the morning to the disorientation of finding himself on his parents' bedroom floor. Worried about his sanity and too groggy to find where he'd put his cellphone, he found the bathroom right where it would be if he were in his mother's home and took his shower in a daze, relieved by the evidence of the bright sunlight that it was still summer.

Then he headed to his childhood bedroom, where he found clothes packed from home and put the pieces together: at some point he had come to his mother's house. He dressed and stumbled into the kitchen to search for breakfast, feeling weird about eating in a dead woman's home. His head felt packed with cotton balls, and the room looked oddly concave. *Am I getting another migraine?*

He stared at Chalsey, who was brewing herbal tea at the kitchen counter. He watched her and pushed against the wall in his mind, trying to figure out when he'd arrived at his mother's house, what day it was, and what he'd been doing. Sometimes, if he concentrated hard enough, he remembered what he'd missed.

Chalsey pulled the tea ball from her mug and watched him with a raised eyebrow. "Fredrick?"

He gave up. If Chalsey noticed him after he switched with Fredrick, then he was taking too long trying to remember on his own. "No, I'm Michael." He glanced around. His mother's obese cat was sunning by the back door, his orange and white fur glowing in the light. "Okay, fill me in. I know you were going to come here with Fred-O on Wednesday. It's not still Wednesday. I woke up in my parents' bedroom. Ew, by the way. Did I miss more than a day?"

"Nope. It's Thursday." Chalsey stirred her tea, the spoon clicking against the porcelain.

"So I lost a whole day, basically. Figures. I didn't wanna be here. But I didn't count on Fred-O sleeping here."

"I was surprised by Fredrick's desire to sleep here as well," Chalsey said. "I expected him to argue with me when I pointed out it was more efficient to spend the night here. But he didn't."

Michael rummaged through his mother's cabinets and wrinkled his nose at the cereal choices. "So, how did Other Me handle it yesterday?" Chalsey had been his girlfriend for years now, so she was used to answering these kinds of questions. It was all part and parcel of dating a guy with DID, dissociative identity disorder.

Chalsey picked up her mug and inhaled the steam.

"Fredrick found an old diary of yours in the cellar. He read part of it."

"Oh, *shit*." Michael plucked out the box of raisin bran, making peace with the least offensive choice. "So he learned our family was in the SOMH, huh?" The acronym stood for Soldiers of the Most High, a White extremist group with freaky religious ideas mixed in for good measure. "I bet he exploded. Is there anything left of him, or am I the sole beneficiary of our body now?" Chalsey would know he was joking. The parts or people inside someone with DID, who were collectively called a DID System, couldn't die or go anywhere. They could internally fall asleep or go dormant, but they couldn't die. And by now, most therapists agreed the parts couldn't integrate, either.

Chalsey trailed over to the table. Today she wore a swishy, green, nylon dress that reached her ankles. Her blonde ringlets hung down her back. "Actually, he learned something I don't think you know. You need to read it, too."

Michael's curiosity flared and burned in his stomach. "Really? Are we finally getting somewhere? I've gotten totally stuck in therapy." He grabbed a bowl, a spoon, and almond milk, whipping himself up a bowl of cereal. At this point in his life, he'd squared with himself the reality that he had dissociative identity disorder. He'd told Chalsey, but no one else. Other people were just so ignorant about it. As far as Michael could tell, people only talked about DID when they wanted to make movies about people with DID being killers. It was offensive, like saying all people with depression were abusers or all people with anxiety were drug dealers. Plus most people still wouldn't call it DID. They insisted on calling it multiple personality disorder, even though the term was defunct and had been for over thirty years.

"I think this will unstick you." Chalsey pointed to a flower-print book on the kitchen table.

Michael saw his purple pill planner and grabbed it. He took an army of medication, including a muscle relaxer, antidepressants, and a proton pump inhibitor for his acid reflux and chronic heartburn. Over half his medicine cabinet was bursting with drugs for stomach acid, diarrhea, and other gastrointestinal complaints. "Well, I wanna know, then. I mean, I'm sure it's bad, but I've gotta know." He carried over his bowl and his pill army and settled at the table. "Do you know where it is?" *No matter what ugliness gets dredged up in therapy or what kind of sick bastard bullshit I find out about in my old diary, it's better than pretending.* Besides, he could watch rated R horror movies and not blink. Nothing got to him. Whenever there was a wasp to deal with and Chalsey wasn't there to save Fredrick, Michael came out. He'd shooed a wasp out of their car for Fredrick just last week at the lake.

"About halfway in."

Swallowing his morning pills first, Michael steeled himself and opened the uber-girly diary.

"You know, kids would've teased me that this thing could turn me gay. If they'd understood I was a boy. I'm sure Mommy Dearest bought this for Fredrick and me. She wouldn't even let us cut our hair or wear it how we wanted. We had to wear it down to our waist. She was a psycho control freak. I'm surprised she didn't count how many breaths we took in a day and make us breathe any 'extra' into a mason jar so that we didn't 'waste' it. Why would she let us pick out our own journal?"

He flipped through the pages, noticing the different styles of handwriting: upright, slanted, condensed, wide, bubbly, spidery, blocky, and even with capitals mixed randomly into lower case.

"Wow. It looks like at least nine kids passed this thing around at a slumber party. I wonder how many parts I have."

So far, Michael was aware of one: Fredrick. But Michael

knew Fredrick had no idea about him or their diagnosis. Fredrick also didn't know Michael was dating Chalsey.

"There could be nine." Chalsey applied herself to her vegan breakfast of fried tofu and vegetables. "According to my research, it's rare for someone to only have two parts."

Michael cringed. "If that's the case, then no wonder I can never balance my checking account." He stopped on a page, icy water seeming to slam into his face. He read silently for five pages, his cereal forgotten.

When he looked up, Chalsey was holding her mug with both hands, sadness elongating her features and dulling her brown eyes. "I'm so sorry," she whispered.

Michael set down the diary and took a bite of soggy cereal. His own childish handwriting scrolled through his mind's eye like a running ticker tape: *touched me there, hurts, slapped me, used his belt, ordered me not to cry, wiped blood...*

Five soggy bites later, Michael lowered his spoon. "I might not have control of the body much longer. Fredrick's going to switch back in. But you're right. This solves a lot of mysteries. My therapist keeps saying I need to dig up my family's dark secrets, just like Dr. John Bradshaw said in his books. And I knew I'd witnessed a lot of violence as a kid. But it still wasn't adding up. I was hoping I'd find my parents' old SOMH regalia in the cellar so I can have evidence I'm not making all this violence up. But I might find something even bigger down there."

"You might." Chalsey set down her mug. "Fredrick already emailed your therapist about the diary and what it says, so you don't have to do that."

"Okay." Michael shook his head and glanced out the window. "I never thought it'd be something like this. And yet somehow, I'm also not surprised." Head pressure and exhaustion slammed into him. *Shit, here we go again.* He didn't even have time to warn Chalsey it was happening.

"Me, neither."

"Hm?" Fredrick switched in and wondered what Chalsey was talking about. For a moment, confusion shot through him. Then he leaped to the most logical conclusion he could fathom. "Oh! You didn't sleep well either? I guess that's no surprise." He glanced down at his cereal bowl, noticed the soggy cereal, and got to work eating. *Damn. I must've spaced out. It's no wonder, though. Who would sleep well in their childhood bedroom after discovering they were assaulted in it? What was I thinking, sleeping here?*

"Yeah, we need to be gentle with ourselves today." Chalsey set down her mug. "Also, I'm going to do a ritual to determine who or what that spirit was last night. Is that all right with you?"

Fredrick snorted. "Mom'd shit if she knew a Wiccan was performing a ritual in her house. But she's dead, and I don't care if it could offend her spirit. Your Wicca offends me less than listening to people tell me for decades that I'm going to hell for being me. So go for it."

Chalsey stood. "Then I'll get right on it."

In the middle of the living room floor, Chalsey sat cross-legged on the throw rug, Fredrick having pushed the coffee table aside. Around her was a circle made of tarot cards, and on the floor in front of her lay the card named High Priestess and a potted plant borrowed from the living room windowsill. Loose-leaf sage burned in a bowl to her left, and a bowl of water sat to her right. Behind her was a lit jar candle. Around her she'd scattered small, raw chunks of lapis lazuli.

Fredrick sat in the recliner, watching in silence. He understood only the basics: Chalsey had represented the four elements with fire, water, earth, and air, the latter of which was signified by the smoke from the burning sage.

"The High Priestess card indicates secrets, secret knowledge, mysteries, and intuition," Chalsey said. "I'm using it to focus my concentration while I ask the Universe to clear up the mystery of the malevolent spirit. The lapis lazuli signifies and amplifies communication."

Icy fingers brushed across Fredrick's lungs, his breathing turning shallow. "Okay." *I pray to a god I no longer believe in, so I can't mock her for trying with the Universe or Goddess or whatever.*

Chalsey stared at the card, falling silent, her eyes unfocused as she fell into a meditative trance. After a minute, she bent over and reached with one hand, touching The High Priestess card with her fingertips.

The steady ticking of his mother's antique wall clock distracted Fredrick. It had been her mother's, and her mother's before her, and her mother's before her: a legacy.

Chalsey straightened and met Fredrick's gaze. "There are three spirits in this house right now. Two are human, and one is malevolent, a demon if you want to call it that. Gaia is trying to explain who the two human spirits are, but the 'demon' is running interference. Instead of hearing words in my mind telling me who they are, I'm hearing a vague wah-wah-wah talking sound like in one of those old *Peanuts* cartoons."

"A demon. Great." Fredrick hopped out of the chair, scanning the entire room. "Well, if what yelled at me during the night was a demon, it did a great job of mimicking my mom when she was angry. And if it's Mom, then she sounds in-character. Either way, it's creepy." Even as he said the words, he wasn't sure he believed there were spirits. Going back to sleep had made his memory of the haunting seem unreal. *Did I make it all up?* All he knew for sure was that he'd fallen down the stairs. He had bruises to prove it. *Maybe I'm just going crazy. I'm only 43, but both my parents are dead. I have no spouse and no children, and I have one half-sibling I barely know. All my grandparents are dead and all my aunts and uncles, too. All I've got left are a couple of cousins I've met briefly at family reunions. So maybe I can't handle the isolation, the lack of a family.*

Chalsey blew out the candle and began picking up tarot cards. "You went into denial, didn't you? Your vibes just withdrew as if you sucked your energy into your body."

"God," Fredrick sighed. "You know I can't help it. It's like my brain is determined to not believe in any of this. I read my own words in my diary. I literally said my father was abusing me. And then I slept on it, and it doesn't seem real. The two spirits I saw yesterday don't seem real."

Grabbing the bowl of water along with the cards, Chalsey stood. "Your brain is insisting that your parents were normal, that you had a normal life, and that you have no problems. You've had two mental breakdowns, and still your brain wants to say your childhood was normal and even boring. I think the answer, or one of them, is clear: reverse gaslighting."

Fredrick squatted and scooped up the jar candle and bowl of sage. "What's *reverse* gaslighting?"

"It's exactly what it sounds like. In gaslighting, children are told they are the problem, not their parents. 'You're just a bad kid' or 'You're just being oversensitive' or whatever. In reverse gaslighting, the child is told they have no problems and everything is fine. 'There's nothing wrong here; you're making it up.'"

Fredrick followed Chalsey into the kitchen, watching as she poured the water from the bowl into the plant on the windowsill. "You're right. My brain is insisting my childhood was normal and my parents average."

"And yet you've been in therapy nonstop for 23 years." Chalsey set the bowl in the drain and faced him. "You can't have depression, anxiety, dissociation, suicidal ideation, suicide attempts, and two mental breakdowns if you had a normal, boring childhood with perfectly good, healthy parents."

Returning to the living room, Fredrick grabbed the potted plant while Chasley picked up the lapis lazuli. "I want to snap at you and tell you how wrong you are. I also want to believe you so I can solve the mystery of why I've spent my life feeling so fucked up."

"Then let's go back into the cellar."

CHAPTER 4

THE LOVERS VI, REVERSED

FREDRICK DIDN'T CARE IF SOMEONE CALLED HIM weak by using insulting terms for female body parts. There was no way he was going into the cellar alone. Not now.

Following Chalsey and her bouncy golden curls, Fredrick descended into the chilly cellar and decided it was a cement hell. His gaze snapped to the far left corner, where a water stain had discolored the gray concrete blocks. Although he saw nothing more than boxes, he felt a spirit's presence. His gaze drew to the corner, and pressure hit his chest, pushing into his lungs. *Something or someone is down here already. Is it Mom? That lady from the 1920s? Or the demon?*

Chalsey marched over to the right-hand corner where they'd discovered the water-stained box. However, she halted a foot shy of the boxes and turned her head, glancing over her shoulder at the left corner.

Fredrick watched. He hadn't said anything, and her back had been to him. Chalsey couldn't know he'd stopped to stare. "What is it?"

"There's a spirit in the corner." Chalsey pointed. "The

feeling I get from it isn't malevolent, but it's making itself known."

Goosebumps erupted over Fredrick's arms, and his scalp tingled. *Independent corroboration. Chalsey experienced the same sensation in that exact spot. Shit.* A dozen childhood memories flashed through his mind: staring at the corner of his bedroom in the night, convinced there was a demon there; being convinced his bedroom furniture would attack him; running downstairs to his parents because he could no longer withstand the terror of the demon; and being reassured evil spirits were not present and that furniture couldn't move by itself.

Along with that was a ten-second memory of the old movie *Poltergeist,* which he'd watched in college. *It's not just movies. People all over the world have reported poltergeist activity for centuries.*

Fredrick skittered sideways across the cellar, staring at the far left corner, but the spirit's presence didn't shift or move. "Okay. So we just pick more boxes and poke around?" Even as he said the words, his gaze snapped to a cardboard box that his mother had covered with checkered contact paper. It was as if the box were calling to him. He gestured to it. "Maybe this one?"

"Or, if all else fails, we resume unloading the water-stained box from yesterday." Chalsey pulled the lid off the checkered box. File folders presented themselves.

"What is it?" Fredrick noticed each folder had a label, and each label bore a family member's name. He pulled out the one marked with his maternal grandmother's name and opened it. "Old photos."

Chalsey picked out one entitled *Grandma's Photo Album* and opened it. Antique black and white photos, some of them blurry or faded, presented themselves for inspection.

"This is so weird." Fredrick thumbed through pictures of

his grandmother as a child. "I never noticed before how much my mom as a kid looked like my grandma as a kid. The resemblance is uncanny. If these photos weren't 30 years older, I'd say these were pictures of Mom instead."

Chalsey held up a black-and-white photo of a young girl standing with an adult woman. The dresses looked like they were from the 1920s. "Who's this? There's no writing on the back to identify them."

Fredrick glanced at them. "Oh, I have no idea." He held up a picture of his grandmother, placing it by the photo from the 1920s. "But they're clearly related. The girl in the photo and Grandma look so much alike it's almost spooky."

"Well, you didn't inherit it." Chalsey closed the folder and put it back in the box. "You look nothing like your parents."

"I always said that." Fredrick shrugged. "Mom said I inherited her grandma's hair, and Dad once said I look like one of my great-uncles, Cecil. Genetics are weird." He shoved his folder into the box and pulled out one labeled *Phillip's Family, Old*. This folder had more black-and-white pictures from the late 1800s and early 1900s. Fredrick slipped out the largest photo, an 8x10 that was printed landscape. Two adults sat in chairs on the front lawn of a white wooden farmhouse. Behind them stood a row of children. The father held a toddler, and the mother held an infant.

"So many children." Chalsey counted them by pointing at each one. "Fifteen!"

Fredrick frowned at the picture. The children looked to be between newborn and roughly 20 years old. "I never knew anyone had 15 children." He flipped the photo over and found the handwriting: *Maurice and Lillian Anderson with their children.* A list of names followed this with ages, marked as starting left to right. "Wait. What? Dad said Maurice and Lillian Anderson had 12 children, not 15. And two of them were a set of twins who died shortly after birth. How are there 15 living children in this photo?"

"Did he misremember?"

"I wouldn't think so. Maurice and Lillian were his grandparents. My grandfather is one of the young children in this photo, maybe the toddler. Wouldn't Dad know how many aunts and uncles he had?"

A hissing, scraping sound erupted from behind Fredrick and Chalsey. Fredrick snapped around so fast he nearly dropped the folder.

The cellar appeared undisturbed.

"I sense energy building in the corner," Chalsey whispered. "The spirit is either excited or disturbed."

The high-pitched scraping sound resumed. Fredrick whirled and crammed the folder and its photo back into the box.

"Fredrick!" Chalsey snapped.

He jerked back around. The corner of an old suitcase stuck out from one shelf. "That wasn't there a second ago." He felt the soaring sweep of hysteria, like a black swan lifting from a black pond into a night sky.

Fredrick, whispered a voice in his mind. *Frontier. Farm. Secrets.*

"Done now!" Fredrick's exit up the stairs mirrored his speed at age 13, as if 30 years hadn't passed. He shot into the kitchen, only to find all the tarot cards on the tile floor. Largo was sniffing them.

Fredrick's brain did the math as he imagined Largo knocking the box into the floor from the countertop. *The top flap on the cardboard box is flimsy now. Maybe a cat could knock them off just right and cause this mess.* He walked over and noticed they were all face-down except one, which was upside down. It showed two naked people, a man and a woman, with an enormous angel standing behind them.

Against his better judgment, he turned to Chalsey as she joined him. "What does this card mean?"

"The Lovers, reversed." Chalsey's brow furrowed, and fine wrinkles erupted from the corners of her eyes, giving away her age. "Generically speaking, that means disharmony, imbalance, conflict, detachment, bad choices, or indecision. The joyous union of the lovers in marriage has been inverted. While it could apply to actual romance, it doesn't have to. To be more precise, I would have to be using the card in an actual reading."

Fredrick picked up the card and stared at its garish colors, the precise hues of blue, yellow, and red being over-bright and clashing. "Well, there's a great deal of divorce in my family, as well as some adultery. If some spirit is trying to communicate with me this way, this could literally be about ruined relationships." He sighed and scooped up all the cards. "I'm going to assume that the cat knocked the box off the counter, though."

"Family secrets." Chalsey stepped over to the refrigerator and opened the door. "Dr. John Bradshaw's books suggest analyzing at least five generations of your family and determining what the secrets are."

Fredrick's brain replayed the spirit's voice: *Frontier. Farm. Secrets.*

"Notice the patterns: divorce and cheating. You've always known what your family's secrets are; all kids do. You notice it even if your family is lying about it." Chalsey pulled out a plastic container and opened the lid, only to wrinkle her nose and slam the lid down. "Subconsciously, you already know the truth. Is the abusing a pattern? Your father dedicated his career to supposedly helping exploited children, but then he violated you. That pretty much guarantees that someone also abused him. Did his father abuse him? And his father before him? Did the mothers?"

What will I find here? The thought came unbidden. Fredrick stood and pushed all the cards back into their box. "Do you think I can find all the answers I'm looking for?"

"You didn't get PTSD out of nowhere." Chalsey pulled out a head of lettuce and set it on the countertop. "And I don't buy the argument that your depression and anxiety are nothing but misfiring brain chemicals. You *can* sort this out." She pulled a bag of carrots and an onion out of the refrigerator drawer. "Both of your parents are dead now. Whatever you've been holding back your entire life, either out of fear of your parents or out of a sense of obligation or duty, will burst out now. You're free."

Fredrick's chest filled with a cold, heavy fog, and ice coated the pit of his stomach. "So I'm going to barf out all my traumas?"

"Probably not all at once." Chalsey pulled out a tomato and a bottle of vinaigrette. "But you can't process traumas if you don't know what they are. Learning the truth means you can heal."

After eating her salad, Chalsey set up her laptop on the kitchen table, preparing to work. Her third career was freelance editor and jewelry-maker. She'd begun her professional life as an English instructor, moved on to a job as an art gallery curator, and now lived a more bohemian life as a freelancer. As a result, she had no problem working out of Fredrick's mother's house, and Fredrick was among her current clients.

Despite his career as a history professor, Fredrick was a prolific writer of both poetry and horror novels. He'd published two poetry chapbooks thus far, as well as four horror novels. Chalsey was currently editing his fifth horror novel before he sent it to the publisher. Chalsey always worked as his developmental editor. The editor at the publishing house had no idea how much easier she had it thanks to Chalsey.

"I'm up to chapter 14." Chalsey scrolled through the document. "Every time the demons attack, it creeps me out. It doesn't matter how many times I read that scene."

"Then I'm doing my job." Fredrick looked up from his phone, having ordered a pizza for himself. *Do I put demons in my novels because I've seen them in real life? I thought I sensed demons as a kid, and I got shoved down the stairs last night. Then there was that short story about ghosts I wrote when I was eight. When I write now, am I writing fiction or lightly altered nonfiction?* "You know, it just hit me how much poetry I wrote about molested children when I was in high school. Do you remember how I wrote an entire novel in middle school about a boy whose father beat and molested him? Then in high school, I wrote a collection of a hundred poems about boys who were molested."

"I remember reading that novel. And those poems." Chalsey pulled her glasses out of her purse and slipped them on. They reflected the laptop screen as squares of white light. "I'm not likely to forget it. The novel was dark and depressing, and the poems were heartbreaking." She glanced at him from over the funky rainbow rims of her glasses. "I wondered that whole time if you'd been harmed, but you kept saying you had normal parents. I didn't want to push."

Fredrick sighed and grabbed his laptop bag, unzipping it. "I know. I couldn't remember anything." He pulled out his laptop and set it across from Chalsey's. He was teaching an online summer course, so he needed to check on his students. "But despite not remembering it, I was coughing it up everywhere."

"Makes me wonder what else you coughed up." Chalsey

tapped on her touchpad and then typed, the ultra-fast clicking showing off her speed. "Do you still have your old books and poems anywhere?"

"All my old notebooks and binders should be in the cellar or maybe still in my old closet." Fredrick had either written by hand or printed out everything he'd composed. "And good point. Maybe I left myself other markers or clues." His numbed-out horror slid aside as his curiosity flared. "I feel almost like a detective now, a detective seeking the truth about my life. What happened to me for real? And why do I have amnesia about it?"

Chalsey shifted her glasses on her nose. "I'd say the amnesia is straightforwardly an act of self-defense. A individual being harmed, violated, and assaulted needs a coping mechanism to handle the terror and pain."

Fredrick knew he was numb when he failed to react to this blunt recounting of his childhood. *But give me a movie showing a person being hit or an individual being harmed, and I melt down. What is it about fiction that breeches my numbness?* He glanced out the window, catching movement in his peripheral vision, and expected to see a neighbor's dog.

A man in a leaf green jumpsuit and a green baseball cap stood in the center of the backyard. He stared at Fredrick, unsmiling.

Then the man vanished.

Fredrick shot out of his chair, and then he wasn't Fredrick. He was Michael. "Demon in the yard!"

Chalsey snapped her head to the side, her eyes narrowing. "Again? Already?" She stood, pushing the chair away, and opened the back door. She stalked outside, crossing the deck.

Impressed by her fearlessness, Michael raced after his girlfriend. With the sun shining down on them and the June heat baking him at 93 degrees, he couldn't feel terrified. Still, his heart raced. "I don't sense anything. Do you? God, this reminds me of high school and your old basement."

"I still have nightmares about that basement." Chalsey glanced around. "I don't sense anything, but I believe you. After all, we know there are two ghosts and one 'demon' in the house."

"We do? Is that what you mean by again?"

Chalsey faced him. "Michael?"

"Yep."

Chalsey filled him in.

Michael cringed, chilled despite the hot sun warming his skin. "Pushed down the stairs? God! That's worse than the night when I was seven and saw the rocking chair sliding across my bedroom floor by itself."

"I don't know which is worse. Sounds like a real toss-up to me. Poltergeists terrify me." Chalsey slipped back inside, Michael following her.

"So if I pissed off some spirits by reading my old diary and looking around the cellar, what are they trying to stop me from knowing?" Michael dropped back into his chair and glanced at his laptop screen. The website for his university's online courses stared back at him. *The students are supposed to submit research paper ideas soon. I wonder if anyone turned it in early.* He co-taught with Fredrick, both of them handling their job, although Fredrick was unaware of that fact by default. Michael clicked on the assignment link before pulling himself back on topic. "Do you think there's some big secret I'm on the verge of discovering?"

Chalsey sank back into her chair. "Didn't you already find a big secret? Your dad was harming you."

"I can't even comprehend that. And yeah, it's an enormous secret. But what if this house contains an even bigger secret?"

"Even bigger than being violated and touched?"

"Okay, you got me there. Fine, an equally big secret." Michael felt a pressure in his chest, as if all the secrets of the multiverse hovered just beyond his grasp. *Gimme, gimme, gimme. I wanna know The Truth.*

A scraping sound erupted from the living room, like the sound of someone pushing a table across a hardwood floor.

Michael and Chalsey stared at each other.

"No way," Chalsey breathed.

The doorbell rang, startling Michael, and with the jumpscare, Fredrick popped back into control of the body. "My pizza's here!" He hopped up, zipping through the dining room and into the living room.

Chalsey followed him.

Once Fredrick accepted the pizza box from a zit-faced teenager, he turned and found Chalsey examining both rooms. "What's up?"

"I thought I heard something a second ago." Chalsey shook her head.

Fredrick carried the grease-stained box into the kitchen. "I'm going to ignore the demons and eat my pizza. It's not like I want to believe in ghosts or demons anyway, and I'm hungry. Time for the comforting numbness of denial and the joy of onions, banana peppers, and mushrooms on a bed of cheese and sauce."

But even as Fredrick set the box on the counter and grabbed a plate from the cabinet, he stung with irony. *How can I act so normal after learning my dad was a predator? Shouldn't I be angry or something?*

The anger will come when the dissociation eases, replied a voice in his mind. *You're still in shock.*

Fredrick deemed his inner voice wise and served himself two slices of pizza.

Chapter 5

THE DEVIL XV, REVERSED

After pizza and some grading of his summer course, Fredrick returned to the water-stained box he'd discovered the day before. Thanks to all the excitement, he'd forgotten to finish going through it, and it was taking up space on the kitchen island. "I guess I better find out what other secrets are hiding in here, other than some letter that implies there was a custody case and a sad but creepy story named *The Child Who Could See and Talk to Ghosts and Scary Spirits.*"

Chalsey, who had remained at her laptop working on Fredrick's novel, glanced up, her rainbow-colored glasses perched on the end of her nose. "Good idea. There's also the suitcase in the cellar that a spirit clearly wanted you to look inside."

"No, thank you." Fredrick shuddered, unfeigned. *That's too damn much for me.* He reached in, pulling out a smaller hot pink box. As he lifted the lid, he found a mint green baby shoe, a pink Minnie Mouse baby hairbrush, and a baggy containing a lock of black hair in it. "These must be mine. Figures Mom would buy me a pink hairbrush. She was so threatened by me being intersex she went overkill on the girl stuff from day one."

Chalsey's fingers flew over the keys for a few swift strokes, and then she looked up again. "Your parents basically played tug-o-war with your body. Despite your dad's statement about letting you choose your gender when you were older, he had you playing softball and soccer and wearing baseball caps. Your mom dressed you in lace and taught you cross-stitching. Honestly, I wanted to beat both their heads in."

"Mom told me when I was six that it was a sin and I'm not allowed to choose my gender." Fredrick set the hot pink box aside and continued digging. "She said God decided for me before I was born and I better face up to the fact I'm a girl." Rage burned behind his sternum like heartburn.

Chalsey snorted. "Yeah, if she meant *she's* God."

"Truth." Fredrick pulled out a manila folder and opened it. A yellowed newspaper clipping fell out, and there was a white envelope with the Tennessee government marked as the return address. Fredrick pulled out the letter inside and discovered it was a death certificate. He scanned it. The name read Timothy Dale Anderson. The birth date was recorded as February 7, 1980, and the death date as March 15, 1980. "God, that's weird."

Chalsey stood and walked to his side. "I'll say. Weird energy is filling the room now. I need to see what that is." She took the certificate from Fredrick and read it. "Wait. This infant would be around our age."

"This baby was born 22 days after I was and only lived roughly five weeks." Fredrick's heart raced, although he couldn't fathom why. "Who were the parents? Clearly, this baby was related to me somehow. His last name is Anderson. But why would my parents have a copy of some random relative's death certificate?"

"This isn't random." Chalsey slipped the certificate back

into the envelope. "I have chills, and this house feels supercharged with energy now. I'm going to burn some sage. I don't know what that is or why it's so important to the ghosts —and maybe the demon—in this house, but I've got to clear out this energy." She marched down the hallway toward the primary bedroom.

Feeling magnetized, Fredrick stared at the envelope with its 15-cent stamp. His stomach squeezed his lunch, whipping the grease and tomato sauce into a storm. *Dead baby. There was a dead baby. Why was there a dead baby?*

I told you to leave all this alone! howled a voice in Fredrick's mind. Like the night before, the intonation and tone matched his mother's.

Fredrick snapped around, scanning the room for a black silhouette.

Nothing.

Behind him, the kitchen table vibrated as if in an earthquake.

Michael smacked Fredrick out of control of their shared body. "We've got a big one this time! Chalsey! Where are you?"

"Coming!" Chalsey ran into the room with a smoking stick of bound and dried sage leaves. "Out! By the wind and the sea, by the sun and the lea, I command you to depart by the power of the Goddess."

Michael jerked open the back door, opting for maximum symbolism. "Yeah, get out! I don't want you here." He made shooing motions with his hand.

The table fell still. The air lightened. The kitchen seemed brighter, as if a cloud had passed between the earth and the sun but had moved on.

"Better." Chalsey's shoulders relaxed. "Michael?"

"Yep."

"Good. Walk through the house with me while I smudge

everything." Chalsey headed down the hallway and into the living room.

Michael ambled after her. "Boy, we kicked up a real storm. But how?"

Chalsey told him the story as she smudged the living and dining rooms.

"Wow, I have no idea who that baby could be." Michael climbed the stairs behind Chalsey. "There's a genuine mystery. And who's even left for me to ask?"

"What about your half-brother?" Chalsey walked through Michael's old bedroom.

Michael stared into the room from the doorway, his mind showing him how it looked in elementary school: pink and white and frilly, with a dollhouse in the corner on a card table and a trunk that held a landslide of Barbie dolls, My Little Ponies, and Cabbage Patch Kids—every toy a girl of the 1980s was supposed to love. "God! Roger and I haven't talked since Dad's funeral. That's, like, 24 years. I mean, I fav his pictures of his dog on social media sometimes, but that's it. It's not like we were ever close."

"Still, Roger might know who the baby was. How old was he in 1980?"

"19."

Chalsey slipped past Michael and headed down the hallway into the office. "Then it's worth asking him."

"Yeah. I'll give it a shot." Michael slipped into the office doorway, taking in his mother's computer desk. A desk calendar filled the space in front of the monitor, and a stack of birthday cards sat on the corner. A semi-orderly sprawl of sticky notes, paperclips, and pens filled out the area. "I guess Mom worked on her latest novel until the end."

"It was her third in a series, right?" Chalsey pivoted and faced Michael, her lips pressed into a tight frown. "I need to read her novel that you found, *The Civil War Ghost*."

Michael realized she meant Fredrick. "Fred-o found some old novel of my mom's?"

"Yes. And I can *sense* it's important. I'm going to read it. Today." Chalsey swept past Michael, her flowing green dress billowing behind her.

Michael followed her downstairs and noticed a newspaper clipping on the floor by the counter. Bending down, he snatched it up. "This is a story about Dad winning an award for being such a great therapist. There's some irony for you: 'Great therapist is actually an abuser.' Damn my life!" He raised his voice to a mocking pitch and set the clipping on top of a manila folder. "'Oh, you don't have any problems, Michael. Your parents are great!' Which is, like, totally why I have DID."

"I'm telling you, it's reverse gaslighting."

Michael felt his control of the body slipping away, and then Fredrick was facing Chalsey from across the kitchen island as she waved a stick of sage in the air, smoke spiraling from its end. "Wow, that makes more smoke that I would have thought." He glanced at the table, but it was still again. "I don't want to believe in demons, but dammit, that was a *shaking table.* I'm never going to sleep again."

"Well, it's gone now." Chalsey set the stick on the edge of the sink. "I'm going to read your mom's old novel." She grabbed the typed manuscript off the counter.

Chalsey: Professional Exorcist. I guess. A splitting headache tore through Fredrick's brain and shot through his left eye. *Never mind all that for now.* "Knock yourself out. I just got a migraine out of nowhere." He headed to his pill army, picking through it for the right medication. "I've got to lie down."

After swallowing some pills, Fredrick climbed the stairs, wondering why the entire house had an aroma of sage when Chalsey had only been in the kitchen.

Since Fredrick set at alarm for 4:30 pm, he was up in time for his weekly telehealth appointment with his therapist. His migraine had downgraded into a normal headache, so he braved staring at a computer screen. He retrieved his laptop from the kitchen, retired to his mom's old office, and set it up on her desk.

Dr. Laurie signed in right at 5:00, her long, brown hair hanging in a straight curtain on each side of her rounded cheeks. She wore tortoise-shell glasses. "I got your email. This was a big revelation. Tell me how you're doing."

"I'm afraid I'm making all this up." Fredrick stared to the side at his mother's bookcase. Since he'd effectively been an only child, this had always been his parents' home office. They changed the paint color five times and replaced the furniture half a dozen times. Now the paint was pale green, the curtains white sheers, and the furniture light oak, an ordinary room that didn't reflect his mother's real mind. "I saw my handwriting. I know what I read. But what if I lied in my journal? Or what if...I don't know."

Dr. Laurie's voice was calm, even-timbered, her expression stoic. "Did you often lie in your journal?"

"Never. Not that I can remember." Fredrick flinched. "But that's just it. I *don't* remember. I don't remember being violated. There it is in my diary, and I wrote dozens of poems and even a novel about being harmed. But..." He trailed off as his mother's blown glass paperweight slid an inch across the desk. He stared at the clear ball with the pale green star inside. *Did I just see that? Am I losing my mind?* A fresh stab of pain shot through his left eyeball.

"If you made it all up, what benefit would it have given you back then?" Dr. Laurie gazed at him, her brown eyes reflecting no suspicion or disbelief.

Fredrick focused on Dr. Laurie. *There are no such things as poltergeists. Right? God.* "Well, considering I apparently didn't tell anyone but my diary when I was a kid, it couldn't have given me any benefits. Maybe it explains why I kept having my dolls and My Little Ponies all beat each other up, though. One day, I had all the My Little Ponies die on purpose by jumping off the dryer and pretending it was a cliff. I think I was eight or nine years old."

The paperweight slid another inch, and all of Fredrick's arm hairs bushed up. *God. I'm being haunted. Why is this happening to me? I never wanted to believe in any of this!*

"Such scenarios during play suggest a problem," Dr. Laurie said. "All right. What benefit would making up molestation give you now?"

Fredrick forced himself to look at her. *I won't let this demon scare me out of talking to my therapist.* "Again, none. I won't get on social media and whine every day about how much my life sucks to get attention and sympathy. About all I would do is make a website educating people about abuse and become an internet activist." He snorted. "Otherwise, the only two people I'm likely to tell are you and Chalsey."

"Then why make it up? You have no reason to." Dr. Laurie shifted in her office chair, which emitted a creak of protest. "I've been seeing you for seven years. You've never engaged in attention-seeking behaviors or lied about being sick to game the system."

The paperweight shot sideways and rolled over on Fredrick's keyboard. Fredrick yelped and shot out of his chair. "And then there's that!" He pointed to the paperweight, although Dr. Laurie wouldn't be able to see it. "I've been haunted ever since I found my diary."

"Haunted?" Dr. Laurie's shock colored her tone, and her brow furrowed.

"That paperweight just rolled over my keyboard. And the

kitchen table vibrated earlier. And a black silhouette pushed me down the stairs. And—"

The electricity died.

A gust of wind hit the office window, rattling it, but sunlight still poured into the room. Fredrick stared at a white laptop screen that read: *Connection lost. Retrying in 10 seconds.* "Shit!"

The house had always had a tumultuous relationship with electricity. Rural electric cooperatives were notorious in his area for random power outages, some only lasting three seconds or fewer. But the timing spooked Fredrick.

"I told you not to air our family secret."

Fredrick jerked around, facing the closet door.

A perfect replica of his mother stared back at him, looking solid and real. Her short, permed hair, dyed brown as if she were thirty years younger, hugged her head, and a frown tugged the corners of her lips. Her eyes seemed unnaturally blue, over-saturated and intense. She wore one of her basic around-the-house outfits: a plain, electric blue, long-sleeved t-shirt and stretchy jeans with an elastic waistband. She sported earrings that looked like orange conch shells, but Fredrick didn't remember her owning such earrings.

"If you continue to tell outsiders our business, I'm going to get furious." Her voice was clipped, snippy.

Then she was gone.

Behind Fredrick, the paperweight rolled off the table and hit the floor, the thud making him jerk. Only the sea-foam green throw rug saved it from shattering.

The electricity fired back up, various electronics beeping.

Numb with fear, Fredrick plopped into the office chair and waited for the internet to be restored.

Once Dr. Laurie's face reappeared, Fredrick explained his encounter, adding, "So, do you want me to take a diagnostic now? Are you going to test me for schizophrenia? But for whatever it's worth, Chalsey is here with me, and she saw some of this stuff, too."

"I rarely use diagnostics." Dr. Laurie frowned. "If you feel comfortable letting Chalsey sit in on your appointment, and if you give her permission to speak, then she can tell me what she's seen."

Fredrick texted Chalsey and invited her upstairs to join the appointment.

Thirty minutes later, Fredrick and Chalsey trudged downstairs. Fredrick couldn't eat supper because of nausea..

"At least Dr. Laurie doesn't think I'm hallucinating." He paused by the refrigerator, his shoulders slumping. "Then again, maybe it's worse that I'm not. That makes all of this real."

"We have to consider what your mother's spirit—if that entity is her and not a 'demon'—is trying to hide." Chalsey leaned against the wall and crossed her arms. "You already told Dr. Laurie about the harming. And the entity said 'if you continue.' That implies there is more. And I believe that's true."

Fredrick nodded and headed to the counter. He'd left out the pizza box, and his stomach lurched as he smelled the spices and grease. "My supper is going to be Pepto."

Then he noticed the tarot card lying in the middle of the box lid. It showed the upside-down image of a Satanic figure with red skin and goat horns sitting on a black pedestal. The pedestal had two human figures chained to it. "Did you set out a tarot card?"

"No, I didn't." Chalsey marched over to his side. "Well, that's not what I was expecting. That's The Devil, reversed. This isn't a bad thing. Upright, The Devil means living in bondage, perhaps to an addiction. Oppression, powerlessness, or excess. But reversed, this card means freedom, reclaiming power, reclaiming control, release, and revelation."

Chalsey probably put that card there herself. She's lying to you. She wants something out of you. Your attention is all she's after.

Fredrick stopped breathing as he realized the voice in his head wasn't his own. He had a flashback, remembering a preacher when he was 11 telling the congregation that some voices in their heads weren't their own. Some were God. Others were demons or Satan.

Your mind is a supernatural battlefield, the preacher had said.

Fredrick skipped right over the theology and shot straight into anger. "Get out of my head!"

Chalsey jerked backwards, her curls bouncing. "What is it?"

"Another damn entity of some kind. An evil one."

Chalsey drew a pentacle in the air using her fingertip. "By these powers I charge you to leave: wind and fire, water and earth, Goddess and God. By the Maiden, the Mother, and the Crone, depart at once!"

A shiver shot down Fredrick's spine, and then Michael stood in front of a pizza box with a tarot card on it. "Great. Just fantastic. What now?"

"Michael?"

"Yep."

"I thought that was you. Your voice and vibes changed." Chalsey sighed. "A stronger entity has arrived, one able to look solid and speak in an audible voice. It took on the likeness of your mother. But a positive entity, one made of Light, left you this message of hope." She pointed at the card. "Something you're doing here is freeing you from bondage."

Michael picked up the card, studying it. "Spirits or entities powerful enough to move physical objects. Didn't you say once that they're rare?"

"Yeah." Chalsey opened a few cabinet doors and then

pulled out a bottle of olive oil. "We need to bless this oil and anoint the doors and windows."

"Sounds Christian to me." Michael leaned against the countertop and crossed his arms. "When I had that decade-long spiritual crisis, I went through at least three different denominations that did that."

Chalsey poured some oil into a cup. "The Pagans and the Christians have had a surprising amount of cross-pollination. The early Christians absorbed a great deal of Greek philosophies, theologies, and worldviews. Christianity didn't form in a vacuum." She stared into the cup, her hand still holding the oil bottle. "Michael..."

"What's up?" Michael set the tarot card aside and opened the pizza box. "Damn, I'm hungry. When did Fredrick eat last?" He pulled out a slice of room temperature pizza.

"You're not nauseated?"

"Nope." Michael pulled out a plate, dropped the slice onto it, and shoved it in the microwave.

Chalsey shrugged one shoulder. "Fredrick was. Do you have a headache?"

"Nope. Why? Did Fred-o?"

"Yeah. It's fascinating how DID works. You don't even share psychosomatic symptoms with each other." Chalsey set down the bottle. "I need to ask you a few serious questions."

The microwave beeped. Michael rescued his pizza. "Sure. Hit me."

"When did you start being afraid you hadn't been 'saved' at church?"

"Age 11. I'd only been baptized for a year when I began worrying."

Chalsey put the oil bottle back into the cabinet. Her eyes narrowed as she stared at a random spot on the wall. "Okay. How many churches or denominations did you try before you gave up on Christianity?"

"Five denominations. At least six different churches. All by the time I was 19." Michael savored the mushrooms, onions, and banana peppers. *Fred-o, you've got good taste in pizza. I don't know what I'd do if I took control of the body and discovered, say, ham and pineapple. I'd even take anchovies over that.*

Chalsey turned to face him, wrinkles creasing her forehead. "And even though Fredrick became an atheist, how many religions have you tried since then?"

"Nine. Buddhism, Hinduism, Wicca, Kabbalah, Kemetic —hey, wait. Why?"

"Stick with me here." Chalsey opened the cabinet where Michael's mother kept her herbs and spices. She pulled out thyme and rosemary, sprinkling a bit of each into the oil. "And you used to have nightmares about demons."

Michael paused with the pizza halfway to his mouth. "Sure. For years and years."

"Any other nightmares like that?"

With hot cheese and mild banana peppers to gird him, Michael pondered what dreams he could remember. Once he swallowed, he tilted his head to the side and gazed at Chalsey. "Well, I had nightmares about animal bones. And blood— like, everywhere. Smeared all over everything. Smoke. Like from a campfire, but it wasn't logs that were burning." He shuddered and set down his half-eaten slice. "I refused to look in the dream. I was afraid it was an animal carcass." He felt cold. Iced over.

"Animal carcasses?" Chalsey's voice was thin with horror.

"And crosses. Not crucifixes. Not upside-down ones. Just regular ones except completely covered in nails. Hundreds of nails." Violent nausea shot through Michael, and acid reflux crawled up his throat. He stared at the tile floor, noting in that disconnected, dissociated way that a single kibble of cat food had settled in one crack.

Chalsey picked up the cup of oil. "I'm going to bless this oil, and we're going to anoint the doors and windows. And then you and I are going to have a serious conversation about your mother's Civil War novel."

"I don't get the connection."

"You will once I tell you about it." Chalsey's jaw rippled. "Someone could have ritually abused you as a child, and we need to consider that possibility. Honestly, it makes sense. Plenty of children are molested, but not all of them develop DID. You did, though. Why? DID is a coping mechanism for extreme, repeated childhood trauma. And sexual violence and ceremonial abuse go hand-in-hand."

Michael felt intense pressure, as if a giant pressed his skull between his hands, and the entire room looked concave. *Severe dissociation. Am I switching? Is Fredrick taking over again?* He turned and jerked open the refrigerator door, pulling out a water bottle and drinking half of it in one shot, trying to force his pizza to stay down. His stomach twisted and roiled. "You've got to be fucking kidding me."

"I wish I were. But this would explain some of your unusual symptoms."

Michael did not want to hear that.

CHAPTER 6

THE TOWER XVI

ONCE CHALSEY BLESSED THE OIL AND ANOINTED THE windows and doors, Michael settled on the living room couch. Largo, seeing an available lap, padded over and hauled his sixteen-pound body onto the couch, climbing onto Michael and kneading his thigh with sharp kitty claws. "Should I switch with Fred-o for this? Or do you want to tell me first?"

Dropping into the recliner, Chalsey arranged her billowing green dress and then rested her hands in her lap. "Either way is fine."

"I'm lucky to have you." Michael never lost sight of the fact his girlfriend handled his DID with aplomb, including the weirdness of being his girlfriend while only being Fredrick's best friend. "All right. I'll take the hit first. What is it?"

Chalsey stared at the pot of mother-in-law's tongue on the windowsill. "In the first half of the novel, your mother's protagonist, Phoebe, loses a baby. The baby contracts measles at eight months old and dies."

A dead baby? Michael felt his brow wrinkle. *Why is everything suddenly about dead babies around here?*

"This shatters Phoebe because she'd already lost her

husband six months earlier. He died in the Battle of Shiloh. The novel is a romance, so at the halfway point, she's falling in love with a new man. But in the meantime, she and her friends, other war widows, have séances in the kitchen to talk to their dead husbands."

Every hair on Michael's body stood up and made itself known, tingles starting on his scalp and whisking down to his ankles. "Oh. My. God. My mom? Write about séances? She spent my whole life screeching about tarot cards, TV psychics, palm readers, séances, witches, you name it. She caught me watching a rerun of *Crossing Over with John Edward* —do you remember him?—when I was in grad school and lectured me for thirty minutes about how God doesn't give humans psychic powers or the ability to talk to the dead. She said Edward was doing the work of the devil."

Chalsey's gaze slid to Michael. "Precisely my point. And she describes the séance. She explains making sacred circles the Wiccan way and details calling the Guardians of the Watchtowers. In a non-hokey way, she even explains channeling a spirit. It's, for lack of a better word, perfect. And I'm only halfway done reading. There could be more."

Michael's fingers and toes went numb. Even his nose felt cold, although it was 75 degrees in the house. He only distantly registered Largo's circling of his lap, turning and turning to make a human nest. "So she did internet research. These days you can read up on anything, almost. There are a billion Wiccan sites that explain how to make a circle and how to Call the Corners."

"You forgot." Chalsey pressed her toes on the floor and rocked the chair, its springs creaking rhythmically. "This novel was typed. Your mom wrote it in the 1980s before she even owned a computer, much less had the internet."

"So she bought a book." Michael felt hysteria climbing up his throat, scurrying up from his stomach like ice spiders.

"Raymond Buckland published his Wicca 101 book back in the '70s, I think."

"Why would she want it? Why include this in her novel?"

Michael picked up Largo and sat him on the cushion. Then he shot off the couch and over to one bookcase. "I don't know. I don't know! She said she hated all that stuff. She said it was a sin." He picked up an angel figurine, this one a blonde girl with a pink robe. There was a matching boy in a blue robe with short brown hair. Kissing angels. "No way, there's just no way—she went to church every Sunday. Made me go. She forced me to tithe. Made me memorize Bible verses. Read me Bible stories every night as a kid."

"You knew at age eight how to make a sacred circle and get inside it for protection against demons."

Michael picked up the boy angel. Pressed them together. Made them kiss. His mother's voice flashed through his memory, random and off-topic: *There are only boys and girls. You must choose. Choose to be a girl. The doctor said you are.* "I don't remember any of this. And neither does Fredrick. I'm sure of it."

"There's another part of you, then." Chalsey rocked the chair harder, faster. The springs whined. "We always knew there should be more. But someone inside of you remembers. And if your mom was hiding her knowledge of magick, and making you hide it, then what was she afraid of? I say more than being found out by a Christian community. You had nightmares about bones and blood and fire."

Michael's head pressure shot high, making him dizzy. "I'm switching!" He set down the figurines. Glass angels filled the entire bookcase to bursting. The entire house was bursting. "I don't think—" His body remained still, but a sudden jerk pulled him backwards, causing nausea as his eyes disagreed with the sensation of falling. Gold and orange sparks exploded across his vision.

With a sharp inhalation, the new person surged up into the space where Michael had been, swiveled to face Chalsey, and stared her down. Thanks to thoughts left over like smoke, they knew who Chalsey was, but they'd never come so far up out of the back of Michael Fredrick's DID System before. It hadn't been necessary. "I get that you're trying to help, but stop."

Chalsey gazed at them, stopping the chair, the squeaking silenced. Her calm expression eased the lines off her face. "Is it not time for Michael and Fredrick to know?"

They tilted their head, examining Chalsey with wary dread. Now that they were in control of the body for the first time in decades, they couldn't remember their name or whether they were a boy or a girl. It felt terrible. "So you know there are many of us?"

"Yes."

Fear crept through their legs and arms, making their muscles twitch. "No one is supposed to know." They'd never counted on needing to do this much damage control.

"I've been friends with you since we were 13," Chalsey said. "It was off and on during college and grad school, but still. We've been friends for 30 years."

The new person frowned, knowing they were eight. *I froze in time. I never met you.* What Chalsey said sounded reasonable. It didn't sound like a trick. Perhaps Chalsey was open to bargaining. The alternative was being at Chalsey's mercy while she and the grown-up boys tore everything apart and ruined everything forever. "Well, maybe that's okay. But it's not time to talk about what Mother did. And Father, too. They did rites. Not Wiccan ones. Other ones. It scared us. A lot. And it was bad. But it's not time yet. So leave it alone."

"I will get you the help you need." Chalsey's expression remained smooth, unruffled. "I will find you a therapist who specializes in treating this kind of trauma. And then you'll have support and help."

The new person snorted. "People said before that they would help." *Teachers. School counselors. Babysitters.* "They didn't. Sometimes they made it worse. And it would take at least a good therapist. Maybe more."

"I understand." Chalsey's voice remained calm.

Chalsey's face didn't turn red or twist. Her brow didn't furrow, and her eyes didn't burn. She didn't scream or accuse or blame. The new person found this odd. *Don't all adults scream when they don't get what they want? Don't all adults hit when kids say no?* "Fine." They dived, having no interest in staying up here in the horrible blankness of not knowing who they really were. Being this far up in the DID System sucked. But they had to pick who to put in their place to fill the empty spot. When they went to grab Michael, he wasn't there. They'd pulled on Michael too hard on accident. The only person they could grab was Fredrick. That wasn't how it was supposed to be. They were supposed to reset things to the way they were before they came up, but there wasn't a choice. So they hauled Fredrick up and pushed him into place before receding into the background of their shared mind.

Fredrick abruptly found himself standing in the living room, Chalsey perched in the rocker recliner. He glanced around the sunlit room with its stack of *Southern Living* magazines, crimson couch, and purring cat. "Wow. I must've spaced out on you. Sorry. We were in the kitchen, and I was talking about Pepto." His legs quivered, as if he'd been terrified a moment earlier. *What the hell? But nothing's happening.*

"This is not the first time something like that has happened." Chalsey began rocking, the chair squeaking. "You need a PTSD and trauma specialist. Dr. Laurie isn't enough anymore. Her specialties are depression, anxiety, and other mood disorders. Now that we know your dad was harming you, this changes things."

Fredrick's shoulders slumped, and he trudged over to the couch, plopping down by Largo, who climbed onto his lap. *Lord, Mom. Why did you overfeed your poor cat until he's obese?* "Okay, fine. I can't argue with you. But you know how it is: I've got to find someone who's never heard of my dad. No one who knew Dr. Phillip Roger Anderson the Amazing Psychologist would ever believe he molested or beat his kid." With sudden clarity, he understood his older half-brother had been mistreated as well. "Or *kids.* God, no wonder Roger moved to California and never visits. He must have never forgotten what Dad did. So why did I?"

"If you're right and Roger didn't forget, then I guess the difference is your mothers." Chalsey grabbed one of her blonde spiral curls and wrapped it around her finger. "Your mom was pushy and dominating. Maybe Roger's was more supportive somehow."

"Maybe." Fredrick knew nothing about her except her name was Janet.

Chalsey reached into her dress pocket and pulled out her cellphone. "Well, anyway. I'm going to research PTSD and childhood trauma specialists. Your dad's been dead plenty long enough for no one to remember him anymore, especially if I find someone in Louisville or Lexington."

"That's fair. And thanks in advance." Fredrick displaced Largo and returned to the kitchen, trying to remember if he had taken Pepto. *Yes? No? Maybe?*

He discovered a half-eaten slice of pizza on a plate and stopped by the refrigerator, his breath crystallizing in his lungs. *Oh, shit. No! I don't remember eating any pizza. In fact, I said I couldn't. And no way would Chalsey eat it, not with cheese on it.*

Fredrick rubbed his face with both hands. *There's*

something more going on here. Something more than PTSD. What am I going to do?

After thirty minutes of Pepto in action, Fredrick settled at the kitchen table with spaghetti covered in pesto sauce. "Maybe I can get this down." He hadn't mentioned the mystery pizza slice. "Just being in this house is ripping up my stomach lining. But Knight Auction Co. is coming in the morning at 8:00."

"How does that work?" Chalsey carried over a plate of noodles with pesto, deciding to "sin" and have some wheat. She was mildly gluten intolerant but dangerously lactose intolerant. "I know we have to unpack the boxes, but what else?"

"They said they'll explain all the fine details once they see what Mom has." Fredrick twirled his fork, catching long strands of pasta. "But we'll need to lay out things on tables for them to take pictures of, and then they'll do an internet auction. They'll auction the house, too." *Goodbye, hideous house full of disgusting secrets.* "I have to remove all personal papers and clothing."

Chalsey settled in her chair and arranged the skirt of her billowing dress. "All right. Time to call in help."

"Being an only child sucks." Fredrick stared out the window, remembered the man in green from earlier, and flinched. But the only sight greeting him was a monarch butterfly resting on the deck railing. "Or being Mom's only child, to be more precise. What kind of help?" Fredrick got along well with his co-workers, but Chalsey was his only close friend. *My introversion is biting me in the ass here.*

"My circle." Chalsey twirled her fork, gathering noodles. "We have nine members. Nine is a sacred number in Wicca."

Fredrick's mind rushed to catch up. *Circle? Oh, your coven. But you don't call it that. Is the term too old? Did it fall out of usage?*

"Three is the most sacred number, signifying the Goddess' three aspects of Maiden, Mother, and Crone. So three times three or nine is also sacred. In this case, that means nine people to help you put out items on tables."

Being used to Chalsey's wide expanse of knowledge, both inside and outside of her specialties, Fredrick smiled. "Maybe you should have remained an English instructor. You're a natural educator."

"Shit pay. Heavy workload. Overenrolled classes." Chalsey shrugged. "Do still miss it from time to time, though. Anyway, is that okay with you? Bring them in?"

"Hell, yeah." Fredrick smiled, relief easing the tension from his shoulders. "If you bring me nine people to help, I'll accept them with open arms."

Chalsey lifted her fork, a noodle escaping. "Nine it is."

Fredrick fought down his pasta with the hope it would digest.

When they stood to take their plates to the sink, Chalsey said, "Plus I want their help dealing with the ghosts and demon in this house. They've been quiet since I blessed the house with oil, but I don't expect that to hold. These entities want something. Their investment level seems high."

"Oh, great. Just what I want to hear." Fredrick's stomach clenched around the pasta, aching. *Wait? When did you bless the house with oil?* "But I can't argue with your interpretation." *Time to come out of denial and face the facts: spirits are real.*

What does that do for our atheism?

Fredrick turned on the water and held his plate under it, watching flecks of basil race down the porcelain and into the drain. Our? *Why did I think* our? *It's my* atheism. *What does this do for* my *atheism?*

Is it my?

Fredrick shut off the water, tingles shooting up his spine. *Are you a spirit? Is a spirit talking to me?*

Silence.

Fuck. I need a new specialist. ASAP. Fredrick opened the dishwasher and shoved in his plate. "Okay. If you want to rest this evening, you should. I guess I can sort through Mom's paperwork. She has three filing cabinets of it in her office."

"You should rest, too." Chalsey rinsed her plate and added it to the dishwasher. "I'm going to finish reading your mom's Civil War novel."

Fredrick's nose wrinkled. "If that qualifies as rest." While he had never shamed his mother for writing romance novels, finding the attitude to be condescending and ridiculous, he hated heterosexual romance stories. *The number of toxic stereotypes is overwhelming. Too many toxic gender roles. Too many abusive tropes.* "You know what? I think I'll play with the tarot cards. The spirits seem obsessed with them. Maybe I'll dive right in."

Chalsey smiled, and despite himself, Fredrick had to admit she was pretty. "Go for it!"

Chalsey retreated to the living room, taking the electric blue three-ring binder with her. Largo waddled after her, his orange and white coon-like tail held high but curved like a candy cane at the top.

Fredrick stared after the cat and his oversized football-shaped body. *The cat has diabetes. Mom had diabetes. The cat is obese, and so was Mom. Dad would have said Mom was eating to medicate her pain. Food addictions are common. But the cat...why spray it all over the cat? She harped on my weight, nitpicking me if I gained too many pounds. But the cat she "pampers"?*

"It's like an internal labyrinth made of psychological clues," Fredrick muttered. He grabbed the tarot deck from the counter and settled at the table. Having read the tiny instruction booklet, he then shuffled the deck. He laid out three cards in a basic spread: past, present, and future.

Looking around the kitchen for ghostly activity first, Fredrick turned over the first card, representing the past. The image showed three women holding up three golden cups in a toast, but the card was upside down. He opened the little white book—Chalsey called them LWB for short—and read the entry for Three of Cups, reversed: "Solitude, loneliness, isolation, gossip, scandal, excess." He stared at the card. "Well, I can't argue with that."

Nope, his internal voice agreed. *Solitude, loneliness, and isolation are a perfect description of the past.*

At this comment, Fredrick scanned the room. No spirits showing themselves. "Okay..." *My internal voice is awfully conversational sounding.* He turned over the card representing the present. It showed a tall stone tower being hit by lightning and two people falling out of windows. "Scary." The card read *The Tower.* "Seems obvious." He looked up the meaning: "Upheaval, sudden change, chaos, disaster, destruction, trauma. Well, I don't need more trauma."

The upheaval doesn't have to be traumatic. His internal voice sounded oh-so-reasonable. *The sudden change can be good. Imagine the tower as a corrupt institution, something you want gone from your life. You might feel like the screaming people falling at first, but it won't be a bad ending.*

"Well, it's true that a trauma has been revealed in the present," Fredrick murmured. As an only child, he had talked to himself his entire life. Excessively. He'd played alone for hours at a time and chatted with himself nonstop. He hadn't stopped as an adult. "And it has caused an upheaval."

Look at the next card.

Fredrick paused. *My internal voice seems different today.*

More like a separate voice. He narrowed his eyes. *Are you a spirit?*

Silence.

Fredrick sighed and flipped over the last card, representing the future. This card showed a disembodied hand holding an enormous golden coin with a star on it. He looked up the Ace of Pentacles: "Abundance, prosperity, resources, new opportunities, security, and stability." His stomach unclenched, cluing him in to the fact he was taking the reading seriously. "Well, I'll accept that."

A strange electric zing snapped through him.

Spooked, Fredrick gathered the cards and the booklet and shoved them back into the box. *What the hell? I don't even believe in magic! Magic with a "c" is illusionary stage magic, and everyone knows that's not real. Magick with a "k" is Wiccan magick or Voodoo or Druidry or whatever, and I've never believed those spells work.*

Fredrick noticed the thought felt flat and dull, as if he'd somehow lied.

You haven't?

"I know you're there," Fredrick hissed. "Stop hiding and tell me who you are."

Silence.

"Tell me."

Fredrick's head suddenly felt stuffed with cotton balls, or as if someone had swaddled his brain with bubble wrap. *Something is going on here.*

Standing, Fredrick retreated to his mother's office, where he'd left his laptop, and joined Chalsey's search for a new therapist. She'd emailed him three links to psychologists, and he filled out their online forms, requesting appointments.

He couldn't wait a moment longer.

CHAPTER 7

STRENGTH VIII

At 7:00 Friday morning, Fredrick stumbled out of bed, showered to halfway regain true consciousness, and then fixed himself coffee to be fully functional. At 8:00, Mark Knight, Jr. arrived with two assistants, and seeing them through the front window, Fredrick groaned.

"I don't know if I can handle this," he told Chalsey as he shuffled across the living room to the door. She had curled up on the rocker recliner with his mom's Civil War novel, sipping on black coffee.

"I'll listen to their spiel, too." Chalsey set the blue binder on the end table. Today she wore a gypsy skirt like a sunset: yellow, orange, and red from waist to hem. Chalsey had matched it to a plain white tank top.

By comparison, Fredrick felt drab in jean shorts and a green t-shirt with his university's logo. "I'll need at least that much support, yeah." *But oh, God, I don't think I can handle this.*

Michael abruptly found himself opening the front door for a man wearing khakis and a polo shirt plus two women, one in a flower print shift dress and one wearing khakis with a checkered shirt. He discovered a mug of coffee in his hand and took a sip, trying to act casual. *Sure, I know what's going on. I wasn't just randomly dumped into a moment.*

Noticing the man's polo shirt had a Knight logo on the pocket, Michael oriented himself. *Oh, right. Auction company.* "Come right on in."

They walked through the house as a group and discussed which items could be auctioned, how to arrange them for photography, and how to auction the house. Chalsey took notes on her phone as they moved room to room. Michael valiantly fought off a panic attack. *Too much shit! Why do humans have to collect so much useless stuff?*

Mr. Knight handed Michael a business card with his email address and company website and then departed with his assistants.

Shutting the door, Michael locked it with a flourish. *Yes, leave. I can't handle any more right now.* "Oh, God, I need an army."

"I told Fredrick I'd call in my circle, and he agreed." Chalsey swiped through a few screens on her phone. "I'll group text them now. It would help if you offered a couple of free pizzas or to let us hold our circle here tomorrow night."

"Right. Tomorrow's Saturday." Michael had trouble keeping up with what day it was. Time jumped around for him too much. But he remembered Chalsey's circle met every Saturday evening. "Sure. Go for it. I doubt Fredrick will mind."

A sharp crack drew their attention toward the back of the living room.

"Did another angel just 'fall' off the shelf and break?" Chalsey asked.

Michael crossed the hardwood floor, coffee mug still in

hand, and stopped by the bookcase. The male kissing angel in his blue robe lay broken into three pieces on the floor, one wing severed and his upper torso and head severed from his lower torso and feet. "Man, that sucks. Now they're not a matching pair anymore." He stooped and picked up the pieces, setting them on the shelf by the pink female angel. Inexplicably, he felt sad. *Why do I care if this angel got broken? Why does it hurt that they're no longer a matching pair? I thought these figurines were ugly when I was a kid.*

Chalsey joined them. "So one of the ghosts or the 'demon' doesn't want us to have a Wiccan circle here. I'd say that's a good thing. They're more likely to do something while my friends are here, and then they can see what we're up against."

"How can you say that so calmly?" Michael rubbed the bridge of his nose with his fingers. "God, you're such a trooper about this shit. I should be running out the door screaming or something."

Chalsey grinned. "Oh, I never let spirits win." She dropped into the beige recliner. "I need to talk to you again about your mom's novel."

"Oh, yeah?" Michael perched on the red couch, unable to relax and sit back. "Wait. I switched yesterday when you were talking about it. Did Fred-o show up?"

"Nope." Chalsey frowned at the binder as she opened it. "A protector state of yours did. They had a high-pitched voice and sounded like a child talking. But they still meant to protect you. I'll try not to make them angry, but I think you should know your mom's novel got even wilder."

"Fine. Hit me." Michael set his mug on the coffee table and scooted back. With the impeccable timing of honed kitty instincts, which he and Chalsey had dubbed cat-dar after the word *radar*, Largo appeared at his feet, hauled his kitty rolls onto the couch, and flopped onto Michael's lap. He scratched

Largo's ears. *I wonder how long it will take your diet to work. I wonder how much a pet's physical condition reveals the mindset of its owner.*

"Two of your mother's minor female characters have 'miscarriages,' and they both imply the 'miscarriages' were actually planned." Chalsey flipped through the typed manuscript. "The protagonist condemns one woman but not the other, which I think is interesting. A pass is given to the woman who induces a miscarriage because her husband was unfaithful to her. The woman who induces a miscarriage because her husband dies in the war and she doesn't want to raise the child without him is condemned."

More dead babies. Michael's brow furrowed. "Okay, that's interesting. Despite being a Fundamentalist about most things —gender, sexual orientation, church attendance, tithing, and the literalism of Scripture—my mom wasn't ever for or against abortion. She always seemed divided on the issue. I wonder why it shows up here, though."

"Good question." Chalsey pointed to a page two-thirds into the novel. "And even weirder, your mom sends her characters into the forest at midnight to summon a demon. The protagonist claims to not want to go, but the other men and women 'drag' her out there without her putting up much of a fight."

"Summon a demon?" Michael's body flash froze, his face stiff, his lips and fingers cold, his breath caught in his chest. "Mom wrote *that?*"

"The ritual she describes isn't a rip-off of anything Wiccan." Chalsey shut the binder. "And you know as well as I do Wiccans don't believe in the Satan of Christianity. Or its God. If she'd described praying to the Goddess to summon a demon, you would have heard me cussing from upstairs. But this scene is something else."

Michael's nose burned, and his ears rang. "Something... else?"

"I once read several medieval grimoires out of curiosity." Chalsey set the binder on the end table and faced Michael more fully. "I discovered a bizarre contradiction: in the Middle Ages, ceremonial magicians used High Magick to summon demons by using all the names of God. The instructions directed them to go to confession first and take communion, and their sacred circles bound the demon and kept it in place. Half the grimoire was about how to control a demon and force it to obey you using Jesus' name. The rest told you which demon to summon for whatever you wanted. Do you want to learn Greek? Summon this demon. Do you want a pretty wife? Summon that demon. Do you want to master geometry? Summon this other demon."

Inhaling sharply, Michael rubbed his face and tried to ground himself. *Nothing is happening. I am safe at this moment.* "So, be a good Christian so you can boss around demons. And, weirdly, learn Greek."

"Knowledge was power." Chalsey shrugged one shoulder. "Your mom's novel sounds closer to that grimoire. They make two circles: one for them to stand inside and another to contain the demon. They summon it using ancient Hebrew names for God. The only Hollywood-style stuff comes at the very beginning and the very end. In the medieval grimoires, animal sacrifice was rare, and none of them say to commit infanticide. If you were told to kill a kid—as in, a baby goat—it was to dry its skin and use it for parchment."

"So the whole Dr. Faustus thing about 'I'll sacrifice a baby and drink its blood' is a reflection of wild Christian terror tactics?" Michael fled to the comforting confines of academia.

Chalsey snorted. "Yes. There was a scholar a long time ago who claimed the word 'kid' meant a human child, but if you read the directions for yourself, it's obvious it's a baby goat."

Michael, having been through Fredrick's history classes, sighed. "Right. Dried animal skins were used as parchment." His body calmed in stages, his fingers no longer cold. "Okay. And the other Hollywood part?"

"Wild sex after the demon is summoned." Chalsey rolled her eyes. "Unless your spell summoned a demon who would fetch you a beautiful woman, there was no sex involved. Most of these demons were supposed to teach you languages or math, physically lead you to a lost treasure, or teleport you to some far-off place. There was no wild orgy."

"More medieval Christian propaganda?"

"You got it." Chalsey folded her hands in her lap. "What your mom did was create an excuse for her protagonist to have sex with her new love interest. Everyone else has wild sex, and the protagonist claims she's not interested. But her love interest ignores her protests and spends the next two pages pleasuring her until she comes three times. It's just an excuse for a big sex scene that attempts to give the readers a safe way to engage in a forced sexual activity fantasy."

Michael felt himself get jerked away. It was like someone hooking the back of his shirt collar and yanking, except without the motion affecting his physical body.

The protector state internally grunted as they forced their way up to take Michael's place. Losing their grip on what their name was and who they were inside angered them, but there was nothing they could do about it. Inhabiting the puny, annoying body that they had to use in the outside world angered them, too. If they were stronger, they could fight better. But this was a situation for words first. The person causing the problem was this Chalsey woman Fredrick liked and Michael dated. *I'll be the judge of whether Chalsey needs to be removed from our life.* The protector state stared at Chalsey. "Don't say the R-word."

Chalsey's face remained calm, the muscles around her eyes relaxed. "I'm sorry. I wasn't trying to upset you."

"I was listening." The protector state waited for the inevitable red-faced screaming, but once again, Chalsey's expression was impassive. *Why is this adult so different from the rest?* Chalsey's behavior mollified them enough to throw her a bone. They wouldn't come down so hard on her. "You were good. You didn't say Mom and Dad did that stuff in real life. But don't talk about the R-word, either."

"Fredrick and Michael found your diary from elementary school and read it," Chalsey said. "They found out your dad is guilty. And I promise they're not falling apart. They're going to talk to a trauma specialist about it. A specialist who has never met your dad before, and since your dad died, they can't ever meet him. So it's safe."

The protector state narrowed their eyes. "It will never be safe!" *Never mind, you're dangerously naïve. I have to stop you from wrecking everything.*

"Both your mom and dad have died," Chalsey said in a composed and even tone. "They can't hurt you anymore."

At this claim, the protector state scanned the room. An unfamiliar, enormous orange tabby sat on their lap. A new TV engulfed half the wall—one slim and flat instead of boxy with vacuum tubes. Their father's brown house shoes were not by the recliner, and neither was his ubiquitous newspaper. The record player was no longer on the fold-down door of one bookcase. Since the carpet was gone, the original hardwood floor was revealed. *The house is different. I could hear Michael and Fredrick talking, but I couldn't see this. And this lady is old like Dad and says she's been our friend for thirty years.*

"Am I allowed to know your name?" Chalsey asked.

The protector state only now noticed that they knew the woman's name, plus lots of other random things. *How?* What they remembered and what they didn't wasn't something that they could control. And now that Chalsey was asking for a name, it didn't take more than a few seconds to realize they could remember it. "I guess. It's Angela. But I'm not a girl. I'm not a boy, either. I'm neither."

"Okay, Angela. I'll use they/them pronouns for you."

"Whatever." Angela petted the enormous kitty. "Just no *he* or *she*." They felt their abdomen unclenching. This was the longest they'd ever been in control of the body. Usually, it was an emergency. They hit someone as hard as they could or they screamed or they lay there and took the pain so no one else had to feel it. But this...this was peaceful. "Mom and Dad are really gone?"

"They're really gone."

Angela sighed. The claim felt true. "All right. You can use the R-word then. But Dad wasn't the only one. And they did the scary ritual stuff first. They—they set up an altar. And prayed to someone not God. And then they took turns hurting me."

Chalsey's face stiffened, her mouth flattening into a line, and her eyes narrowed. "I'm very sorry. And that was very wrong of them."

Since Chalsey seemed sincere, Angela decided she wasn't doing that fake polite thing adults did when they pretended to take a child seriously but didn't. *Adults think they're so smart. But I can see right through them.* "Don't tell Fredrick and Michael. They're not ready to know yet. And Dietrich says not to tell them. It's bad enough that they read our diary. We don't want them to fall apart."

"I understand."

The kitty nuzzled Angela's hand and purred. Angela supposed this new world wasn't so bad. There was a cat, and their parents were dead. "All right. Just be good, okay?"

"I will."

Angela let go.

When Michael switched in, he found himself petting Largo. "Oh! I'm back." He gazed at Chalsey. "Who did you get?"

"A child who says their name is Angela. They're agendered." Chalsey ran both hands back into her blonde curls.

Given Michael's BA in psychology, he wasn't surprised to hear that. *Not all my self-states can be male. Carl Jung said everyone has both anima and animus. Eastern philosophy holds that everyone has both yin and yang. I should have both male and female parts—and even agendered or third gender ones.*

"Angela has trusted me with some information," Chalsey said, "but they specifically ordered me not to tell you or Fredrick, and I don't want to violate their trust. I need to build rapport with each of your parts or self-states. Your inner people."

Michael leaned his head back against the couch. "Then don't tell me. It's more important for my child states to learn they can trust you. Whatever it is, I'll cough it up in therapy, eventually. In a worst-case scenario, I could take you to an appointment with my new therapist, give you permission to talk, and then leave the room. That way, my therapist could know and make plans to help me, but you wouldn't have broken your promise."

"Sounds like a plan."

Michael's stomach grumbled at him, reminding him he'd only had coffee for breakfast. "Okay. Food and then more unpacking. We've got to get all this ready to be photographed."

"You got it."

"You've always got my back." Michael gently lifted Largo, collected the broken angel, and faced the painful knowledge that Chalsey was the only person who had ever loved him for real.

Fredrick stared into his bowl of raisin bran. *I remember showing Mr. Knight around Mom's house, but I don't remember drinking my coffee. I know Mr. Knight had two assistants with him, but I remember nothing we discussed. What the hell is wrong with my memory?*

"One of my friends from my circle has today off." Chalsey settled across from him with a plate of fried tofu and vegetables. "He's got Fridays and Sundays off instead of Sundays and Mondays. So he's offered to come help today, too."

"Mondays?" Fredrick focused on Chalsey. *I can tell either Dr. Laurie or my new therapist about my memory problems later.* "Is he a barber? Or a tattoo artist or massage therapist?" Mondays off were specific to a subset of jobs in their area of Kentucky, so he felt he could guess.

"Reiki practitioner." Chalsey smiled. "He went to our high school. He was a senior when we were freshman, so you might not remember him: Anthony Michael Stevenson."

Fredrick cast back his memory to the boy slumped in the corner of chemistry class, drawing comic book characters in the margins of his class notes. "That kid who sang in an indie band." He saw a flash of their talent show performance when they'd covered the then-popular "Loser" by Beck.

"Yep. That's him."

"Okay, sure. I'm not turning down help."

Chalsey whipped her phone out of her skirt pocket and texted him.

After choking down raisin bran, Fredrick poured a second cup of coffee to replace the mysteriously missing first cup and resumed unpacking the water-stained maroon box that had held a baby's death certificate and his mother's Civil War novel. "Most of this is trash. Would you pull over the garbage can?"

"Sure." Chalsey grabbed the can and set it at his feet. Then she washed the skillets she'd used.

Fredrick tossed in old letters, recipes cut out of magazines, and an issue of *TV Guide* with a dog-eared article, and fifteen issues of *Writer's Digest.* "God, Mom used to make me read *Writer's Digest.* As soon as I got serious about writing a novel —do you remember the one I named *The Desperate*?—she drowned me in articles."

"Yeah, I remember that novel. It really showed your pain." Chalsey frowned at the skillet she scrubbed. "Your mom was abusing you with that. The more articles about 'The Right Way to Write' that she shoved at you, the more insufficient you felt. The more articles about publication she forced on you, the more intimidated and hopeless you felt."

Fredrick stared at the decades old article he now held. Someone had taken it out of a magazine, possibly *Writer's Digest,* and stapled it in the corner. The title was "15 Things to Never Say to an Agent." A flutter of panic shot through his chest, contracting his heart, even though he'd published four novels and two poetry chapbooks. "You're right. I've never stopped being afraid. She said she was helping me, but I was only sixteen. It overwhelmed me."

"She knew that. She saw your fear. And she did it anyway. That's abuse."

Fredrick wanted to argue, but he remembered telling his mom how much the querying process scared him.

Her only response had been, *"Well, it* is *scary. It's hard. I'm worried I'll never be published, either."*

Fredrick tossed the yellowed article into the trash. "Mom never said, 'I believe in you. I know you'll persevere. I know you'll be good enough.' She just said, 'Everyone rejects me. I think it's all hopeless.'"

Snorting, Chalsey slammed a cabinet door shut. "But notice that she got published and was even on her third novel when she died. And you know what she didn't say? 'I got published, so I know you will, too.'"

Fredrick met Chalsey's gaze, knowing he had survived the querying process with her help. She had given him courage, told him he was good enough, and told him to never give up. She had queried for him until he got accepted by three different publishers and his career had launched. "You're right. She never said that."

"She got jealous of you. Your writing quickly became stronger than hers. So she competed with you."

The doorbell rang, and Fredrick headed into the hallway. "I know you're right." *And I both do and don't want to admit it.*

Reaching the front door, Fredrick opened it. A man in his mid-forties stood on the porch, smiling. He had curly blond-brown hair that hung an inch below his jaw, blue eyes, and full lips. Stainless steel body jewelry decorated his face and ears: a nose ring, a stud in his right forward helix, and a ring through his left ear in his daith. He wore jeans and a faded green t-shirt with the Celtic Tree of Life on the front.

He's handsome. Gorgeous, even. Fredrick opened the screen door as well. "Hey."

Chalsey swooped up behind Fredrick. "Hey! Fredrick, meet Anthony Stevenson. Toni, meet Fredrick."

"Nice to meet you. Call me Toni."

Fredrick shook Toni's hand. "Nice to meet you." He stepped aside so Toni could enter. A faint whiff of patchouli incense accompanied him.

"Goddess! The energy in here." Toni scanned the living room with a frown and a furrowed brow.

"This is what I was talking about," Chalsey said. "I

anointed all the doors and windows, but the spiritual muck is terrible."

Fredrick closed the door, locked it, and stared at Toni and Chalsey. *Toni is like a male Chalsey: a beautiful, earthy kind of person.*

So they're both beautiful? the conversational voice asked inside Fredrick's mind.

Okay, yeah. But I don't think Chalsey wants me thinking about her that way. We're just friends.

You sure?

I prefer men. Fredrick wondered why he was being so chatty with himself. But a flashback overran the thought, the pain shooting through his gut. His mind replayed the image of his mom standing over him while he sat on his frilly bed in his pink bedroom. He'd been twelve and fighting the traumas of puberty.

"The fact you like boys proves you're a girl." His mom had propped her fists on her hips.

"What if I like boys while I'm just me?" he'd asked.

His mother had slapped him.

Fredrick jerked. *Wait! I didn't remember that before. Mom slapped me.*

She did that a lot, the conversational voice groused.

Toni stood in front of the bookcase that had lost two angels. He picked up the pink female kissing angel and examined it.

Well, it doesn't matter, anyway. Fredrick's shoulders slumped. *I've never gotten off of "second base" with anyone. An adult doesn't want to date someone who's too terrified to have sex.*

Toni whirled around, looking toward the doorway between the dining room and the kitchen. "There's a malevolent spirit in here right now." He pointed. "It looks like a green blob in my spirit vision."

"Green again, huh?" Chalsey drew a pentacle in the air with her finger. "By the Maiden, the Mother, and the Crone, and by fire, water, earth, and air, I banish you from this house."

Toni set down the angel, a frown tugging his lips again. "It's gone for now, but I'm worried it'll come back—or one just like it. It'd be best if we set up an altar."

"No!" Fredrick startled himself with his shout. "No altars in this house!" He hadn't even known he was going to speak.

Toni flinched and paled. "Oh, God. I'm sorry. I wasn't trying to offend you. And of course, I would never set up an altar in someone's house without their permission."

"And no sacrifices!" Fredrick realized his voice sounded high-pitched, almost child-like. *What am I saying?*

Chalsey held up both hands as if warding off an attack and turned toward Toni. "Fredrick actually knows Wiccans don't sacrifice black cats or whatever."

"Ah, right." Toni's brow furrowed again as he studied Fredrick. "Your energy just totally shifted."

Fredrick pressed his hands to both sides of his head as if he could hold his brains in by sheer physical force—and more to the point, that he needed to. "I have *no idea* why I said that. The words just popped out of me from out of nowhere." *I'm gonna die of embarrassment here. I meet a beautiful man and then accuse him of animal sacrifice? Jesus Christ, I totally just lost it!*

One of Toni's eyebrows arched high. "Stress, maybe? I mean, your mom did just die and all."

"I mean, maybe. I guess." Fredrick shivered and didn't know why. "I let Chalsey set up a temporary altar on the floor yesterday. At least, I think it was yesterday." He couldn't remember clearly now. "I know about the whole 'represent the elements' thing."

Chalsey stared at the bookcase. "Guys, we're actually—"

She paused and rotated on one heel, the movement sharp and robotic. "Never mind. I can't talk about that yet, so we'll deal with that later. Fredrick, you inherited this house to do with what you will. If you like, I can help you make an altar to any friendly spirit of your choice: Jesus, Mother Mary, St. Christopher, St. Michael the Archangel, the Buddha, Kwan Yin the bodhisattva, you name it. You could even make an ancestor altar and decorate it with pictures of family members you loved. It's all up to you. All Toni and I would ask is that you see the recipient of the altar as being a positive force: a light-bringer, a source of truth or enlightenment, and/or a protector for the occupants of the house."

Fredrick's heart raced, his hands turned cold, his face grew numb. He felt the wideness of his eyes, his shallow breathing, his trembling knees.

"But only if you're interested," Toni said. "Wicca does not proselytize—or we're not supposed to, anyway—and I never want anyone to practice a religion they didn't choose for themselves. The best minds in Wicca say to choose the path that suits you and will fulfill your spiritual needs, whatever path that might be."

Fredrick's knees straightened, and he inhaled more deeply. *My choice. My path. Okay.*

Do it, said the conversational voice. *Choose whatever you want. But I can feel it's important.*

Understanding that a separate voice was, in fact, addressing him, Fredrick looked away. *Who are you?*

I'm your—

The voice was cut off, silenced. Fredrick felt cotton balls in his skull, packed around his brain. *That feeling again. Brain Bubble Wrap. That isn't normal. And the voice was trying to tell me the truth!* Frustration fired through him, hot coals in his veins. He looked back. "When Mom and I went on vacation to England, we visited a couple of cathedrals. And for a moment, only for a moment, as I stared up at a Mother Mary statue, I thought I felt something. I'm *not* saying the God of Christianity is real. I walked away a long time ago. But if I'm going to do this, I'm going to have to break the rules of my Baptist upbringing and use a Mother Mary statue. Or something."

"A fine choice," Toni said.

"But we need a statue," Chalsey said.

Fredrick shot through the living room. "I inherited a Miraculous Medal from my grandma's best friend." He zipped into the kitchen and thundered down the cellar stairs. Eyeing the pink boxes in the corner, he marched over and began pulling off lids.

Chalsey and Toni joined him.

"A Miraculous Medal?" Chalsey echoed. "What's that?"

"A Mother Mary pendant," Toni said. "It's probably the most popular pendant of a saint that Catholics wear."

Fredrick opened three boxes and then saw his childhood jewelry box: white and pink with roses and a ballerina pictured on the lid. *More girly-girl stuff I didn't ask for.* "Helen was my maternal grandma's best friend, and she had no children. When she died, she left things for my grandma, mom, and me. I don't know why, but Helen willed me her Miraculous Medal and her cross necklace. Mom made fun of the medal. She hated Catholics. She mocked all their beliefs. But she let me keep the medal for sentimental reasons." He pulled out the jewelry box, opened it, and lifted out the pewter Miraculous Medal on its pewter chain. The pendant was the size of his pinky nail.

"That'll do." Toni smiled. "I can feel the power radiating off the medal from here."

Although confused by this declaration, Fredrick nodded and marched back upstairs, Toni and Chalsey following. *You're Wiccan. Why do you believe a Catholic Medal can have power?* "Where should I put this—" He couldn't say the word *altar.* Trying to caused him a pulse of terror. "—this medal? And what else should go with it?" *Not a dead animal. Clearly. Duh.*

"Catholics are fond of incense and candles," Chalsey said. "Catholic churches are filled with such things. Most religions around the world have used incense and candles since ancient times."

"Right." Fredrick swept into the dining room and considered the ledge of the china cabinet. "This'll work. Right?" He set the Miraculous Medal in the middle and began removing the collection of glass bells his mother had inherited from his grandma.

Toni joined him, helping. The bells tinkled as they moved them to the dining room table. "Sure it will. Almost any flat surface will work."

"I'll get my sage and a bowl." Chalsey whisked down the hallway to the primary bedroom.

"I'm sorry I yelled at you." A miserable blush burned Fredrick's cheeks. "I really am not sure why I did."

Toni gave him a sideways look and a smile. "Hey, no problem. I got ahead of myself and flipped you out. I'm sorry about that, too. But it's all good now."

Overwhelmed by the need to keep apologizing, Fredrick held his breath for a moment. *No, stop. One apology is enough. You don't need a dozen.*

That's our parents' fault, the conversational voice said. *They would demand an apology for some imagined slight, and then they'd beat us anyway, no matter how many times we apologized.*

"Our"? Fredrick echoed. *"We"? Can't you tell me who you are?*

Silence. The Brain Bubble Wrap resumed.

"Candles." Fredrick snapped himself out of his near-trance. "Mom had plenty of candles." He retreated to the kitchen. One lower cabinet had a built-in Lazy Susan in the corner, and he opened the door to rotate it out. Three shelves of candles met his inspection: tea lights, votives, tapers, and pillars in a variety of colors, along with candle holders.

"Wow. There's a fantastic collection." Toni entered the doorway and leaned against the doorjamb. "Your mom was serious about her candles."

Fredrick half-smiled, one corner of his mouth ticking up. "Yeah, I guess she was. Any suggestions on what color to use?"

"White for purity." Toni hummed to himself. "Maybe blue. Most paintings of Mary show her in blue, I've noticed. Oh, wait—blue is also for protection, so that's a great choice."

"Blue it is." Fredrick pulled out a blue votive and found a white holder. He grabbed a box of matches. "Anything else?"

Toni stepped back into the dining room. "Nah. If any of us think of something later, you can add it. But this is a good start."

Fredrick nodded and carried the candle to the altar-but-don't-call-it-an-altar. Chalsey joined him, placing a bowl of lit sage incense to the left of the Medal. Fredrick set the candle to the right and lit it. "Now what?"

"Evoke Mother Mary," Toni said. "Ask her for protection. Do you know the Hail Mary?"

"Nope. Not a clue. My half-brother Roger converted to Catholicism in his forties, but everyone else in the family has been Baptist or Presbyterian." *Our black sheep, the Catholic. Mom about melted down, and he's not even her son.* Fredrick pulled his phone from his pocket and googled the Hail Mary. "Okay, here we go: 'Hail Mary, full of grace, the Lord is with thee. Blessed art thou among women, and blessed is the fruit of thy womb, Jesus. Holy Mary, Mother of God, pray for us sinners now and at the hour of our death. Amen.'"

Chalsey shivered and rubbed her arms. "Wow. You invoked a lot of power there. Good job."

"Huh?" Fredrick stared at her. "I'm not even sure Mother Mary is real."

Toni chuckled. "Well, she clearly knows she's real."

Although Fredrick grew confused again, he set it aside. *Whatever.* "Mother Mary, if you are real, then please help me. Protect me. Protect this house and its visitors. Um, amen."

Chalsey blinked several times. "Again, wow. That was powerful. Do that every morning and night, and we may have less of a problem."

"Okay, you lost me." Fredrick faced Chalsey. "If you don't believe in the Christian God or Satan, then why do you think Mother Mary responded?"

"Soft polytheism." Chalsey shrugged. "It's simple. In hard polytheism, you believe every single god and goddess is a distinct, separate person who must be evoked and worshipped. In soft polytheism, you believe there is one enormous Divine Spirit who will answer to many names, including Jehovah-God and Mother Mary. This Divine Spirit has many names for the sake of all the people on Earth—and, potentially, elsewhere, if there is other sentient life in the universe."

Toni stepped up to the altar. "And why wouldn't there be? With our limited technology, we can already detect something like 100 million galaxies, and you know we can't see them all. That's an enormous universe. A living one. And the Divine Spirit is everywhere, all at once."

"A Divine Spirit who must figure out how to take care of its enormous creation," Fredrick mused. "Well, I hope it's engaged and caring rather than detached and ambivalent. I need the help." He faced the altar-but-don't-call-it-an-altar. "Divine Spirit and Mother Mary, if you exist, I want to be my true self, my real self, devoid of masks and healed of traumas and free of everyone else's opinions and constraints."

Toni's face softened, easing the lines on his forehead. "That's a beautiful prayer."

So says a beautiful man. Fredrick smiled. "Thanks." He carried the matches back into the kitchen.

Waiting for him was the box of tarot cards spewed on the floor again, a single card face up, showing a woman pressing a lion's jaws shut: Strength, VIII.

Being my real self will make me strong. Fredrick wanted that outcome with all his soul.

Chapter 8

THE HIEROPHANT V

With the altar made, Fredrick returned to work. He led Chalsey and Toni back into the cellar, where they retrieved three card tables and tucked them into the corners of the living room and dining room. Then they filled the card tables and dining room table with items for Knight to photograph for the online auction.

"I'll need more tables." Fredrick assessed the dining room table. Even with both leaves in, the table didn't hold enough.

"You'll need a table just for the photographer." Toni stationed himself between the dining room table and the china cabinet. "Most of the tables can hold items that are waiting to be photographed, but one table should otherwise be empty. You don't want the photos to look crowded."

"True. Okay, I'll make that the kitchen table, then." Fredrick glanced into the kitchen. Largo had hopped onto the table to stare outside. Unable to bear chastising the poor cat, Fredrick let it go. *Mom nitpicked you and yelled at you, just like she did me. But it's an easy fix: I'll just clean the table later.*

Chalsey pulled out her phone and fired off a message. "I'll ask everyone to bring a card table tomorrow, if they own one."

"I've got one," Toni said. "But where will we set them up? Space is at a premium here."

"The back deck." Fredrick shrugged. "The neighbors won't bother them. We'll cover it all with tarps in case it rains, and we won't put out anything super expensive. And as far as I know, there's no rain in the forecast."

Chalsey slipped her phone into her skirt pocket. "No, none. And good idea." She turned to the two bookcases. "Let's move all the angel figurines to the kitchen island."

A bad feeling wafted through Fredrick's gut. *Why am I so uneasy? Everything has to be rounded up. It's not like we can spare the angels.* "Sure. If you two transfer the ones downstairs, I'll go up to Mom's office and the guest bedroom. This house is exploding with angels."

"On it." Toni whisked over to join Chalsey.

Fredrick reported upstairs to his mother's office. Besides the computer desk, which filled half the room, his mother had three bookcases. Mixed in with all the writers' workbooks and reference books were antique copies of classics like *Jane Eyre* and *The Scarlett Letter*. But regardless of the books, every shelf had angels: porcelain angels, wooden angels, painted angels, and plain ones. Singing angels, kneeling angels, kissing angels, and flying ones. Some were chipped antiques and others collectors' items.

Finding an empty Amazon box by the trashcan, Fredrick loaded up as many as he could, but it still took him three trips up and down the stairs. In the end, the island counter looked like the heavenly host that filled the sky the night Jesus was born.

"How many angels is this?" Toni's tone betrayed his bewilderment.

"44," Chalsey said. "And two got broken, so there were 46."

Fredrick's mind did the math. "46. 4+6=10. And I

learned that in biblical numerology, ten signifies perfect. Symbolically, my mom owned the perfect number of angels."

"Now there are 44, and 4+4=8." Toni raised an eyebrow. "So what's eight mean?"

"New beginnings and hope," Fredrick said. "Most Christians associate it with Jesus."

Toni nodded and gazed out the window. "Interesting. Were your parents devout Baptists?"

"My dad went to church every Sunday, but I think it's only because Mom dragged him there." Fredrick opened the refrigerator. *Is there something other than water or milk?* He picked up a bottle, discovering it was sweet tea. *40 grams of sugar? No wonder Mom couldn't keep her diabetes under control.* "My maternal grandma and mom both taught Sunday School. Mom sang in the choir, and Grandma played the piano. Mom made sure I tithed exactly 10 percent of my weekly allowance, and she read me Bible stories every night until I was 10, mostly from the Old Testament. The scary ones."

"Pretty devout, then." Toni slipped into a kitchen chair. "I wondered. But despite the 46 angels, there's not a single cross, painting of Jesus, or statue of Jesus."

Fredrick gave up and poured a glass of water. "You know, good point. We never had crosses or paintings of Jesus or anything. Mom hated them."

"A devout Christian who hates crosses and artwork of Jesus?" Toni's eyebrow shot back up. It seemed a habitual mannerism for him.

"She didn't even display the family Bible my dad inherited from his mother. She stuffed it on the bottom shelf of the coffee table."

Toni and Fredrick shared a gaze, the silence filled with unspoken thoughts.

My mom's behavior is contradictory, Fredrick admitted. *But why?*

Why, indeed? drawled the chatty inner voice.

"What kind of scary Bible stories?" Chalsey opened the pantry doors and frowned at its contents, her nose wrinkling.

"Oh, the famous ones: God murders all the firstborn sons of Egypt, including the ones of the servants and the livestock, literally punishing everyone for Pharaoh's decisions. Samson captures foxes and sets their tails on fire so he can burn down the fields of his enemies. God drowns the world. God kills a man for trying to steady the Arc of the Covenant and keep it from falling over. God murders David's newborn son because David committed adultery. You know, all that warm-and-fuzzy stuff."

Toni leaned forward and propped his elbows on his knees. "And these were your bedtime stories? Weren't you too terrified to go to church?"

"Well, yeah." Fredrick leaned against the refrigerator and sipped his water. "Not that I got a choice in the matter, of course. But I sat in the pew every Sunday, listened to the preacher, and felt I had to be failing God with every breath I took. Supposedly, Jesus died to 'save' me, but I always felt like I'd end up in hell anyway because I was too much of a failure."

"It's called Religious Trauma Syndrome by several therapists." Chalsey glanced over her shoulder. "The diagnosis isn't official yet, but they consider it a form of Complex PTSD. I'm pretty sure you have it."

Fredrick had the nagging sense that there was a pattern in his life, one just beyond his mental reach. *I feel like I'm climbing a mountain toward a revelation. But what kind?*

Chalsey swept her hand toward the pantry. "Have you really stopped to look at this?"

"No. I admit it." Joining her, Fredrick peered into the pantry. A bag of Hershey's chocolate bars greeted him, along with a bag of marshmallows and a box of Graham crackers. Beside them were cans of fruit in heavy syrup, candied nuts, and chocolate syrup. Under this was a shelf of five different brands of potato chips. On the bottom shelf were cans of vegetables, boxes of dried pasta, and jars of spaghetti sauce. Across the floor were two dozen rolls of paper towels, like a Covid-19 run on toilet paper.

"Sugar," Chalsey said. "It's mostly sugar and potato chips, two things really dangerous for a diabetic."

"Passive suicide?" Toni asked.

Fredrick sighed. "An inability to tell herself no. Wait. Dad would say she had a food addiction—one she couldn't give up even if it killed her." His gaze slid to Largo, who lay sprawled on the kitchen table, his kitty rolls spread out. "Christianity taught me bodies are inherently evil and have out-of-control appetites. It said I must discipline my body and deny it what it wants. But psychology reveals that traumatized people can have food addictions and that body mindfulness will help you stop overeating."

"Also, sugar is technically a drug," Chalsey said. "Sugar can become an addiction by itself." She pointed to Largo. "Meanwhile, cats will eat out of boredom and stress. Your mom didn't play with him, and he got no exercise. So being cooped up all day with nothing to do, Largo became bored and overate. Especially since she constantly shoved food his way."

"No animals, including humans, were meant to live indoors." Toni leaned back and offered Largo his fingers to sniff. "Now that we do, we need to consciously compensate both in terms of food and exercise." Once Largo sniffed his fingers, Toni scratched under his chin.

Fredrick slumped. "I admit it. I'm angry with my mom. She died from complications from her diabetes, and it could have been prevented. She spent my whole life telling me she hated how fat she was, but she wouldn't exercise because it was boring and it made her sweat. I pointed out to her she was eating 1500 calories for supper alone, not counting breakfast or lunch, and all she said was that I didn't eat *enough*. She complained to me about how bad the high blood sugar made her feel, and then she ate herself to death." His voice rose as he unleashed the pent-up rage, startling Largo into sitting up. "All I can think is, 'But you refused to ever do anything about it! You never took care of yourself. Grandma lived to be 89, and Grandfather lived to be 86, but you died at 76 because you were childish and stubborn.'"

"You have a right to feel angry," Chalsey said. "You don't have to bury or dismiss your feelings."

"And yet now you're wondering if she had a food addiction." Toni scratched Largo's ears in a slow, soothing pattern.

Fredrick trudged over to the other kitchen chair and flopped down, setting his water glass on the table. "Yeah. Mom told me all these horror stories about her childhood. And Dad's death crushed her. But she refused to go to therapy until age 69, and then when she finally went, she said it did no good."

Chalsey pulled out two cans of vegetables. "So what did your mom refuse to work on in therapy? What traumas did she refuse to touch? Whatever they were, she tried to cope with them using a food addiction."

"I know her father cheated on her mother and then divorced her when Mom was only a year old. That was 1947, before it was acceptable to divorce." Fredrick stared at Largo's fur, which shone yellow, orange, and red in the sunlight. "Grandfather was never really part of her life, and he refused to pay child support. Mom grew up poor because Grandma worked as a teacher, and her pay was underwhelming."

Chalsey pulled the can opener from one cabinet. "That's

the surface trauma. She always spoke of it openly, and that means it's not what we're looking for. She could talk freely about her bitterness toward her father, and we need to know what she found too painful to discuss. What was unspeakable?" She plugged in the can opener.

The electricity died.

Fredrick's mom appeared in front of the pantry doors. Like the day before, she wore jeans with a long-sleeved blue t-shirt. Orange conch earrings still dangled from her ears. She narrowed her eyes at them.

"Holy shit!" Toni shot to his feet, and Largo jumped off the table and scrambled out of the room.

Chalsey froze, her can halfway to the can opener.

"I *told* you it's none of your business!" Marilyn Smith Anderson snapped. Also like before, her short, permed hair was dyed brown in a perfect imitation of life. "Quit digging around in my life. All three of you have secrets you want to keep. So stay out of mine." She pointed at the angel collection. "And put my angels back where you found them! I didn't give you permission to get rid of my possessions."

The entity vanished.

Fredrick stared at the empty spot, too numb to panic. *Sounds just like her. Can't be her. But sounds just like her.*

Toni had pressed himself into the kitchen corner.

Chalsey set down the can with a *thump*, as if her arm muscles gave out.

The electricity popped back on, a dozen electronic devices beeping.

"Well. That happened." Fredrick turned toward Toni and discovered he was pale and sweating. *I bet he'll leave and never come back.* "My life: the sudden horror novel. I *write* horror. I didn't expect to *live* it."

You already have lived it, said the conversational voice. *That's why you write it.*

Fredrick cringed. *Touché.* "Okay. Why don't you go outside into the sunlight?" *Behold the power of shock. Now I'm as calm as Chalsey. Or fake calm, anyway.* "Can you stand or sit on the grass and ground yourself?"

"Mmm," was the extent of Toni's reply. He edged out of the corner, slipped around Fredrick, and shot out the back door.

"*That's* what you saw yesterday?" Chalsey's tone was sharp.

"Yeppers."

Chalsey shook her head. "That's the most powerful evil entity I have ever seen. Or even heard of." Her voice was strained. "That *has* to be the 'demon.'"

"My mom died and became a demon?" Fredrick was only half-joking, and he burst into laughter. "God, that's amazing!" Even to his own ears, his laughter sounded hysterical. *My mom, the demon!*

Abruptly, with no warning inside of himself, Fredrick grabbed an angel off the counter and hurled it at the floor with all his strength. It shattered, tiny white shards flying everywhere. "You fucking bitch! Child exploiter! You tortured me!"

Chalsey jumped and knocked into the refrigerator.

Fredrick didn't know why he'd accused his mom of harming him. *I thought that was my dad.* "God! Sorry. I'll clean that up in a minute." He raced out the door after Toni, needing fresh air and a large, open space.

The blasting heat of the June sun hit Fredrick's face, and he inhaled the thick, humid Kentucky air. *Get it together, man. You've got to get it together. Throwing things like an angry teenager isn't gonna cut it.*

Fredrick closed his eyes and lifted his face, the sunlight halfway piercing his eyelids. *Mother Mary, if you're real, deliver me.*

An hour later, Fredrick, Toni, and Chalsey sat on the deck chairs in the oven-like Kentucky heat. Coping with seeing the evil entity had meant leaving the house and eating lunch at a restaurant.

"We can't just sit outside all day." Chalsey fanned herself with a new *Southern Living* magazine Fredrick had pulled from the mailbox. "If we all march in together and go to the primary bedroom, I'll get my sage, and we can smudge the house. Again."

"I'm outside, and I still feel cold." Toni stared at his lap. "This is humbling. I've spent years thinking of myself as hot shit at dealing with spirits, and then I see *that thing*. It looked solid! And talked out loud. That's not supposed to be possible."

Chalsey held the magazine over her head like a visor. "That's true. People have heard a voice but not seen a spirit, or people have seen silent, solid-looking spirits. But a solid-looking spirit that talks? Nope. Not on my watch, anyway." She peered at Fredrick. "How did you even sleep in the house last night?"

"Denial. Shock. Dissociation." Fredrick shrugged. *The same way I apparently went most of a lifetime not remembering my dad violated and mistreated me.* "Well, anyway. Strength in numbers, right? I like your plan. Let's do it."

Chalsey stood and marched to the back door. "'We few, we happy few, we band of brothers. For he to-day that sheds his blood with me shall be my brother.'"

"Shakespeare's *Henry V*." Fredrick stood and followed her. "The St. Crispin's Day Speech, I think."

"You think right."

Toni brought up the rear, silent and radiating tenseness.

The kitchen proved blasé and spiritless. All 43 angels

remained crowded together on the island counter, and Fredrick's shoes crunched the remains of angel 44. They jogged down the hallway from the kitchen to the primary bedroom, which was in the front right corner of the house.

Chalsey grabbed her bundle of sage and lit the stick. As soon as the flames burned lustily, she blew them out, leaving the sage to glow. "Toni, say a Wiccan blessing of protection over each room. Fredrick, I suggest you recite the Hail Mary over each room."

"You got it." Fredrick whipped out his phone and pulled up the webpage from earlier.

They covered the entire house, including the bathrooms, the pantry, the cellar, and even the closets. Then Chalsey herded them outside to walk around the house three times, the number three being sacred in both Christianity and Wicca. Fredrick felt self-conscious at what had to be a weird show for the neighbors, but he repeated the Hail Mary four times, once for each side of the house.

Once back inside, Fredrick grabbed a broom and a dustpan and swept up the shattered angel. "So Chalsey asks what secret my mom was really hiding, and the 'demon' loses its shit. Why?"

"So you don't think it was your mother's ghost?" Toni leaned against the back door and crossed his arms.

"Nah." Fredrick leaned down and ushered the broken glass into the dustpan. "I barely believe in ghosts at all, and I don't believe a human ghost could get that powerful. That entity has to be something else."

Chalsey grabbed the trashcan and walked it over. "I agree. And while I'm not sure why it's so invested, I'm sticking with my best guess: It doesn't want you to know the truth because, to borrow a Bible verse, 'The truth will set you free.'"

Fredrick dumped the glass into the trashcan. "Seems like a sound theory for now."

"Well, let's not talk about the entity until the circle gets here tomorrow night," Toni said. "It'll take all nine of us, ten including Fredrick, to deal with such a thing."

"Works for me." Fredrick returned the broom and dustpan to the hall closet and then faced Toni. "Sorry you got blasted by an evil spirit. That's not exactly the experience I want to give my guests."

Toni smiled and dropped his arms, his shoulders relaxing. "Hey, it's okay. I know. I think I'd better consider this a learning experience or something. I'll be up until midnight researching high-level entities now." He glanced at the kitchen table. "Weird. I didn't see this earlier." He picked up a tarot card.

"So the Tarot Ghost is hard at work again," Fredrick said. "What did I get this time?"

"Tarot Ghost?" Toni looked between Chalsey and him.

Chalsey downloaded the story of the tarot messaging.

"So there are two high-level entities." Toni held out the card to Fredrick. "And the second one can move physical objects."

Fredrick accepted the card, which showed a pope-like man wearing a red robe and sitting on a throne. Before him stood two men who appeared to be lower-ranking priests. At the pope's feet were two golden keys crossed over each other. The text read *The Hierophant*. "So what's this one mean?"

"It can mean tradition, conformity, and conventions," Toni said. "But it also means education, knowledge, and beliefs. To understand the meaning, we'd need more context."

Fredrick glanced through the doorway into the dining room, his gaze resting on the altar-not-altar. "Did the Tarot Ghost leave it because we saw the evil entity? Or did it leave it because I set up an...ah, a sacred space for Mother Mary?"

"Good point." Toni rubbed the bridge of his nose. "Okay, considering how much power you generated praying the Hail

Mary, let's assume it's that. What does the Tarot Ghost want you to know about it, then?"

"Educate yourself about Mother Mary?" Chalsey's tone was thoughtful. "Or gain knowledge about Catholic beliefs? I think Catholic priests will still perform exorcisms—or at least some of them do—so maybe educate yourself about exorcisms?"

"Or call on a priest to perform one?" Toni pointed to the priests and pope on the card.

Fredrick held up the card again, his gaze returning to the two golden keys. "I think it must be about educating myself or gaining knowledge. I seem drawn to the keys, and I assume those are keys of knowledge based on what you've said."

"Yes," Chalsey said. "And follow your gut feelings about this. If something seems to draw you in, make a note of it."

"The key is knowledge." The words rang in Fredrick's mind. "Feels right. I'm going with the answer 'all of the above': learn about Mother Mary, exorcisms, and, like we said before, my mother's secrets."

"Sounds like a plan," Toni said.

Fredrick returned the card to its box and submerged himself into the cool, relaxing waters of denial about The Demon Mother. "Despite it all, I'm getting back to work." He met Toni's gaze. "But you don't have to stay. You didn't sign on to get screamed at by someone else's dead mother."

Toni laughed. "Um, no. I didn't. But I'll stay awhile longer."

Three hours later, three-fourths of the cellar's contents had been catalogued on a legal pad, and all the photo albums and paperwork had been moved to the upstairs office, centralizing their location. And thanks to Toni's hard work and good nature, Fredrick officially had a crush.

Fredrick stood at the front door as Toni backed his little green 2016 Ford Fiesta down the driveway. *I feel like I'm back in high school. I'm totally cooking up a burning infatuation here.* He closed the door once the car vanished from sight.

"You like him." Chalsey dropped into the recliner, extended the footrest, and kicked off her sandals.

"Guilty as charged." Fredrick fell onto the couch, jerking off his sneakers and resting his feet on the arm. His feet throbbed with silent condemnation: *What the hell do you think you're doing standing on concrete for hours?*

Chalsey turned a smile Fredrick's way. "Well, he likes you, too. And I do mean in 'that way.'"

"That's too good to be true." Fredrick stared up at the swirls in the plaster ceiling. "But I hope you're right."

"Bet'cha twenty bucks."

Fredrick summoned half a smile. "You're on."

CHAPTER 9

THE EMPEROR IV

MICHAEL AWAKENED ON THE COUCH, CURLED ON HIS side with his forehead pressed against the back. *I guess Fred-o took a nap.* He groaned and sat up, checking his activity tracker for the time: 6:03 pm. The activity tracker informed him it was Friday still. *I don't know what I'd do without this thing. For the rest of my life, I'm going to need a watch that tells me the day of the week and the date, not just the time.*

Chalsey was asleep in the recliner, its back pushed down and the footrest up. Her face had relaxed, easing away stress lines, and her natural spiral curls had spilled over the cushion.

You're beautiful. Michael smiled. *You always were.* He still remembered when Chalsey had asked him out. They'd been friends for fifteen years by then and were both 28. Michael, or more accurately, Fredrick, had been finishing up his PhD. Chalsey had finished her MA and was an English instructor.

They'd been in Michael's apartment, eating takeout sushi. Given it was June, they'd been swimming at the lake earlier that day, trying to relax despite their teaching summer courses.

Chalsey had dipped a piece of salmon maki into soy sauce, paused, and then caught Michael's gaze. "I've been holding this in for a long time, and I don't think I can hold it in any longer. I think I'm in love with you."

Those basic words had silenced a longing in Michael's soul. "I think I'm in love with you, too."

And with that, they'd begun the negotiation process around Michael's DID: Michael would date Chalsey, but Fredrick wouldn't. Michael knew; Fredrick didn't.

And 15 years later, we've mastered this process. Michael stood and stretched. *We're so kick-ass.*

The movement seemed to awaken Chalsey. She peered up at him. "I guess we both passed out, huh?"

"Yeah." Michael's feet ached, the arches throbbing. *Must've worked hard.* "You've got Michael now. Did I miss anything interesting?"

Chalsey filled Michael in on The Demon Mother and Fredrick's crush on Toni while Michael fixed them both tacos for supper—beef tacos for him and tofu tacos for Chalsey.

"Well, damn." Michael bit into a crispy taco shell and enjoyed the spicy beef. Fredrick and he had mostly given up beef and pork. *Time for a nice treat.* "Fred-o's gotten a crush on someone? About damn time. Let's see...he hasn't been interested in anyone for eleven years now. He might count it as twelve."

"Yeah. Tara burned him bad."

Michael set down his taco. "True. But I think the worst problem is our sexual trauma. It's not like we didn't notice we have it. We just had no idea what caused it. All we could figure out is that the boy who violated us for two weeks in sixth grade must have somehow won first place in the trauma Olympics and given us permanent sexual dysfunction."

Chalsey fought her lettuce and diced tomatoes back into her taco shell. "And now you know it's your father's fault."

"It makes way more sense." Michael gazed out the kitchen window at the detached black wooden garage. It was a converted barn. His father had worked all summer long to fix it up when Michael was six. "I should read the entire diary word for word. Maybe I can get more insights." He knew Fredrick was more sexually frozen that he was, and it worried him. *Did Fred-o get more of the abuse than I did? Or is my reaction to being violated different from his?* "In fact, maybe I should reread all my journals. I maintained a journal until I graduated with my master's degree." Some of them were in boxes in the cellar and others at his own house.

"Just be careful. You might trigger yourself badly."

Although Michael accepted the warning, he grabbed the flower-print diary after supper and settled on the couch with it. Chalsey sat on the couch by him with a book, Dr. John Bradshaw's *On the Family,* another text about dysfunctional families and their toxic behavioral patterns. Such books had turned into Chalsey's specialty.

Michael read some benign diary entries discussing Field Day or gymnastic contests. Other entries were menacing but vague, mentioning angry men who came to the house and how Michael's dad left with them to "take care of business."

I bet those were Dad's SOMH buddies. Michael grimaced. *God, I wonder if they killed people. I'm sure they terrified people. Probably beat people. But did my dad ever kill anyone?*

About a third of the way in, Michael reread the entry he'd found about "touching." His chest burned, but he forced himself to continue. The handwriting changed from entry to entry, revealing that different self-states had recorded their experiences. At least three different inner people talked about "touching": one with wide, bubbly handwriting; one with tall, thin, spidery handwriting; and one with short, squat, blockish handwriting.

Between the entries about "touch" were other complaints about the late Dr. Phillip Roger Anderson. Michael also discovered that someone had ripped out three pages. *That's a bad sign. What was I—what were we—so determined to hide?*

"I never liked my father." Michael closed the flower-print diary and set it on his lap, finished. "I always remembered he only had two modes: stoic and angry. I always remembered that he'd whipped me with his belt a few times. I was terrified of the man. Terrified of his anger. And he got angry easily."

"Correction: He chose to let go of the control of his anger. He used it as a weapon to control you. It was cold and calculating on his part." Chalsey set aside her book. "Dr. Lundy Bancroft said the distinction is important in his book *Why Does He Do That?: Inside the Minds of Angry and Controlling Men.*"

Michael inclined his head, accepting the insights of a psychologist who specialized in treating abusive men. "Very well. He purposefully unleashed his anger on me often." He lifted the diary and waved it back and forth. "But what I just learned is that my dad was much worse than I remembered. My self-states described an absolute tyrant: rigid, dominating, stubborn, distant, and violent." He tossed the diary onto the coffee table. "My dad once threatened to belt me because I was crying over having no friends to play with."

Chalsey took Michael's hand and squeezed it gently. "That's cruel."

"I only had one real friend in the whole neighborhood when I was in elementary school: Connie. Angie didn't count. All we did was fight." Michael stared at their clasped hands. His parents' house was on a rural highway in a line of other Craftsman houses and old farmhouses. But behind them was a newer subdivision built in the 1970s. "Connie didn't live here; her grandma did. She visited her grandma every two weeks on Sunday afternoons. Mom and Dad decided, without even asking Connie's grandma how she felt, that I was spending too much time playing with her. They told me I couldn't play with her that Sunday. That meant I'd have to go a whole month without seeing my best friend, which to an eight-year-old is forever. I was just so lonely. I spent almost my entire childhood playing alone in this house. So I cried. He told me I was using my tears as emotional manipulation and said he'd beat me with his belt if I didn't stop."

Chalsey leaned over and gave him a one-armed hug. "Emotional abuse. It's just as severe as the physical abuse of whipping you. It's just as severe as the exploitation, too. Abandonment, rejection, isolation—all those things create deep wounds. Your father attacked you in every way he knew how. Those are acts of genuine evil."

Wrapping one arm around Chalsey's waist, Michael inhaled and sighed. "I know you're right. I always felt alone. Always." He felt a stirring sensation in his gut and then the strange internal feeling of someone moving inside his mind.

Michael pulled back, releasing Chalsey. "Someone's coming up! I don't know if it's Angela again, or if you'll get another new self-state. But—"

The new person popped into control of their shared body and scanned the woman. *She seems familiar.* They glanced around the living room. "Everything changed. Why?"

"Many years have passed," the woman said.

The new person recognized her voice. "Wait. Are you Chalsey Montgomery?"

"Yes." Chalsey was much older, sporting fine wrinkles around her eyes. "How old are you?"

"13. How old are you?" The new person crossed their arms, intimidated. *What's going on? How did I lose time? Why is everything so strange?*

"43. You're 43 now, too."

Too weird. Moving on now. "Where's Mom?"

"She passed away. So did your dad." Chalsey wore a red, orange, and yellow gypsy skirt with a white tank top. Her silver necklace was a pentacle, and the outer circle of the pentacle showed the phases of the moon. "It's safe now."

I like her outfit. "Is it really?" The new person stood and walked through the living room, dining room, and kitchen. "We're rounding up Mom's things?"

Chalsey followed. "Yes."

"Then where's Mom's altar? If she's dead, then we've got to get rid of it." The new person faced Chalsey. "Did I tell you my mom does magick?"

Chalsey grew still and gripped the back of a kitchen chair. "No. What kind of magick?"

"Only the bad kind. She hurts people." The new person stared down the hallway toward the primary bedroom. "Her altar might be in her bedroom. But she moves it around." Their stomach clenched, squeezing until it hurt. "I'm scared to go in there alone. Bad things happen in there."

"I'll go with you. Do you know your name? I mean, the name you have on the inside? There's Michael, Fredrick, Angela, and someone named Dietrich I haven't met yet."

"Laura." She frowned. "So we told you about all of us on the inside, but we didn't tell you about the magick?"

Chalsey shook her head. Her blonde curls bounced.

"Weird. But okay, fine, whatever." Laura held out her hand. "Let's go check for the altar."

Chalsey took her hand, and Laura led her down the hallway, her heart racing. "Scary things happened in here. Always scary things." She halted at the door and stared at the open suitcase on the floor. An enormous orange and white tabby cat had curled up on the clothes inside, napping.

"I see I forgot to close my suitcase lid." Chalsey's voice was dry.

Laura chuckled, her tension broken. "You'll be all covered in cat hair." Her fear bounced back. "So you're sleeping in here right now? Well, Mom's definitely dead, then. No way would she allow anyone to sleep in her bed." She shuffled two steps into the room and stopped, her heart pounding. *I can't stand to go inside any farther.* "I don't see it. But we have to find her Bible, and we have to find the glass pyramid, the pine box, and the white candy dish."

"Those are your mom's altar items?"

Laura nodded.

"I saw a small pine box in the guest bedroom," Chalsey said. "The bedroom that used to be yours."

Goosebumps flashed over Laura's arms and down her back. "She put it in my room? Even scarier!" She led Chalsey upstairs, the third step creaking under her foot, as always. *One thing didn't change.*

"What kind of scary things happened?" Chalsey asked. "Do you want to talk about it? Or are you not ready yet?"

"Not ready yet," Laura whispered. She halted in her bedroom doorway, shocked to see neither the old pink paint nor the new blue paint on her walls. An unfamiliar dark yellow had replaced it, although the pine furniture remained. All the dolls, pictures of unicorns, and frilly curtains were gone. Muted paintings of Venice, the Eiffel Tower, and Big Ben adorned the walls of the room. A Chinese floor vase held imitation pussy-willows. "What an upgrade."

"Your mom redecorated after you grew up and moved out."

Mom even let me move out? There's a shocker. The chest of drawers drew Laura's gaze. "There!" She marched over, her pulse racing until her arms and legs quivered, and pulled Chalsey along by the hand. When they reached the chest of drawers, she pointed. "This. This is Mom's altar."

An antique white candy dish stood in the center, tiny pink flowers painted on the sides. In the back left corner sat a pine curio box five inches long by three inches wide. In the back right corner stood a three-inch-tall jade pyramid.

Chalsey touched the altar, then jerked her hand away. "The energy is so faded I couldn't feel it from the door. But when I touch it, I can sense rank energy. Whatever your mom was praying or whatever spells she was casting, it was all black magick."

"You're not allowed to call it magick. Or spells." Laura stared at the pine box. It held pins, rings, and a brooch, all of them with terrifying energy oozing off them. She knew. She'd seen them. They had forced her to wear them. Reaching out, she opened the box, but the jewelry was gone. Inside, she found a folded white piece of paper. *Where's the nasty jewelry?*

"You're not? Seriously?"

Laura snapped the lid shut. "Nope. She'll slap your face if you do. And you can't call this an altar, either. But it is. She prays here. But not to God. It has a different name. I'm not allowed to say its name. She doesn't call it a demon, and she won't let you call it a demon, either. But it's an evil spirit."

Chalsey shuddered. "I see. Have you ever seen it?"

"Yes." Laura felt her gaze unfocus. She both did and didn't see the pine box. "I've seen several. That one is the scariest. Most of them look like black blobs. The big one with the name shows up looking like a human, though. It talks. Usually its lips don't move, but you hear what it says inside your mind. It says to do bad things and hurt people." She turned to stare at Chalsey. "I bet you don't believe me."

Chalsey's face had lost color until her lips were a faded pink. "No, I believe you. I saw something earlier today. A spirit. It was evil, and it looked human and solid. Did the spirit look like someone you know?"

Laura shook her head. "It was some old man. He had a beard, and he was mostly bald on top. He had a bit of a beer belly, but he wasn't super overweight or anything. And he had a big, crooked nose."

Laura felt herself slipping, as if her brain were greased and her consciousness could slide out of her skull.

Another new person found himself standing before the altar. He took in the items and pondered what Laura had been saying. He had internally overheard the conversation. "But one time the spirit looked like Dad. That was when I was 19. Dad had been dead for three months. All this was downstairs on Mom's chest of drawers, and she was praying. And then that entity showed up. It was *so* obvious it was the same spirit. It's so evil you can't miss it. But she called it Phillip and began crying and asking why he'd left her."

Chalsey peered at him. "And how old are you?"

"23." He felt a warmth in his hand, looked down, and discovered their clasped hands. "Oh, God! Sorry." He released her. "Why—why...Wait. When did you move back to Kentucky? I thought you were still in Washington state."

"You lost time." Chalsey's brow furrowed. "You have the same energy as Michael."

Michael blinked as a strange sensation zinged through him. "Well, I am Michael. Yeah, that's my name. I mean, not legally. Obviously. But I hope it will be someday."

"I've been talking with another piece of you, Michael." Chalsey sighed. "I feared this might be the case. Your spirit is fragmented. Or your mind, if you prefer."

"Fragmented?"

"Yes. Thanks to trauma, there are multiple pieces of you inside your own mind." Chalsey ran one hand back into her spiral curls.

Despite his confusion and building panic, Michael noticed Chalsey was beautiful. "Multiple pieces? In what way?"

"Well, for example, there could be a five-year-old Michael, a 13-year-old Michael, and you're a 23-year-old Michael. There's also a Michael who's 43, your current age." Chalsey dropped onto the side of the bed. "Basically, every time you got severely traumatized, a piece of your mind broke off, each one named Michael. And each one remains frozen in time, stuck at the age they were when the trauma occurred. Fortunately, EMDR therapy can help them grow up to match your current physical age and combine into a single Michael. But there are still other parts of you beyond just you as Michael: one named Fredrick, one named Angela, one named Laura, and one named Dietrich."

Michael glanced down and discovered a boring university t-shirt with jeans shorts. "So am I psychotic?"

"No." Chalsey held up both hands. "Definitely not. You have dissociative identity disorder. It's not a psychosis. It's a dissociative disorder, just like its name says. It's a coping mechanism for severe childhood trauma. Most psychologists now believe you can only develop it when you're very young. No older than nine, maybe not even older than five or six. And it happens because you're being severely traumatized repeatedly."

Michael crossed his arms over his chest. "Oh, you mean like my dad raping me all the time?" His voice was sharp and hot, like a fire poker. "Yeah, that totally happened. I wondered why he even bothered to have a wife. I was like a blow-up sex doll that could talk. He was all over me all the time."

Chalsey's lips pressed into a thin line, her eyes narrowing. "Hypocritical, piece-of-shit tyrant."

"And Mom knew it, too." Michael jabbed his finger toward the altar. "And then there she was, sobbing all over her hidden-altar-in-plain-sight and telling some entity that looked like my dad how *much* she *missed* him." His words lilted with mockery. "Yeah, thanks, bitch. Miss my harmer. Miss the predator living in your own home with you—the one who preys upon your own child. Traitor. Soulless monster." He raised his voice into a farce of his mother's voice and clasped his hands by his cheek like a cartoon woman. "Oh, Phillip!

How I miss the way you violated our only child together! Please return and mistreat them some more!"

"There's no forgiveness for something like this." Chalsey stood and lifted her chin. "I was never Christian, and I never will be. And I'm glad. I don't want to believe that God can just whisk that away. I don't want to believe that all your mom had to do in the ER was say, 'Jesus, I'm just so sorry I tortured my child for 43 years. Please forgive me!' And die and go to heaven, all sins washed away as white as snow." She sneered, her nose wrinkling. "Your mom doesn't deserve a get-out-of-jail free card. And neither does your dad."

"They sure as hell don't." 23-year-old Michael turned and yanked open the two top smaller drawers. "I knew it. Here's Mom's old Bible. Or, really, we should call it her Curse Cookbook. She cursed the shit out of people with this thing." He pulled out a battered black leather Bible with red-edged pages. The corners of the cover had cracks and frays.

Chalsey drew backward, bumped into the mattress, and flopped down. "Burn it! There's so much evil blasting out that thing we've got to destroy it."

43-year-old Michael found himself in his old bedroom holding his mom's worn-out Bible. "Huh?" He glanced down, felt the tar-like ooze of evil energy seeping over his fingers from the Bible, and dropped it into the open drawer. "God! What the fuck?"

"We have to burn that and destroy this altar." Chalsey stood and grabbed the Bible. "Get the candy dish, would you? And is that you, Michael? As in, current you?"

"Current me?" Michael grabbed the candy dish and followed Chalsey downstairs as she filled him in.

They walked to the barn-garage, grabbed an old grill, and filled it with coals. With the help of some lighter fluid and matches, they barbequed the Bible out on the gravel driveway. Michael watched it burn with horror, the edges of his mind flashing images of his mom reading from the Bible and yelling verses at him.

Once the Bible was half-burnt, Michael got a trash bag, put the candy dish inside, and then smashed it with a hammer. A single strike caused an internal dam to burst, and he smashed it a dozen times, every *crack* sending tingles down his spine. Then he collapsed onto the grass and cried.

"What did Mom do to me?" he sobbed into his hands. Chalsey knelt by him and hugged him. "What did she *do*?" His mind exploded with facts, names, and images: a lit candle, a solemn prayer, and his mom's hand gripping the Bible until her knuckles turned white. His mother slapping him in the face with the Bible and screaming she would curse him like God did Ham. Chalsey's voice as she explained about Laura and 23-year-old Michael. Chalsey holding up the electric blue binder of his mother's Civil War novel. Chalsey saying, *Sexual violence and ceremonial abuse go hand-in-hand*.

"I'm sorry." Chalsey caressed his back. "I'm sorry. No one can ever deserve what happened to you."

Michael allowed himself to be soothed. His sinuses ached, and his head pounded. "You said sexual violence and ceremonial abuse go hand-in-hand. Why?"

"One theory psychologists have is that adults use the trappings of rituals and pretend to summon Satan or whatever in order to terrify the child and subdue them prior to the violence or assault." Chalsey continued to stroke his back. "Another theory I read said that adults engage in ritual abuse as a form of psychological warfare upon the child. They terrorize the child into mindless obedience, telling them things like 'If you don't obey me and do what I say, I'll summon Satan to kill you' or whatever other nonsense. As far as twenty-first century psychologists can tell, these people aren't literally performance infanticide on altars to Satan while older children are forced to watch. It's more like an evil 'game' to psych out a child, dominate them, and break their will."

Break their will, huh? Michael stared at the grass, green and thick and vibrant and so at odds with his anger, panic, and shame. "I spent my entire childhood and early adulthood saying I was a doormat that everyone walked all over. I drew almost nothing but bullies at school. I couldn't stand up for myself, or if I did, all that happened was that I had a panic attack and assumed the other person would destroy me. I hated myself for being so miserably spineless."

"If you were a doormat, then you can lay the blame at your parents' feet." Chalsey caressed his hair back from his forehead. "They consciously set out to destroy you on purpose."

Michael nodded, fell into numbness and dissociation, and stood, exhausted and hallow, his chest empty like a rusted oil drum. "Please make sure the Bible is done burning. I'm going to take some aspirin."

"Sure."

Michael trudged inside and found a tarot card lying alone on the kitchen floor, displaying itself proudly: The Emperor, reversed. It pictured a domineering tyrant of a man in a suit of armor entombed upon his throne.

In that moment, Michael wondered if the card referred only to his father or if it encompassed both of his parents. *My parents, the freaks.*

CHAPTER 10

THE MOON XVIII

FREDRICK AWAKENED TO DARKNESS AND THE FAINT sound of Chalsey's breathing, heavy in her slumber. He checked his activity tracker. 3:01 am. Sitting up, he scooted off the couch cushions and repositioned them. The downside to sleeping on cushions on the bedroom floor was the way they slipped around as he squirmed in his sleep.

Bowing to the needs of his 43-year-old body, he crept into the bathroom. His mother had renovated the house so that the primary bedroom connected to the first-story bathroom, like in a modern house. Replacing the tub with a standing shower had been necessary, but his mom had powerful feelings about bathrooms. She demanded convenience, a good-sized vanity, and twenty-first century fixtures and tile.

Marilyn Smith Anderson had demanded a lot about many things.

Wide awake and aching from the subpar sleeping conditions, Fredrick grabbed his phone, slipped into the living room, and turned on the light. As soon as he settled in the recliner, Largo stood from his bed on the cushionless couch, stretched with a trembling back, and walked across the end table. Fredrick accepted a lap full of sixteen pounds of cat. *I'll pet Largo and listen to meditation music on YouTube. Then maybe I can go back to sleep.* He vaguely recalled a nightmare about fighting in World War II and being an Ally soldier spying on the Germans. Germans had chased him around, trying to kill him. Cold tingles shot across his skin. *Okay, I don't want to dwell on that.*

In front of him on the coffee table sat the flower-print diary.

Fredrick stared, his heart jumping inside his chest. *I didn't move that in here. And Chalsey would never read it without asking my permission first. She's not that kind of person. Did the Tarot Ghost move my diary?*

Turning his head, Fredrick scanned the living and dining rooms. He could barely breathe. *Just don't be The Demon Mother. God, I can't handle that twice in one day.* An innocent collection of hard rock maple and light oak furniture met his inspection. *Maybe I should light the candle on my new Mother Mary altar.*

The word *altar* caused a spike of fear in his chest.

Fredrick searched his memories of his therapy sessions with Dr. Laurie, recalling her explanation of "inner children" or "child ego states." She had said, *"We all have child parts of ourselves—the child inside who got hurt. They get abandoned or rejected by our parents, bullied by our peers, or attacked by our teachers or preachers. Their pain stays with us as we grow up, and sometimes we have to negotiate with that part of ourselves. We need to heal that part of ourselves."*

Fredrick stared at the altar-not-altar across the room. *So the inner child is terrified of altars.* A new spike of fear. *Or even the very word. Why?*

Movement in the corner of his vision caused him to gaze back at the living room. The female ghost from the 1920s, with her white flapper dress, long string of pearls, and Mary Jane shoes, stood in front of the TV. She smiled and pointed at the diary.

You want me to read it? Fredrick couldn't move his lips, couldn't speak. Her appearance startled him so badly he jerked and upset Largo.

She pointed to the diary again and vanished. Unlike The Demon Mother, she had been transparent, the outline of the flatscreen TV obvious through her body.

With cold, half-numb hands, Fredrick leaned forward and grabbed the diary. *I won't piss off a ghost.* Largo shifted in protest, but Fredrick ignored him and read the entire diary. As he read, he saw flashes of memories that made no sense: hugging Chalsey on the couch, standing in the guest bedroom and pointing at the chest of drawers, burning his mother's old Bible in a grill, and smashing his mother's candy dish with a hammer. Each flash lasted perhaps two seconds. *What is happening to me?*

When he finished, Fredrick set the diary on the end table. *I can't even comprehend this shit. My brain is peeling like an onion. And I don't feel real.* The room looked concave, and Fredrick felt dizzy as the dissociation kicked in. *My dad, the award-winning psychologist, nonstop harmed me.*

No one will believe me. Except Chalsey.

Fredrick absently petted Largo, his elderly fur smoothing down only for a moment before sticking out again. *Did Dr. Laurie believe me? My parents just look so "normal." They were just a middle class, white-collar couple with a two-story house and a kid and a cat. Church-going, hardworking, as sweet and stereotypically American as apple pie.*

Largo purred, unaware of how Marilyn Anderson's food addiction had destroyed his pancreas, and tilted his head to demand a scratch on his chin.

Maybe I should keep this to myself. I can tell Chalsey.

Maybe Dr. Laurie. But no one else would ever believe that a solid, hardworking couple like Dr. Phillip and Marilyn Anderson would be child abusers. Everyone's told themselves a cute little fairytale about how people like my parents don't harm or violate their kids.

Fredrick felt less and less real as the dissociation deepened. The TV wasn't real. The living room wasn't real. Largo wasn't real, and neither was Fredrick. It was all a dream, a simulacrum of life, a mystery play inside the mind of a far-off deity, once known but forgotten. A wish and a prayer couldn't awaken such a deity and deliver Fredrick out of the hell called life.

"That's right. Don't tell."

Snapped out of his trance, Fredrick looked around, his heart pumping great draughts of blood. *It's The Demon Mother.* But a black blob hovered in the doorway between the dining room and kitchen, nonhuman and indistinct.

"'And the rest is silence,'" the entity said.

Fredrick recalled the quote from Hamlet's death scene.

Wake up, whispered a voice in Fredrick's mind.

Hear me, said another.

We need you to hear us.

Ignoring the confusing voices, Fredrick stood with Largo, transferring him to the recliner seat. "But I must shatter the silence."

The black blob oozed forward, shadow to shadow, and hovered in the corner of the dining room. "I told you what would happen if you ever told."

Goosebumps erupted over Fredrick's body, and he wheezed for breath. "No! For once in my goddamn life, I'm standing my ground against you! I must tell." He felt as though someone else spoke through his body, but he threw in his lot with them.

"You're cruisin' for a bruisin'." The entity regurgitated

Fredrick's least favorite childhood phrase: His dad's promise to spank him.

Abruptly, Fredrick experienced a flash of memory: his dad grabbing his arm and jerking him across his lap, whaling on his ass as hard as an adult man could hit someone.

Phrases popped into his mind, all of them said in his parents' intonation:

You just wait until we get home!

Aw, just backhand that brat!

If you don't stop crying, I'll spank you again!

And then Fredrick remembered standing in the shower at the age of eight or nine, crying under the hot spray, and begging God to save him: *Please, God. I'm sorry. I'm so very sorry I sinned! I know I was bad. I know I'm a terrible sinner and that all humans do is sin and sin and sin because we're all fallen and bad. But please, please convince my dad not to spank me again. I don't think I can take it. I don't think I can take that much pain again. I'll do anything for you, God. Anything. Just please spare me. I can't. I just can't. I can't stand that much pain again.*

Fredrick stared at the black blob.

A sheet of reality, like wallpaper falling out of his parents' hands, crashed down inside of Fredrick, hitting his mind's floor. The dissociation snapped away, bringing the world into focus. "My parents were both harmed me. And all their graduate degrees, singing in the choir, tithing to the church, and Puritan ethics can't change that. Whoever or whatever you are, fuck off."

"I'll kill you."

The voice was cold. Factual. Calm, even.

Fredrick laughed. "Kill me? Really? Come on, then! Do it! Do it, I dare you! I've attempted suicide four times! I've been trying and trying to die and get off this fucking hellhole of a planet! I don't care if there's nothing on the other side. Or are you going to tell me there's a hell? Well, I've been there, too. This *is* hell. My violating, harming, over-controlling, authoritarian, dominating, oppressive parents made this place hell. I've spent my entire life having panic attacks! I'm terrified of everyone everywhere all the time." His yells shattered the silence of the night, filled the living room, and scared Largo from the room, but he only yelled louder. "So kill me, motherfucker! Take me out of my goddamn misery! I've spent my entire life *afraid to live*."

The blob hovered.

Silence.

"Didn't expect that, did you?" Fredrick smirked. "Let's try this: Hail Mary, full of grace, the Lord is with thee—"

The blob vanished.

Fredrick felt lighter inside his chest, as if someone had ripped an entire skyscraper off of his heart. "Holy shit. That worked."

Chalsey burst into the room wearing sun- and moon-print white PJs and looked around. "What is it?"

"Actually, make that 'what *was* it.'" Fredrick felt a surge of a rare emotion: satisfaction. "It was some kind of demon or entity. I kicked its ass out with the Hail Mary. I guess Mother Mary doesn't mind dropkicking demons."

Chalsey visibly relaxed, her shoulders lowering. "Well, the Catholics call her the Mother of God, the Queen of Heaven, and the Queen of the Universe. Surely, in their estimation, she does more than simply stand around and look sweet."

Fredrick laughed. "Okay, I would hope so." His chest felt clear, as if he'd beaten bronchitis. "My parents were child abusers." The words felt freeing. Despite the dark topic, Fredrick smiled, uplifted. "My parents were predators. That's the truth. Or that's the first truth I need to know. I can *feel* the truth of it now. My numbness isn't in the way."

"That's great." Chalsey smiled. "Take that truth with you into therapy. You can beat this. We'll get you the right therapist and the right therapy."

Fredrick nodded and followed her back into the bedroom. *Every night I tell whatever Divine Spirit might be out there that I want to be me, the real me, with no one else's opinions and demands in the way. Is this the answer? Am I finally on the right track?*

I want to be really, truly me.

In the morning, Fredrick stumbled into the kitchen, a zombie seeking brewed coffee, and fired up the coffeemaker. Waking up had become increasingly difficult as he grew older, and not in a way he associated with age. It was like his brain struggled to flip the "on" switch. Also, functioning had gotten more difficult. Every day after teaching, he had to take two-hour-long naps, and yet he still slept eight hours a night. Even doing something as simple as attending a committee meeting before teaching his classes threatened to smash him for the whole day. He was only 43, but he felt 83. *Is this what they call chronic fatigue?*

Through the haze of morning grogginess, Fredrick stared out the window at the driveway and saw his mother's small grill. A memory flashed through him: the image of burning his mother's old Bible.

With a surge of heart-pounding adrenaline, Fredrick shot fully awake and ran out the door. When he reached the grill, he jerked off the top.

The burnt, curled remains of a book greeted him.

"Oh, God!" Fredrick's heart thudded so hard his arm and leg muscles trembled. He slammed the lid back on. A second flash fired through his mind: beating a trash bag that contained his mother's candy dish. *It's those weird images from last night.* He ran into the garage and opened the outdoor trashcan. A battered white bag sat on top. Fredrick picked it up by the top, and glass tinkling noises erupted. He dropped it again.

There's another me. Another me who does things I then don't remember! Fredrick shut the lid with shaking fingers. He remembered his eleventh grade English class and the book report he'd written for Mary Higgins Clark's *All Around the Town.* The protagonist had been severely traumatized as a young child and had multiple personality disorder, which psychologists had later renamed dissociative identity disorder once they'd studied the condition more. One of Fredrick's ex-friends had loaned him the book despite their wrecked friendship, insisting he had to read it. He'd thought that mysterious, but he'd accepted the book and even enjoyed it. *Did Kris insist I read the book because he thought I had DID?*

With a wave of panic, Fredrick gave in to the inevitable. He ran back inside. "Chalsey!"

"Coming!" came her voice from the primary bedroom.

Fredrick paced in a circle inside the **U**-shape of the kitchen counters and appliances. Largo hovered by the pantry, looking hopeful for more food. "I can't have DID. Right? My dad would have noticed. He would have taken me to a dissociative disorder specialist and had me diagnosed and treated. He would have—"

Fredrick stopped pacing. *He would have done anything to hide his abuse of me and keep the family's secrets.*

A blue splash of color caught Fredrick's attention from the corner of his vision. The morning tarot offering awaited him at the edge of his mother's Heavenly Host of Angels gathered on the kitchen island: The Moon, reversed. The dark blue night sky held a bright yellow moon with a frowning face.

Chalsey swept into the room and joined him. "Reversed,

huh? You can take that two ways. The Moon upright can mean things that are secret or hidden. So reversed, The Moon can mean clarity and understanding."

"Clarity and understanding." Fredrick faced Chalsey. "All right, then. You've known me for 30 years on the nose, and for the last 15 years, we've either hung out or talked literally every day. We spend so much time together everyone thinks we're dating or that we should get married. So please, for the love of all things holy, level with me. Do you think I could have DID?"

For an instant, Chalsey's face seemed to freeze, her lips set in a perfect line and her eyes unblinking. She looked like a goddess statue with her free-flowing curls and her gauzy white dress that reached her ankles. Then she blinked, and her face relaxed. "I think that's possible." Her voice was its smoothest and calmest, what Fredrick had dubbed Soothe the Spazzing Cat Voice. "Why are you suspicious?"

Fredrick exploded, telling her about his experiences with missing time, feeling like he'd dropped into the middle of a conversation, and the moved diary. Then he added the nuclear bomb of the burnt Bible and the smashed candy dish. "And don't I have the right pieces?" he finished. "I discovered that I experienced severe abuse as a young child. I was a psychology major. I got a BA. I'm no expert, but I remember what the textbook and Dr. Hadley had to say about DID and its causes."

"Let's sit down." Chalsey gestured to the kitchen table.

Fredrick rounded up his cup of coffee, prompting Chalsey to do the same, and then they faced each other over the sunlit table.

"I believe what you have is DID." Chalsey took a sip of her black coffee. "I have talked to other parts of you."

Fredrick felt the stampede of a thousand wild horses in his chest. "But I don't feel like I'm missing *that* much time." He stared into his coffee cup and watched the steam rise like his panic. "But then again, I'm apparently missing all my memories of being molested. God!" He met Chalsey's gaze. "What—what do the other parts of me act like?"

"The one I talk to the most is very kind." Chalsey reached out and patted his arm. "I've also met two who are children. They're all otherwise perfectly normal. Just traumatized."

Fredrick stared at her in numb shock. "Then...you've known for sure."

"Yes. The other adult you I speak with is sure it's DID. And he knows you don't know. He's marginally aware of you." Chalsey took another sip of coffee. "He'll be glad you caught up with him."

Tears burned Fredrick's eyes. *You were friends with me all this time, knowing I have the most severe dissociative disorder a person can have. You may be the only person in my life who really loves me—as in, unconditionally.* "So this is why you pushed me to get a new therapist. I need a DID specialist."

"Exactly." Chalsey's brow furrowed. "See if you can reach out and sense your other self. His name is Michael. You're the Fredrick, and he's the Michael, of Michael Fredrick Anderson."

Fredrick sat back in his chair. "Okay. I mean, I can try." He stared off to the left, his gaze resting on the doorjamb of the door into the dining room. He felt pressure. *Hey, is there really a Michael in here?* Faint dizziness washed through him as he reached inside. *Michael? Are you the one who's been talking to me for the last few days?*

His vision turned concave, the doorjamb appearing farther away than it logically was. The sense of internal pressure grew. "I'm going to try to switch places with Michael. I don't know if I can, but if it works, then I've got my proof." He pressed again, reaching out to Michael. It felt like brushing up against a second mind.

"Try to relax control of yourself," Chalsey murmured, her voice still soothing.

I can do this. I will do this. Fredrick released control. *Dr. Laurie says not to grasp at things too hard. Release control. Be more flexible. Let events flow like water.* A strange sliding sensation erupted inside his mind, and the room looked distorted, as though he viewed the doorjamb through a glass Coke bottle.

The second consciousness pushed toward him.

"He's here. I can tell he's here now." Fredrick fought to loosen his internal reins. *Radical acceptance. Whatever will be will be. It's safe here. It's only Chalsey. I can let go.* The advice of two dozen self-help books flowed through him.

"Good." Chalsey and her words seemed only half-real. "Urge him toward the sound of my voice."

Fredrick imagined he was scooting toward the right on a couch and that Michael was sitting on the left and taking his place at the center. Fredrick felt bubble-headed, as if someone were blowing glass inside his brain.

Michael slid into control of their body. "He did it. I'm Michael." Everything around him looked concave, reminding him of playing with the different lenses of his dad's old camera.

"Wonderful!" Chalsey straightened her shoulders and smiled. "Does Fredrick still seem aware of you?"

I can hear her, Fredrick said.

"Yes." Amazement shot through Michael, piercing Fredrick's numbness and shock. "Oh, my God! This changes everything. We can stop losing time now, and we can help each other." He grabbed Chalsey's hands and squeezed them. "Thank you!"

Fredrick internally jolted at the sudden knowledge that Michael and Chalsey were dating. *Oh, my God!*

Michael laughed. "Okay, so now he knows we're a couple."

"Oops." Chalsey laughed, too. "It's okay, Fredrick. You don't have to date me just because Michael is. I'm fine with dating Michael and being your best friend."

Holy shit! You've been dating for 15 years. Fredrick received another download of information as Michael's thoughts joined with his. *And you tried out Wicca. You went to circle meetings with her. You—you've done some sexual things without blowing up on the landing pad! Fucking hell! I have this whole second history with Chalsey that I knew nothing about.*

Michael cringed. "Poor Fred-o. He's getting pummeled with all my knowledge now."

Well, I'm not mad. I'm just stunned. Fredrick flared with alarm. *But I just got a crush on Toni!*

"I don't care," Michael said. "Chalsey, would you explain that it's okay if Fred-o dates Toni?"

"I truly don't care if you date Toni," Chalsey said. "You didn't ask to get abused until your parts got disconnected from each other. And everyone has parts. Psychologists have known that since the 1970s. There's a whole therapy technique called Internal Family Systems that helps people negotiate with their various parts in order to reduce internal conflict and indecision. It's not just for DID. It wasn't even pioneered with DID. Think about it. People say stuff like this all the time: 'Part of me wants to get married, and part of me doesn't. Part of me wants to change careers, and part of me doesn't.' We *all* have parts."

Fredrick's calm permeated Michael. *Oh. Yeah. Good point.*

"He gets it," Michael said.

"So your parts are just pulled farther apart than normal. So far apart they couldn't talk to each other anymore. That's all." Chalsey shrugged. "I never want to get married again—marriage was hell—and I'm polyamorous. And I don't think it's fair to ask someone with DID to unnaturally narrow themselves to dating a single partner if they're not all interested in the same person."

Fredrick's peace caused Michael to relax, and their stomach muscles unclenched. *Chalsey is the best person ever.*

Into that peace fired Fredrick's earlier realization: *Our father had to know this.*

Michael released Chalsey's hands and spoke for both of them. "Our father knew we have DID. No way did he fail to notice. Missing time? Losing memories? Wild fluctuations in personality type? I mean, think about it. When Fred-o takes the Myers-Briggs, he scores an INTJ. When I take it, I score an ESFP. Plus I had other markers of extreme trauma: night terrors, bedwetting, panic attacks, and suicide attempts. Fuck it all! He knew perfectly well we were traumatized, so he had to notice the DID, too."

"Makes sense that he would." Chalsey took a long swig of coffee and glared out the window, her entire face creasing. "It's like he got a PhD in psychology just to learn how to hide his own child's trauma. Or—shit. His *children's*. What about Roger?"

Fredrick abruptly remembered that he'd forgotten to text Roger and ask him about the mysterious dead baby who would have been his own age and the death certificate his parents had kept.

"Roger moved across the nation, majored in psychology, and has spent his entire life treating abused children." Michael sighed. "I assumed he was just being Phillip Roger Anderson II. You know, living up to the name Dad gave him. What I hope now is that he did for real what our dad only pretended to do: help abused children because he was abused."

Chalsey nodded and took another swig of coffee. "Goddess, I hope so."

There is so much I have to tell you, whispered a voice in Michael's mind.

That wasn't me, Fredrick said.

They both felt ghostly internal movement, a shifting inside their shared mind.

There is so much I have to tell you now that you know we're all here inside you, whispered the voice. The intonation sounded like a child's, and the energy with it felt young.

"Like what?" Michael asked. He held up one finger, signaling Chalsey to wait.

There's a box in the attic and a suitcase by the cellar stairs. And Mommy and Daddy did—

The voice fell silent. Fredrick and Michael felt as though their brain had been packed with cotton balls.

It's that Brain Bubble Wrap feeling again, Fredrick said. *I kept getting this sensation when you tried to talk to me. Wait. That was you, right?*

Yeah, that was me. Michael stood and headed for the refrigerator. *I was trying to get through to you and warn you about our past.* "A third self-state tried to talk to Fred-o and me, but we lost them. It could have been Angela or Laura." *I guess we better check out the attic and the cellar later.*

From Michael, Fredrick caught up with the existence of the other self-states.

"Now that Fred-o and I can talk to each other, maybe we can work toward talking to the other self-states on purpose." Michael opened the refrigerator and frowned at the contents. "We need to make a grocery run."

"EMDR therapy should help with that," Chalsey said. "It physically 'rewires' your brain to help you heal from trauma using bilateral stimulation. Even walking is a mild form of bilateral stimulation. You could go on a long walk and try talking to your other parts."

Michael pulled out the almond milk. "Sure. I'm game. I'll try most anything once."

Brave, Fredrick sighed.

"We could go to the nature preserve this weekend," Chalsey said. "After grocery shopping."

"You're on." Michael pulled out the box of raisin bran and wondered how his life would change now that his parts were speaking to each other again.

CHAPTER 11

THE SUN XIX

BECAUSE OF THE DAY'S TIMING, MICHAEL AND Chalsey only accomplished grocery shopping before members of Chalsey's Wiccan circle began arriving with card tables. A Latina woman in her mid-thirties arrived first. Fredrick, who had switched with Michael, opened the front door as she climbed onto the porch with a card table tucked under her arm. She had a long, teal ponytail, blue eyes, and a blue sundress.

"Come on in." Fredrick held the storm door open.

Chalsey whisked into the room. "This is Heather Torres."

Heather and Fredrick shook hands. "Nice to meet you," she said. "Thank you for hosting our circle tonight."

"Thanks for helping me with my mom's stuff." Fredrick liked her vibes, which were calm but peppy around the edges.

Chalsey led Heather to the back deck for set up.

The second person to arrive was a man with long auburn hair and green eyes. He was taller than Fredrick, perhaps five foot nine, and carried two card tables, one under each arm. His long hair and laidback vibes contrasted with his beige slacks and white Oxford shirt with black pinstripes.

Chalsey joined them. "Corey Lewis, meet Michael Fredrick Anderson."

They likewise shook hands, and then Chalsey ushered him to the back.

Toni arrived next with his card table. Like the day before, he wore jeans and a t-shirt, this one royal blue with a retro Mentos logo on it. "Hey!"

"Hey." Fredrick smiled and felt the heat in his cheeks. Toni's gorgeousness hit him straight in the gut with those honey brown-blond curls and the surprisingly full lips.

So you found a male Chalsey, Michael commented from inside, his amusement wafting through Fredrick.

God, I feel thunderstruck. Fredrick blushed as he led Toni back to the deck. Corey and Heather were hanging out and drinking sodas Chalsey had bought during their grocery run.

Fredrick and Chalsey took point in the living room again, welcoming the next member. A gray-haired Asian American woman arrived in a sedan and carried up two card tables, one under each arm. Like Heather, she was around five feet tall.

When Fredrick opened the door for her, powerful vibes hit him. This woman, with her tiny stature, wavy hair, and sharp brown eyes, had an aura of solid titanium. She looked to be in her early 70s and, unlike Fredrick's mother, used no makeup to hide her wrinkles. She wore black slacks with a red, traditional Chinese silk shirt covered in a dragon pattern.

"This is Wendy Yuan, our high priestess." Chalsey took one card table.

Fredrick shook her hand, and an electric current shot up his arm, as though her spirit had given him static shock.

"We'll help you with your ghost problem." Wendy's firm tone rendered the words a proclamation.

I believe you. Fredrick smiled. "I welcome the help."

Chalsey led her to the back.

The last vehicle to arrive, a pale blue van, brought two

people. The driver was a woman who appeared to be in her late twenties and had brown hair and brown eyes. She wore a brown jumper-dress over a white shirt. With her was a man around forty years old who was six feet tall. He had short, orangey-red hair and wore jeans and a green polo shirt. Each of them carried a card table.

Chalsey returned in time to introduce them. "This is Gina Peterson and James Brooks."

Fredrick shook their hands, and then they all gathered on the back deck. Largo had slipped outside and was sniffing the deck and people's shoes. Alarmed, Fredrick rushed to his side but didn't grab him. For now, Largo wasn't in danger. *Fine. Sniff the great outdoors. It's probably a kitty sensory overload.*

"This is everyone for today," Wendy said as James and Gina set up their tables. "Jeremy and Pamela aren't able to come."

"We have food and drinks," Chalsey said. "Everyone help yourselves."

"James and I brought snacks, too," Gina said. "They're still out in the van."

"And I brought beer," Toni said.

Wendy clapped her hands together. "Then we're all set. Let's help Michael with his chore, and then we can have our circle."

When Wendy used his name, she jerked Michael into control of his body. *Oops. Well, that happened.*

"I think it's Fredrick," Toni said.

"It's both." Michael felt the tug as Fredrick almost switched with him. *We should warn Chalsey later that saying our names can now induce a switch.* "Different people call me different things. Chalsey calls me both. Then again, she's known me forever."

Wendy turned to him. "Well, which should I call you?"

"Fredrick," Michael said.

"Fredrick it is, then." Wendy headed inside, a woman on a mission.

Fredrick regained control of his shared body with a sudden jolt. He picked up Largo and followed her in. "Basically, just grab anything not already set out on a table. Knickknacks, books, Tupperware, whatever." He set Largo down. "Anything but electronics."

The circle members swarmed inside like an army of worker bees and zipped through the house, talking as they grabbed items.

Fredrick tucked himself into the corner of the kitchen long enough to text his half-brother. The extent of their texting was usually a group chat that included both Roger's and Fredrick's mothers and Roger's step-father: *Merry Christmas, Happy New Year,* and *Happy Birthday.*

We're dropping on him out of nowhere, Michael said. *But we've gotta know what he knows.*

Fredrick typed out the text in Standard English, fighting the autocorrect: *Do you know anything about a baby in the family who died? I'm cleaning out Mom's house, and I found a death certificate that says Timothy Dale Anderson, February 7, 1980-March 15, 1980.*

Not expecting an answer soon, given it was Saturday and early afternoon in California, Fredrick stuffed his phone into his back pocket and joined the group. As everyone worked, Fredrick gave away a few things to his helpers. Corey found a book he wanted and Heather a necklace. Gina discovered a knickknack and James a toy ship in a bottle. Far from being offended, Fredrick was happy to get rid of some stuff. Gina even expressed an interest in adopting Largo.

During their snacky supper, which they ate standing up in the kitchen, Fredrick checked his phone, but Roger hadn't responded. *I hope I didn't piss him off by asking.*

I don't know why you would, Michael said.

It's important, said a third voice, the same child from earlier.

Why? Fredrick asked.

Silence.

Not this routine again, Fredrick groaned. He walked over to the kitchen trashcan and tossed in the paper plate. On the counter beside him sat an innocent tarot card, as if it were perfectly normal for a Tarot Ghost to pepper one's day with messages. This card showed a brilliant yellow sun with a smiling face hanging over a smiling child on a horse.

Well, I don't need the Little White Book to know what this one means, Fredrick told Michael. *Let me guess: happiness, confidence, optimism, and joy.*

"All right. Let's get our circle started." Wendy herded everyone from the kitchen into the living room.

"You can join us," Toni said, smiling.

Fredrick couldn't pass that up. "Okay."

Thatta boy, Michael said. *Explore something new. Jehovah isn't gonna strike you dead with a Zeus-like lightning bolt to the head.*

Fredrick and Toni settled on the couch side-by-side, along with Heather. Toni sat in the middle, and Fredrick felt eleven years old again. *Our thighs are touching!*

I'm glad you're this engaged, Michael said.

Gina took the recliner, and everyone else pulled over dining room chairs except Wendy, who stood.

What a trooper, Michael said. *Do you think she's a vet? She's got a soldier's endurance.*

Maybe. What I really think is we have chronic fatigue from PTSD, Fredrick said.

"We'll be starting with breathing techniques and meditation," Wendy told Fredrick. "That will be followed with visualization exercises and some yoga."

Chalsey set her chair by the couch, positioning herself on Fredrick's other side. "Wendy is a martial arts instructor."

"I learned yoga, tai chi, and other such techniques of my ancestors after I returned from the Vietnam War," Wendy said. "I came home with PTSD, and Western medicine wasn't cutting it."

Dude, we were right. She's totally a vet, Michael said. *Maybe she was a nurse.*

"Fair enough." Fredrick kept an open mind and followed along with everyone as Wendy led them through what seemed to be a set practice session. Although his mind wandered during the meditation, he visualized every object Wendy asked for and even kept up with the yoga poses. Mostly.

"Have you practiced yoga?" Wendy stopped by Fredrick, who had picked out the spot by the front door. Everyone had haphazardly strewn themselves across the living room, dining room, kitchen, and even hallway.

"I bought three VHS tapes of yoga while my dad was dying and did at least one a night." Fredrick felt a flash of remembered panic. His dad's death from lung cancer had taken eleven months, and Fredrick had suffered panic attacks the entire time. *Why did I flip out when he was actually my abuser? Shouldn't I have been relieved the one who harmed me was dying? But I couldn't remember any trauma, and instead I melted down.* "I used it for stress relief. That was 24 years ago, but I kept doing a few of the stretches. My psoas muscles are crazy tight."

Wendy inclined her head. "It's no wonder. Our psoas hold our stress and trauma. Our entire pelvic floor can hold stress. Yoga poses for your psoas can release stress from your body."

That news hit Fredrick squarely. "I'll look up some videos on YouTube for it, then." *I must have shit tons of trauma in my psoas. No wonder my hips hurt all the damn time.*

"It should help you." Wendy glanced out the front

window. "The moon has risen. Let's head outside and worship the Goddess." She smiled at Fredrick. "You're free to join us in this as well. You'll just need to follow along as best you can and stay inside the sacred circle once we cast it."

"Sure." Fredrick peeled himself off the floor and followed everyone outside, curious.

You might like it, Michael said. *I never could find a replacement religion that really aligned with my own personal beliefs and spiritual needs. Wicca was probably the closest. Maybe it's our Celtic blood calling out to us.*

Maybe. Fredrick allowed himself to have a sense of adventure. *I mean, Grandma said we're Scots-Irish.*

Chalsey fell into step beside him as they crossed the back deck and headed into the grass. "Heather is leading this part of the circle tonight." She pointed toward the Latina woman with teal hair. "Wendy has us all take turns. It's basic. We'll sing and give praises to the Goddess and pour a libation of water onto the grass. We do this at every full moon, and the name of June's full moon is The Moon of Life. June is associated with oak trees in the Celtic nature calendar, and oak is associated with cleansing, strength, self-confidence, and optimism. That'll be our focus tonight."

"I could use some of that," Fredrick muttered. He settled on the ground and stayed out of everyone's way.

Several people made trips to their vehicles, and then they began their set up. Toni made an enormous circle out of river stones. James grabbed the grill, tossed the burnt book out of it, and carried it inside the circle, filling it with a collection of broken sticks from the yard. Gina carried over the small outdoor table from the deck, the one Fredrick's mom had used to hold drinks. She set it in the center of the circle and piled on a few raw chunks of agate and topaz in one corner, creating an altar.

Corey set a bowl of water on the altar, and Chalsey added

a bowl of incense. Fredrick understood: They were representing the four elements, with the flames from the grill as the fire.

It's pretty standard, Michael agreed.

I'm sure it's fine as long as I don't use the "a" word. Fredrick showed Michael his memory of a child state's fear of the new Mother Mary altar.

Heather took over, having everyone stand inside the circle. She held a hand drum, and she directed them to move in a circle as they sang a song praising the Goddess' wisdom.

Fredrick wasn't able to sing along, but he walked and clapped his hands with the beat of the drum. Excitement built in his chest, tingling, and both Toni and Chalsey seemed to glow, their faces lit with joy as they smiled and sang. *They both look radiant. Peaceful, even.*

"Ask the Goddess to cleanse you or give you strength," Heather called between verses.

"I pray for strength to find a new job!" Gina said, raising her voice over the singing.

"I ask to be cleansed of old fears," Toni said.

"I pray for more optimism," Wendy said.

Corey fell quiet, apparently making his request silently.

"I ask for help to get closer to my sister," James called out.

Fredrick jumped in. "I ask to be myself, my true self, free of lies and masks!"

"I pray to deepen the love of my life," Chalsey murmured, her voice nearly lost under the singing.

Fredrick felt Michael's answering pang of love for Chalsey.

"I ask for strength—freedom from fear." Heather halted, and with her, everyone stopped and threw up their hands, stretching their fingers toward the full moon.

Fredrick followed suit as Michael explained, *The symbol of the Goddess is the moon, but they don't believe the Goddess is literally the moon. It's just symbolism.*

Well, every religion has a symbol. I'm less concerned with the symbol than whether they can access the Divine Spirit. Fredrick felt a burst of tingles race over his scalp, his atheism taking a pounding.

We sent energy out into the Universe somehow, Michael said. *May the Divine Energies accept our prayer.*

Everyone settled on the grass, and a discussion of crystals and their healing properties broke out. Fredrick had tried both reiki and crystal healing once as a variation from his weekly massages, so he listened with half an ear. His gaze fell upon the flames inside the open grill. *Man, I can't believe we burned Mom's Bible.*

It was soaked up with evil energy, Michael said. *It was terrifying.*

"—green stones for the heart chakra," Heather was saying. "Balancing the heart chakra is essential for—"

A flash of an image shot through Fredrick's mind as he stared at the fire: a different fire with bigger flames. Fear thundered in his chest. *What was that?*

I'm not sure, Michael said.

The third voice returned: *I've been trying to warn you that—*

Fredrick saw another flash of memory: His mother standing by the flames, holding her open Bible and singing. His entire body erupted into goosebumps. *What the hell?*

The image grew sharper, the memory clearer. Fredrick could hear his mother's words as she sang: "*—upon this litany, until our deaths, that you may bring us more power, and that our deeds should always glorify you.*"

Fredrick saw a flash of The Demon Mother, except in his memory it was The Demon Grandfather: a half-bald man with a slight beer belly and a bulbous nose.

No! screamed the child's voice inside Fredrick, and he panicked so hard his heart skipped a beat. He tasted aluminum, and his teeth ached, and he scrambled backwards, knocking into the river stones behind him. "No!"

"Michael!" Chalsey shouted.

Michael was jerked into control of their shared body, and he tumbled backwards onto the grass, heart pounding, two stones poking his ribcage. "God! Oh, God!"

Chalsey ran to his side and knelt, grabbing his hand. "What is it? Is it like before?"

Fredrick saw Michael's memory of a previous circle and a previous panic attack. Michael had been staring at the bonfire, warming himself on a chilly fall night, and then had panicked without knowing why.

"Yes," Michael gasped. "It's fire. It's about fire somehow."

James jumped up and snapped the lid shut over the already dying flames.

Toni scrambled over to Michael's side and squeezed his shoulder. "Fire? Are you pyrophobic?"

"Not especially. Okay, kind of." Michael and Fredrick had both been terrified of fire as children, unable to even light a match. "I thought I got over it as I grew up. But this..." He met Chalsey's gaze. "This was a PTSD flashback about fire. I'm sure of it."

"Okay. Let's get you inside." Chalsey helped him sit up.

Michael reached back and rubbed his back where the stones had jabbed him. "Note to self: Fire bad."

"Then don't play with fire," said a snide voice.

Michael jerked toward the voice.

The Demon Mother stood on the deck, arms crossed, still wearing her electric blue shirt and jeans.

"It's the entity!" Chalsey turned to Wendy. "We destroyed the altar Fredrick's mom used to summon it, but it still came anyway."

Fredrick switched places with Michael at the sound of his

name. His terror converted into rage. "Go away! I don't want you here."

"What you want is useless and pathetic," The Demon Mother said. "Get out! All of you. I don't want you in my house or my yard."

"You're dead," Gina drawled. "None of this is yours anymore."

Wendy held up her hands and made a triangle with her fingers, pressing her thumbs and index fingers together. "By the wind and the waves, the trees and the streams, and by the power of The One, I command you to depart. You are Uninvited."

The Demon Mother propped her hands on her hips. "You can't—"

She vanished mid-tirade.

Wendy's shoulders slumped. "That was enormous. Your mother was summoning it? She must have been summoning it for *decades*, then."

Raw terror shot through Fredrick, making his teeth ache again. "Yes." He felt certain it was true, although he had no direct memories.

Wendy walked over and knelt by him. "I will have to do research and confer with other high priestesses. Removing such an entity will not be easy. This isn't some prankster spirit. This is the closest thing I've ever seen to a demon-god. Not that such things exist. It's just—it's the worst evil entity I've ever seen."

Fredrick felt every cell in his body convert to ice. He turned to Chalsey. "We're not staying the night tonight."

"Agreed."

Fredrick stood and helped everyone clean up the circle, and then everyone left.

Only as Fredrick drove away with Chalsey did he realize that Roger still hadn't replied to his text.

CHAPTER 12

JUDGMENT XX

FREDRICK AND CHALSEY ARRIVED HOME AT 9:00 AS the sun set, casting the horizon into a bloody glow. The town of Ashleigh, Kentucky, lay 45 minutes west of their old hometown of Careyville and was three times larger, boasting a population of 33,000. During the school year, the population swelled to 45,000 as Ashleigh University's campus filled up.

Parking his car in his driveway, Fredrick stared at the rainbow-tinted sky, the crimson staining the horizon. The sky spread overhead in bands of orange, yellow, and even a faint swath of green before the blue and navy that signaled the onset of night. The full moon hung opposite the sun, Venus sparkling to her right.

"Mom summoned that entity all my life." Fredrick broke the car's silence. "I don't remember a damn thing, but somehow I still know that. I *feel* it. Like gut instinct."

"A self-state named Laura said as much," Chalsey said. "Part of you remembers."

Fredrick nodded and climbed out of the car. His little 1100-square-foot house awaited him, quiet. It was a gray stone building from the 1940s with no garage but thick oak trees in its yard. With two bedrooms, one and a half baths, and no basement, its only claim to luxury was its large living room. "You want to just head home? Spend the night in your own bed?"

Chalsey shut the passenger door and leaned against it. "I will. But I'll hang out with you another hour if you still feel off balance."

"I'm still a little knocked sideways, yeah." Fredrick headed to his side door and let them in. Chalsey had left her 2012 white Prius parked in his driveway, enabling her to head out whenever she liked.

Fredrick flopped onto his white suede couch and stared around his living room, analyzing what he'd accidentally said about himself. The walls, carpet, and couch were all white, with only the tables and a tan recliner to break up the monotony. "I surrounded myself with white. Almost my entire house is white." The kitchen and bathroom floors were white tile, the appliances were white, and even the towels were white. "White symbolically means purity and innocence, and I feel safer with everything white. Was I subconsciously reacting to that *thing*?"

"Maybe." Chalsey plopped down beside him.

Michael switched with Fredrick. "It's Michael. Can I rest my head on your lap?"

"Sure."

Michael shifted and lay on his back, resting his head on her thighs. He draped his knees over the couch arm and stared at the white plaster ceiling with its swirls. "Fred-o and I are admittedly confused. Why would our mom—maybe even both our parents—be summoning demons?"

They never called them demons, said a third voice. This voice and its matching energy seemed to belong to a teenager rather than a younger child.

Are you Laura?

Silence.

Michael pushed ahead. "I don't get it. My mom always seemed like such a dyed-in-the-wool Christian. How does a woman who reads me Bible stories every night, chews my ass out if I don't tithe, and attends church every Sunday for her *entire life*—barring illness—turn out to be a demon-summoning freak?"

"It could have been a ruse." Chalsey ran her fingers through his hair. "This is Kentucky. There's a church on practically every street corner, and in a town of 11,000 people, everyone is up inside everyone else's business. And back when we were kids, Carveyville was more like 8,500 people. Your mom once said Christians are still going door-to-door in Careyville and inviting people to their church. Your mom would want to fit in. Also, despite U.S. law, her employers had the potential to fire your mom for not being a Christian. Kentucky is an 'at-will' commonwealth, after all. Her employers wouldn't have had to list a reason for firing her, or they could lie and say it wasn't religious-based."

Michael focused on the breathing exercises Wendy had taught him earlier, forcing his belly to expand and relax. "Okay, true. And then there's Grandma Smith. I know you have to remember what a bossy, controlling narcissist she was. If Mom had stopped attending church, Grandma Smith would have crawled up her ass." His maternal grandma had died in 2003, only four years after his father had passed. "But even with Grandma Smith dead, Mom still went except during the pandemic." With diabetes, morbid obesity, and a heart murmur, Marilyn Smith Anderson had obeyed her doctor's orders to attend church via TV or the internet.

"A ruse, then." Chalsey shifted her hand and massaged the muscles under Michael's eyebrows.

"God, that's sore." Michael was stunned by the amount of stress around his eyes. "Okay, so Mom pretends to be

Christian. Then why did she still argue with me about Christian concepts? Is the Bible literal or not? Is the Earth only 6,000 years old? Are you 'once saved, always saved' or can you 'fall from grace?' She picked fights with me about theology as if she cared. Like a True Believer."

Chalsey shook her head. Fine wrinkles sprang forth around her eyes and mouth. "But you just said it: picked fights. She argued religion with you because she wanted to argue about something. Didn't matter what. She nagged, she harped, she nitpicked. You hit forty, and she was still inspecting your inner ears for blackheads, complaining that your hairstyle is too messy, and harassing you that you're too skinny. A person like that, whether male, female, or intersex, is arguing to argue. She wanted to you feel wrong. Feel ugly. Be self-conscious."

Our mom was never Christian, whispered the teenager.

Michael swallowed the nasty truth, the bitter pill of his mother's mockery of her childhood religion. Of all the things he'd ever swallowed—chalky milk of magnesia, uncoated aspirin, or sulfur-laced antibiotics—nothing had gone down as hard as this. "My mom flogged me for not following a religion she herself never believed in. I can't even *look* at a church without wrinkling my nose with horror, much less set foot inside of one, but when she lashed out at me, she didn't believe a word she was saying."

"This is your new reality, the actual reality." Chalsey leaned down and pressed a kiss to his forehead. "May it set your free."

At 10:00 in broad daylight, the June sun beating Kentucky with 90-degree temperatures, Fredrick unlocked his mother's front door and slipped inside. A scan of the living room showed everything was as he'd left it, the dining room table and card tables filled with items to auction.

Largo raced into the room, his kitty belly swaying back and forth with each step, and meowed a diatribe at being made to wait for breakfast.

"Seems clear." Fredrick stepped in, allowing Chalsey and Toni to enter behind him. "Largo isn't hiding. Let's put in about an hour's work and then get the hell back out of here while the gettin' is good."

"Sounds like a plan," Chalsey said.

Fredrick swept through the right archway into the hallway and then into the kitchen, Largo on his heels. The sunrays lit dust motes lazing in the air, the morning peaceful and quiet. The house's undisturbed energy hadn't yet fully broken, lulling the unsuspecting into relaxation. It was as if an enormous evil entity didn't live in the house, ready to scream at anyone it didn't like.

Mom's dead, and a demon with her face is still nitpicking us, Fredrick groused to Michael. *Fuck our life.*

You just wait. That bitch'll show up and demand we put on a pink, frilly dress, Michael said.

Fredrick laughed. It wasn't funny, and yet somehow it was.

"What's up?" Toni joined him, hovering by the sink.

Opening the cabinet, Fredrick pulled out Largo's kitty kibbles and poured an appropriate serving into the food bowl. *Poor cat probably thinks I'm starving him.* Largo charged in so fast the last two kibbles hit him on the forehead.

Michael switched with Fredrick to answer. "Some freaky-ass demon-monster-spirit-thing shows up with my mom's face and snarks me. Now I'm thinking, 'Dude, she's dead, and she's still riding my ass, anyway.' Wasn't death supposed to fix this problem? Shit, man."

Toni tilted his head to the side, one eyebrow arching, and smiled.

Oops. Did he notice I'm different? Michael said to Fredrick. *Sorry, Fred-o. Get back out here and woo yourself a boyfriend.*

Oh, my God! Don't say it like that. Fredrick found himself in control of the body again. He got Largo's insulin shot ready and administered it to the scruff of his neck, like his mother had taught him.

"I'm glad you can have a sense of humor about it," Toni said. "I'm not sure I could do the same if it was me."

Fredrick glanced down the hallway toward the primary bedroom. "I believe I was exposed to a lot of scary entities as a kid, and I just don't remember it yet."

"Really?" Toni crossed his arms, his brow puckering. "What makes you think so?"

Fredrick explained about the oozing Bible, carefully omitting his DID.

"Hell, man." Toni wrinkled his nose. "That's some evil mojo. I guess some people would say your mom was abusing Hoodoo, but that can't be right. You're White. Hoodoo's a Black tradition, and it doesn't exist to summon demons. All that evil Hoodoo bullshit's just a Hollywood horror movie thing."

"I don't know anything about Hoodoo," Fredrick said. "I mean, I watched *The Skeleton Key,* but that's a work of complete fiction."

Sweeping into the kitchen through the dining room archway, Chalsey still looked every inch the goddess, even wearing jeans with a white t-shirt. A vague female form with a spiral on its tummy filled the shirt. "I want you to read something." She held out a blue three-ring binder to Toni.

"You're going to torture Toni with my mom's novel?" Fredrick mimed a shudder. "What did Toni ever do to you?"

Chalsey barked a laugh. "Well, I won't make him read the whole thing. Just the important parts."

Fredrick abruptly learned from Michael that the novel

contained séances and a demon-summoning orgy. "Holy shit. Okay." *Our mom wrote that? What the fuck?* "I'm going into the cellar. Would you cover my back?"

"Sure." Chalsey opened the binder and pointed. "Read from here until chapter 23."

"This oughta be rich." Toni plopped into a kitchen chair. "What is it? An evil grimoire for summoning Satan except in novel form?"

Chalsey stared at him.

Fredrick paused at the top of the cellar stairs. "About that..." Instead of finishing his sentence, he skipped down the stairs.

After a moment, Chalsey joined him. "What's up?"

Although Fredrick scanned the cellar, he sensed no ghosts. "A suitcase, apparently."

"You mean the one the ghost wanted you to open?" Chalsey pointed at the red suitcase that halfway protruded off the bottom tier of the storage shelves. "You never came back for it."

"Today's the day, I guess. Or one of me thinks so, anyway." Fredrick marched over and tugged it onto the floor. It was a hard plastic Samsonite suitcase from the 1970s. Kneeling in front of it, he opened it. "I was told to check a suitcase in the cellar and check the attic, although I don't know for what."

A musty clothing smell wafted up. One side held three dresses from the 1960s or 1970s: a navy dress covered with white flowers and a built-in, flared miniskirt; a chartreuse ballroom gown with enormous white, lacy bell sleeves; and a navy-, pink-, and purple-swirled sleeveless dress. With them were two white leis from Hawaii and a pair of white pumps. "I think these are all keepsakes from Mom's Hawaiian vacation." Fredrick refastened the straps over them and turned the suitcase the other way, opening the solid flap. Solid purple fabric met his inspection.

"Terrifying energy is wafting up off of that," Chalsey whispered.

The memory of the ghost in the cellar talking to him fired through Fredrick's mind: *"Frontier. Farm. Secrets."*

Unsure what that meant, Fredrick ignored the memory, grabbed the top, and pulled. A robe began unfolding, and he stood and shook it out. "It almost reminds me of a purple graduation gown."

Dude, that's a SOMH robe. Michael's fear shot through his sense of victory. *We found it. Proof! I remembered it right. Our crazy parents were totally in the SOMH.*

Stunned into a state of dissociation, Fredrick turned the robe in his hands, which felt half-numb. On the front breast was a symbol: three white crosses superimposed over a Bible. "Holy *shit*." His voice emerged croaked and mangled.

"The hood." Chalsey pointed.

Fredrick glanced back into the suitcase and saw the pointy tip of a purple hood. "Oh, God, why!"

A million pieces flew together in his mind, the memory of his parents' voices clamoring in his head, and built a picture:

If the Blacks don't like it here, they can just get on a boat and go back to Africa.

Ugh, you have illegal Mexican immigrants living down the street from you now. Your property value will plummet.

Well, I hope Trump builds that wall.

I have a homosexual cousin, but I can tolerate that he's gay if he keeps it behind closed doors.

Phillip! How can you say that? It's disgusting. It's an abomination.

Welfare only exists for lazy Black people and illegal immigrants, and they get more of it by having as many children as they can.

I can't believe Roger converted to Catholicism! I'm so disappointed in him. Everyone knows their beliefs are sinful.

They call priests "Father," they pray to saints, and they turned Mary into a goddess. I'm telling you, it's blasphemy.

What is the world coming to? Those Muslims built a mosque in our town. It was bad enough when they started taking all the doctors' jobs—you can't even get a White doctor around here anymore—but a mosque! God in heaven must be crying. I wish he'd just strike them dead!

Fredrick dropped the robe back into the suitcase and stared at the gray cement block wall. "Mom taught me a song when I was a kid:

"Jesus loves the little children,

All the children of the world.

Red and yellow, black and white,

They are precious in his sight.

Jesus loves the little children of the world."

He faced Chalsey, the lyrics bothering him for more than one reason now that he was an adult. "She lied! Dad told me all people are actually equal, but he lied. Out of one side of their mouth, they said race didn't matter. But here's the reality." He jabbed his finger toward the robe. "I've spent my entire adult life listening to my mom hate on immigrants, Blacks, gays, and Catholics, and somehow I didn't put it together."

Chalsey laid a gentle hand on his shoulder. "Plenty of people are racist, homophobic, and anti-Catholic without being card-carrying members of the Soldiers of the Most High. You couldn't have guessed without your memories intact."

For the first time since he was 11, Fredrick rage-cried, his sinuses burning. The horror and pain and fury exploded outward, detonating in his stomach and shaking his body. "Goddamn fucking bigot!" In his mind, he could see his mother's wrinkled nose and curled lip. "No wonder you never accepted me. I'm intersex and agendered, but you hate everything LGBTQIA! Dad insisted I choose for myself, but you hated him every second of every day for that. Didn't you?"

Chalsey hugged him, and he slipped his arms around her in return.

The truth might as well have shattered all the tiny cellar windows, emitting the sun to glare in Fredrick's eyes. "I'm actually agendered. Under all this pain, the reality is I never wanted to be male or female. Mom hated me for not being female. And Mom hated Dad for not having me cut up as a baby to suit *her* desires for *my* body."

Thundering down the stairs, Toni shot into the cellar. "Oh, my God, what is it?"

Shame stabbed Fredrick through the ribs. *Great! My adult crush walks in on me screaming and crying. There's a winning strategy for getting a boyfriend.*

"Fredrick just found this." Chalsey released Fredrick and picked up the robe by her fingertips, only to drop it again. "Disgusting! The energy's so bad I can't even touch it."

Toni's gaze fell on the SOMH symbol, which had landed face-up. "Shit. I'd have a total meltdown if I found that in my parents' cellar. In fact, I'd never be the same." He held out his arm toward Fredrick.

Stunned by the offer, Fredrick edged over. Toni gave him a one-armed hug. *Okay. You're officially boyfriend material now.* "I feel tainted." He had always been the type to level, even with strangers, and he didn't see any reason to stop now. "I feel guilty by association." He shuddered in Toni's embrace. "Oh, *God*. Did my parents parade me around in some kiddy version? A little purple robe for five-year-olds?" His stomach churned and flopped over. "I'm gonna puke."

"You don't know?" Toni rubbed his back with slow caresses. "You don't remember?"

Fredrick shook his head. "My memory's all shot to hell. Totally full of holes."

Toni's hand paused in the middle of his back. "Damn!" Fear laced his voice. "Okay, you need a therapist. ASAP. That is *not good*."

"I contacted several and asked about openings." Fredrick calmed at Toni's show of sanity. *You're not anti-therapy. You aren't telling me to have a stiff upper lip. You're not mocking me for crying.*

"And you're not guilty by association." Chalsey knelt, shoved the robe back in, and shut the suitcase. "You were already fighting all those beliefs and attitudes when I met you back in middle school. Somehow, you figured out it was wrong, and you dismantled it piece by piece. In fact, I remember telling you in tenth grade I thought *my* dad was in the SOMH, although I never could prove it, and we both made fun of him together."

The memory flashed through Fredrick, calming him further. "Okay, that's true. No later than tenth grade, I was attacking all White supremacy ideologies. I never understood the anti-Catholic stuff; I had two Catholic friends in elementary school. And in eleventh grade, I kicked my homophobia."

Chalsey stood and smiled. "You killed it in one day flat."

"One day?" Toni looked between them.

"I came out to him as bi," Chalsey said.

"Faced with a real person who wasn't straight, I couldn't keep screaming about all gays going to hell." Fredrick cringed. "Hurts to even think about it now. *I'm* bi."

Toni squeezed Fredrick's shoulder. "See? You can't be guilty like your parents. You thought for yourself."

Struck by the words, Fredrick stared at the suitcase. *I thought for myself. Roger, did you do that, too? Am I not alone?* Roger still hadn't responded to his text. "I'm a history professor, and I spend a lot of time talking about slavery: what led to it, what it was really like, and how it still affects the U.S.

today. I've always wondered why I ended up focusing on it so much. I never imagined that the answer was my parents were trying to cram hate of everyone not White, straight, and Protestant down my throat."

"And preferably male," Chalsey drawled. "At least in your dad's case."

"Definitely that." Although Fredrick had always remembered his mother's loud bids to make him a girl, he now wondered what he *didn't* remember about his father's efforts to make him a boy. *Leave me the fuck alone! I don't want any of your stupid gender roles.* The idea of letting it all go, of having no gender at all, was a proverbial siren's call. He wanted to board a three-mast, wooden ship and sail into the sunset, vanish into the Agendered Seas, and never return.

Chalsey headed upstairs. "Well, we can't auction the old dresses, so that'll have to wait for the yard sale. Do you want to check the attic?"

"If I can handle the shock of what might be up there," Fredrick mumbled. He reached out and clasped Toni's shoulder, consciously trying to flirt. *I always sucked at flirting. God, awkward.* "I'll leave you to the questionable pleasure of reading Mom's novel, poor sod."

Toni laughed.

Fredrick followed Chalsey upstairs and grabbed an unsweetened green tea from the refrigerator, green tea being his vice. He remembered his mother's cringe when she tried it, the lack of sugar repelling her. "Let me drink my version of liquid courage first." He opened the bottle of Ito En, the only green tea he would drink.

"The Tarot Ghost has visited." Chalsey pointed to the countertop. "It's like having a Secret Santa in June or something."

Snorting, Fredrick glanced at the card, which showed an enormous angel blowing a trumpet and men, women, and

children standing up out of coffins. The card read *Judgment.*
"Okay. So, like, Judgment Day?"

"Yes." Chalsey picked up the card. "Think of self-evaluation, awakening, renewal, reflection, and even reckoning."

"I'll say this is a reckoning." Fredrick took several swigs of tea. "Awakening and renewal, huh? You mean like finally realizing you're non-binary and third gendered?" Even the phrase *third gender* felt wrong. "No, I need to stick with agendered. God, why did it take me this long to figure that out?"

Toni settled at the kitchen table and picked up the binder. "Life can be complicated. And I think many people don't figure out things like that until they're in the forties."

"Mid-life crisis. Well, fine, that's fair." Fredrick headed upstairs. "I spent my whole life living in other people's boxes. Time to get out." *Time to climb out of the boxes, burn down this house, and get on with my real life.*

CHAPTER 13

THE HANGED MAN XII

Fredrick stepped into his old bedroom, his gaze landing on the chest of drawers. A memory flickered through him, showing him one of his selves grabbing the white candy dish, and he glided over to stare at what remained: a pine curio box, likely handmade, and a green jade pyramid.

Mom's altar, the teenager said inside his mind. *Remove it all.*

Not questioning this wisdom, Fredrick pulled off the pyramid and the box, first setting the pyramid on the nightstand and then opening the box. There was a piece of white paper tucked inside.

It should hold jewelry. But is that a letter? asked the teenager.

Chalsey stepped up beside him. "What's that?"

"Dunno." Fredrick pulled out the paper and tossed the curio box onto the bed. "Before I crawl into the attic, let's check it out." The attic crawl space could be accessed through his old bedroom closet.

Chalsey rubbed her arms. "I feel something like an electric charge coming off of that."

Unfolding it, Fredrick discovered words in perfectly slanted cursive. "This is definitely Mom's handwriting." He felt a stab of morbid curiosity and read it aloud:

April 15, 2004

I don't know why I'm writing this. I think it's stupid. But Phillip always said to follow my instincts about these things, so here I go: The house isn't right. I'm wondering if Martha did a working in here. She visited this weekend, and ever since she left Sunday night, I haven't been able to summon The Wanderer, and I can't seem to get any peace.

Michael switched in. He lowered the letter and stared at Chalsey. "The Wanderer? God! That gives me a terrifying feeling. Do you think it's what she called the entity?"

I told you they never called them demons, said the teenager.

"Maybe." Chalsey shivered. "Just you reading it is affecting the energy in the house." She frowned. "Also, you'd been male and Fredrick Michael for four years by 2004, and here she is calling you Martha and she."

Michael groaned. "I remember she called me Martha to my face for three years after I legally changed my name. I'm not even sure I can call that passive aggressive. It was just aggressive." He held up the pseudo-letter again. "Also, why is she saying I did 'a working?' I never told her I converted to Wicca for a while. Why would she assume I was casting spells?"

"Great question."

Steeling himself, Michael resumed reading:

It's almost like my offering is no longer working. I'm going to move the offering to the guest bedroom, start over, and see if that fixes it. Maybe Grandmother's brooch would help. But I must do something, anything, to put vitality back into the offering. It's not like my commitment has wavered.

Michael's grip wrinkled the letter, and his heart rate kicked up. "Is the word *offering* supposed to be a stand-in for the word *altar* here?"

"Could be." Chalsey crossed her arms over her stomach and hunched forward. "The energy of her letter or journal entry or whatever is terrible, and I can believe she's replaced all words she associates with witchcraft with synonyms or euphemisms."

With a pounding heart, Michael resumed reading:

I will give the standard three Bible readings and prayer, but past that, I'm not sure what to do. I can't do it Grandmother's way, and I can't do it Phillip's way without him here to help and guide me. I must do this on my own. It still breaks my heart that Phillip died.

Michael's stomach clenched. *Grandmother's way? Phillip's way?* He forced himself to keep reading, given there wasn't much text left:

I will make this as simple and bearable as possible and leave this journal entry as a relic of my dedication:

Dear Wanderer, I beseech thee to grant –

Michael stopped reading. "Oh, hell no! That's an actual spell." He scanned the final three lines, seeing a Christian-style prayer that wasn't addressed to the Christian God, plus a fancy, unknown symbol like a magical seal. It was a circle with a diamond inside and letters of a foreign language. A brown dot covered the center of the seal.

"That's evil." Chalsey's voice emerged flat. "Destroy it."

"It's dried blood." Michael's neck tingled, and goosebumps shot from his neck down his arms. "But you never—" He paused, not sure what he had started to say.

A different self-state shoved him aside. "It's Laura. You never use blood in a working. Grandma Anderson and Grandma Smith both taught me that. Never, ever use blood. Not your own, and not from an animal, either. Mom broke the rules. She used blood." She narrowed her eyes, glaring at the seal. "She broke the rules all the time." She tore the paper in half, then into quarters, and then into eighths. "We'll have to burn it, too."

Chalsey lowered her arms and straightened. "Laura...your grandmas taught you magick?"

"You can't call it magick, remember?" Laura turned and headed downstairs. "They'll slap your face if you do."

Chalsey followed her. "What did they call it?"

"They told me not to call it anything." Laura marched into the kitchen, grabbed the metal tongs from a drawer, and pulled a box of matches from another drawer. "But they said if I absolutely *had* to call it something, to call it The Way." She handed the matches to Chalsey. "I'm scared of fire. Please light the match for me, okay?" She grabbed the pieces of paper with the tongs and held them over the stainless steel sink.

"Sure." Chalsey lit a match and touched the flame to three paper corners.

Toni set down the binder and joined them. "What's this?"

Laura sized Toni up. She'd watched Fredrick and Michael talk to him from the back of their shared mind, and she wasn't sure she trusted him yet. He didn't put off evil vibes, though. "An evil, magical seal my mom made to summon that entity-thing."

Toni's eyebrows scrunched together. "You sound different."

Laura shrugged one shoulder and stared at the flames. As the paper curled and blackened, she dropped the pieces into the sink to finish burning and set aside the tongs.

"Sorry," Toni said. "So your mom made magical seals of some kind?"

"Yep. She mostly didn't draw them. Dad did. But Dad was dead when she drew this one. I tried to destroy her altar to the entity using my magick." Laura's shoulders drooped. "But she figured it out."

Chalsey traded a look with Toni. "That's high-level magick. I'm going to look up *The Greater Key of Solomon* on the internet later and show it to you. I want you to tell me if you recognize any of the seals or symbols."

"What's that?" Laura asked.

"It's a medieval grimoire that was attributed to King Solomon," Chalsey said. "Supposedly, you use the grimoire to summon spirits of the dead and demons to do your will using the power of God. The spellcaster is referred to as the 'exorcist' and the spells are called 'experiments.'"

Toni wrinkled his nose. "I've never used it. It requires belief in God and the purging of sins, and I have no interest in summoning demons, if they exist as such, or bothering the dead."

"The foreign language on your mom's seal looked like Transitus Fluvii, which is the alphabet used in *The Greater Key of Solomon*." Chalsey rubbed her forehead. "This isn't Wicca. It's medieval ceremonial magick."

Laura turned on the water and washed the gray ashes and fragments down the sink. "I've heard of Wicca, but I don't know anything about it. What's the difference?"

"Wicca is mostly 'low' or root magick," Toni said, "like working with herbs and roots, making salves or teas, and preparing poultices. 'High' or ceremonial magick is mostly stuff like *The Greater Key of Solomon*. I admit I'm giving you the TL;DR version here, but the truth is the English witches whose practices were adapted into Wicca were root-workers and herbal healers. They weren't out at midnight summoning demons."

Laura stared into the drain, her memory pulling her back into her childhood. She would stand on a stool in front of the stove and stir herbs in a pot. "My grandmas did that kind of stuff. They'd grow herb gardens, boil the herbs, and then mix them with things like oil. Then, if you got a cold or cut yourself, they'd grab their homemade medicine and treat you with it."

"Appalachian folk magick," Chalsey said. "They taught you that?"

"Sure." Laura faced Chalsey. *It's still weird seeing you so old. You're supposed to be in eighth grade like me.* "They taught me all sorts of stuff, like hanging a lucky horseshoe over your door or tying knots in a rope to bless someone with a happy marriage. You'd recite Bible verses over it while you tied the knots. They also tied different colors of ribbons on trees to keep away evil spirits." She clenched both fists over her chest.

"And it's *not* what Mom and Dad were doing. Everything my parents did was *scary*."

Toni glanced toward the binder. "About that. In what I've read so far, the stuff in your mom's book is some kind of fake demon-worshipping bullshit. Sounds like Salem Witch Trial stuff. But the *way* she talks about it...And now you're saying your parents were doing rituals of some kind. It sounds like your parents were messing around with magick they didn't really understand."

Laura lowered her fists, her hands still clenched. "Well, you don't need to do it right to call them. The evil entities *want* to come. All you have to do is ask, and they'll show up. And then they tell you to do evil things."

"And you saw this?" Toni asked.

"Mom and Dad *made* me," Laura said. "They made me pray to those things. They made me—"

You're saying too much! Angela hissed inside their shared mind.

"Never mind." Laura fled into her own subconscious.

Fredrick found himself back in control of his body. "I heard her talking," he told Chalsey, throwing in the towel about hiding his DID from Toni. *He's only known me for a few days, but I'm going to toss him into the deep end. If he can't accept I have DID, then we can't date anyway.*

"You did?" Chalsey squeezed his arm. "That's important! It's a sign of progress."

"Her?" Toni echoed.

Fredrick met Toni's gaze. "I have DID. Have you heard of it?" Thanks to his BA in psychology, he couldn't panic about his diagnosis. *I'm fascinated by my mind. This is a plus.*

Well, that'll help us deal with it, Michael said.

"Yeah." A look of wonder crossed Toni's face, easing the wrinkles from his brow. "I've never met anyone who has it, though. I saw the movie *Sybil* when I was 13, and I thought it was fascinating. Probably not fully accurate. But fascinating."

Fredrick stared at the window. "Well, my name as a self-state is Fredrick, but I'm not the 'real' Michael Fredrick Anderson. That movie is so old that people were still clinging to the idea that there is a 'real self' with a bunch of 'false selves' called alters. That's really offensive. We are all parts of one person, not internal imaginary friends. I didn't make up the teenage girl who was just talking. She's part of me. All of us together are Michael Fredrick Anderson." Although he couldn't speak for everyone with DID, he hated the term *alter*. "I'm not an alternative personality. I'm still real."

Chalsey patted Toni's arm. "I know it's a lot of information, but this is important. What psychologists know now is that *all* people in the world are comprised of parts. The concept of a single ego is simply wrong. The human psyche isn't made that way. You can call them parts, selves, or even energy patterns."

"I'll go read up on it, then," Toni said.

"I suggest the book *Embracing Our Selves: The Voice Dialogue Manual*," Chalsey said. "Psychologists Hal and Sidra Stone wrote it. They got a lot of backlash for it because people don't want to accept the fragmentation inherent in human personality."

Toni snorted. "Okay, whatever. Modern human *life* is fragmented. Postmodernism drew attention to that back in the mid-twentieth century. Why pitch a fit about it now?"

Fredrick fell head-over-heels into infatuation. *I'm going to ask this guy out.*

Go for it, Michael said. *Wait for a good moment and ask for his number. Then go get coffee together.*

"Beats me," Chalsey said. "I've been using voice dialogue therapy, internal family systems therapy, and EMDR therapy for almost twenty years now to deal with what my crazy-ass parents did to me. I turned my whole life around this way. I saved myself from alcoholism this way. I don't *care*. It works, and that's all that matters to me."

"Fair enough." Toni squeezed Fredrick's shoulder. "So one of your other selves was talking just now?"

"Yeah." Fredrick's mind had moved on to showing him images of Toni and him at Ashleigh's family-owned coffee shop, relaxing on a sofa and chatting. "Her name is Laura. She's thirteen. Michael and I are adults. And Chalsey's met one named Angela who's a child, but Michael and I haven't connected with them yet."

Plus there's apparently someone named Dietrich, Michael said.

"Okay, so there're four." Toni rubbed his chin with his thumb and forefinger. "What's getting me is that this is evidence your parents severely abused you at a young age. And clearly, that involves some kind of weird ritual stuff."

Michael switched with Fredrick. "I think I remembered part of that at your esbat last night. Just a single image with fire and Mom holding her evil-oozing Bible, but it was enough to blow me up." He paused. "And hi, I'm Michael."

"Hi, Michael." Toni smiled. "I'll keep up with you as best I can. I'm noticing that each of you has different vibes and a different tone of voice, and I'm hoping that helps me."

Michael waved his hand through the air in dismissal. "We can always announce ourselves when we switch. You know, as long as we're in private. I don't consider it a big deal."

"Oh, wow. This is like a whole new world." Toni shook his head, still smiling. "You're brave. You're just marching forward with all this. And whatever happened when you were a child, you survived it."

"You have a point there." Michael hadn't considered his

actions brave, but now he was forced to reconsider it. *Apparently, I survived physical abuse, sexual abuse, and ritual abuse. I'm a badass survivor.* "Okay. I never made it into the attic. I got waylaid by the creepy seal thing Mom made. I better try again and get this done."

Toni nodded and walked back to the table. "I'll finish reading up to chapter 23 of your mom's novel, then."

"Lucky you." Michael climbed the stairs, clinging to the railing this time. *Dealing with all this weird shit's wearing me out.*

I feel you, Fredrick said. *We've just got to hold out until Wednesday when Knight shows up to take pictures for the auction.*

Michael steeled himself as best he could, but the real comfort was the sound of Chalsey's footsteps behind him on the stairs.

In the bedroom, Michael opened his old closet door and pulled on the chain for the bare bulb overhead. The closet was five feet long with a single rod that held Marilyn's off-season clothes. Michael shoved them to the side, revealing the small door to the right. The door was four feet tall and three feet wide, which had been perfect for a small child. It had a sliding lock that was latched.

"Creepy as fuck," Michael said. "This door always scared me as a kid. I was afraid some evil entity was hiding behind it. A different self-state thought it was cool and pretended it was a doorway into a fantasy land. Good for them, I guess. But not me."

Let me handle it, Laura said. She switched with him. "I was the fantasy land daydreamer. I'll do this." She slid the latch open and peered inside. The crawl space was barely large enough for an adult man to squeeze into, and all she saw was an old red train case. She grabbed the dusty handle and pulled it out. Like the suitcase in the cellar, it was hard plastic Samsonite luggage. "Why put it here?"

"As it concerns your mom, who knows?" Chalsey said.

Laura carried the train case over to the bed and opened it. The top tray had partitions for makeup, and below that was a larger space for a brush, hairspray, and other such items. However, Marilyn had filled the top tray with old jewelry: five lapel pins, four rings, two brooches, one necklace, and two pairs of earrings. "Part of this used to be in the curio box."

"Nasty energy." Chalsey stepped back. "She was using some or all of that during black magick rituals."

"I remember," Laura murmured. "Some of this stuff is connected to the SOMH." She pointed at a gold ring with a purple and white cross-shaped emblem. "Some of it went on Mom's altar." She pointed to a gaudy, oversized reindeer brooch. "And some of it she wore during rituals." She picked up a plastic button pin with a magical seal on it. "Dad made two of these with a button-making machine."

Chalsey stepped back another foot. "I don't know how you can stand to touch any of it, and I think you should purify it and then throw it all away. Other than that gold ring, is all of it costume jewelry?"

"Not all of it." Laura set down the button pin and picked up a white gold ring with a jade stone. "This one is real. If I purify it, I could sell it. It was my great-grandma's. But I don't want it. Mom used to make me wear it when she summoned them."

Chalsey bowed her head. "I wouldn't want it either, then."

Laura tossed the ring back in. "Isn't the symbol for Wicca a pentacle?"

"Yes. One of them. Why?"

Laura stepped aside. "Look it over. See if you find anything Wiccan. I'm curious."

Wrinkling her nose, Chalsey inched closer and scanned the jewelry. "None of it. In fact, I don't recognize any of the symbols here except the cross necklace."

"Okay." Laura pulled out the tray. "I didn't think so, but I wanted to be sure." In the bottom of the train case was an antique hand mirror, a 5x7 spiral-bound book, and a black plastic pencil box.

With a gasp, Chalsey retreated to the doorway. "That energy is even more rank."

Goosebumps shot up Laura's arms. "Mom used the hand mirror in some of her workings. I don't recognize the book." She picked it up. The book was an inch thick, and someone had overlaid the cardboard cover with green linen. "This book wasn't bought. Someone used a hand machine to punch the holes." She opened it to the middle, picking a random page.

Black cursive handwriting leapt off the page at her, and Laura yelped and dropped it onto the bed. It took a moment for her to realize that the evil energy emanating from the book had stabbed her psychically, somehow ordering her not to read the contents. She glanced at the page and saw something like a recipe—two tablespoons of rosemary, two rosehips— and a square-shaped drawing under it. Every cell in Laura's body demanded that she look away, and she smacked the book shut.

Chalsey had pressed her body against the bedroom door. "What is it?" Her voice was wispy.

"I think it's a grimoire. I didn't even remember Mom had one." Laura tossed it back inside the train case. "We'll burn it. It's sad that there could be perfectly normal herbal tea recipes in there, but Mom clearly added something *else*. This book feels like them now."

"I'll burn it right now." Chalsey's face had drained into a

sickly complexion, making the fine wrinkles around her eyes and mouth stand out.

Laura grabbed the black pencil box. "Sure. Just let me check this." The top slid long-ways, so she slid it open. Then she snapped it closed, ice lightning shooting down her spine. She tossed in the box, put the tray back in, and closed the train case.

"What was it?"

Although Laura stared at the bright red lid, in her mind, she still saw a little knife with its wooden handle. "A pocket knife. Mom defiled it. I can feel it. Let's go." *I don't want to remember. I don't want to remember. I don't want to remember.* She grabbed the handle and carried the case downstairs, Chalsey following her.

When Laura reached the kitchen, she felt a spirit standing by the kitchen island. Despite the spirit's invisibility, Laura had the impression of a woman no older than Chalsey and perhaps a decade younger. "What do you want?"

The spirit's energy vanished.

Toni looked up from the binder. "What is it?"

"A spirit of some kind. Didn't feel evil." Laura edged up to the island and discovered a tarot card. "Oh, wait. This is what Fredrick and Michael have been talking about." The card showed a man in tights hanging upside down from a tree, one leg crossed behind the other. The letters read *The Hanged Man.* "Well, he wasn't executed. He looks pretty calm, considering."

Chalsey stepped up beside her. "There are a few different readings for this card, like indecision, sacrifice, or waiting. I don't prefer to think of it that way. In Norse mythology, the head god, Odin, hung upside down on a sacred tree for three days in order to gain knowledge and wisdom. I prefer to see this card as suggesting perspective, contemplation, and insight."

Laura felt the interpretation click inside of her spirit. "You're right. That ghost wants me to have perspective about something. I need to contemplate something and get insight about it."

"But what?" Toni asked.

Laura held up the train case. "My mom's abuse of black magick, maybe. Or why my mom was summoning evil spirits but insisting they weren't demons. Why build an altar and refuse to call it an altar? Why do magick and refuse to call it magick? Why say all spirits are neutral and it's only how you apply their advice? Why claim that your rituals, which you don't call rituals, will help you and your family when you're hurting me in order to do them? Why any of this?"

"Psychosis?" Toni closed the electric blue binder and set it on the kitchen table.

"Maybe. But Mom was still making sense when she talked." Laura headed to the back door with the train case.

Chalsey opened the cabinet over the stove and grabbed the salt.

"Back in the '90s, Dad always said psychosis was obvious." Laura paused with her hand on the doorknob. "A psychotic break means someone can't answer one or more of five questions: Who they are, when they are, where they are, and two other basic checks, like who is the current president of the U.S. So they'll say, 'I'm King Henry VIII, and this is England. I just executed Catherine of Aragon. And I don't know what this U.S. is that you speak of.'"

Toni gazed up at Laura from his chair. "And your mom could answer all the questions."

"Right." Laura shook her head. "I know my self-state name is Laura, but my legal name is Fredrick Michael now that I'm grown. I'm 13 as a self-state, but my body is 43. I'm in my mom's house in Careyville, and it's 2023. The current president is Joe Biden. I'm not psychotic, and Mom wasn't psychotic. So what the hell was she doing and why?"

"Important questions," Toni said.

Laura was glad for the validation, so she nodded at him and jerked open the door, marching into June heat with Chalsey and Toni. *I'll use magick, I'll call it magick, and I'll use it right. White magick to make the world a safer place.*

CHAPTER 14

THE MAGICIAN

OUTSIDE, CHALSEY, TONI, AND LAURA, STILL IN control of Michael Fredrick's shared body, purified the contents of the train case, threw most of it away, and burned the grimoire in the grill. With that chore done, they began cleaning the house to prepare it to be auctioned. Fredrick switched in, dwelling on Toni as he scrubbed his mother's toilets. *If Toni's sweeping this house, he's got to be infatuated with me.*

At noon, they left and returned to Ashleigh, where they met Wendy for lunch at a Japanese sushi and hibachi restaurant. Sushi was Chalsey's favorite food, and Michael took control of his shared body in order to enjoy it with her. Although Toni wasn't required to stay and hear what Wendy had researched, he opted in.

The Sunday lunch crowd was still in force, voices bouncing off the white tile floor and all the tables full. Three enormous TVs, all showing different sports games, hung over the sushi bar and detracted from the charm of the bamboo water fountain.

Wendy had arrived first, secured a table, and ordered hot green tea. After they joined her, Michael ordered one as well, Chalsey water, and Toni a Japanese beer.

"Okay, hit me." Michael wrapped his hands around his warm cup. "How bad is my mom's infestation?" He didn't worry about anyone overhearing them. The clamor of voices would cover any conversation.

"Your mom *is* an infestation," Chalsey muttered.

Toni laughed, and Michael grinned. *You hated my mom the instant you laid eyes on her. You had a kid's keen sense Mom was a crazy bitch.*

"Bad." Wendy sipped her tea. "The other high priestesses got back to me right away. For a spirit to appear solid and speak audibly enough for multiple people to hear means one or more occupants of the house had to have worshipped it by name, made offerings, and also promised some kind of payment, payoff, or reward for the spirit's 'services.'"

Michael felt Laura's sudden surge of fear as if it were his own. His heart raced. "Made offerings?" *Like the journal entry said?*

She totally did, Laura said. *I don't even want to think about it, and Dietrich doesn't want me to talk about it.*

Who's Dietrich?

Our captain. Or CEO. Or director. Whatever you want to call it. He controls what we remember and in what order we remember it. Or he's trying to. Now that Mom and Dad are both dead, our memories are trying to all burst out at once. He's trying to slow it down so we don't drown.

Michael's stomach clenched. *Well, that's good! I don't want to drown.*

Toni leaned forward, his voice low. "When you say 'offering' and 'payment,' do you mean human sacrifice?"

"I doubt it." Wendy stared into her teacup. "Unless one of

Fredrick's parents was a literal serial killer. Some serial killers engage in highly elaborate ritual murders, often using common religious symbols like crosses and pentacles."

"No, not that," Laura said, breaking through Michael's control momentarily. "I never saw a person die." When she pulled back, Fredrick found himself in charge because Wendy had said his name.

"What did you see?" Wendy asked. "Are you willing or able to say?"

Fredrick's gaze slid to the floor. *Me personally? Nothing.*

You can say she used her own blood, Laura said. *I'm not ready to talk about anything more, though.*

"Mom used her own blood." Fredrick's stomach clenched tighter until it ached.

"Blood is an incredibly powerful spell component." Wendy sipped her tea. "I refuse to use it myself. Too dangerous."

Fredrick met Wendy's gaze and frowned. "I suppose it's that way the world over, isn't it? Almost all ancient cultures engaged in animal sacrifice, like the Jews, the Hindus, the Egyptians, the Greeks, and the Romans. Christianity embraces the concept of human sacrifice, or god sacrifice, if you will, since Jesus sacrificed himself for everyone for all time. Some modern-day religions still use animal sacrifice, some with more ethical constraints and considerations than others. So in the end, it's always about blood, isn't it?"

Silence enveloped their little table. Around them, Fredrick heard the blast of cheers from one TV, a woman complaining about her preacher's sermon, and a man making a dirty joke. Snippets washed over him: "—preachers shouldn't be preaching politics. This is supposed to be about the Word of God, and there he is—" overlapped with "—was walking through her apartment naked and covered in peanut butter."

This was punctuated with "—a score of 51 to 30!" The noise threatened to give Fredrick a headache.

"I'm afraid so." Wendy set down her cup. "Not just inside of religious rituals but also using women's menstruation to bar them from both religious and community fellowship. And euphemistically, the word *blood* is used to mean your race. In every way possible, we've weaponized blood."

Fredrick's gaze flicked up to one TV, which showed a soccer match in a foreign country. "Of course my mom would use blood." *For my mom, being in the SOMH meant harassing people for what "blood" they had. Why not also use it in rituals?* "Is an entity that is summoned by blood and given blood offerings harder to exorcise than one that isn't?"

"Absolutely," Wendy said. "And we need to destroy all the altars she had."

Fredrick's gaze flicked back to her. "Well, I destroyed one."

Two, said a voice inside, but Fredrick wasn't sure which.

"I want to talk about that." Chalsey paused as the server returned to take their orders. Once he left, she leaned forward. "I think the house was actually full of altars. Marilyn had collected 46 angels and decorated every flat surface in the house with them. I think there were at least eight angel altars, each one either a bookshelf or a table."

Tingles erupted over Fredrick's arms and then flashed up his left shoulder to his scalp. "Shit! That appears to be accurate. I think that's true."

"In that case, we started dismantling the altars by collecting the angels in the kitchen," Toni said. "We need to go back and purify them with salt."

Fredrick stared at the sushi bar, only halfway seeing the three men working side-by-side. *Angels?* Pressure swelled in his chest and then in his mind, as if a revelation would burst out and make his nose bleed. "Angel worship? Did my mom call what she was doing angel worship?"

Chalsey's hand paused an inch shy of her water glass. "What?" Her eyes widened. "I sense an overwhelming pressure engulfing my entire body, as if I am being forcefully submerged in the ocean."

"Kali, *kreem*," Wendy said.

Although Fredrick recognized the name of the Hindu goddess, he couldn't guess what *kreem* meant. However, the room suddenly seemed brighter, as if clouds had been over the sun and then departed. *I've experienced that before. Did she dismiss evil spirits with a Hindu prayer?*

"Better," Chalsey said. "Angel worship?"

No! screamed a voice in Fredrick's mind. *No! You're not allowed to talk about that!*

Ignore that, Laura said. *That's not Dietrich. In fact, that wasn't one of us. An evil spirit is probably yelling at us.*

Trusting Laura, Fredrick charged forward. "She wouldn't have called it worship. Mom always melted down about Catholics, claiming they worship saints and Mother Mary and saying what a sin it was." With burning determination, he decided to make a Mother Mary altar in his own house. *Fuck you, Mom. How about I make an altar for the Holy Mother? Would that blow you up?* "And she wouldn't call her made-up ceremonies rituals or magick, either. Someone like that would have to come up with a euphemism. 'Angel honoring'? 'Angelic protection'? I mean, in my memory, she called them decorations and knickknacks."

Chalsey frowned and traced the rim of her water glass. "Something like that, but not exactly that. The phrase 'angel worship' seemed closer. Perhaps that's how she secretly thought of it."

"But 'angelic protection' had a bit of a ring to it." Toni fiddled with his beer bottle, tipping it back and forth. "Okay, so she says she's simply inviting angelic protection or something. Or—wait. She says that in the daytime. I noticed that in her novel, all the séances and demon-summoning happened at night."

"So she had two faces like a Janus statue," Wendy said. "In the daytime, she puts on the face of The Good Christian Woman, goes to church, and tries to get other people to follow Jesus. At night, she's using black magick."

Fredrick's lungs froze. "I never once saw my mom witness to anyone." He forced himself to breathe, to not lock up. "In 43 years, I never saw her 'walk someone down the Romans Road,' never saw her go canvassing, and never saw her even invite someone to our church. I kept witnessing to my friends, trying to convert them to Christianity, but she never once said anything except to a friend I'd already 99 percent converted."

"And you draw what you are," Chalsey said. "Like draws like. That's the Law of Attraction."

Fredrick met Chalsey's gaze. "But I've never once attracted a single Christian friend. I always drew friends who used to go to church as little kids but didn't anymore—the whole 'I'm Christian, but I haven't gone to church since I was three' thing —or kids who were agnostic or even atheist, like you were. I fought to be the best Christian I could be, read the Bible on my own, and prayed on my own. But I only drew non-Christians."

"Pay attention to that," Wendy said. "Your energy didn't tag you as a Christian. Other Christians didn't gravitate towards you, despite your devotion. What you said with your mouth couldn't make up for the fact that the energy following you around wasn't Christian energy."

Fredrick shivered and picked up his teacup, sipping the green tea. "God, creepy. What kind of energy *followed* me?"

"Meanwhile, your mom writes demon-summoning orgy scenes," Toni said. "And she's doing blood magick using Solomon's seals."

"Right." Chalsey pulled out her phone. "Let me google a few and show them to you. See if you recognize any."

"Angel worship." Fredrick felt a strange reverberation every time he said it. "In Christian cosmology, demons are fallen angels, and she wouldn't call the evil entities demons."

And she wouldn't even admit they were evil, Laura said.

"So she got around it by calling the demons angels?" Toni lifted his beer bottle and took a swig. "That's brazen."

"We need to consider that your mother had a personality disorder," Wendy said. "Someone with narcissistic personality disorder can be brazen."

Fredrick snorted and took another sip of tea. "She always said her father had narcissistic personality disorder. My dad was a psychologist, and he agreed with her."

"Then your mom easily could have had NPD," Toni said. "There's a line of NPD running down one entire side of my family, so I should know. I only have three types of family members: the NPD ones, their enablers or 'flying monkeys,' and the runaways, like me."

Fredrick studied Toni with ballooning interest. *So you come from a fucked up family, too, huh?*

Chalsey handed Fredrick her phone. "Here's a page with five seals."

Fredrick accepted the phone. *Laura, you're on.*

Laura switched with him and used her finger to scroll down. "Three are mostly familiar. I'm not sure Mom and Dad copied them correctly. Maybe they had a notebook where they'd hand-copied seals and spells and stuff from someone else's book. Can you buy *The Greater Key of Solomon?*"

"Sure." Chalsey accepted her phone back. "These days, there are a thousand copies on Amazon alone. But back in the early 1980s when this was happening? And in rural Kentucky? It's more likely one of your parents met someone in college who had a copy and then copied down the seals by hand."

Laura curled her lip. "Well, I'm not sure they copied it down right. Or the rituals, either. Or it's possible they made stuff up on purpose because they thought they were so *clever.* Who knows?"

The server arrived with their plates. Laura fell silent, worried he'd overheard, and switched with Michael, who wanted his sushi.

"Saying you'll summon angels using mis-copied seals from *The Greater Key of Solomon.*" Toni shook his head. "There's a disaster waiting to happen."

Laura is right, said a fourth voice to Michael. *There was a third book, a book of seals and spells. Find it and destroy it.*

Michael paused in the act of pouring soy sauce into his dipping bowl. *Who are you?*

Your captain, Dietrich.

Holy shit! You can talk to me now? Joy punctured Michael's stress about the black magick. *That's progress.*

We're bursting out of "hibernation" and self-imposed isolation, Dietrich said. *We're waking up and coming out to talk because both our parents are dead now.*

"No wonder this entity is so powerful." Wendy picked up her package of chopsticks, pulled them out, and snapped them apart with a sharp *crack.* "My only question now is what your mother or both your parents promised it as payment: 'Do this for me, and I'll do that for you.'"

A chill snapped through Michael as he poured his soy sauce. "I have no idea." The burning in his chest, like someone had lit oil on fire in his lungs, convinced him he didn't want to know.

All in good time, Dietrich said.

Never is fine by me, Michael said.

No, I want to know, Fredrick said. *But not until I find a good therapist first. We need a specialist ASAP. I hope I hear back tomorrow from the ones I messaged.*

"Better yet, how do we get rid of it?" Chalsey asked. "Destroy all the altars, and then what?" She popped a piece of avocado and cucumber maki into her mouth.

"We'll have to purify the entire house." Wendy poured herself soy sauce. "It would be best if we used dirt from Marilyn's fresh grave. We can use the dirt to attach the entity to and then return the dirt to her grave, attaching the entity to its summoner. Or we can cast a purification ritual directly on the dirt and then use it as a symbol to sever the spiritual thread between Marilyn and the entity."

Toni lowered his chopsticks. "We'll need the entire circle to do something that big, at least as it concerns this entity."

"I can't promise it'll be enough." Wendy picked up a piece of her salmon maki. "But it's a place to start. Without knowing the exact rituals Marilyn and her husband did, and without knowing what they promised the entity, it may take a while to figure out how to banish it."

Michael ate a piece of spicy tuna roll, mulling over the issue. "Well, I don't want the new owner of the house to be terrorized. But there's still another problem to consider: If I sell my mom's house, will that entity follow me home instead?"

Wendy set down her chopsticks. "That is my number one concern. It's possible, and we have to make sure it doesn't happen."

Inside of Michael, Fredrick and Laura both detonated with terror, their fear shooting down Michael's arms and legs and making his teeth ache.

Anything but that! Laura yelled.

"Oh, fuck no," Michael said. "I would do anything at all to stop that. Except kill someone, of course. Past that, basically anything."

Neither Michael nor the rest of his DID System could imagine anything worse.

Later that afternoon, when Michael got home, he opened the door to his attic. The ceiling in the bedroom hallway held the attic access door, which had a foldable ladder attached to it. The springs on the hinges groaned as Michael lowered the door by tugging on the pull-string. Then he unfolded the ladder and climbed into the attic, the June heat blasting over his head as he did.

What are you after? Fredrick asked. He imagined them on the bridge of *The U.S.S. Enterprise,* having grown up watching reruns of the original *Star Trek* series. In Fredrick's imagination, Michael sat in Kirk's captain's chair, being the one in control of their body, and Fredrick stood to Michael's left like Spock or Scotty sometimes would. Behind them, Laura sat at the communications console like Uhura. Fredrick couldn't sense the relative position of either Angela or Dietrich.

"My old Wiccan stuff." Michael sat on the attic floor and flipped on the lights. A light switch had been affixed to one support beam by the previous owner. Two bare light bulbs flared to life, revealing boxes and an old wooden chest. Michael's Christmas tree, some old books, and an old light fixture filled the area. "I hid it in a box up here, hoping you'd ignore it. I just wrote 'old college junk' on the outside."

Holy shit! Seriously? Fredrick was stunned by what he'd hidden from himself.

"If you'd opened it, you might've even assumed the previous owner left it behind." Michael stood and walked stooped over to avoid the ceiling beams. "After all, my handwriting looks different from yours. I've got the big, boxy, square handwriting."

Okay, fair enough. Slants and loops filled Frederick's

handwriting. *So you tried out Wicca with Chalsey but didn't like it?*

"I couldn't wrap my mind around the divine feminine, even though I wanted to. Too much Protestant Christian brainwashing where the divine is only allowed to be male." Michael knelt on the floor in the back corner of the attic, sweat already running down his temples from the heat. "And I felt like the insistence on a divided male and female divine grated too much on my personal experiences as an intersex person. Chalsey said I could conceive of the divine any way I wanted, that Wicca has a lot of space to experiment with such concepts, but I was already reading up on Buddhism." He opened a weathered, faded microwave box that looked forty years old.

Fair enough. Fredrick watched with interest as Michael unpacked a royal blue handbook entitled *Buckland's Complete Book of Witchcraft,* a black leather Book of Shadows, a wand, a piece of onyx, a Celtic ceremonial dagger, and a wooden goblet with a pentacle on it. Under them were three boxes of tarot cards, including the same deck their father had owned: the classic Rider-Waite-Smith.

Laura edged forward, scanned the energy of the contents, and relaxed. *Well, you didn't do any black magick, or I'd sense it.*

"Hell, no." Michael pulled out the RWS deck and then repacked the box. "Okay, I'm going to run an experiment. I'm going to leave out this tarot deck and see if our Tarot Ghost has followed us home."

A shot of fear fired through them like an arrow.

She's okay, Laura said. *But if she followed us home, I'm afraid the evil entity did, too.*

Michael closed the box, stood, and walked back to the ladder. The air was so humid he had trouble breathing, and he had sweated through his shirt and boxers already. "Let's hope it's just the Tarot Ghost."

You think it's a woman? Fredrick asked.

Felt like a woman to me, Laura said.

Then I wonder if it's the 1920s flapper, Fredrick said.

Michael flipped off the lights and climbed into the cool waiting arms of air conditioning. He folded up the ladder and shut the door, sealing away the heat. "Chalsey thinks there are three spirits total, but we don't know what the third one looks like. Or makes itself look like, anyway."

I packed the old family photo albums in the trunk on Saturday, Fredrick said. *We could flip through them and see if any picture jumps out at us or something. Or see if anyone is dressed like a flapper.*

"Sure. Why not?" Michael left the tarot deck on his kitchen counter. *Look. Bait. Come and get it.* Then he slipped out the side door and got the box of albums from his car trunk.

In the brilliant light of his all-white living room, glowing in the June sun, Michael flipped through album after album, studying pictures with Fredrick and Laura. Half of the antique black-and-white photos were mysteries. The photos didn't have any familiar faces, and no one had written names or dates on the back. The pictures from 1950 onward were more helpful, often having names and dates. They passed over pictures from 1961 of Roger as an infant and faded, red-tinged, color photos of themselves as a baby.

"God, we look sickly." Michael ran one finger over a picture of them labeled "three days." Their bare thighs were too thin, and the attached card from the hospital read, "19 inches. 6 pounds & 12 ounces."

We didn't even weigh seven pounds? Fredrick felt a flash of concern. *But Mom said we weren't premature.*

Look at us. We're clearly sick, Laura said. *Were we a crack baby or something?*

More like a smoker's baby, Fredrick said.

"But Mom never smoked." Michael curled in on himself. "And Dad gave up smoking before he married Mom. I've got a bad feeling about this."

Where's the picture with the bandage on our tummy? Dietrich asked, coming forward. *I remember asking Mom about the bandage, and she said it was to hide where our umbilical cord was.*

Seriously? Fredrick asked.

That doesn't feel right, Laura said.

Michael flipped back and forth through a dozen pages and couldn't find it. Instead, there was a picture of their school portrait from first grade stuffed in the middle of all their baby pictures.

Mom took out the picture showing the tummy bandage and threw it away, Dietrich said. *Why?*

I have no idea, Fredrick said. *And no one ever said we were sick as a baby. If Mom'd had her way, we would have had surgery to be a "typical" girl, but Dad intervened. So what gives?*

The System fell silent.

"I have a terrifyingly bad feeling." Michael snapped the album closed. "I'm literally spooked now." He tossed the album back into the box. "We find two pictures of flappers from the 1920s but with no names, and our baby pictures from the first three weeks of our life look awful."

But then at six weeks, we look healthy. Even slightly chubby, Dietrich said. *Whatever it was, they turned it around in about three weeks.*

Michael shoved the lid back on the box and carried it into the guest bedroom, which they'd converted into an office. "I don't know, but these pictures give me the creeps."

And we never saw a picture of a baby named Timothy Anderson, either, Fredrick said.

"That's it. Let's try calling Roger and picking his brain." Michael pulled his phone out of his pocket. "Maybe I'm rushing him. Maybe he intends to text us sometime today. But I'm calling." He opened the contacts list, selected his half-brother, and hit "call."

As the phone rang, Michael returned to the living room, needing its brilliant, nearly blinding white light to calm him.

After four rings, Roger picked up, and they traded greetings.

"Sorry I didn't text you back." Roger's sigh carried over the phone. "I always do Saturday afternoon mass, and there was a parish picnic afterwards. I spaced it. How are you?"

"Cleaning out Mom's house is more of an adventure than I bargained for." Michael's tone was dry.

"I get that. Cleaning out my mom's house was a nightmare. I'll never forget it."

Michael wondered if Roger had done battle with ghosts or demons. The heavy quality of Roger's voice made him suspicious. "Yeah. I found some stuff I didn't expect." *Like SOMH stuff.*

Silence.

Michael counted to ten. Roger still didn't reply. "And I found that weird death certificate that I texted you about. Do you know anything about a Timothy Anderson?"

The call dropped with a little *snick* of a sound.

Michael lowered the phone and stared at the home screen with the large white digital clock reading 4:11. Behind it was his chosen wallpaper of a pink and purple nebula. "Um, was that natural? Did he hang up on me? Or..." He stared at the room, terrified The Demon Mother would pop into the room to scream at him.

Movement to his left in the doorway into the hallway

made Michael jerk and yelp. The flapper ghost in her slinky white dress and long strand of pearls stood staring back at him. She pointed toward the kitchen and vanished.

I feel pressure, Laura said. *It's like someone's pressing on our body with a board.*

What did Wendy say earlier? Fredrick's panic flared through them, sharp and spiky.

"Kali, *kreem!*" Michael snapped.

The pressure vanished.

The phone rang, and Michael jerked again. Roger's name popped up on the caller ID. "God!" He answered it, his fingers trembling slightly. "Did the call drop?"

"Seems to have." Roger sounded puzzled. "Well, anyway. I was trying to say I do. I don't know what Mom and Dad told you, but this is the truth. Your mother lost a baby. She was inconsolable, and our dad just told her to try again. She had you less than a year later."

Michael was instantly confused. "But Mom and Dad married in February 1979, and I was conceived that May 1979 —or maybe in April, I was never sure—and then born the following January 1980. When did Mom have time to lose a baby?" He folded in on himself, propping his feet on his couch and hugging his legs to his chest with one arm.

"Michael...I'm sure your mom was trying hard to look like a good Christian woman in front of you, especially when she was still grooming you to be a good little Christian girl. But your mom got pregnant in October 1979, only two months after she and Dad started dating. That's why she and our dad only dated six months before they married. They arranged their own shotgun wedding. But your mom lost the baby before she was even really showing."

Michael's confusion only got worse. He dropped his arm and unfolded, but his knee began bouncing. "But the death certificate I saw was for a baby who got born and then died, like, a month later. And that baby was born after I was."

Roger groaned. "Look, I'm not sure how much I should say. I'm not sure how much you want to know, and I'm not sure what you remember. I don't want to overwhelm you."

"Mom couldn't have had a baby only one month after I was born." Both of Michael's knees began bouncing.

"No, it's not that," Roger said. "Our dad had two wives. Simultaneously. One lived in Tennessee, and your mom, obviously, lived in Kentucky. The other wife, Nicole, and your mom were pregnant at the same time. He'd been with Nicole since 1975, so that was four years of marriage when he met your mom. He'd secretly married Nicole before he even divorced my mom in 1978. It was Nicole who lost a baby, and it's that baby's death certificate. I'm not sure why he had it in the house he shared with your mom. Maybe he hid it like he did everything else." Roger's tone turned bitter. "Or maybe he said it belonged to one of his many, many cousins. Who knows? That man was full of lies. So full I could never tell when he told the truth."

Michael couldn't even feel his body. His lips were numb, his fingers numb, even his tongue. Both his knees stilled. "Another...wife?"

"I'm sorry." Roger's voice sounded constricted, as if his throat had tightened. "That's probably too much, especially since your mom just died. I should have waited to tell you. But when you asked, I wondered if you should know the truth. And it's there. It's everywhere—all over our family in enormous explosions of dysfunction. My mom found out and divorced him, and then Dad accused her of being the one who cheated instead. What a load of crock! But your mom believed Dad and married him."

Fredrick took control from Michael, who sank into stunned silence. "And did Dad stay married to Nicole?"

"Yeah. For another three years. Then she got wise and divorced him. Nicole never had another child with our dad, so there's no missing sibling here. And she was glad she didn't have a child when she found out the truth." Roger snorted, and it burst into a harsh laugh. "Nicole got my mom's name and number and called her. They were friends for a few years, just based on both hating our dad."

Fredrick felt tension in his lungs, as though he might cry. The oak coffee table in front of him wavered in his vision. "But no one warned my mom?"

"They tried. Your mom called them liars and accused them of being jealous and wanting to end her marriage with our dad."

With a sickening crack, Fredrick remembered the day in grad school when Chalsey, as his current best friend, and Kris, his former high school best friend, had teamed up together for a single day to convince him his fiancé was cheating on him. Fredrick had resisted them at first, insisting Tiffany would never do that because she was too crushed by the fact her ex-boyfriend had cheated on her. But while Kris had walked away, Chalsey had persisted until Fredrick could see the truth. "It repeated, just like psychology says it does. Family secrets and patterns repeat. My fiancé cheated on me when I was in grad school."

"My first wife cheated on me," Roger said. "I don't know why I was so surprised. She cheated on her first husband to be with me, and then after I married her, she cheated on me."

"My mom's father cheated on my grandma and then abandoned them when Mom was only a year old," Fredrick said. "And then my mom married a cheater. God!" He realized he'd dissociated. Nothing in the living room felt real. The chair and front door looked impossibly far away. Fredrick wasn't real and had never lived at all. Roger wasn't real. His voice was a scrap of meaningless noise, like static in a radio station.

"But Michael..." Roger paused. "Your mom's gone now. Come out and see me some time. I'd love to have you. My wife would love to meet you. I admit I don't think I can stand to set foot in Kentucky ever again. Too many terrible memories. But if you wouldn't mind seeing California, then head my way."

"I'd love to visit California," Michael said as the sound of his name pulled him back into control of his body. "I'll be dealing with Mom's estate all summer, but next summer should work."

"Next summer it is." Roger's voice sounded more upbeat.

Michael let him go and stared out the window at the oak tree filling his front yard. Thick branches and green leaves offered shade to a set of cardinals. "Two wives at once. I thought that bullshit was reserved for *America's Most Wanted, Cold Case Files*, or some thriller movie: Man with two wives summons demons, harm his kids, and then murders 27 children in the community! Or some shit."

My life the horror movie? Fredrick asked.

I told you that you write horror novels because you lived one, Laura said.

Unable to comprehend this turn in their life story, they did what they always did in such moments: they called Chalsey.

As they filled her in, they remembered the Flapper Ghost and headed into the kitchen to see what she had pointed to. On their counter was a single card: The Magician, reversed. A man in red robes pointed one finger down toward the ground and lifted a wand toward the sky with his other hand—the connection between heaven and earth. Before him stood an altar.

"The Tarot Ghost followed us home," Michael said.

"Interesting." Chalsey's voice was low, almost distracted, as if she were already drumming up a dozen psychological theories for him. "At least she seems to help. The Magician reversed means manipulation, cunning, trickery, illusion, and deception."

"This morning I would have sworn that referred only to Mom and her summoning of that entity through abusing magick," Michael said. "Now I feel like it's referring to Dad and his two wives."

"Or both," Chalsey said. "It could definitely be both."

Michael was forced to agree.

CHAPTER 15

THE STAR XVII

ON MONDAY, FREDRICK AWAKENED IN HIS OWN BED, safe in his own house, and wanted to see Toni. Toni, however, didn't get Mondays off, being the reiki practitioner in his workplace who took off Fridays instead. *What a bummer! And I've got it bad.*

I'm pretty sure Toni wants to see you, too, Laura said.

Somehow, Fredrick could feel her smiling on the inside. It was impossible to miss her teasing energy. *Well, I hope you're right.*

Although Chalsey had planned for them to take Monday off, there was the issue of feeding Largo until he was re-homed. So Fredrick steeled himself with 24 ounces of coffee, picked up Chalsey, and headed to Careyville.

The rural highway to Careyville was a curvy, hilly, two-lane affair, its only boast being its widened shoulders. Major efforts to make the road safer had helped in 2006. For all of Fredrick's childhood and adulthood, it had been a shoulderless deathtrap. With the improved driving safety, Fredrick could enjoy the wheat and cornfields they passed and the swaths of untouched forest full of maple, oak, and walnut trees. Old farmhouses, new mansions, and decaying trailers lined the road between farms.

"I have to admit something." Fredrick shut off the air as they approached the pig farm, reducing the dose of manure stench. "I'm totally flipped out that Mom wasn't a virgin. I spent my entire middle and high school years being terrorized by Christian ideology about being a virgin on your wedding night, and I got slammed in the face with the whole True Love Waits campaign when it exploded in the '90s. I knew my parents would kill me if I ever messed around, much less had sex. And then I find out they had sex before marriage!"

"You don't see it yet, but your whole childhood is filled with signs of sexual abuse." Chalsey turned from the window and took a sip of her homemade fruit smoothie. "It's not just controlling whether you had sex. But that's bad enough. Even after you were in college, people other than you were still dictating the terms of your private sexuality."

Fredrick opened the vents again. "Yeah. I *felt* something was wrong with it when the youth minister stood in front of the church and asked all the youth to come to the front and sign a True Love Waits card. Somehow, I understood it was a violation. I felt like a freak sitting there with all these other kids and teens, ages 11 to 19, standing up and parading their virginal commitment in front of the entire church. It was like writing the word *whore* on my forehead in red letters. But I couldn't do it. I remember thinking, *You're asking me to swear to God himself that I won't have sex before marriage, but I can't know the future. And if I mess up, then I've broken an oath to God. I'd feel so much shame I'd be suicidal.*"

"I'm glad you listened to yourself." Chalsey set her tumbler in the car's cup holder. "And there's a pattern of premarital sex in your family, although it's been kept secret until recently."

Fredrick slowed as he approached a tractor on the road.

Summer in rural Kentucky meant having to pass tractors. "You know, you're right. Mom and Dad did it. My maternal grandfather's autobiography, which he wrote but didn't publish, claimed that he and my grandma had premarital sex in the backseat of his car. When Mom read it, she blew up and swore he was lying."

"But your mom had to say he was lying," Chalsey said. "She told me once that when she was in college, her mom saw her kiss her boyfriend at the end of their date, and then her mom and her grandma teamed up together and screamed at her about her 'sexual sin' for forty minutes."

Fredrick's stomach clenched. "Yeah. Mom was 21, and they browbeat her about it. Hearing that her own mom was having sex before marriage after being browbeaten about a kiss would blow her up."

"Exactly."

"And Roger had sex before marriage. I know that much." Fredrick shook his head as he surveyed the damaged contents of his own sex life. "Michael's had sex with you twice, despite our massive trauma, and I had oral sex with two of my exs. And Michael's had oral sex with you. That forms an obvious pattern of premarital sex. But what about the sexual violence?" Fredrick saw a clear stretch, pulled out, and passed the tractor. He and the tractor driver exchanged a wave. "What am I not seeing?"

"You told me once that your mom and grandma would come into the bathroom when you were using it."

Fredrick's brow furrowed. "Yeah. All the time. What about it?"

Chalsey held up one finger. "Any psychologist these days would say that's a form of sexual abuse. I always thought it was weird and wrong. There were two bathrooms in your house, and they could just *wait*. But they would walk in and wash their hands or get a towel or grab a Band-Aid or whatever. They didn't give you any body privacy at all."

The muscles around Fredrick's eyes ached from his sudden tension. Michael, Laura, and he all fought to comprehend this new worldview. "So Mom and Grandma having me follow them into the bathroom in order to finish a conversation was also wrong? And when I was taking a bath, and they came in to pee, that was wrong?"

"Absolutely!" Chalsey groaned and tugged on one of her blonde curls. "There were *two* bathrooms. And even if there was only one, they needed to wait."

Fredrick's mind replayed hundreds of images of his mother and grandma changing clothes in front of him. "Because I was considered a girl, they didn't hide their bodies from me. I saw them naked all the time. I have a brain full of saggy boob memories."

Chalsey shuddered. "That's so wrong that I don't have words for it. Fredrick, you had proof you were being molested this whole time. It's not just that you've been sexually frozen and spent your whole life having nightmares about being violated. Lack of bathroom privacy, inappropriate discussion of sex—"

"You mean like my mom telling me my dad developed ED?" Fredrick slowed as they entered Careyville, taking a left onto a tiny country road that would wind its way over to his mother's road. "Or my mom complaining to me that my dad always just rolled over after sex and didn't cuddle afterward?"

"Totally inappropriate." Chalsey reached into the backseat and grabbed Dr. John Bradshaw's book, *Healing the Shame that Binds You*. "Even if you don't have time to read anything else, I think you should read what Bradshaw says about sexual violence and incest."

"I will, then." Fredrick fell silent as he wound his way to the familiar red brick Craftsman house.

When they parked and climbed out, Fredrick discovered Largo in the front window, his face pressed against the glass. "I'm going to get cussed out by the cat."

"How dare you be late, meow!" Chalsey said.

Fredrick opened the front door, stepped in, and halted. The dining room chairs had all been pushed away from the table. Icy spiders scurried up his spine. "Um, I know we didn't leave the room like that."

Chalsey stepped up beside him. "We didn't. The Demon Mother must have had a tantrum. I left some sage here. Let's burn some on your Mother Mary altar."

Fredrick flinched at the word *altar*, the usual fear firing through him. "Yeah. Let's do that."

While Chalsey got her sage stick, Fredrick fed Largo and gave him his insulin shot. "You're going home with me today, boy. Gina might adopt you, and that's great if she does. But I can't leave you in a house with an evil entity, and it's not fair to make you wait until 11:00 or noon to get your first meal of the day, especially since you have diabetes."

Largo blissfully ate his kibbles, unaware of the 45-minute Car Ride of Hell now in his future.

"You know, you love cats," Chalsey said, entering the kitchen. "And you're okay with dogs. But you've never owned a single pet. Michael always said it's because I'm allergic, and I've always said I'm not *so* allergic that you need to refrain for my sake. But is that the real reason?"

Michael switched in at the sound of his name, and then Laura switched in over the top of him. "No." She walked to the Mother Mary altar with Chalsey and tried hard not to think of it as an altar. "That's Mom and Dad's fault. It's what they did."

"Is that you, Laura?"

"Yep." Laura remembered Catholics crossed themselves, so she touched her finger to her forehead, her stomach, and each of her shoulders. "Um, let's see. Mother Mary, pray for me? Is that a good prayer?"

Chalsey lit the sage stick and balanced it on the incense bowl. "Whatever feels meaningful to you."

Dietrich switched in. "Hi. I'm Dietrich, the captain or director of our DID System."

Chalsey smiled. "Nice to meet you, Dietrich. I recognize your energy or vibes. I think we've met before."

"A few times. I melted down once about a rape scene in a movie, and you comforted me." Dietrich stared at the smoke rising from the sage stick. "For me, the Universe is clearly all one entity, a Supreme Being whose energy fills everything everywhere: us, the earth, every blade of grass, and every tiny ant. But that entity feels female. I can't worship the God of Christianity. He's too male. I can only do this if I see the divine as female."

Chalsey nodded. "Then you have Michael's opposite problem. He struggles with escaping the concept of an only male god."

Unlike everyone else, Dietrich didn't switch away at the sound of Michael's name. As the captain, he could stay in the captain's chair at will. "Yes. At least Catholicism offers me this small pittance: Mary the Mother of God, the first disciple and the foremost of all the saints." He pressed his hands in prayer posture. "Mary, Queen of Grace, comfort me. Release me, set me free, and enable me to be me."

Chalsey gasped, her shoulders jerking faintly. "That was powerful. It was a massive surge of divine magick, if you want to call it that."

"Thanks." Dietrich inclined his head, pleased. "I don't want to talk about why we can't have pets yet. Fredrick can try to take Largo home, but it would be better if Gina adopted him. I think we'll trauma barf everywhere."

"You need to do what's best for you, and Gina seems

pretty interested." Chalsey picked up the sage stick. "I'd love to take Largo, and I'm much less allergic to him than some other cats. It varies cat to cat. But I still think my allergies would get me in the end."

"Yes, don't torture yourself." Dietrich switched Michael in.

Michael was surprised by how much power Dietrich had over switching, but it didn't scare or threaten him. Michael believed they all had roles to play. "Would you mind texting Gina later, then?"

"Not at all." Chalsey started through the house, smudging it, and Michael followed her, finding nothing else out of place.

However, his fear was also a distraction. *What does it mean that I can't handle having a pet? Just what did Mom and Dad do?*

Laura and Dietrich were conspicuously silent, and Michael didn't like what that suggested.

Thirty minutes later, Michael rummaged through boxes in his mother's office closet while Chalsey picked through the filing cabinet drawers. Michael was following the advice to find his parents' grimoire of badly copied seals and destroy it.

"We've catalogued basically everything in the cellar." Michael opened a file folder box covered in white contact paper with rainbow-colored lines. "All but the last twenty-five percent, I'd say. But if we can't find it up here, I guess we're going back to the cellar."

The filing cabinet hinges groaned as Chalsey opened the bottom drawer. "Yeah, we won't have a choice. I suppose she could have hidden it in a unique place, but I hope not." She sat on the floor, folding her legs. Today, she wore jean shorts and a tank top with a maple leaf pattern. Given she mostly avoided shorts, it was an unusual sight.

"Makes me wonder if she's been using it lately or if her usage declined after Dad died." Michael fingered through folders, finding old cellphone and credit card bills, plus a few warranties on electronics. "It wasn't with her nasty, ruined Bible." He'd already checked all the drawers in the chest of drawers.

Chalsey pulled out a folder and thumbed through it. "*Ruined* is a good word for it." She tilted her head, speed reading. "You know, I feel like your parents' behavior should somehow all add up to a coherent picture, but I know it doesn't have to. Still, I keep asking myself what two people who use the seals of Solomon to summon demons and who are members of the SOMH are seeing as a connection between their 'interests.'"

"Ask demons to kill all people of color?" Even as he said it, Michael could feel that was wrong. "No. Let's boil it down to something simpler: fear."

Chalsey looked up. "You're right. I can feel it in my heart. It all has to do with fear."

Michael closed his box and pulled out another one, this one covered in solid red contact paper. "Fear turns into hate. Plenty of ex-SOMH and ex-Neo Nazis admit they joined because of desperation, trauma, fear, and hopelessness. They wanted a place to aim all their negative feelings, so they used entire races, all gays, and all Catholics as scapegoats. Usually women, too." He pulled off the lid and began fingering through the files. "Then, when they're older and wiser and they've sorted out their lives, many of them leave. It's well-documented."

"And fear could lead to demon-summoning." Chalsey stuffed her folder into the drawer and flipped through two before pulling out another. "In medieval times, people supposedly summoned demons for wealth. Your mom and dad both accrued enormous college and grad school debts, and your mom was vastly underpaid her whole life, but especially when she was younger. Maybe they feared bankruptcy."

Michael's fingers touched a folder, and icy tingles shot into his hand and up his arm. "Or maybe Mom was trying to have a second child, and she miscarried a second time." He yanked out the folder and paused, afraid to open it. "Would someone summon a supposed 'angel' for help conceiving? Or to ensure a live birth?" His heart pounded even though the folder was the same boring pine green as all the others.

"Maybe." Chalsey lowered her folder. "What is it?"

Steeling himself, Michael opened the file. His heart slammed against his ribs. His mother's perfect handwriting, slanted and loopy and pristine, filled the page. "I—don't—" *know.* His fingers seemed to move without him, turning pages as if he were possessed. Seals and circles and squares and a foreign language like ancient Hebrew jumped off the page at him. English phrases also stood out to his gaze, his brain reading them against his will: *a yew branch, only at dawn when Jupiter is in the House of—*

Abruptly, Fredrick found himself lying on the floor, staring at the white ceiling fan in his mother's office. "Hm? Did I switch? It's Fredrick."

Chalsey sat beside him on the floor, and she leaned over him. "It was almost like you passed out, except your eyes remained open and glassy. It scared me. I'm glad you're okay." She held up a green folder. "We found it. We're going to burn it."

Fredrick felt foreign energy burn through him and jump out, arcing like invisible lightning. "You can't do that!" He smacked the folder from her hand, his entire body twitching with anger and hysteria. "Who do you think you are?"

Chalsey's eyes narrowed. "Kali, *kreem!*" She pressed her

hand to Fredrick's chest, and he felt heat pass from his sternum through his lungs and exit from his back.

The anger and hysteria evaporated. Fredrick had no idea what had happened or why. "I'm so sorry! Was that another self-state? That wasn't me. I would never smack something out of your hand."

"Oh, it *totally* wasn't you." Chalsey picked up the folder, stuffing the papers back into it, and stood. "It was like you channeled a spirit just for a second. The *wrong* kind. That means this can't wait." She marched down the hall. "Let's go."

Fredrick pushed himself off the floor and followed her downstairs. "That was scary. I had no idea I could channel spirits like a medium or something."

I knew we could, Laura said.

There's a reason our mom wrote scenes about séances, Dietrich said, *and not a benign one like mere fascination with the occult.*

Fredrick's brain felt paralyzed with shock, and the information seemed to drop right out of him. He felt the knowledge draining away. *In a second, I won't even remember you said that.*

Chalsey reached the end of the kitchen island, and The Demon Mother appeared in front of the back door, still sporting her electric blue shirt, jeans, and orange conch earrings.

"I've had enough of this." It held up its hand, and Chalsey appeared to trip on thin air.

Chalsey fell hard onto her knees on the white kitchen tile, crying out, and the folder flew from her hand, the pages scattering again. "You can't stop us." She slid sideways, sitting on her flank. "You don't really have a body. That's all for show."

"Perhaps," The Demon Mother drawled. The doors blew

open, and wind whipped through the house. "But I still have this."

The papers scattered as wind buffeted the kitchen, making the angels tinkle against each other and napkins fly. Fredrick's fear iced him into a statue, cementing his feet to the floor. The wind blew against him so hard it stole his breath. Two papers soared out the door, several down the cellar stairs, and the rest across the kitchen and dining room.

"You'll never find them all." The Demon Mother smirked. "And unless you do, you'll never get rid of me. Then again, I'll assure that you never get rid of me, anyway. I'm a permanent fixture in your life: an immortal mother, undying and always at your side." She snorted and vanished.

Chalsey pushed to her feet and rubbed both knees. "God, I hope I didn't crack a kneecap. That really hurts." She limped toward the back door. "We have to catch the two blowing around outside."

Go! Dietrich shouted at Michael, switching him into control of the body.

Michael raced around Chalsey. "No, I'll get it. You sit down." He dashed across the deck and out into the yard, where the papers floated in the breeze.

An immortal, undying mother? Fredrick echoed, too horrified to process anything else.

Great! An Evil Mother Mary straight from the Abyss. Just what we need. Laura's sarcasm burnt their lungs.

Michael caught the first paper and sprinted after the other, catching it before it blew into the neighbor's yard. Then he stumbled back inside, woozy and winded, as though he'd run ten miles instead. "What the hell? An entity that can control air? Make it into an invisible stone for you to trip on or summon a mini tornado?"

Chalsey had settled on a kitchen chair, still rubbing her knees. "I've seen 'demons' use air and water pretty easily. Fire, too. I think anything that flows or spreads on its own is easier for them to manipulate. But this one is so strong it can open doors and move furniture. Wood, stone, and earth are usually much harder to move, but here we are."

"Want some ice packs?" Michael set the papers on the counter. "I'll burn every paper I can find here in a second. But I'm worried your knees will swell."

"I'm pretty sure they will, yeah."

Michael opened the freezer and pulled out his mother's readymade ice packs, handing them over to Chalsey along with two hand towels for comfort. Then he began gathering the other papers.

"How will you know you got them all?" Chalsey asked.

"This is my mom." Michael held up a page. "She put page numbers on them. She had her entire life organized, numbered, color-coded, and indexed."

Chalsey shook her head. "Well, her Type A personality benefits us now."

Once Michael gathered every page he could find, he arranged them numerically. "Okay, yeah. We have a problem. Pages eight and 15 are missing."

"I'll help you look as soon as my knees stop hurting so much. Just burn what you've got."

"Yep." Michael headed outdoors to the little grill. He poured on charcoal, lit it, and tossed in the pages. "This thing's being put to good use. Finally."

It's a wonder the pages don't scream with demonic voices, Dietrich quipped.

You mean like those old stories about Ouija boards "screaming" if you burnt them? Laura asked. *Because supposedly the demons in the boards screamed as they died in the fire.*

Exactly. There's an urban legend for you.

Michael stared at the curling, blackened paper, which was blessedly silent, and the lapping flames.

Don't watch the fire for too long, Dietrich said. *You might have another PTSD flashback.*

Michael looked away. "Yeah, no thanks."

Once the task was complete, he headed inside. Chalsey had returned the ice packs to the freezer and was limping around the dining room, searching.

"There's this weird thing I keep noticing about The Demon Mother," Michael said, joining her. "I mean, in every way it just looks like Mom: face, hair, and clothes. They'd identical except for one thing."

"What's that?" Chalsey limped into the living room.

Michael followed her, and they looked behind the entertainment center. "It's wearing orange conch earrings. Mom never owned anything like that. She didn't do shell jewelry."

Chalsey halted and stared at him over the top of the flatscreen TV. "What? From my viewpoint, it's wearing pear-shaped sapphire earrings."

Michael felt his stomach drop out, as if he were in an elevator. "Wait. Seriously? What is it wearing? I see jeans and a long-sleeved blue t-shirt."

"Yeah, I see that, too." Chalsey's eyebrows pulled together as she frowned. "And it's wearing blue sandals. It's a real outfit your mom owned."

Puzzlement wafted through Michael as Fredrick, Laura, and Dietrich all grew curious. "Okay. What do conches symbolize? And orange? Maybe it's a message of some kind."

"Nothing bad." Chalsey resumed her search, checking behind the curtains. "For example, a conch in Buddhism means hope, optimism, willpower, and courage. And in the Buddhist flag, orange means wisdom, strength, and dignity."

Michael snorted.

Angela switched in over top of Michael. "It's Angela. And I'm here to tell you that my parents would *never* want me to have hope, optimism, willpower, or courage. All my parents wanted from me was blind obedience, subservience, and fear. My parents wanted me to act toward them the way our preacher at church said to act toward God: Don't ask questions, just obey. Or God will punish you. Fear God, and be a servant of Jesus Christ. If not, you're sinning against God. Except my parents were human and wanted that behavior from me, anyway."

"Spiritual poison on all counts." Chalsey stopped by the couch. "I'd check under the couch, but I can't get on my knees right now."

Angela got on the floor and looked. A clump of cat hair and a mouse toy greeted them. "Nothing. Just a cat tumbleweed." They pushed to their feet again. "I wasn't allowed to have strength or dignity. And the only wisdom my parents wanted me to gain was about money."

"So why see conch earrings on The Demon Mother?" Chalsey perched on the back of the couch, given it wasn't pushed against the wall. "Is it to draw attention to all the things you should have had but were denied?"

"Maybe." Angela switched places with Michael, who ran his fingers back through his hair. "It's the 'greatest hits' of authoritarian parenting, huh? Be a mindless little puppet until you're 22, and then when you graduate college, magically turn from an ugly duckling into a swan and sprout adult skills out of your ass."

Chalsey slumped. "Well, that was the version we got, anyway. One day, you were still a kid. The very next day, you were dumped on your ass. I mean, at least your parents taught you to balance a checkbook first. My parents failed to even do that much." She held up both hands. "Not that I want to compete for the title of the worst parents ever. No one should want to win that contest."

"We're friends and lovers because we understand each

other." Michael stepped over and ran his arms around Chalsey, hugging her to his chest. "We believed each other about how shitty our parents are."

Chalsey hugged his waist tightly. "You were the first person to ever believe me. I'll never forget that."

After searching the entire first floor and the cellar, Michael and Chalsey gave up for the day and retired to the kitchen for a late lunch. Waiting for them was the daily tarot card: a naked woman pouring out two vases of water, one into a stream and another onto land, with an enormous star over her head. The card read The Star.

"That's a positive message." Chalsey grabbed the ice packs from the freezer and the hand towels. "The Star means hope, inspiration, renewal, healing, and rejuvenation." She limped over to a kitchen chair.

Michael jerked open the refrigerator and pondered the contents. "I'm not really feeling that one today. Most of the cards have made sense to me. But why this card today?"

"Think of it this way: the more you understand about your trauma, the more you can heal." Chalsey positioned the ice packs. "You can't heal something you know nothing about."

"I can't argue your point, but that doesn't feel right somehow." Michael pulled out raw vegetables so he could make a salad for Chalsey. "It feels like it should be more specific."

The woman on the card looks like a goddess to me, Dietrich said.

We made a Mother Mary...um, sacred space, Laura said. *And we burned incense on it today. Although Catholics don't refer to her as a goddess, people worldwide venerate her as the mother of Jesus.*

And the evil entity claimed it was an undying, immortal

mother, Fredrick said, *which is the exact opposite of what we want.*

Michael pulled out a cutting board and a knife and began chopping lettuce. "Could there be hope or healing in me finally grasping the divine feminine?"

"Absolutely." Chalsey propped her feet on the other chair, positioning the ice packs better. "You need the healing badly. They taught you that only masculinity can be divine, and you were trying to be a boy as a child. But your mom forced you to be a girl while your religion and your entire society told you women are second-class citizens and the source of original sin and corruption in the world. From your point of view, you mother shoved feminine inferiority up your ass, so you rejected all things feminine. Including me for about six months back in high school when I went all super-girly for a while."

"Sorry," Fredrick said, switching with Michael. "I still feel bad about that."

Chalsey waved one hand through the air. "I forgave you decades ago. And I'm only bringing it up to say you never recovered. You got surgery to be a man, but you've realized you're agendered. And it's great that you finally see that you have no gender. But deep inside, you still bleed from wounds caused by your mom forcing you to be female, especially when society doesn't value women for anything other than sex, emotional labor, cleaning, and childcare."

"I'll work on it in therapy. I promise." Fredrick washed off a tomato and chopped it up.

"But the divine feminine is another way to do healing work." Chalsey gestured at her own torso. "I rejected my body because I was molested as a child. I hated everything about my body, especially having my period, and I overfed my body to cope with the pain. I've done a lot of therapy, but converting to Wicca also helped. I threw my arms wide open to the

Goddess, to the celebration of women's bodies, and to the power of creation. Instead of being despised for being female and locked away when I was menstruating, I was asked to rejoice in menstruation, sex, and pregnancy. It was freeing."

Fredrick grabbed a package of shredded carrots and sprinkled some over the salad. "It's true. I hated my breasts. I hated my body. Doctors talked about me being intersex as a disorder or a dysfunction, and that hurt enough by itself. But my female 'bits' made me a target for chauvinism. And let's not forget the sexual assaults on the school bus."

"Throw in your parents' mistreatment, and you have a nasty, pus-filled wound in your heart." Chalsey's tone was soft, despite the words. "But healthy people are both yin and yang, anima and animus. And being happily agendered means healing the trauma. Maybe accepting the divine feminine is a steppingstone along the way."

Glancing over his shoulder, Fredrick stared at the Mother Mary altar in the dining room. "I'll consider what you're saying." The acid burning behind his sternum told him Chalsey was onto something.

After lunch, Fredrick and Chalsey packed up the cat supplies and insulin, caught Largo in the cat carrier, and spent 45 minutes tortured with anguished kitty cries. By the time Fredrick got to his house, he had to take a valium to handle his stress meltdown. Only once Largo forgave him and curled up on his lap could Fredrick cope. The valium induced an afternoon nap, so he fell asleep on the couch with Largo and had a nightmare that the vet forced him to put Largo to sleep because of his diabetes.

And so went Fredrick's first few hours of having a pet.

CHAPTER 16

THE HERMIT XIX

IN THE PEACE OF HIS OWN HOME, FREDRICK GRABBED his laptop after supper, settled at his kitchen table, and checked his online summer course. He'd filled the course with links to video lectures he'd filmed, reading materials, forums, and other interactive activities, but that didn't mean students didn't have questions. Other than three student messages, everything seemed fine. Largo lay at his feet as he answered the messages. Fredrick considered that progress. Largo had spent the first thirty minutes hiding, the next two hours napping, and then had toured the entire house after eating his kibble, sniffing every room and meowing.

Somewhere in the back of Fredrick's mind, he felt pressure building about Largo. As Fredrick closed his laptop, he tried to determine what it was. *I'm a grown-ass man. Or an agendered person. Fine. I'm a grown-ass adult. I can take care of a cat.*

That has nothing to do with it, Dietrich said.

An inexplicable surge of shame billowed through Fredrick's torso and made his intestines cramp. *Okay. Maybe I don't want to know what this is about. Yet.*

Fredrick's phone dinged, and he pulled it out of his pocket. An unfamiliar local number topped the text message:

> HEY, IT'S TONI. CHALSEY GAVE ME YOUR #.
> SAID YOU HAD A NASTY DM INCIDENT. WANNA
> GRAB COFFEE & TALK?

Fredrick's heart tried to smash through his ribs and run away. "Holy shit! He asked me out for coffee."

Doooooo it, Michael said.

Fredrick typed out a response, agreeing to time and place, and ran to the bathroom to double-check his appearance. *I need to look casual, but not like a slob. Maybe a fresh shirt. Oh, and run the electric shaver over my face.*

I see this part is the same between guys and girls, Laura said. *The whole 'I gotta look good for my date' thing.*

"Totally." Fredrick spiffed himself up and zipped out to his car, arriving ten minutes early to Ashleigh's family-owned coffee shop, The Ashleigh Brew Co. The shop was in the town square, surrounded by boutiques, the old courthouse, and lawyers' offices. Fredrick parked on a side street and entered the coffee shop, where wall lamps over each table offset the dim overhead lighting. Mixed in with the tables were brown leather couches and chairs and even a take-one-leave-one bookcase filled with used books. The dark wooden flooring was original to the building, which had been built in the 1820s. The ceiling sported antique tin inlaid with a fleur-de-lis design, and earth tones filled the entire space: taupe walls, brown furniture, and green accents.

Toni stood by the pastry case, gazing in. His honey-colored, brown-blond curls framed his face nicely, and he wore jeans with a casual button-up shirt, navy blue with white pinstripe squares.

Despite the coffee-only status of this event, Fredrick felt a shot of arousal, the warmth blooming through his lower abdomen. *He's beautiful. I'm on a date for the first time in... Oh, God. How many years? Twelve? Something like that.*

Go get 'em, Michael said. *I'm rooting for you.*

Butterflies flapped up and down Fredrick's throat and swarmed in his stomach. He ambled over and tried to look cool. *Yeah. I'm not flipping my shit or anything.* "Hey."

Toni turned to him with a smile and sparkly blue eyes. "Hey."

That was all it took. Fredrick was slain. *Shit, it really is like I'm 11 again or something.*

Doom, Laura joked.

Toni stepped into line, and Fredrick joined him. "You come here a lot?" Toni asked. "I'm so bad I'm on a first-name basis with all the workers."

Fredrick chuckled, trying to blow off the tension. "Not that much. But I've been here enough to know what I like." *Right now, I'd just like to have you, though.*

Whoo, Michael said. It was like having an internal teenager cheering him on and adding commentary.

If you say that out loud, he might take you up on it. Laura's internal voice was dry.

"Yeah. I'm stuck on one of three drinks." Toni stepped up to the counter. "Although I try anything new they come out with." He ordered a cinnamon latte and a raisin and almond bagel.

Fredrick ordered an Ethiopian Yirgacheffe and a square of their homemade dark chocolate fudge. *I'll be up until 2:00 now. Oh, well.*

Once they picked up their orders, they settled on a brown leather couch, the seating not crowded on a Monday evening. Most people ordered to-go, although an older woman read a book in one chair, and a college-aged woman typed on her laptop, no doubt taking advantage of the free wi-fi.

"So you tried to burn another grimoire?" Toni kept his

voice low. "But that got you some serious fireworks." He took a sip of his latte.

"Yeah." Fredrick shared his observation about the conch earrings, then added, "I think I've gone into permanent shock. I should be too scared to even walk through the door. But somehow, it doesn't seem quite real."

Toni nodded and set down his coffee cup. "Maybe you're dissociating away all the fear." He took a bite of bagel.

"Maybe. Probably." *Well, he seems nonchalant about that part.* "Did you read up on DID or something?"

"Yeah." Toni lowered his bagel. "I can tell there's a lot of misinformation out there about it. But I found two decent websites, and then I watched some YouTube videos made by people with DID. I think that helped more. There's a big difference between having some clinical psychologist analyze you from the outside like a specimen and talking about your real-life experiences for yourself."

Fredrick sipped his coffee, his mind showing him his father bent over his desk at home, flipping through numerous clinical tomes. "An enormous difference. I'm not sure psychologists even understand what their clients are telling them about DID. Especially if they go in with preconceived notions and don't keep an open mind." He gave Toni half a smile. "My dad was a psychologist, and he always struck me as pretty confident that he already knew what was up and already had all the answers."

"An insider's view, huh?"

"Yeah. And my experience with DID seems different from what my textbooks taught me in college." Fredrick took a bite of fudge, relishing the smooth, chocolaty goodness. *Strong hints of vanilla. Their cook is excellent.*

Toni nodded. "There seems to be a lot of personal variation. Everyone's brain is unique."

Angela surprised Fredrick by switching in. "Hi. I'm Angela. I'm agendered, so call me they/them."

"Hi, Angela." Toni took a sip of latte as if watching someone switch was the most ordinary, quotidian experience in the world.

"You don't have to date all of us." Angela considered the half square of fudge between their fingers. "You can just date Fredrick. But we should all try to be friends."

Fredrick nearly died. *Don't use the word "date!" What if he's not up to wanting to call it dating?*

Toni rested his cup on his knee. "That would make everything go smoother." His other knee bounced faintly but quickly. "Are you okay with me dating Fredrick, Angela?"

Wait, he just rolled with it? Fredrick was tentatively relieved.

"As long as you're nice to him and respect all of us," Angela said, filled with an eight-year-old's common sense. "You can't be nice to him and then mean to one of the rest of us. Just like it wouldn't work if Fredrick is nice to you, but then one of us is mean."

"You're being wise about this."

Angela shrugged one shoulder. "Adults make it too hard. It's dumb." They popped the rest of their fudge into their mouth and then licked their fingers.

Toni laughed. "Okay, true."

"Everyone should have an internal kid to keep them on track." Angela took a sip of coffee and wrinkled their nose. *Why ruin the chocolate with something bitter?* "If they did, adults would make less stupid mistakes."

Toni grinned. "You're probably right." He took another bite of his bagel, the wrapper crinkling in his fingers as he shifted it.

"I can tell you one other thing about The Demon Mother," Angela whispered.

Shifting to face Angela better, Toni leaned forward. "What is it?"

"She made us to do séances for her all the time." Angela leaned forward as well. "She used us like a human telephone to call the afterlife."

What? Fredrick and Michael shrieked together.

"She wanted to talk to the three babies she miscarried, but that didn't work," Angela said, ignoring them. "I don't know why."

You mean like in her Civil War novel? Fredrick asked.

Yep, Dietrich replied. *Or similar, anyway.*

"So she made us channel her grandfather for her," Angela said. "Her dad abandoned her when she was one, and her grandfather died when she was two. She said, 'I didn't get a dad, so it's only fair that I at least get to talk to my grandfather.'"

Toni set his coffee and bagel on the coffee table. "How old were you?"

"Four. She saw me channel a spirit by accident during one of her rituals with Dad, so she jumped all over it. She made me do it all the time. I went into a coma inside my brain when I was eight. I couldn't take it anymore, and I told her so. She got mad and started beating me, and that was the last thing I remembered until I woke up a few days ago."

"That's very wrong." Toni held out his hand. "No one should ask their child to channel spirits, and no one should harm a person, either."

Angela took his hand and squeezed it. "You're nicer than any adult I've ever met. Stay that way. Don't get mean later. All adults know how to do is scream."

Toni squeezed her hand in return. "I won't get mean and scream. I'm not a screamer."

We'll see, Angela said to Fredrick, and they switched with him.

Fredrick abruptly found himself holding Toni's hand. He blushed. "Thank you for being so patient and kind to them. Angela hasn't come out to talk much yet." He was so stunned by the revelation he didn't know how to react. "And God, if you weren't Wiccan, you'd think I was psychotic right now."

Toni squeezed his hand and released it, rescuing his coffee and bagel from the table. "I've seen all sorts of crazy shit. I spent part of my childhood living in an old farmhouse, and it was absolutely haunted. I converted to Wicca when I was 13. My parents weren't happy, but they didn't disown me or anything. They were lapsed Methodists. They only went to church on Christmas." He shrugged. "I started having more experiences with spirits after that—less scary ones. Then I got into reiki in 2009. I've seen other kinds of interesting energy phenomena since then."

"I guess you would, yeah." Fredrick sipped his coffee and felt his mind fighting to reject Angela's story. His brain tried to nope out of this trauma. "I tried reiki once. I didn't feel anything while it was happening, although I felt better at the end. But right in the middle, my water bottle fell off the middle of the bench, popped open, and gushed water all over the floor."

"Yeah, stuff like that." Toni sipped his latte. "Sometimes when I go to help my clients, some*thing* gets angry and fights back. It's not every client. But I've built up a few stories over the years."

Fredrick gazed at Toni, struck hard. *You can understand this part of my experiences. I'm not either a freak show or a liar in your eyes.* "I'm struggling with what Angela said. It's nothing that Michael or I knew about our life. Have you met anyone before who can channel spirits?"

"Heather can," Toni said. "James can hear and see spirits if they show up. So can Wendy. Corey can summon spirits with no rituals at all. It's like his brain is constantly connected to

Samhain or the Day of the Dead or something. But channeling the spirits so that they can talk through her body? That's Heather's specialty."

Fear and fascination tingled in Fredrick's lungs. "Who does she channel?"

"Ancestors and deities," Toni said. "She only does it for holidays like the Day of the Dead. It takes her a lot of energy."

Fredrick's gaze wandered around the room. A man now sat at the table nearest theirs, scrolling down his phone screen. Two teenagers stood just outside, smiling, laughing, and chatting. A bumblebee flew up to the window and bounced off it twice before lighting on the maroon and white petunias in a concrete planter by the teenagers. A steady stream of cars whisked past, circling the town square on the way to their destinations. *Do I have the ability to channel spirits? What would my life be like if this ability returned?*

Don't tell anyone beyond Toni and Chalsey, Angela said.

It's only safe now that Mom and Dad are both gone, Dietrich said.

"I don't have a fancy spiritual ability like that." Toni finished his latte and set down the cup. "And neither do the two members of our circle you haven't met yet. But everyone has something they're good at. It might be herbs or spell work. For me, it's reiki and crystals."

Fredrick realized he had an opening. "I'd like to try reiki again. What's your schedule like?"

"Not bad. I can probably work you in next week." Toni whipped out his phone and opened his calendar app.

Fredrick made an appointment and hoped he would also get a second date.

In the morning, Fredrick awakened with Largo at the foot of his bed. Fredrick hadn't had the heart to lock Largo out of his bedroom, even though Largo's coming and going had awakened him twice. *I'm okay. I can handle a pet.*

Fredrick stumbled through his morning routine and dragged into the kitchen to fix coffee and feed Largo. He gently pinched the nape of Largo's neck and gave him his insulin shot. *See? Having a pet isn't so bad.*

As he capped the needle and tucked the syringe into the biohazard box, Fredrick noted the tarot card waiting for him: an elderly wizard-looking man wearing a gray robe and cloak and gripping a lantern. He held a staff in his other hand. The text read *The Hermit.*

I remember liking this card, Michael said.

Fredrick pulled out the LWB and read the meaning: self-reflection, introspection, contemplation, withdrawal, solitude, or search for self. "Well, I can't argue with that. I'm searching hard for myself. I'm contemplating my entire life, including parts of my past I just learned about." He set down the booklet and watched Largo pad out of the kitchen into the living room. Fredrick had left the blinds open so Largo could have a "cat TV" view of all the juicy birds in the front yard: robins, cardinals, red finches, mockingbirds, and even the occasional blue jay.

With no warning, Fredrick felt a psychic snapping sensation. The pressure from the day before swelled, filling his lungs and constricting his stomach. He saw a flash of memory: going with his ex, Paul, to an animal shelter to pick out a new cat. It was a kill shelter, and Fredrick saw dozens of cats in tiny cages, some with kittens. Each one had a date of arrival, which determined their date of death. Paul had adopted a kitten, and Fredrick had driven home and melted down.

Fredrick still remembered sobbing into the phone to Chalsey, screaming hysterically as grief, pain, terror, and shame had exploded out of him. *"I wish I had never been born! I wish I had never even existed at all!"*

Kill shelters had always bothered Fredrick, but he'd had no insight into his reaction beyond the fact all those innocent cats and dogs would die unwanted. Unwanted, abandoned, and alone.

A layer of reality peeled back, and Fredrick saw a second memory: a bloody patch of grass and brown fur matted with blood. He could feel how young he was; he could feel sobs shaking his chest. Words flew through his mind, although he wasn't sure if he'd thought them or said them: *"I'd rather die! I would rather be the one to die!"*

Shit! Laura howled in their mind. *Don't press into that memory. Stop. Shake it away.*

Angela jumped into control of their body, pushed into the captain's chair by Dietrich. They shut down the memory, the images fading away. "It's not time. Not yet. We don't have a new psychologist."

Neither Fredrick nor Michael was fooled.

Was that an animal sacrifice? Fredrick asked. His words to Wendy fired through their consciousness: *Some modern-day religions still use animal sacrifice. So in the end, it really always is about blood, isn't it?*

The image of blood-matted brown fur flashed through their mind again.

I don't kill animals! a child's voice shrieked, but no one was sure who it was.

"No fucking way." Michael took over. "That's too Hollywood. Too grim-dark. Too Southern Gothic horror. My parents didn't—they didn't..."

Michael stood still, watching Largo hunker down on the back of the couch and chitter at a bird in the yew bush just outside the window. With no warning, his stomach turned, and he dry-heaved, retching sounds filling the kitchen. He knelt on the floor, bracing his hands on the cool tile as his stomach violently contracted.

Once the retching stopped, Michael leaned against the bottom cabinet, curling into a ball and hugging his legs to his chest. "It's too horrible. I can't stand it. Take it away! Make me forget it again."

Fredrick sat at the kitchen table, his morning coffee steaming in a cup at his elbow and his laptop open. He couldn't remember entering the kitchen, making coffee, or grabbing his laptop. The last thing he remembered was taking a shower. "I lost time."

I'm not sure what happened. Michael's concern washed through them.

Don't press on it, Laura said.

It's not time to touch that yet, Dietrich said. *Do you want to make a Mother Mary...ah, sacred space today?*

"Sure." Fredrick checked his personal email. One psychologist he'd messaged had emailed him back, so he stopped and made an appointment. Then he got Gina's number from Chalsey and texted her about adopting Largo. Gina agreed, and they set up a time to meet. The mere idea that someone not him would be responsible for Largo's safety, health, and happiness relieved Fredrick immensely. "Man, that was really stressing me out."

We're just not ready for a cat yet, Michael said. *Whatever that means.*

"I guess not." Fredrick sipped his coffee and roused himself to make breakfast. He opted for a ham and cheese omelet, going fancy for the day, and swallowed his daily pill army as he waited for the omelet to finish cooking.

Movement in the corner of Fredrick's vision drew his

attention. He glanced toward the living room, assuming he would see Largo, but the Flapper Ghost stood in the doorway instead. Her slinky white dress, strand of pearls, and high-heeled Mary Janes remained consistent, but today she frowned. She pointed toward the floor.

What does she want? Dietrich asked.

Here, let me. Angela took over. *I'll handle it.* "I can channel spirits. Hold on, and then you can talk through me." They moved the skillet off the burner and shut off the heat. Then they faced the ghost. "Okay, focus on me. Aim your words my way."

The Flapper Ghost didn't move. Her frown eased, and then Angela felt a sliding sensation, as if they were switching, but Angela was still in charge of their body. Angela let go of their control, words flowing out: "'You must return to the cellar. You left behind my scrapbook. Go back to my scrapbook and read— '"

The ghost vanished, and Angela felt pressure in their head.

Is this what Chalsey was talking about at the restaurant? Michael asked.

"Kali, *kreem!*" Angela snapped. The pressure eased away. "I don't know what that means, but it clearly works."

The Flapper Ghost reappeared and pointed to the floor.

Read my letters, Angela heard in their mind, and then the ghost vanished again.

Fredrick switched back in. "*My* scrapbook? *My* letters? If she means the one I found, then I'm totally confused. I found Grandma Smith's scrapbook. But she was born in 1918 and was too young to be a flapper."

Maybe it's a different scrapbook. We still have the last corner of the cellar to go through, Michael said.

"Who would be old enough to be a flapper?" Fredrick tried to do head math.

Grandma Anderson was old enough. She was born in 1909,

Dietrich said. *But no one ever said she was anything other than a rural girl who grew up to be a farmer's wife.*

"Our great-grandma had two sisters," Fredrick said. "They were both younger than our great-grandma. And Mom was named after her great-aunt Marilyn, who supposedly had a fantastic sense of style. In theory, our great-great-aunt Marilyn could have been a flapper."

Well, we'll find out when we get to Mom's house today, Laura said.

Fredrick groaned and rescued his omelet. Knight Auction Co. was coming the following morning to take pictures, so he and Chalsey had to make sure all remaining items were set out or close by in boxes. "Yeah. I'll find the scrapbook and hopefully the missing pages of the grimoire. And this time tomorrow, Knight will get everything else about this process underway."

CHAPTER 17

JUSTICE XI

ONCE FREDRICK AND CHALSEY ARRIVED AT HIS mom's house, he packed the Mother Mary altar into a small box, deciding to take the candle holder and candle and not just the Miraculous Medal.

"I'm sure there're a million Mother Mary statues to choose from online," Chalsey said. "I'd say scan their energy using their picture and see which was feels like a good match for you. Or there's an antique store in Glendale I visited once, and it had an extensive selection of Mother Mary statues. We could make a trip to Glendale, and you could handle the statues and read their energy that way."

"Either." Fredrick could no longer argue about items having vibes or "energy" all their own, not after touching his mom's corrupted Bible and her two grimoires. He carried the box out to his car, determined not to leave it behind by accident, and then reported to the cellar.

Chalsey joined him, and they faced the last corner where the Christmas decorations were stored. They'd gone through some decorations, but there were twelve boxes, so they hadn't finished. Plus there were boxes with fall, Easter, and Fourth of July décor.

"Somewhere in here might be a scrapbook." Chalsey grabbed the first red box. "Well, let's move all the decoration boxes out of the way and see if a non-decoration box is under them."

"Sure." Fredrick tagged in Michael, finding that the decoration boxes bothered him, although he didn't know why. Michael grabbed the Christmas tree box, and in short order, they cleared the corner.

At the bottom were two unmarked boxes, one a plastic tub and the other cardboard. Michael discovered an old light fixture in the cardboard box, but when he opened the plastic tub, a blast of nasty energy hit him in the face.

"God, what was that?" Chalsey stepped back. "Be careful."

"I have no idea." Michael lifted out his maternal grandma's jewelry box, her Bible, and two framed awards. Then he lifted out an old plastic jewelry box, cheap but antique, that was turquoise with a clear lid. The lid had a horse-drawn buggy etched on it. "I wonder who this belonged to." He could see a butterfly broach and some hatpins inside.

Chalsey folded her arms over her stomach. "You might figure it out with time. But something in there has been contaminated."

Behind Michael, Laura tensed. *She's right. I feel stagnant evil energy coming out of this box.*

Michael lifted out a stapled book entitled *A Brief History of the MacCarthy and Peace Families,* a manila envelope filled with three pairs of white kid gloves, and an envelope with two white handkerchiefs, both with **M** monograms. At the bottom were two high school yearbooks, one from 1962 and the other from 1964, and a black scrapbook. "Evidence I'm not crazy or making this shit up." He pulled out the scrapbook.

"No energy is coming off the scrapbook itself." Chalsey accepted it from Michael. "Let's take it upstairs. I want sunlight, and I don't want to be near whatever has the nasty energy."

"Right." Michael stood and followed Chalsey upstairs.

At the kitchen table, with the sunlight pouring in through the window, they sat side-by-side and flipped through the scrapbook, which seemed to belong to a teenager. It contained drawings of ladies in fancy flapper clothes, apparently cut from magazines, and newspaper clippings about births, deaths, and marriages. There were antique report cards and a high school graduation program.

Michael inspected a report card. "Marilyn Avalon MacCarthy, tenth grade, Buffalo Memorial, 1926." The card showed all *A*'s except for a *B* in handwriting. "This is my maternal great-great-aunt." *We were right.* "I don't know much about her, except she married a doctor and had no kids."

"I guess she left her belongings to her sister or her niece, then." Chalsey flipped another page. "Or maybe directly to your mom as her grand-niece." An envelope was glued to the page, and Chalsey pulled out a yellowed invitation. "Well, there's the wedding, Marilyn marrying Zeke L. Carson: October 24, 1932 at First Baptist Church."

Michael flipped the next page and discovered two envelopes stuffed between the pages, not glued in. "She said to read her letters."

He slipped one out, discovering pink roses at the top of the stationary.

"It's addressed to my great-grandmother."

April 22, 1934

Dear Kate,

I know you will understand my pain as others can't. I have miscarried my first child. I remember trying to comfort you when Michael was stillborn, and here I've lost my child, too. I can't seem to stop crying. I try not to let Zeke see me. As a doctor, he understands medically what happened, but I don't care about the details. There is only a pain in my heart where my love for my child should have been.

Michael's throat closed, and he tucked the letter back into its envelope. "God, I can't." His voice was rough. "Her pain's still seeping off the page, even after all this time."

"That's so tragic," Chalsey murmured. "Since I could never conceive, I'll never know what it feels like, not to lose a child and not to give birth to one. I genuinely can't imagine."

Michael moved on to the second envelope, which seemed at odds with the wedding announcements and birth announcements glued to the page. He slipped out the letter, this one on blue stationary. "God, here we go:

January 4, 1936

Dearest Kate,

How can I express the pain I feel? How can I find the words? I wish to pray, 'Let this cup pass from me,' but if God wills a thing, how shall I deny my Lord? I have miscarried again. I had been so hopeful when I reached four months, but it was not to be. I wonder what pain Mary felt seeing her son die on the cross, but at least her son lived first and fulfilled His divine mission in life. My children never breathed. How can I endure this pain when—

Michael fled the captain's chair, and Laura switched in. Tears tracked down their cheeks. "She was in so much pain." Laura folded the letter and tucked it into the envelope.

"And she honestly believed her god would curse her to suffer such a thing." Chalsey shook her head. "There is no solace in your religion if you believe your god is the one hurting you. What are you supposed to do? Thank your oppressor for hurting you? I can't imagine following such a religion."

Laura inhaled, willing away fresh tears. "Not all Christians believe that way, but some do, yeah." She flipped two more pages and found another envelope tucked between the pages, this one white with red roses in one corner. She opened it and slipped out the letter, which had matching red roses. "Let me guess. Another miscarriage. Here we go:

March 11, 1937

Dear Kate,

I know you will chastise me, but I will not hold my tongue. My God has abandoned me once and for all. Perhaps the Baptists are wrong. Perhaps God predestined and determined us to be the Elect and the Reprobate. If so, I am clearly the Reprobate, for now I find I can no longer believe. I gave birth; I held my baby in my arms, and by nightfall, she was dead.

I know I seemed strong at the funeral. I listened to my preacher's sermon about God's will, God's grace, and all the souls in heaven, including my daughter's. I told myself my daughter is with Jesus and to take comfort in that. But my heart broke. I felt it shatter. It will not return. Now I side with Macbeth:

'Out, out, brief candle! Life's but a walking shadow, a poor player that struts and frets his hour upon the stage and then is heard no more: it is a tale told by an idiot, full of sound and fury, signifying nothing.'

Life is nothing, Kate. My life, my baby's life, Zeke's life. All our lives. It is all full of sound and fury, signifying nothing.

Laura lowered the letter, unable to read further through the tears in her eyes. "God, I feel that. I feel that pain." Angela switched in. "Fredrick and Michael don't know it, but we've attempted suicide thirteen times, not four. We tried for the first time when we were six. We didn't want to see—" Angela halted, remembering how Fredrick and Michael had reacted to Largo earlier. "Well, we didn't want to see anymore horror."

Chalsey pulled a napkin out of the napkin holder and dried her eyes. "So much pain and heartbreak. And so many miscarried and stillborn babies. Your maternal grandma, your maternal great-great-aunt, your mom, and even your dad's secret second wife."

Fredrick switched back in, feeling his brow wrinkle as he frowned. "Okay, yeah. Nicole isn't related to us, but Mom, Grandma, and Marilyn were all related. Did they inherit a condition that made pregnancy difficult? Just how many dead babies are in this family?" Michael switched in next. "And Mom wrote a book about séances for dead babies, which is apparently tied to Mom asking us in real life to channel her dead babies for her, although we couldn't."

"Grief," Chalsey said. "The séances are about grief, perhaps out-of-control grief."

Michael tucked the letter back into its envelope. "Like when Dad died, and I was watching episodes of *Crossing Over with John Edward*, wishing I could go to L.A. or wherever it was taped and be a person in the audience. I wanted Edward to channel my dad for me." He snorted. "My mom was such a fucking hypocrite. She chewed me out about watching *John Edward* when she, herself, had already used me as a medium. How do you even get that bold?"

"A personality disorder. I'm still betting on narcissistic personality disorder."

The Flapper Ghost appeared by the table, her young face melancholy, her eyes lowered and her shoulders slumped. She still wore her slinky, white dress and long strand of pearls.

Michael jerked, his heart racing. But so far, she hadn't hurt him. "I read your letters. Are there more?"

The Flapper Ghost nodded and pointed at the scrapbook.

Fredrick, still terrified of Christianity even 24 years after leaving the faith, switched in. "Are you in hell?" *You said you no longer believed in God.*

The Flapper Ghost drew her head back with a look of obvious surprise and then shook her head. Her image faded.

"Couldn't help asking," Fredrick muttered. He flipped several pages and found a plain white envelope yellowed around the edges. He slipped out the letter, which was likewise plain and yellowed. "Oh, God. I hope it's not another dead baby. She says:

April 6, 1948

Dearest Kate,

I just must tell you what Madam Jefferies said. I can't tell you how much peace it gives me to hear news from the other side, to hear from Zeke and my babies. As skeptical as you were about Madam Jefferies, you must admit it has done me some good, and this time Zeke said he's been talking with Grandfather.

Just imagining our beloved family gathered together, in whatever heaven or afterlife exists, and free of tears, eases my soul. And Madam Jefferies says there is already a place prepared for me. When I pass on, I will once again be at Zeke's side, and I will hold all my babies at long last! If I were to say 'Glory be!' one more time, it would be for that.

Admittedly, I have had little luck with the Ouija board on my own, but the tarot is much more effective. I got a message from Zeke myself using the Visconti deck.

. . .

Fredrick stopped reading, his heart pounding, and Michael switched in. "Oh, my God! Seriously? My great-great-aunt was using the tarot? And going to séances? And using a Ouija board? Plus she told my great-grandma?"

"And your mom held her own séances using you." Chalsey crossed her arms over her chest. Today she wore a white prairie shirt with ruffles and a spring green gypsy skirt, and the ruffles covered her arms. "Michael, it's obvious to me now. You had people in your family die in World War I and II, probably including Zeke, and you had someone die in the 1918 flu pandemic. There are all these lost babies. There are séances and spirit summonings. I think the pattern is clear here."

"Death." Fredrick switched in and set down the letter. They were rapidly cycling between self-states. "It's all about the inability to accept death and loss. I mean, think about the losses on Dad's side, too: my paternal grandfather committed suicide when my dad was eight. He never got over that. It's why he went into psychology, or so he said. My paternal great-grandma supposedly lost a set of twins who died the day they were born."

Chalsey stared out the window. The sun lit the grass into a neon green glow. "And your dad had more than one wife who miscarried a baby. You've got unprocessed, unresolved deaths on both sides of the family."

Dietrich switched in. "The others don't know it, except Angela, but Grandma Smith lost five babies, not one. She only ever mentioned it once. She got married in 1938, but she didn't give birth to Mom until 1947. And then, after finally succeeding, her husband left her a year later. Not that Mom would have been better off if he'd stayed. Hector Smith was an evil man."

"Five lost babies." Chalsey shifted her gaze to Dietrich.

"But why did Marilyn Avalon MacCarthy's ghost fight so hard to get you this information? You no longer have your female 'bits,' as you call them. You can't have babies that way, or lose them, either. Why bring attention to this pattern of loss in your family?"

A sharp slapping sound drew Dietrich's attention, and he discovered his dad's tarot deck on the floor behind them, the cards halfway out of the box. Michael switched in and stood. "I think Flapper Marilyn sent us another message." He picked up the only card that was face up. "It's Justice." The card showed a man in red holding a sword in one hand and scales in the other.

"That can mean literal justice or law," Chalsey said. "Or karma. Consequences, accountability, cause and effect, truth, integrity, and honesty."

"Cause and effect," Michael echoed. "Flapper Marilyn wants me to know the truth about cause and effect, about consequences. All these deaths, all these séances, all this unprocessed grief—it led to the moment my mother summoned a demon to do her will. It led to a grown-ass woman asking her four-year-old child to channel spirits for her. All this ritual abuse. It wasn't just to scare me, to subjugate me, to break my will and make me too terrified to tell anyone I was being violated and assaulted. My mom also wanted to raise the spirits of the dead. And she wanted an unpaid medium to give her access to her dead loved ones any time she pleased."

Chalsey stood and hugged Michael. "Children don't exist to give adults free labor. Or even paid labor. We have laws against child labor for a reason. And you weren't born here to be your mom's telephone to the afterlife. What she did is egregious spiritual abuse."

Michael hugged Chalsey's waist in return, trying to wrap

his mind around this new picture of his family and its dysfunction.

"You're such a bleeding-heart liberal," drawled a grating voice.

Michael and Chalsey released each other and turned to face The Demon Mother with her blue shirt and jeans. She stood in the hallway from the kitchen to the primary bedroom.

"You and your sappy whining about the rights of children, Blacks, and gays." The Demon Mother wrinkled its nose. "By all means, don't make a child useful. Let the Blacks sit on their asses collecting welfare. And let the gays—"

"Shut up." Despite the words, Chalsey's voice was calm. "I don't need a speech about abusing others from a 'demon.' I couldn't care less about what your opinion is. No human being is born to be a tool."

The Demon Mother laughed. "Oh? A tool, now is it? I put in all that work being pregnant for nine months, put up with the labor pains, and toiled to provide for my child for 18 years plus college, but I'm not entitled to a little payback? Martha Fredrick *owes* me respect, love, and hard work for all my time, pain, and effort."

Laura burst into laughter, accidentally knocking Michael out of the captain's chair. "So love isn't freely given? You have to *owe* your parents? That's called *conditional* love, bitch, and it's not real love. If you feel that way about children, then don't fucking have any!"

Angela charged out next. "Oh, yeah, I totally *owe* you for being molested, raped, forced to summon demons, forced to channel your grandfather, forced into being a girl, and watching you *murder innocent animals*!"

Fredrick's and Michael's horror shockwaved through their shared body.

Although Angela suspected they shouldn't have revealed

that part yet, they continued. "By all means, let me pay you back for my outstanding, wonderful childhood. I'll pay you back, you self-righteous, sanctimonious freak, as soon as I get to the afterlife. Don't you worry about that."

Fredrick popped out next. He was surprised Angela knew the word *sanctimonious,* but he ignored that for now. "My name is Michael Fredrick, not Martha. And I don't owe you anything, not even being at your hospital bed when you died. Since family is nothing more than a financial transaction to you, this is simple: You didn't pay in, so I don't have to pay out. You would have to have loved me first, but you didn't. I was your chew toy, your sex doll, and your free psychic. If there's a hell, I hope you're in it."

The Demon Mother drew back her shoulders, her blue eyes glowing. "Why, you ungrateful, disrespectful, hateful little brat! How dare you accuse me and your loving father of such horrible things. I oughta—"

"Kali, *kreem!*" Chalsey shouted.

"You can't get rid of me, you tree-hugging pretend witch," The Demon Mother snarled.

Fredrick felt his rage snap. "Hail Mary, full of grace, the Lord is with thee." A chant popped into his mind, and he ran with it: "I didn't make *you, you* made me. You're not my responsibility!"

The Demon Mother vanished without even a gasp.

A stabbing pain shot through Fredrick's left eyeball. "Instant migraine." *I know that isn't really the ghost of our mother, but damn, that still felt great to say.*

I agree, Angela said. *I needed to vent that.*

"We hit upon something important and powerful," Chalsey said. "That's why The Demon Mother attacked so hard. Your parents' death-denying refusal to grieve goes back for generations, and it's hit you and negatively influenced your life. I watched you struggle with anger over your dad's death for 20 years. Your inability to accept it really isn't yours. It's your family's. And you express it by writing horror novels about death and ghosts. If you face this wound at its source when everyone before you refused, you will heal for real."

Fredrick felt the power of the words hit in his heart. "I'll accept it. I'll work on it in therapy, I'll process it, and I'll accept it precisely because they wouldn't."

The words were like a spell vibrating the air.

CHAPTER 18

TEMPERANCE XIV

THE FOLLOWING MORNING, BEING WEDNESDAY, meant Knight Auction Co. was coming. Fredrick awakened at the ungodly hour of 6:30 and took peace only in the fact the sun was awake alongside him. By the saving grace of coffee, he picked up Chalsey at 7:00, and they arrived with fifteen minutes to spare. Knight arrived precisely at 8:00.

For hours, Knight, Jr. and three assistants teamed up with Chalsey and Fredrick to take pictures. To preserve his sanity, Fredrick switched with Michael, who then switched with Dietrich, who clarified he was an adult and could handle it. Even though she was 13, Laura insisted on taking a turn. All of them kept out an eye for the two missing pages of the grimoire, but they found nothing, just like the previous two days.

The event remained blissfully ghost-free.

Once Knight left, Michael ordered a vegetarian pizza with no cheese, Chalsey agreeing to have some wheat. Chalsey and Michael collapsed on the couch and waited for the delivery driver, silent with exhaustion.

Staring at the snake plant in one window, Michael dredged

up enough energy to speak. "What if I'm just making all this up?"

"What do you mean?"

Michael's gaze traced the yellow outer edges of the snake plant's leaves. It was a tough, hardy plant, hard to kill. "The fear has been building up in the back of my mind all day: What if I'm making all this up? My parents never missed church, but I'm accusing them of summoning demons. My dad's entire career was treating trauma children, but I'm accusing him of harming, mistreating, and violating me. Yesterday, Angela even said our parents sacrificed animals. Isn't that just too overboard? What if I'm making all this up?"

Chalsey squeezed Michael's arm gently. "I think you remembered too much, too fast, and now you're pulling back. It's like extending a rubber band. You're trying to snap back into your familiar shape. But no, you're not making it up. Having DID is proof of severe childhood trauma. You can't even have a cat. You can barely engage in sexual activity. And you can't stand to hear the word *altar*."

A flash of fear shot through Michael, right on cue. "Okay, yeah. I guess. I just..." He wasn't sure what to say about it.

"It's a lot to absorb." Chalsey rubbed his arm. "And your mom has only been dead for two weeks. That's not much time considering how many revelations have popped out. And of course, your other self-states weren't willing to come forward and reveal what they know until your mom died. They didn't feel safe. It makes sense that you didn't remember anything before now."

Fredrick switched in. "I see your point. I guess my issue is that it doesn't seem real. These memories belong to Angela, Laura, Dietrich, and, to a lesser extent, Michael. I can't see these memories for myself. I'm going off what they're saying." He gave Chalsey a wry smile. "The voices in my head say I was mistreated horribly."

"You don't have schizophrenia, and these voices aren't auditory hallucinations." Chalsey lowered her hand. "Also, keep in mind that you found physical evidence for part of what you're saying: two grimoires, a SOMH robe, SOMH jewelry, and two spirits that other people can see."

Fredrick glanced around the room. "You know, you sensed a third spirit, but we haven't seen anything else."

"Maybe it doesn't want to be seen." Chalsey leaned her head back against the couch. "You know, I went through a phase where I feared I'd made up the trauma I suffered. I had memories, but I was still worried. I think the human mind tries to push away and negate severe traumatic material."

The doorbell rang, and Fredrick stood. "I'm sure you're right." He retrieved their pizza from the delivery driver, and they moved to the kitchen.

Waiting on the kitchen table was the day's first tarot card, which was inverted: Temperance. It showed a blond angel with red wings and a white robe pouring water from one cup into another.

"All right. What does Temperance mean when reversed?" Michael asked, switching in. "I never could remember this one."

"Imbalance." Chalsey grabbed two plates. "Excess, extremes, discord, recklessness, or hastiness."

Michael settled at the kitchen table and opened the box. The scent of hot tomato sauce and grilled vegetables filled the air. "Okay. So I'm imbalanced now. I found my diary on Wednesday of last week, and I've been proceeding at a reckless pace in uncovering all these traumas. It's excessive."

"Seems right." Chalsey handed him a plate and sat across from him. "What you've realized and learned is incredibly important, but now your brain is flooded. Do you think there's any way to slow down how fast you remember more details?"

"I have no idea." Michael pulled out two pieces of pizza, discovered they were still hot, and tore into one.

I've already been trying to slow it down, Dietrich said. *This is all unfolding much faster than I ever imagined it could or would. But even as the captain, I don't have full control. To a certain extent, our brain will simply do what it's going to do.*

Chalsey pulled out a piece as well. "Well, hopefully your new psychologist will have more information and can help. When you're first appointment?"

"Next Monday at 5:00." Michael found the lack of cheese to be strange-tasting, but he decided he liked the pizza. *It's like a spicy vegetable soup on bread.*

"That's actually really fast, so I'm thrilled," Chalsey said. "Most psychologists have a three-month-long waiting list."

Silence returned as they ate, tearing through the pizza like it was a Friday night party. Michael and Fredrick resumed worrying that they'd made up their traumas.

I'm sorry I blurted out the thing about animal sacrifice, Angela said. *You both made it clear you weren't ready to know that, but I got so mad at The Demon Mother I blurted it out anyway.*

You don't need to apologize, Fredrick said. *We're all just doing the best we can here.*

I just don't want to go back to a mental hospital, Michael said. *Of course, we would have never ended up in a mental hospital if they hadn't given someone who has depression a drug for bipolar disorder. Seriously. I hate this new fad of treating depression with antipsychotics. It ripped our damn brain out of our skull. But what did they expect? I'm not bipolar, and I don't have schizophrenia. Of course it ripped out my brain.*

A lightning bolt seemed to shoot down Michael's spine, and he tossed his leftover pizza crust onto his plate. "Oh, God. I just had a gut-wrenching thought."

"What?" Chalsey pulled her last piece of pizza from the box.

"What if my mother was bipolar? Even if she had narcissistic personality disorder, it doesn't mean she didn't have a co-morbid diagnosis. Dad always said half his clients had a co-morbid diagnosis, like having borderline personality disorder and depression at the same time." Michael glanced around the house. "And think about my mom's cleaning habits. She either had the house as perfect as a showroom, or she was complaining of depression and could barely wash the dishes."

Chalsey set down her pizza slice. "Great Goddess, I think you're onto something. She would write an entire novel in two months, maybe less. And then she'd complain about depression and write nothing."

"She would plant an entire garden, and then she'd let the weeds eat it, saying she felt depressed."

"She'd stay up until 3:00 or 4:00 in the morning writing for an entire month."

"And then she'd spend a month sleeping fourteen hours a day."

"She'd spend thousands of dollars on some fad in one month, and then turn around and say she was too depressed to shop even for groceries."

Michael and Chalsey stared at each other.

"It has to be a possibility," Michael said. "She spent 58 years on different antidepressants and said none of them helped. But no one tried her on lithium or one of the newer bipolar meds. Instead, they threw *me* on four different bipolar meds, and all that happened was I got really sick every time."

Chalsey rubbed her face. "Because you have DID, not bipolar. You weren't fast-cycling through mania and depression. You were switching between self-states."

"God, that's so unfair!" Michael's frustration burst

through him so hard he stood and grabbed the broom from the closet, cleaning just to burn energy. The explosion of people through his mother's house had dirtied the floor, so he felt productive. "They put *me* on bipolar drugs, and I spent five days in a fucking loony bin, submitted to plastic mattresses and pillows, an egotistic head psychiatrist who's convinced everyone has OCD, and talked down to by nurses who make grown-ass adults fill out worksheets about their favorite color and favorite vacation. But Mom complains for 58 years about her antidepressants not working, and all they do is change which one or up her dose. That sucks, too, but at least she didn't spend five days as an adult coloring in children's coloring books with fucking crayons and playing Connect 4 like a fucking toddler. I've never felt so condescended to in my life."

Chalsey stood and got the dustpan. "I'm so sorry. I never imagined such a nice facility would still be so subpar here in the twenty-first century. If I'd had a clue, I would have talked you out of checking yourself in. Then again, I also blame Dr. Laurie for leaving for a month on vacation without referring you to an on-call or substitute psychologist while she was away. You were suicidal, after all."

"You don't need to feel guilty." Michael let it drop. They'd had this same conversation a dozen times since 2017. "The bigger point is I was raised by a woman who probably had both bipolar and NPD. And my dad, the award-winning psychologist, insisted it was depression and that some antidepressants and talk therapy were all she'd need."

Chalsey knelt, positioning the dustpan so Michael could sweep in the broken leaves, random cat kibbles, dead bugs, and fur tumbleweeds. "Yes. You'll need to explore how your mom's untreated conditions affected you and your life." She stood and dumped the contents into the kitchen trashcan. "In the end, this is perhaps the only thing you two had in common:

she spent her entire life, and you've spent your life until this point, misdiagnosed and mistreated."

"I'm still not forgiving her," Michael said. "I don't care what her diagnosis was. I don't care if she and Dad both experienced sexual violence as children, too. They still paid it forward. I didn't deserve to be harmed and violated just because they were."

"No, never." Chalsey stored the dustpan back in the closet. "I firmly believe there is justice in the afterlife, even if I don't agree with Christianity's claims about what it is and how it works. Your parents will face justice, and their pathetic excuse of 'But I was violated by my parents first' won't cut it. No real deity would ever accept such a ridiculous excuse."

Michael returned the broom to the closet and inhaled through his diaphragm, trying to calm himself. "I have to believe you're right. I have to believe there is justice in the next world. Because I'm gonna lose my mind if I think there's not."

Chalsey hugged him, and he took what comfort from that he could.

Around 7:30, Michael and Chalsey arrived at Michael's house, having treated themselves to a matinee and supper at a fancy restaurant. For a blessed four hours, Michael and his System had avoided thoughts of their parents, their childhood, and even the auction.

Now Michael lay on the living room floor, flipping idly through his old creative writing journal that had been in the cellar. Largo stretched out on the carpet beside him, purring, and Chalsey lay on the couch, studying Michael's baby pictures in the family photo album.

"I was seriously obsessed with vampires and ghosts," Michael noted. His eighth-grade creative writing journal looked like his earlier diary: seven distinct handwriting styles, from blocky to loopy and from tiny to huge. "No matter who wrote in this journal, they only wanted to talk about the supernatural. Also, all the dads in these stories are abusive or absentee, and all the moms act like selfish little brats."

"You were shouting at the top of your lungs." Chalsey lowered the album. "You were telling yourself the truth about your life."

Michael reached out and scratched under Largo's chin. He rolled over onto his back and wiggled, but Michael didn't pet Largo's stomach. Most cats hated that, Largo included. *I wish people understood cats better. This position doesn't mean what people think it means.*

I wish people understood kids better, Laura said. *Like a tantrum doesn't mean your child is being a brat. It means you failed to communicate, or you ignored what they needed until they melted down. But nooooo, it has to be the kid's fault.*

That's so the adults have an "excuse" to hurt their kids, Angela said. *Or at least an "excuse" to yell at them. All adults yell.*

Chalsey set the album on the coffee table. "After seeing your baby pictures, I have a basic question: was your mom on drugs? You're underweight and visibly scrawny."

"I suppose we'll never know. Until death." Michael flipped a page and found an illustration of the ghost character from one of his short stories. "I admit, I'm curious. I don't really look like a normal baby until I'm about six weeks old. And Mom could have tried to self-medicate her bipolar disorder—assuming we're right—with drugs. If not, then she could have self-medicated her depression."

"Is there anyone else with bipolar in your family that you know of?"

"Not that I know of. But I have depression and anxiety running down both sides of the family. You know my paternal grandfather committed suicide, but you don't know my maternal grandfather's first wife also committed suicide, although I'm not related to her. However, there've been other suicide attempts in the family. We also have self-harmers."

Chalsey shifted onto her side and gazed at him. "What else?"

"Drinking, drugs, and minor criminal behavior, like stealing candy bars." Michael flipped another page and discovered a bloody vampire illustration. "For example, Roger admitted to me when I was a teenager that he drank and smoked pot all the way through high school and most of college. He didn't stop smoking pot until he nearly flunked out. As far as I know, he still smokes cigarettes despite repeated attempts to stop." He flipped the page. Another vampire story. "Plus we've got less obvious addictions in the family: work addiction, sex addiction, and religious addiction. And food addiction, although that's more obvious. And I won't be the first person with a PTSD diagnosis."

Chalsey fingered one ruffle of her shirt. "You have a BA in psych. I'm not going to surprise you when I say this: both sides of your family are exploding with trauma. Technically, you've been surrounded by evidence this entire time."

"It's funny how you can take this kinda stuff for granted." Michael flipped several pages and found a mafia story he didn't remember writing.

That's mine, Laura said. *We already couldn't share memories with each other by then.*

"People have been saying depression and anxiety are common for a long time now." Michael scanned Laura's mafia story. "And there were kids at school who were cutting or making suicide attempts. When I was in high school, one guy succeeded. Kids in the 1990s had more awareness, I think. And lots of kids at our high school drank or did drugs. So I wasn't thinking my family was in any way unusual. Weren't all families like that?"

Chalsey sat up and straightened her skirt. "Lots of kids do that. They think whatever they see at home is normal." Her phone dinged, and she pulled it out of her skirt pocket. "It's Wendy Yuan. She says the circle has agreed to help kick out the evil entity. We'd need to meet at your mom's house on Saturday night again, and we'll need dirt from your mother's grave."

Michael laughed. "Wow. Grim. But sure."

Laura switched with Michael. "This is the kinda stuff Angela and I remember doing with our grandmas. There was a working you could do to keep evil away from you or your house that involved fresh graveyard dirt. I guess every family's got variations, but for Grandma Smith, you got dirt from the grave of a person you knew had been good. A local saint. She never needed much. Just a few teaspoons. How much does Wendy want?"

Chalsey typed the question on her phone. "She says about a fourth of a cup. Exact measurements aren't necessary. But she wants us to tie a white string or ribbon around the jar once we get it and pray a blessing over the dirt to make sure it remains sanctified. The soil should already be blessed, coming from a cemetery. But we'll make sure."

"No problem," Laura said. "Mom's got all sorts of ribbons in her sewing kit."

Chalsey typed another message. "All right. It's all set up. This weekend, we'll kick 'demon ass.'"

Fredrick switched in. "Thank God there's an end in sight. Let me take this opportunity to text Toni and ask for a second coffee date. Just hearing a solution is on its way boosts my morale enough to text him."

Chalsey grinned. "Go for it."

To Fredrick's vast relief, he and Toni agreed on Friday night.

CHAPTER 19

THE EMPRESS III

On Thursday, Fredrick slept in until 11:00, woke up, and wished it were Friday already so he could go on his date. After coffee and checking on his online students, he followed through on a fragment of Michael's memory. During Michael's almost three years of being Wiccan, he had read half of the book *When God Was a Woman* by Merlin Stone, based on the advice from the circle's high priestess.

It was supposed to help me push past patriarchal notions of divinity, Michael said as Fredrick pulled up a digital copy. *It's a book that explains how and why patriarchal notions destroyed goddess worship. Matrilineal, goddess-worshipping societies were once all humans knew, but now we believe goddesses never really mattered at all except to be the wives and daughters of the gods.*

Fredrick bought the book and downloaded it. "Let's see what she has to say, then. Why did you stop reading?"

Grad school. We had too much homework.

"Fair enough." Fredrick grabbed his tablet and moved to the couch. Largo joined him, and a pulse of sadness fired through Fredrick that Largo would be leaving that evening to live with Gina. He petted Largo's head. "It's all for the best," he told Largo. "Gina can take good care of you without melting down from ritual abuse." He still couldn't wrap his mind around this detail of his childhood.

Before he could get caught up in the fear that he was making up all his trauma, he stuffed his nose into Stone's book and read. By page 152, he estimated his blood pressure was 220/170, and he needed antacids to calm the acid storm in his stomach. He set down the tablet and stood, heading for the bathroom medicine cabinet. "The level of open, wanton destruction and conscious abuse of power by men...I don't think I can read anymore today."

Makes sense of our childhood experiences as someone who was forced to say they were a girl, Michael said. *When your patriarchal, woman-hating religion tells you a woman ruined the world and that all women for all time deserve to be punished with childbearing pains and permanent subjugation to men, how can you ever love yourself? According to the Abrahamic religions, women were made as an afterthought, and Jesus as a god-man had to come along and fix a woman's mistake by dying horribly.*

Fredrick took two Tums, shut the antique medicine cabinet door, and stared into the mirror. His masculine face gazed back at him, stubble covering his cheeks. Reaching up, he ran his fingers over the sharp, bristly hairs, relishing in the rough reminder he had a fully male body now. "We felt more like a boy than a girl, even as a toddler. Even agendered, I'm more comfortable with men's clothes. But goddammit, it's so obvious now. I rushed to get surgery because it saved me from the damnation of Christianity. And even after I left the church, I couldn't leave a culture that is founded on Christian beliefs. As long as I had any female 'bits' left, I wasn't *really* human, and I didn't *really* have any value."

Maybe that's why Christians hate trans people so much, Laura said. *The transmen have escaped the curse of Eve, so they have fewer women to abuse and condemn. And the transwomen are "insane" because they're giving up their God-given right to domination, oppression, and abuse to live under the curse of Eve.*

"One of many reasons, I'm sure." Fredrick snorted and grabbed his electric razor. The soothing sounds of male shaving soon filled his ears. "Also, the stupid claim God makes no mistakes, even though babies are born with birth defects all the damn time."

It's the same hate that drives the SOMH, Michael said. *They're all like, "Stay in your box!" Either you were born superior—White and male and straight and Protestant—or you can go die for being born inferior, which is everyone else on the entire planet.*

Fredrick smirked and put up the razor. "Because hate is the heart of the One, True God. And people wonder why I left Christianity." He marched out and rescued the small box of altar supplies from his car. He'd gotten the box home but had struggled to put up an *altar* in his home. "I suppose my attitude makes this a hilarious contradiction."

We live in the Bible Belt, Laura drawled. *There's a church on every corner, all the cemeteries are filled with Jesus statues and crosses put there by the cemetery owners, and some stores still close on Sunday. I mean, seriously. Have you ever seen a star of David in a cemetery around here? Freedom of religion here just means the freedom to choose which denomination of Protestant you are.*

Amen, Michael said with conscious irony.

"Well, let me violate everyone's sensibilities and go Catholic." Fredrick swept through the house to his office and cleared off a space on the desk by his printer. "Here we go: the divine feminine. Mary, the Immaculate Conception. Since we're not allowed to be any other religion than Christian—do you think they'd burn down our house if we put a pentacle in our front yard the way our neighbors put out crosses?—this is our only way in."

With the efficiency born of anger, Fredrick laid out the Miraculous Medal, the white candle holder, and the blue candle. Then he hopped on the internet and ordered a statue of Our Lady of Lourdes, the Mary figurine that seemed to call out to him. A trip to the store enabled him to buy cone incense and a holder. In short order, he was standing in front of his desk and its sacred space with lit incense and a lit candle.

Four Hail Marys later, Fredrick felt calmer.

I think Chalsey was right about this, Michael said. *We need to heal. Even agendered, we need to embrace the yin and the yang. We don't have to be one or the other. All the energies are inside us. But we were taught to hate one, to despise it as inherently inferior and evil, to believe it's innately weaker, dumber, and more gullible. And according to Merlin Stone, this flies in the face of 22 millennia of women rulers, judges, lawyers, physicians, advisors, and priestesses who followed the Supreme Goddess. Women who have been mostly erased from time as if the world began with the Greeks and Aristotle and their chauvinism.*

"Yeah, the hundreds of civilizations that existed before Abraham did," Fredrick muttered.

Merlin Stone even pointed out there were female pharaohs that male archeologists insisted were male because a woman ruler was so unthinkable, Laura said. *I'm female inside of us. I want to hear more about what I can do instead of constantly being told I exist only for men to fuck and use as an unpaid maid.*

I'm with Laura, Dietrich said. *I'm male inside of us, but I still want to hear about how I wasn't born to be a fuck toy and a "helpmate" just because our body had female "bits," too.*

Galvanized by the agreement of the System, Fredrick grabbed a pair of scissors and headed outside to their tiger lilies. "I say we cut three lilies and take them to the enormous Mary statue in the Catholic cemetery. We can lay them at the statue's feet and pray to Mother Mary there. I get that it's only a statue, but I like the symbolism."

All magick is symbolic, Michael said. *Even Communion relies on bread and wine to be the symbol for Christ's body and blood. You don't perform the Eucharist with actual human flesh and blood.*

"Fair enough." Fredrick cut three lilies, grabbed his keys, and hopped into the car.

The drive to the cemetery eased Fredrick's stress, all the maple, oak, and walnut trees providing a glowing green contrast to the clear blue summer sky. The sun lit the world, seeming to promise Fredrick a new beginning. He drove five miles outside of Ashleigh on a rural highway, turned off at an ubiquitous Dollar General, and zipped down a road to the old Catholic cemetery. Established in 1791, it held some of the oldest graves in the area.

When Fredrick parked the car and stepped out, he felt waves of peace wash over him like the warm ocean. A scant memory of visiting Panama City Beach when he was 11 flitted through him, waves lapping over his feet as he looked for seashells. Thanks to less traffic, the cemetery was spared the roar of cars. Birdsong mixed with excited chirps and the buzzing of a bee. Fredrick retrieved his three lilies and strolled toward the solid white Mary statue.

Antique limestone tombstones lined Fredrick's way, some leaning or toppled, the names and dates mostly or fully worn away by the rain and elements. Moss spotted the stones green. A small sarcophagus was mixed in, perhaps three feet long.

Someone's toddler, Laura sighed, and they all thought of the pattern of miscarriages and stillbirths in their family.

Fredrick halted in front of the Mary statue, her arms

spread wide and her head faintly bowed. A small, sweet smile upturned her lips.

Welcoming, Michael noted. *I suppose for millions of Christians, she's The Good Mother.*

There's a friendly spirit here, Angela said. *It could be a cemetery guardian spirit.*

Fredrick leaned into Angela's awareness, and he sensed a presence by the statue. Unlike The Demon Mother, it didn't feel threatening. "Interesting. I just assumed spirits of place, like river spirits or cemetery spirits, were myths."

Once you can access my abilities better—our abilities—you'll learn differently, Angela said.

"Wow. We have such a different life than I thought." Despite his shock, Fredrick focused on his mission. He lay the tiger lilies at the statue's feet. "Mother Mary, I stand before your relic and offer you flowers. For Catholics, you are The Immaculate Conception, the one whom God allowed to be born without sin so you could carry Jesus in your womb. You lived and died without sin, you bodily ascended into heaven like Jesus, and you restored honor to the name of womankind. While Jesus was the Second Adam, you were the Second Eve. And as Jesus died on the cross, he gave you to all humans as their mother, the Queen of Heaven, the one we can ask to pray for us."

Fredrick took a deep breath to steady himself. He felt tears burning in his eyes. "But I was born into a Baptist family, and this was not what I was taught. There was no positive female role model for me. Mary was just some virgin who was selected to be special for nine months and who faded to the corners of time, no longer useful or wanted. She had a normal human family with Joseph. And under the weight of evangelical chauvinism, I was taught I was a second-class citizen, an object of permanent scorn."

Behind Fredrick on the internal command deck, Laura

and Michael began crying, and it caused Fredrick to cry externally. "I was born intersex, but the doctor ruled me to be female. So my mom forced me to be a girl, to be something I was taught I should hate. Mother Mary, pray for me. Save me from my hate. I have no interest left in the divine masculine. If God is real and is pissed off, you'll have to step into the gap and pray for his mercy. Because you alone are all I can stand to pray to now. But if God won't forgive me for it, then I guess I'll just go to hell."

A massive surge of energy filled the cemetery, powerful and sweeping. Fredrick fell silent, looking around, but all he saw were lush trees, silk flowers, and gravestones. Feminine energy washed over him, comforting and gentle. The fear and pain and hate eased from his chest.

Someone answered, Michael said. *Someone real.*

Fredrick sat at the feet of the statue, closed his eyes, and focused on the loving energy. *I'll call her Mother Mary. She answered to that name, and she offered me love and compassion. That's good enough for me.*

Once the stress drained away, Fredrick stood. "I leave with you my terrified obedience and self-hating subservience to the divine masculine. May the sacred energy of this sacred space cleanse the negative energy I leave behind."

Fredrick turned and marched back to his car without looking back. He felt something painful tear out of him, as if on a string tethered to the statue. He climbed into his car and drove away, still without looking in the rearview mirror. Once he reached the rural highway, he felt a second pain tear out of him, again as if on a string tethered to the statue.

Then, when Fredrick reached his home street, he felt a third and final tear, another layer of pain ripped away, and he felt made of Light.

On the counter in his kitchen, he found the tarot card The Empress, showing a woman with a crown of stars sitting on a throne outside in nature—the divine feminine, creativity, abundance, nature, and fertility.

Fredrick picked up the card and smiled. "I've come home."

The following evening, Fredrick met Toni at The Ashleigh Brew Co. at 5:30. They curled up on a couch again, both with lattes, and shared a mammoth-sized cinnamon cookie. Since Fredrick had spent the day reading article after article on Mother Mary and the Catholic church's theology about her, he felt peaceful and relaxed.

The Bible still relies too much on The Virgin vs. The Whore, Michael had said around noon, *and I want to find myself a warrior goddess to commune with. But this is a good start.*

"I'm looking forward to the circle tomorrow night," Fredrick said without irony. He'd learned on the internet that there were self-fashioned Christian Wiccans who used Mother Mary as The Goddess and Jesus as The God in their Wiccan rites. "But kicking out The Demon Mother will probably be a real shit show. I'm glad we can relax together tonight." Not that Fredrick had dressed in a relaxed manner. He wore his nicest khakis and a green polo shirt with a horizontal white stripe. He'd also donned his new sterling silver Miraculous Medal, which he'd purchased from one of the three Christian bookstores in their small town.

Toni smiled, his entire face lighting up and his blue eyes all sparkly again. "Hey, I'm thrilled we could hang out first and just kick back." He wore jeans and a black t-shirt with a dream catcher and a wolf on the front. An understated silver pentacle hung around his neck. Although the outfit was simple, Toni still looked heart-slayingly gorgeous in it.

Struck by the nearness of their bodies, Fredrick blushed. *Dammit. It's only a second date, but I want to kiss him already.*

Is that fast? Or slow? I haven't dated anyone in a typical way since I was 18. I don't think I ever knew.

I can't help, Michael said. *Chalsey and I had already been best friends for 15 years first. We just hopped right to it.*

"This has all been hell on you. You deserve a break." Toni reached out and squeezed Fredrick's arm.

Shit, now I want to kiss him right here in public. Fredrick thought he'd explode.

You're 43, Laura said, internally smirking. *You're old now. You've got to be sexually frustrated as hell.*

Hey! Michael replied for both Fredrick and himself. *We're not that old.*

With a pounding heart, Fredrick reached up with his other hand and squeezed Toni's hand. "Thanks. You've been great about all this. You didn't even know me—probably didn't remember me from high school—and you just charged right in and helped."

Toni glanced away, his smile broadening. His cheeks flushed. "Ah, I just did what I hope someone would do for me. You've gotta put good energy out into the universe if you ever want good energy to reach you."

You flustered him, Dietrich said.

"Well, I'll help when the time comes, then." Fredrick lowered his hand. "Assuming one or both of your parents are still alive."

"Both." Toni lowered his hand as well and then offered it to Fredrick.

Fredrick accepted, his heart pounding. *Okay, fine. I feel like a horny teenager here.*

Desperate middle-aged man, Laura teased him.

Hey, you're in this middle-aged body with us, Michael said.

Laura laughed inside their mind, and it made Fredrick smile. He was glad Toni would think the smile was about holding hands.

"I don't talk to my parents much." Toni held his hand snuggly. "I call on Mother's Day and Father's Day. I only show up in person on Christmas day."

Fredrick recalled what Toni had said about NPD running down one side of his family. "One of them a narcissist?" He sipped his coffee, holding the cup in his free hand and trying to pretend he was unruffled while holding Toni's hand. *Yeah, it's just simple affection. My heart's not trying to race right out of my chest or anything.*

"Yeah." Toni snorted into his cup as he took a sip. "Dad's a grandiose narcissist. Mom's his dedicated flying monkey, always excusing his behavior and saying everything's my fault. No thanks. I've got better stuff to do with my life."

"God, totally." Fredrick noticed a man and woman two tables away now glaring at them. *Will we get lynched? This isn't Louisville or Lexington. A metropolitan mindset won't save us.*

Our own parents would have shown up in purple hoods and killed us in the alley, Angela said. *They would have killed us harder just because we're their child.*

Fredrick's stomach turned to a lima bean-shaped ice chunk. "Do you think we're safe here?" he whispered, leaning closer to Toni.

Toni glanced at the glaring couple and stared back.

Both the man and the woman looked away.

"I'm guaranteed life, liberty, and the pursuit of happiness." Toni met Fredrick's gaze again. "I don't know if we're safe, but I refuse to hide. That said, if you feel threatened, we can go somewhere more private. Or we can catch a movie and hold hands in the dark." He grinned.

Fredrick suffered a flashback of the "I'm not gay seat" that teenage boys and even adult men used—the insistence that there be an empty chair between two men in a theater to prove they weren't gay together. He laughed. *It all seems so stupid now that I'm older.* "A movie would be good. Or we could go to your place or my place." *So I can kiss you.*

"Either is fine." Toni chuckled. "My apartment's not too wrecked right now. I might be a bachelor, but my pad isn't constantly junked up."

"Okay. Let's head out, then." Fredrick stood without releasing Toni's hand, and they strolled out hand-in-hand.

Toni offered to drive, so Fredrick rode with him to his apartment behind the mall, finishing his coffee on the way. The complex, which included a community pool and playground, was built of orange brick.

After parking in front of row O, Toni hopped out and led Fredrick inside. The building contained two stories and four apartments, and Toni had the one on the bottom left. The front door opened onto a combined dining nook and living room with a sliding glass door. A hallway led to the two bedrooms and bathroom. Glancing around, Fredrick sized up the owner via his space: the earth-toned chair and sofa were offset by floor pillows, crystals covered the coffee table, and beside the TV stood a small table set up as an altar. A white goddess statue sat centered at the back, and before her rested a bowl of water, a feather, a wand, a raw amethyst geode, and a dagger.

A pulse of uneasiness swept through Fredrick as Laura and Angela noticed the dagger.

In Wicca, an athame is a ritual dagger, Michael told them. *You direct energy with it, like a wand. You never cut anything real with it, not even herbs. There's a different tool to harvest herbs with.*

Laura relaxed slightly. *Get closer. Angela and I will scan it for bad energy.*

Wanting to reassure them and himself, Fredrick walked to the altar while Michael tossed their empty paper cups into a recycling bin. Once he was closer, Fredrick discovered a sprig of a green herb in the center plus a golden coin.

The gold coin could be a sun symbol, Michael said. *The summer solstice is coming up, after all.*

The altar's clean, Angela said. *No negative energy here.*

The goddess statue has good energy around it, Laura said. *Whoever the statue represents, she's a positive force.*

"Like it?" Toni joined him.

"Simple but lovely." Fredrick pointed to the statue. "Who's the goddess?"

"Brigid." Toni smiled at the statue. "She's the Irish goddess of the forge, poetry, and healing. She's a sun goddess and a sovereignty goddess, which means the tribal leaders had to have her favor before they could rule."

Leaning closer, Fredrick examined her. In one hand, she held a sword and the other a bowl that emitted flames. A wreath encircled her hair. "She's credited with a wide range of abilities, then." He thought of Merlin Stone's commentary. "She's not just a goddess of fertility and sex. And she's not an enshrined virgin, either."

"Ancient peoples didn't narrow down their women that way." Toni plopped on a floor pillow in front of his altar and gestured to the one beside him. "Think of the diversity of the Greek goddesses: Athena, goddess of wisdom, and Artemis, goddess of the hunt. It wasn't just Aphrodite, the goddess of love and sex."

Fredrick settled on the pillow by Toni and offered his hand. "It matters to me. I'm fighting to accept the yin inside."

"That's beautiful." Toni took his hand and kissed it. "I spent 12 years fighting that war, and I finally won it."

Shock fired through Fredrick and his System. "Won it? How?" His hand tingled where Toni had kissed it.

"Therapy. Reiki. Meditation. Study." Toni sighed. "My father spent most of my childhood attacking me for being 'too effeminate.' He went into high gear when I was seven, and he still hadn't let off when I moved out at 18. He hates my piercings. He hates my longish hair. He hated that I wrote poetry and composed music and sang in a band. He hated my long-haired, 'hippy' friends, as he called them. When he found out I'm bi, he nearly died." He shook his head. "I ended up a wreck. All obsessed with my masculinity."

Fredrick gave Toni's hand a squeeze. "Your dad tried to terrorize you into being hyper-masculine." *Just like my mom tried to terrorize me into being hyper-feminine.*

"I got to the point I was all yang and no yin." Toni snorted. "It made me an asshole. I lost a friend that way, and that was a real bomb. Woke me up fast. I got a machete and started hacking my way through the jungle of gender lies. I had so much blocked energy from it that during my first reiki treatment I cried from the release."

"Does worshipping the divine feminine help you with it?" Michael asked, micro-switching with Fredrick for a second.

Toni smiled at the Brigid statue. "Yes. I pray to Brigid every night to help me keep balanced, and I meditate on her many roles. The gender binary is so restrictive. Gender roles in both the East and the West are too restrictive. I needed to borrow a Buddhist phrase, The Middle Way."

"I understand." Fredrick jumped in with both feet. *Love me or leave me.* "I was born intersex. But the doctor who delivered me recorded me as female, and my mom fought a war to make me a girl. I was never comfortable being a girl, and I was trampled by both secular sexism and the innate sexism of Christianity. Finally, I gave in to the demand to make my body into a cookie-cutter 'standard,' but when I did, I had surgery to be a binary man, not a binary woman."

Toni turned toward him, his brow furrowed, and took his other hand, squeezing both his hands gently. "That sounds so hard."

"It *is* so hard." Fredrick looked toward the Brigid statue and thought of the Mother Mary statue and the feeling of her presence in the cemetery. "Now I'm sure I'm agendered, but I've violently rejected everything female. I hate it. It disgusts me. I hated my female body parts, I hated my female social training, and I hated my female identity. I couldn't leave it behind fast enough. But if you reject the yin, the anima, completely..."

"You become all yang," Toni murmured. "It's unhealthy."

Fredrick met Toni's gaze. "I dedicated myself to the divine feminine yesterday. It's the first step in what I know will be years of work. But I want to be free of this gender prison. I want to be free of the hatred of the anima." His vision blurred, and then he felt the wet heat on his cheeks. "I'm tired of believing women are inferior. I'm tired of feeling like I was born *wrong*."

"You weren't born wrong," Toni whispered. "Not as someone who was intersex, and not as someone ruled—by whatever definitions that doctor applied—to be female. You're just you, and that's fine, whatever that is." He slipped his arms around Fredrick.

Fredrick sniffed, fighting off the tears, and hugged Toni in return. Then Toni's understanding and compassion, his act of caring and acceptance, lit Fredrick's passion into a blaze. He pulled back, met Toni's eyes, and let him see the desire there.

Toni's gaze dropped to Fredrick's lips, and Fredrick took the hint. He leaned in and kissed Toni, mouthing his lips. His kissing skills were rusty, but Michael's weren't, and the kiss seemed to flow out of him gracefully.

A *ripping* sensation in Fredrick's chest signaled his desire tearing free, released from its prison of self-hatred and trauma, at least for a moment. He clutched Toni to his chest, kissing him more passionately, moaning as he slipped his tongue past

Toni's lips. Toni moaned sharply and met Fredrick's tongue in a caress.

The arousal firing through Fredrick's body transcended any he had ever known. More than the throbbing heat, more than the need to make love, it was an unthawing, an unfreezing, an escape from the dungeon of trauma. Fredrick pressed Toni backward, and he accepted, lying on his back on the floor as Fredrick lay over him. With their bodies pressed flush, Fredrick felt Toni's answering arousal, and he let go, pinning the beautiful man to the floor and kissing him senseless.

Only once they both lost their breath did Fredrick relent and caress Toni's flushed cheek. He dropped a kiss on Toni's neck. "I don't normally run this hot."

Toni gasped at the kiss. "I'm not afraid of your passion. I'm not afraid of your yin or your yang. Your energy is beautiful. I don't go to bed with people on a first or second date, but I don't think sex is shameful or evil, either. I think it's natural and wonderful. You can rain your arousal down on me."

To someone who had spent his life frozen, Toni's words were more gorgeous to Fredrick than his good looks. "I want to rain it down." *Without panicking. Without shutting down. Without going numb. How far can I get?*

Just ease in, Michael said. *Stop if you panic or go numb, but give yourself rein until that moment. We'll stay out of your way.*

Fredrick felt somehow more alone in his head, as if Michael and the others had drawn away, and reassured, he lapped up Toni's neck. "Is your neck a good spot?"

Toni moaned and tilted his head to the side. "*Very* good."

Reminding himself to breathe so he didn't lock up, Fredrick followed his instincts, lapping and kissing and sucking on Toni's neck. Toni moaned, holding Fredrick tightly and running one leg behind Fredrick's knee.

Encouraged, Fredrick slipped one hand under Toni's t-shirt and caressed his chest, finding a nipple and stroking it.

Toni cried out and pressed his chest up into the touch. "God! Yes, amazing. Touch me there."

Happy to please, Fredrick lifted Toni's shirt, baring his chest, and lapped over one nipple. Toni cried out again and clutched his shoulders. Being free to express himself as a man to another man, one who could accept both his yin and his yang, Fredrick sank deeper into his passion, running his hands under Toni's back and sucking on his nipple. Toni shouted his pleasure, squirming under Fredrick, and Fredrick made love to that nipple, licking and sucking and even nibbling lightly.

"Oh, God, I'm almost gonna come just from this," Toni gasped. He kneaded Fredrick's shoulders with both hands.

"I could slip my hand down." Fredrick didn't lift his head to speak, and his lips grazed Toni's nipple.

Toni shivered. "If you're ready, I'm ready."

Fredrick snaked his hand between them, found the hard, hot bump, and caressed it through Toni's jeans. "Tell me if that's not enough." He switched to Toni's other nipple and sucked on it, moaning.

With a cry, Toni pressed against Fredrick's palm. "It's enough!" He rocked his hips faintly, meeting the stroking of Fredrick's hand.

Fredrick felt memories flow through the back of his mind, sensed but not seen. Ugly memories. All his fear of rape. All his nightmares. This time, he let the flood pass unchecked and stayed in the moment with Toni, his cries, his moans, and Toni's pert nipple against his tongue. *Come for me. Be beautiful. It's beautiful. We're beautiful. And the goddess watching over us doesn't judge us as obscene for love or pleasure. I have the right to feel pleasure, too.*

At the triumphant thought, Fredrick sped up his strokes,

and Toni wailed and came, his hips jerking against Fredrick's hand.

Fredrick felt a new reality crash down into his chest, into his world. He lay his head on Toni's chest, stunned and breathless. *My parents harmed and violated me until I could never see sex as anything but the evil preached by The Church. "True Love Waits. Be a virgin until marriage. No, be like Mother Mary: a virgin until the day you die, never sinning, never sullied." But I have the right to pleasure. My body is not evil. My body did not tempt them to sin by violating and harming me. I am not the evil here.*

Toni caressed Fredrick's back and relaxed under him. "That was fantastic. Your passion is beautiful. Natural. A desirable trait. Since I know you used to be Christian, let me say this: Please don't be tempted to retreat into shame later."

Tears burned Fredrick's eyes, but he held them in. He lifted his head and smiled. "I refuse to give into shame." *Okay, so I'll be working on that in therapy for years, but I won't give in.* "I want to see sex as natural and good and lovely."

Toni smiled and caressed Fredrick's face with both hands. "It is. And I want you to reach that truth." He pressed a gentle kiss to Fredrick's lips.

Since Fredrick wasn't ready to be touched in return, given his trauma was still too unprocessed, he sat up so Toni could go change clothes. Then they curled up on the sofa, talking and trading kisses before heading out to catch dinner and a movie.

By the end of the night, Fredrick's thoughts solidified on a single mantra: *You can't even stop me with sexual trauma, Demon Parents. I will defeat everything you did. I will be the real me.*

I will be free.

CHAPTER 20

WHEEL OF FORTUNE X

On Saturday, Michael and Chalsey headed to Careyville in the afternoon and searched the house again for the missing two pages of the grimoire. Chalsey found the first page in the cellar's corner where they'd already checked five times. Michael found the other behind the entertainment center, which they'd searched three times.

As they walked to the grill, Michael clutching the pages and a lighter, a basic question burned behind his sternum. "Okay. Now I have to know. Can evil spirits hide things from humans?"

Chalsey's sigh was gusty. Today she wore a moo-moo style, tie-dyed dress in blue and white that reached to her ankles. Pentacles were stitched along the hem. Her blonde curls bounced in the wind. "I've been forced to conclude the answer is yes. People report problems like this all over the planet and have for centuries. I've had the experience of searching my apartment for my keys or wallet, only to find them right where I left them. It's like they can temporarily trick you into not seeing what's right in front of your face."

"So you don't think they literally move the item?" Michael

dropped two fresh charcoal briquettes into the grill and lit them. *I don't know if I can cook food in this thing again. It's turned into an evil artifact grill.* Once the flames leapt up, he tossed in the papers.

"No." Chalsey crossed her arms and stared at the burning pages. "I've never found anything in a place that wasn't logical. It's usually where I expected it to be. I just somehow managed to not see it. And it happens even when I'm not stressed out or rushing."

"That's more like a classic Jewish folkloric demon," Michael said. "They're imps, little troublemakers."

Chalsey glanced around the backyard, frowning. "Yeah. Honestly, there seem to be all sorts of different evil spirits, from imps to Cthulhu-like massive entities."

Pressure built in Michael's head, and he scanned the yard as well. "Oh, God. Here we go." Even with the brilliant June sunlight, the thick grass, and the chirping birds, Michael felt only violent thunderstorms in the night. "It's here. I can *sense* it."

For an instant, Michael suffered a flash of memory: the yard as it had been in his childhood, the wooden fence standing seven feet tall, a solid brown barrier between his backyard and the neighbors'. The kiddie pool had been on the concrete patio where the deck now stood, and a fire pit had occupied the center of the yard, surrounded by dirt and stones.

And then a second flash intruded upon Michael's mind: a fire in the pit at night, bloody brown fur, and his mother's voice intoning Bible verses.

"Oh, God!" Michael turned toward the gravel driveway, wrapping his arms over his stomach and closing his eyes. *I saw it again! Some poor dead animal.*

"Don't be so melodramatic," said a familiar, grating voice. "Animals must die for the greater good of humans. And even if it's some stray dog, what kind of life would it have had, anyway?"

"Michael!" Chalsey hissed.

Fredrick and Laura both tried to switch in, and somehow, they crammed into the captain's chair together. They turned to face The Demon Mother, who stood on the deck, and were jolted by the orange conch earrings. This time, the earrings were the size of human ears instead of the mini shells normally used for earrings. "There was no greater good in what you did," Fredrick-Laura said, "and even animals deserve rights."

The Demon Mother swept one arm through the air. "Oh, plenty of religions still use animal sacrifice. You said so yourself."

Fredrick-Laura froze, horrified that The Demon Mother knew what they'd said in a restaurant back in Ashleigh, just like it had replied to their thoughts about their flashback of a dead animal.

"Murdering a squirrel or a rabbit on your homemade altar is not the same," Chalsey said. "Take Vodou or Voodoo, for instance. If animal sacrifices are made, the killing is done by a trained butcher, and the meat is then cooked and eaten on the holiday at hand. Phillip and Marilyn Anderson were not trained butchers, and they apparently left the dead animal to either rot or buried it in the yard."

"Also, they sacrificed these poor animals to demons, not deities," Angela said, breaking through Fredrick-Laura for a moment.

The Demon Mother laughed. "Well, the God of the Christians murdered his own son, but no one's pitching a fit about the human sacrifice. Or does that count as suicide? God and Jesus supposedly being the same person and all? Anyway, if the God of most the planet can kill his own offspring, then surely I can kill a few mice, squirrels, and rabbits."

"You're not really Marilyn Anderson," Fredrick-Laura

said. "And we destroyed the grimoire with the seals of Solomon. Why are you still here?"

The Demon Mother laughed again, sharper this time. "Oh, honey. Bless your little heart. Did you really think I told you the truth? I'm made of lies. If I ever told you something that was mostly true, it would only be to trick you into doing something stupid." She propped her hand on her hip. "My favorite is, 'You can climb the ladder and fix the roof yourself. You don't need to waste all that money hiring a professional.' Although I usually just score broken bones with that one, I got a man killed once."

Fredrick-Laura were stunned by the entity's sheer bluntness about its evil.

It just told you it always lies, Michael said. *And that's probably the only truth it can ever tell. So in this case, I think it's safer to assume the truth is more than one person died.*

"Well, destroying the grimoire is still a good idea," Chalsey said. "And we won't stop until we kick you out of Michael Fredrick's life."

"Good luck, sweetheart." The Demon Mother smirked. "You'll never get rid of me." The entity vanished.

Fredrick-Laura turned to Chalsey. "If it said that, doesn't that automatically make it a lie?"

"Good point." Chalsey closed the grill lid to snuff out the flames. "Because it said that, there must be some way to kick it out. Time to visit the cemetery."

Laura stepped back, leaving Fredrick in control. "Just let me get some white ribbon from Mom's sewing kit, then."

They retreated inside, and Fredrick grabbed an empty spaghetti jar from his mom's supplies and the ribbon. On the way back out the door, he spotted the daily tarot card on the kitchen table.

"Here's our message." Fredrick studied the image: an

orange-brown wheel in the sky surrounded by clouds and various winged creatures. The text read *Wheel of Fortune.*

"Okay, that means change," Chalsey said. "Cycles, fate, luck, fortune, and the unexpected."

"The unexpected," Fredrick echoed. "Well, I want to change my fate and get rid of The Demon Mother, but I'm going to stay on guard for the unexpected today."

"Good idea."

They left for the cemetery and gathered the grave dirt for Wendy's spell.

That evening, Toni arrived first. He wore his usual jeans and an olive green t-shirt with the original *G. I. Joe* cartoon characters on the front. Fredrick smiled at the warm memory of one of his childhood cartoons and opened the door, ushering Toni inside and into his arms for a hug.

Toni pressed a kiss to Fredrick's cheek. "Ready to get rid of the entity?"

"Past ready." Fredrick found he didn't want to release Toni, and they settled on the couch, Toni's arm around Fredrick's shoulders. Fredrick left the front door open and the storm door unlocked so he could wave people in from the couch.

Wendy Yuan and Heather Torres arrived together, Wendy's gray hair tucked up into a loose bun and Heather's teal hair back in a ponytail. Wendy's black shirt was kimono-styled, and she wore it with black pants and a belt. Fredrick wondered if her devotion to martial arts inspired her wardrobe. In contrast, Heather wore a blue t-shirt with jeans.

Fredrick waved them in, and they each entered carrying bags. "Come in. Make yourself at home."

"Were you successful in getting the grave dirt?" Wendy asked.

"Yep. It's in the kitchen." Fredrick leaned against Toni's side, trying to stay calm. *There's no way The Demon Mother won't attack. But what will it do?*

Wendy and Heather headed to the kitchen, where Chalsey was already smudging with sage.

James Brooks and Gina Peterson arrived together again, James nearly having to duck as he entered the door. James's orange-red hair was windblown, and he was working on a tan, despite his pale complexion. He wore jeans and a crimson *Star Wars* t-shirt. Gina wore a green khaki jumper dress over a white shirt with green pinstripes. They, too, carried bags.

"How's Largo settling in?" Michael asked, switching with Fredrick for a moment.

"Just fine." Gina smiled. Her brown hair curved down to tuck under her jawline. "I got him a cat tree, and I put it by my sliding glass door. He's been watching the birds from it."

Michael switched back with Fredrick, and they relaxed deep inside. "Good. I want him to be healthy and happy."

James and Gina reported to the kitchen as well.

Arriving last, but not late, was Corey Lewis. His long auburn hair hung down freely, and he wore a retro white 1970s-style leisure suit with a magenta button-up shirt. While the effect might have failed on some men, especially ones in their early 40s, Corey looked dashing.

"Classy," Fredrick murmured to Toni as he waved Corey in.

"Corey always dresses with style," Toni said.

"Do I?" Corey chuckled, apparently caught off-guard. He likewise held a bag.

"Snazzy," Toni said.

Corey blushed faintly. "Thanks." He headed into the kitchen, where voices now filled the air.

"Oops. Didn't mean to knock him off-balance." Toni leaned in and pressed a kiss to Fredrick's lips. "I don't think our other two members are coming again this weekend, so it's time."

Fredrick groaned but stood. "Yeah. Let's go face the music. As in the horror movie soundtrack."

When they entered the room, Fredrick discovered that the angel-free kitchen island had been converted into an altar. A white tablecloth covered it, and various items encircled the jar of dirt in the center. A fancy silver chalice sat in the west, a geode of green aventurine in the north, a lotus-shaped incense burner in the east, and a pale blue goddess-shaped candle in the south. A Scottish dirk rested by the incense burner. Chalsey's cream-colored goddess statue stood in the north with the aventurine, its features nonspecific and a spiral carved on its torso.

Toni pulled an antique pocket watch from his front pocket and set it in the south. He frowned and moved it to the east and then to the west. "West it is. The energy's best here."

"You use a watch on your altar?" Gina leaned closer, studying it. "It's beautiful."

"Thank you, and yes. It's my maternal grandfather's. He was a Cunning Man who lived in the mountains of North Carolina. He was excellent at healing work." Toni smiled at the watch as if relieving fond memories. "I always have his watch on my main altar."

Fredrick assumed Toni's main altar was in his bedroom, given the watch hadn't been on the living room altar.

Wendy turned to Fredrick. "We've all brought items we consider the most powerful for us. Do you have anything you'd like to add?"

Reaching up, Fredrick unclasped his Miraculous Medal and set it on the altar.

Toni moved it a few times and then left it in the east by the incense.

"Excellent." Wendy clapped her hands. "Let's get to work. I've prayed to the Goddess repeatedly about our best option, and her answer is to trap the evil entity's energy in the grave dirt and take it to Marilyn Anderson's grave."

Fredrick felt like a bus parked on his chest. *I can already feel that thing coming.*

The negative energy in the room tripled, Angela said.

"Here it comes." Chalsey grabbed the saltshaker and sprinkled salt on the altar. "I bless this altar by the power of the Stag of the Deep Forest and the Moon Rising in the Heavens."

Inside of Fredrick, Angela gasped at the surge of power, as if white energy blasted off the altar. It made Fredrick's lungs hitch for a moment.

Whoever Chalsey's calling on, they totally responded, Laura said.

With a crack, the electricity died, the hum of the refrigerator silenced. The summer sun slanted through the windows, lighting the room.

"It's here," Angela whispered, breaking through Fredrick's control for a moment.

They didn't have time to finish casting the sacred circle, Michael said. *This is bad!*

Chalsey lit the sage incense stick and candle, her fingers trembling around the match.

"My, my," drawled the grating voice. "Such a party in my kitchen."

Fredrick turned toward the doorway between the kitchen and dining room. The Demon Mother stood there, shoulders straight and chin held high. She wore her signature blue shirt and jeans, but the orange conch earrings had grown again until they were each half the size of her head. Had the situation been less dire, Fredrick would have laughed at the ridiculous image.

"You might as well appear." Wendy unscrewed the jar lid, a picture of calmness. "We're going to get rid of you now."

Corey, James, and Gina all backed away, and Toni appeared to have stopped breathing, his face growing pale.

Only Heather stepped forward. "Your torture of Michael Fredrick is over! I don't care who summoned you here or why. This ends now."

Her gumption impressed Fredrick. *Tough as shit.*

"I'll kill you all if you don't stop." The Demon Mother's voice fell flat.

Laura yanked control away from Fredrick. "But you admitted earlier that you always lie. That means you won't kill us. And kill us how? That body of yours isn't real."

The Demon Mother narrowed her eyes. "You always were such an impetuous child. Hateful, petty, and immature."

"Sounds exactly like you." Laura narrowed her eyes. "I learned from the best."

Wendy held her hands over the jar of dirt and began chanting.

"I said I'd kill you!" The Demon Mother snapped.

"So do it." Laura propped her hands on her hips, purposefully evoking her mother's favorite pose in life. "Kill us. Do it. Do it. Do it." *I'm tired of being afraid of you, bitch. Let's have it out once and for all.*

The kitchen window shattered, and everyone jumped, screamed, or both.

Wendy resumed chanting.

The Demon Mother smirked. "What? That little taste of my power is not enough for you yet?"

"You can't kill us or you would have already," Laura said.

The Flapper Ghost appeared beside Laura, glared at The Demon Mother, and pointed at the door.

"Not you, too," The Demon Mother drawled.

Switch with me, Laura told Angela.

Angela took over and looked to Flapper Marilyn. "Speak through me."

Flapper Marilyn nodded, and Angela let go of control over her mouth. Words immediately popped out: "Your time here is through, and you know that. My great-grand-niece and her husband offered you something they could never give. Even if they still lived, they couldn't pay you. But now they've passed on. There's nothing else you can do."

The Demon Mother pointed at Angela. "Michael Fredrick's blood was also used in the rite. I can make him pay up."

"It's not something a human can give," Flapper Marilyn said.

Angela lost control of the body to Fredrick, who looked between them. "Just what exactly did my parents claim they would pay you?"

"Everything," The Demon Mother snarled. She slashed her arm through the air, and Flapper Marilyn vanished.

Wendy faced The Demon Mother, picked up the athame, and pointed the tip at the jar. "I seal you to the dirt of Marilyn Anderson's grave. Your work and time here are finished forever. Go silently to the grave, and may your energy be reborn into something clean and new."

"No!" The Demon Mother shrieked. It pointed at the jar. It shattered.

Wendy jerked backward, and everyone gasped or yelped.

Another spirit appeared where Flapper Marilyn had stood. At first, it looked like fog, but then it coalesced into an image of Fredrick's father. Phillip Anderson's boxy jaw, broad face, and aquiline nose remained familiar to Fredrick, kept fresh in his mind from pictures. The man had died at age 60, his black hair mostly gray, and he looked the same now: gray, tall, stately, and broad-shouldered.

Terror shot through Fredrick, freezing him like liquid nitrogen.

He'll beat me, Angela said. *He'll scream at me and then beat me for not getting rid of The Demon Mother on my own.*

He'll hit us, Laura said simultaneously. *He must be so pissed that we didn't solve this problem by ourselves.*

However, Phillip bowed his head and stared at his feet. *It's my fault.*

Angela, realizing she could hear him, jumped back into control. "I'll channel you, but only if you don't scream at me." Rage supplanted her fear. "I won't harm myself for your pleasure."

Phillip nodded and then faced the Demon Mother.

Angela took a deep breath and mentally relaxed, letting his words through: "It's my fault. You're here for me. Leave my son out of it."

"You have nothing I want," The Demon Mother said.

"But that is all you have," Phillip said through Angela. "You were promised things. Marilyn and I promised you anything you asked for because we thought we could control you with magick. But you must know we can't deliver, and honestly, we never intended to. And no one can. Whatever anger you have, it should be aimed at Marilyn and me. Michael Fredrick owes you nothing. He did not consent to have his blood spilled. Marilyn and I took it from him by force."

Angela pulled away, flashbacks exploding her concentration. She felt pain in her groin, felt hands gripping her, hurting her, holding her down. She heard heavy panting in her ear. And she felt the rage, the volcanic lava rage, of knowing her mother stood there and watched her father harmed her in front of their demonic altar, focused only on getting what she wanted and not caring what price her child paid for it. Angela closed her eyes and turned away, curling in on herself.

Michael found himself in control of the body, and he shuddered as Fredrick's, Laura's, Dietrich's, and Angela's pain, fear, and anger exploded through him, volcanic ash in their shared soul. He uncurled and glared at the specter of his father. "You betrayed me in every way a father can!"

Phillip's shoulders slumped, and he stared at the floor, not arguing. *There is punishment for me. Not the Christian hell, as you were taught. But a punishment I can't deny, avoid, or contain. I must bear this sentence like a prisoner. I must pay you what you're owed.*

"There's no way you can pay a debt for what you did to me," Fredrick said, bursting into control of their body. "You beat me, raped me, and used my blood to summon evil entities like that." He pointed at The Demon Mother. "And you made me watch you sacrifice innocent animals on altars. I'll never forgive you."

You don't have to, Phillip said simply, more calm and rational than he ever had been in life.

"Touching, I'm sure," The Demon Mother said. "But I'm bored now. All of you are going to leave, and you won't be coming back."

No, don't let it go! Phillip shouted to Fredrick.

"I don't know what to do!" Fredrick yelled back. "I've got DID, you dumb fuck, and it's your fault. If you taught me what to do, then I can't remember it now!"

The back door blew open, and gale-force winds blasted through the kitchen, aided by the broken window.

"Out! Out! *Out!*" The Demon Mother screeched.

"Kali, *kreem!*" Wendy shouted.

Toni, Corey, Heather, and Chalsey yelled dismissals as well.

Fredrick grabbed his Miraculous Medal off the altar and clutched it in his hand. "Hail Mary, full of grace, the Lord is with thee!"

The entity vanished, along with Phillip Anderson, and the winds died out. Silence descended upon the room, unnatural-feeling after the storm. Fredrick finally detected heavy breathing from several people.

"I will meet with my fellow high priestesses and discuss this outcome," Wendy said. "I don't scare easily, and I never quit. We will find a way. It's important to know your blood was used to summon that thing, Fredrick. I don't blame you for not remembering, but it changes things."

Fredrick nodded and exhaled. *Goddammit, I wish this had ended it. I wanted this to be over.*

I don't know if I can sleep tonight, Angela said.

We'll stay at Chalsey's apartment and let her cast an enormous sacred circle around the bed, Michael replied.

Reassured by this plan, Fredrick helped the circle clean up the altar.

CHAPTER 21

THE CHARIOT VII

IN THE MORNING, MICHAEL AWAKENED IN Chalsey's bed, finding her still asleep. It was 8:00, the June sun already blasting the morning hot, and all over Ashleigh, girls were being stuffed into dresses and hauled off to church to be reassured that their God thought they were unworthy.

Grumpy but calmer than he had expected, Michael climbed out of bed, waking Chalsey. "I'm going back. I'm going back to Mom's, and I'm going to talk to Dad's spirit. We know who the second human spirit is now: Phillip Anderson I. I'm going to give him a piece of my mind, and then I'm going to ask him to help."

Chalsey sat up, her curls half-flattened and tousled. Gray smudges decorated the inner corners of her eyes. "You sure you won't wait for Wendy?"

"Yep." Michael stepped over the circle of tarot cards Chalsey had made around her bed and headed to the bathroom.

Two hours later, Fredrick pulled his white Camry into his mother's gravel driveway. Chalsey and Toni had both opted to come with him. "I need to be alone first. You two have a nice Sunday morning drive for thirty minutes and come back."

"You're not going inside by yourself, are you?" Toni's voice was sharp.

"Nope. I'll stay outside. I mean, The Demon Mother can appear outside, sure." Fredrick climbed out of his car and tossed Chalsey the keys. "But I have a gut feeling that the front yard is the safest spot on the property. They didn't kill any animals out here." *Not that Angela and Laura can remember, anyway.*

"Okay." Chalsey didn't sound fully convinced, but she transferred to the driver's side, and she and Toni left.

Fredrick crossed the grass to the towering oak tree in the front yard. Sitting between two roots, he gazed up into the boughs, remembering the tire swing he'd had as a kid. Painful, sweet memories returned to him: His father hanging the tire swing, his father putting together his toys on Christmas morning, his father teaching him how to ride a bike, his father teaching him how to drive. "I don't understand you," he murmured into the warm breeze. The leaves tossed and whispered. "Who were you people? Mom would stay home with me when I was sick and dote on me but then also make me channel spirits for her. She would cry over a dead cat on the road but murder a squirrel on an altar. You built me a tree house in the backyard but then slipped into my bedroom at night and raped me. You make no sense. Come here and explain yourself."

The spirit of Phillip appeared before Fredrick. *I'm sorry. I drew arbitrary lines in my mind, telling myself I would do this, but never do that. I considered myself morally superior to men who harmed their wives and children because at least I only harm my children. The instant I died, my non-logic was ripped away. I saw myself exactly as I was. I experienced everything I ever did.*

"So your life flashed before your eyes?" Fredrick didn't worry about the neighbors seeing him talk to himself. They'd be at church, anyway. "And you saw all the evil you committed?"

I saw both the good and the evil. Phillip walked over and pretended to sit by Fredrick. His ghostly form stretched out its legs on the grass. He wore a gray pinstripe suit, an Oxford shirt, and a black tie, looking like his typical working self. *More than seeing it, I relived it from the viewpoint of everyone whose life I touched. I felt myself help traumatized clients. I felt myself violate both you and Roger.*

Fredrick's stomach lurched, clenching and roiling and tumbling. A flash of fear burned him at the idea of reliving everything he'd ever done. "I guess it pays to do more good than harm."

Considerably. Phillip gazed at Fredrick. *I'm dead, but I will still try to help you now. If you wish it.*

"You gave me DID, you know." Fredrick went back for it, needing the acknowledgement. He felt his System with him, all of them demanding answers.

Yes, I know. I knew before I died. Phillip glanced over the yard. *I could tell by the time you were two that you were already neuro-divergent. By the time you were six, I was sure you had developed DID.*

"Didn't stop you for a second, huh?" Fredrick's bitterness climbed his throat as acid reflux.

No. I had an undiagnosed condition of my own, and I hid deeper and deeper inside of it. Phillip peered back at Fredrick. *I knew I needed help, but I refused to get it. It was a matter of my pride, my hubris. Your mom knew I needed help, too. She never once confronted me about it. Not that I'm putting the blame on her. My mental health was my responsibility. I'm just explaining.*

"Was Mom bipolar?"

The psychologists still alive would diagnose her as such, Phillip said. *Human psychology is clearer once you're on the other side.*

Fredrick nodded. "You noticed, but you did nothing."

I thought she had three or four co-morbid personality disorders, and I did nothing to help her. Nothing real. I painted myself a martyr: the psychologist who even takes a severely wounded person as a spouse.

"Disgusting. Arrogant."

And more. Phillip remained calm, unruffled, a hundred times more the man in death than in life. *It was abusive.*

Satisfied for now, Fredrick pointed at the house. "How do I get rid of that entity? I know that's not Mom."

No. It's the creature we summoned. Even if you wished to speak with your mother, you wouldn't be allowed yet. Or, more to the point, she wouldn't be allowed to talk to you yet. I've been dead for 24 earth years. That makes a difference.

Fredrick felt Phillip mentally snort. It was an odd sensation.

We were incredibly arrogant. And stupid, Phillip said. *We had no idea the seals were copied wrong, and we wouldn't have cared even if we had known. We were brash enough to think that our abilities combined were enough to control the spirits we summoned. So we summoned That Creature repeatedly. It was already powerful, but it fed off of us spiritually.*

"Your abilities?" Michael and Laura asked together, switching in. "What abilities?"

The ones you inherited, Phillip said. *I had the Scottish second sight, as we called it. I also could channel spirits, but I didn't understand that while I was still alive. I misinterpreted what I was experiencing. My extra sensory "sight" gave me flashes of psychic insights and knowledge.*

Angela switched in. "So you gave me the ability Mom abused."

Phillip bowed his head.

"And Mom?" Laura asked. "What could she do?"

You would say she was a powerful spell-caster. Phillip shook his head. *She could make any spell she found work for her, and she could write new ones. It was her confidence that overcame the botched half-copy we had of* The Greater Key of Solomon. *She was breathtaking in her strength, but sadly, she only used it for abusive and cruel ends.*

Fredrick switched in again and sighed. "I don't remember any of this yet, but the others do. And I've lived with the trauma, regardless." He stared at the apparition. Like Flapper Marilyn, Phillip was see-through. "You seemed to think yesterday that I knew how to contain the entity, but none of us remember how. What do we do?"

Laura switched in again. "Better yet, do you really think I inherited Mom's ability to cast any spell she laid eyes on?"

I know you did, Phillip said. *You cast three-fourths of every spell we did. We made you do it for us because you were stronger than your mother.*

Outrage fired throughout Laura and the entire System, flashing through their body and leaving an internal sunburn.

"Fucking user pieces of shit," Angela spat, making use of their adult vocabulary.

I'm hardly able to deny that, Phillip said, *much less take offense to your assessment.* He pointed at the house. *Your older friend is right. Use the grave dirt. And whatever you do, don't spill your own blood. Get red wine and use it as a symbol. Pour it over the dirt and command the evil entity to attach itself to the dirt. You must be the one to do it. It must be your spell, your casting power. You have what it takes. Then take the dirt to the cemetery. And don't believe anything the entity says when it comes.*

"Because it always lies," Fredrick said.

Always. Phillip stood, or perhaps mimed standing. *Call*

me back if there is trouble, but you are burning your spiritual energy by talking to me. Save the rest for your spell.

"Wait," Laura called. "There's one last thing we don't know. What did you offer that entity in payment?"

Phillip stared at his feet for a moment and then met Laura's gaze. *We promised it an end to its suffering by giving it its own life and its own body.* He vanished.

Dietrich's horror struck through the entire System. *But that really is impossible!*

Fredrick understood immediately. "The whole point of all of this is that The Demon Mother wants *our* body. The real Marilyn Smith Anderson wanted our body to be female, but this thing just wants our body regardless of its shape."

Fucking hell no, Michael said.

"Definitely hell no." Fredrick leaned his head against the tree trunk and considered the directions. "Mom has a bottle of red wine for cooking."

Let's do it, Laura said. *I can remember casting a few spells for them. Apparently not all of them, but a few. We can do this.*

I remember casting a few, Angela said. *Like Laura, I know it can't be everything Dad referred to. But some. I agree we can do this.*

"Then we'll wait for Toni and Chalsey, and we'll do it," Fredrick said.

When Chalsey and Toni returned, Fredrick and Michael took turns explaining the conversation and the directions. They all stood under the oak tree, both for shade and apparent protection. The Demon Mother hadn't appeared to disrupt Phillip.

"Well, it can't go worse than yesterday." Chalsey clutched

her purse to her chest. "And the dirt is still in the house, sealed."

Toni bowed his head. "I won't lie. I think this is the most terrifying thing ever. Chalsey, you've got the most badass lady balls I've ever seen."

Chalsey chuckled.

"I feel like a shrieking 1930s cartoon woman by comparison." Toni lifted his head and met Fredrick's gaze. "But I won't leave your side. No way. This is too serious."

I'm falling in love with you. Fredrick squeezed Toni's shoulder. "You've been hanging in there just fine. And thank you."

Toni cringed, clearly not convinced.

Fredrick released Toni, and they marched up to the front door, Fredrick letting them inside.

The Demon Mother stood in the doorway into the hall. Each orange conch earring was the size of her head and looked like malformed antlers. "I won't let you do it."

"Mother Mary, keep it out of my way." Fredrick stalked through the living and dining rooms and into the kitchen, where the dirt was sealed in an old jar. The jar sat on the kitchen island, a tarot card waiting beside it. This card showed a man standing in a chariot that was drawn by two sphinxes, one white and one black. *The Chariot,* it read.

Chalsey stopped at Fredrick's elbow. "Determination, willpower, control, focus, and success."

"Message received and understood." Fredrick turned toward the cabinet over the stove and pulled out his mother's cooking wine. Michael wiggled into the captain's chair with him, transforming them into Fredrick-Michael. *Let's do it.*

Toni grabbed the pentacle around his neck and pointed with his finger as if it were a wand. "By the power of Brigid, I cast our sacred circle." He drew a circle in the surrounding air.

Chalsey pulled a vial of ashes from her purse, having

taught Michael long ago that ashes from altar incense were sacred. She uncapped the vial and sprinkled their circle with ashes.

Fredrick-Michael opened the jar.

The Demon Mother appeared on the opposite side of the island, just outside the sacred circle. "You can never stop me! You can never get rid of me! I'll haunt you for all time!"

It always lies, Angela said.

Fredrick-Michael ignored the entity. "Mother Mary, bless this wine and empower it with my blood. My blood for my blood. I will break this contract."

"No!" The Demon Mother shrieked. "You can't do that! It won't work."

"Thanks for telling me it will." Fredrick-Michael smirked at her. He poured red wine over his hand, imagining that his palm had been cut, and held his hand over the dirt. He continued to pour the wine slowly, letting it drip down into the jar like blood.

With Dietrich's help, Angela crammed herself into the captain's chair and then Laura as well. Dietrich shifted everyone around and then hopped in after them, momentarily fusing them into a single consciousness.

The Combined Fredrick-Michael felt a spell form and flow out of them.

"Mother Mary, full of grace, take this creature from this place,

Take this creature, take its soul, forge it into Earth below.

By my blood, this is set, the blood conditions have been met,

To the grave it will go, its face again to never show. Amen!"

The Combined Fredrick-Michael sneered at the screaming entity. "I command you to depart into this soil!"

The Demon Mother vanished, its screams and its spirit pressure popping away. Using their free hand, the Combined

Fredrick-Michael smacked the lid on the jar and screwed it shut. The jar was hot to their touch.

"Holy shit!" Toni gasped, shuddering. "That was awful."

"But it worked." Chalsey squeezed the Combined Fredrick-Michael's shoulder.

Fredrick and his fellow self-states peeled back apart, reaching their limit of staying combined.

That was amazing, Laura said. *I didn't even know we could do that.*

Toni squeezed Fredrick's other shoulder. "You completely kicked ass."

"Thanks." Fredrick washed his hands. "Now let's get this thing to the cemetery."

Chalsey drove, and Toni and Fredrick sat in the back seat, both of Fredrick's hands wrapped around the jar of wine-soaked dirt. Fredrick vibrated with tension. *This has to work.*

The Careyville Memorial Cemetery was mostly modern and filled with granite gravestones, angels, and obelisks. The grass was neatly mowed, and flowers decorated half the graves. Chalsey drove around two loops to Fredrick's parents' plot, and they all climbed out.

As Fredrick walked to the grave, a sense of finality filled his chest. *I won't come back here again. I refuse.* The grave was still covered in flowers, little U.S. flags, and even an angel figurine.

Chalsey snatched the angel and hurled it against the granite gravestone. "Sorry, whoever left that, but we can't let images of angels anywhere near this grave."

"Definitely not." Fredrick knelt by the dirt, and Michael joined him in the captain's chair again. Together, they dug up a corner and then emptied the jar's contents into the hole they'd made. "I command you to be bound to this grave forever." They covered the wine-soaked dirt with fresh earth. "There."

"I can feel the entity is anchored now," Chalsey said.

Fredrick stood and walked away. "Don't look back."

Chalsey and Toni fell into step beside him, and none of them glanced back. They piled into the car, Chalsey driving again, and left.

Just like with the Catholic cemetery, Fredrick felt something dark and heavy rip out of his back as they drove away. Out on the main road, Fredrick felt something else dark and heavy rip away. And finally, when they turned onto Fredrick's childhood street, he felt a final dark, heavy lump rip free.

"'Free at last, free at last,'" Fredrick quoted the same song as Martin Luther King, Jr. had. "'Thank God almighty, I'm free at last.'"

When they entered the house, the entire structure seemed to glow with sunlight, the air lighter and cleaner somehow. And before them, on the kitchen island, were 21 of the 22 major arcana of the tarot laid out in an arc, in order from The Fool, card 0, to Judgment, card 21.

"There's only one left." Chalsey smiled. "I wonder when you'll get it."

"And the final one is fitting," Toni said.

Fredrick wasn't sure what Toni meant, not understanding what the last card would be. But Flapper Marilyn appeared by the island and smiled at him.

Thank you, she said. *You did it. Now heal, so this cycle can end for good.*

"I will," Fredrick said.

She bowed and vanished.

CHAPTER 22

THE WORLD XXI

FREDRICK RECLINED ON THE PLUSH SOFA IN HIS NEW therapist's office. The room was earth-toned: brown carpet, two brown-striped couches, and a green chair. Ferns sat in two corners of the room, a desk in the third, and a water fountain in the fourth. This was Fredrick's second appointment, and he found the room just as relaxing the second time as the first.

His therapist, Dr. Jane, sat across from him on the other sofa. Her short brown hair was parted on one side, and her black cat eye glasses sat perched on the end of her nose. She had a nose ring, pentacle earrings, and a dozen tattoos that were offset by her ruffled crimson shirt and black gypsy skirt. She was like Chalsey, except with tattoos. Fredrick liked her.

"So what's been happening since your last visit?" Dr. Jane asked.

"Mom's house sold in the auction and at market value, too," Fredrick said. "The internet auction went great. Between my mother's bank accounts, stocks, and property, I've inherited $750,000."

"That's a lot of money."

Fredrick gazed at the water fountain, which was fashioned

out of bamboo. Water trickled out of the top stalk down into another two. "Well, it means I can pay for the next 30 years of therapy that I'll need thanks to what my parents did to me. In a sense, I guess I could say they owe it to me. But I may donate part of it to animal shelters or animal rescue organizations in honor of all the animals they sacrificed." He had given Dr. Jane an overview of his trauma history.

"Do you feel that would help you achieve a measure of peace?"

"Perhaps. And it seems fair to me." Fredrick glanced back at Dr. Jane. "I know it will take the rest of my life to heal from this, but I'm determined to succeed. My parents' horror show doesn't get to ruin my whole life. And I always felt that there should be a way to heal from my panic attacks, not simply to learn how to live with them."

Dr. Jane nodded. She held a notebook in one hand and a pen in the other, and she tapped the pen against her jaw. "Determining the source of the panic attacks and using EMDR therapy to process that originating incident is the answer. Sometimes there are multiple incidents to process, but there's a technique called Float Back we can use for that. You don't have to live with panic. Or depression. You and your brain can both heal."

For the first time in his 43 years of life, Fredrick took hope. "I prayed the same prayer every night for 14 years: 'God, whoever and whatever you really are, help me discover the real me. Who I am should be between only you and me, and no humans should weigh in on it.'" He snorted and resumed watching the flowing water in the fountain. "I never imagined the answer would be that I have DID, I'm agendered, and my parents were demon-summoning individuals who caused harm to many people and were in the SOMH." He laughed. "Summarizing it like that really makes it funny in a grim-dark way."

"Are you glad you prayed the prayer?"

Fredrick focused on Dr. Jane again. "Yes. Even though I no longer believed in any deities, I prayed it because I was tired of living in nonstop anxiety and suffering debilitating panic attacks and depression. Now I can begin my healing journey for real. Although the truth is horrifying, it was worth it. Not knowing my fear was really about sexual violence and animal sacrifice made the fear unmanageable."

"It always works that way," Dr. Jane said. "We simply have to be careful not to push our minds faster than they can handle once we work on the traumatic material. Which reminds me, would you consent to take the MID 6.0? It's a diagnostic that will assess your level of dissociation and PTSD."

"Sure. Give me more insight into myself." Fredrick paused, checking with Michael and the others, and everyone was on board. "All my self-states agree to it."

Dr. Jane jotted down a note. "Perfect. All right, let's discuss what your first EMDR target will be, then. By 'target,' we mean the negative belief you wish to get rid of. You'll select a specific traumatic memory, determine what negative belief you accepted about yourself because of the trauma, and then use EMDR to process that trauma and get rid of the negative belief."

"Let's start with the sexual trauma, then," Fredrick said. "Michael has a girlfriend of many years, and I have a new boyfriend. I'd kinda like to be sexually functional."

Forty minutes later, Fredrick left with a treatment plan and a new life underway.

<hr>

At 7:00 that evening, Fredrick stood over his stove, watching supper cook. He was fixing spaghetti and garlic bread for his

date with Toni. The weekend before, Toni had blown him away with a homemade meal of *cacio e pepe* potato gnocchi. Fredrick wasn't a fancy cook, but he was doing his best.

As Fredrick pulled two plates out of the cabinet, he saw a tarot card on the counter. "Finally!" Flapper Marilyn had visited him twice in the intervening eight days, but she hadn't delivered the 22nd card. Fredrick set down the plates and grabbed the card. It showed a woman surrounded by a victory wreath and holding two staffs or wands. Fredrick smiled. He'd already memorized the card's meaning: completion, achievement, fulfillment, a sense of belonging, wholeness, and victory.

The doorbell rang, and Fredrick swept to the door, admitting Toni and giving him a hug. Toni carried a brown paper bag.

"God, that smells good." Toni held Fredrick's hand as they returned to the kitchen. "And I'm starving."

"Good. I fixed enough for four people." Fredrick grabbed the pot of pasta and poured it into the colander.

Toni set the bag on the counter and pulled out a bottle of merlot. "Well, here's my contribution."

"Awesome. Works for me." Fredrick turned off the burners and then served the noodles. "Every time I see red wine for the rest of my life, I'm going to think of defeating that evil entity." He laughed, a sound of pure joy.

"There's a great association." Toni uncorked the wine bottle.

As they sat down at the table with spaghetti, garlic bread, and merlot, Fredrick became pensive. "I keep thinking of a Robert Frost poem. I feel like I'll be 70, or maybe only 60, and saying:

> *"I shall be telling this with a sigh*
> *Somewhere ages and ages hence:*

Two roads diverged in a wood, and I—
I took the one less traveled by,
And that has made all the difference."

Toni smiled. "Because you took the road to healing when your parents refused? And now you have this long tale that makes all the difference?"

"Exactly." Fredrick took a sip of wine and savored the complex flavor of blackberries, plum, and a note of chocolate. "The evil entity aimed to terrorize me more and more, and I just kept seeing increasingly large orange conch earrings on it: symbols of hope, optimism, willpower, courage, strength, and wisdom. Even with my memory fragmented and my self-states disconnected and unable to communicate, I—or rather we— continued to fight."

"That's beautiful. And you won." Toni held up his wineglass. "I propose a toast, then: To hope, strength, and wisdom."

"Cheers." Fredrick clinked his glass against Toni's. *And to both Chalsey's and now your love.*

It made all the difference.

Author's Note

I would like to comment upon the journey of writing this novel. My life partner, Keith, and I both have been clinically diagnosed with dissociative identity disorder (DID). However, there are almost no positive or realistic portrayals of DID in the media. Therefore, I set out to write a novel in which the protagonist has DID and to realistically portray that character's experiences using a mixture of Keith's and my experiences.

I particularly was interested in showing how someone with DID can still be capable of working a fulltime job, having romantic relationships, and having a normal life. Not all people with DID are incapacitated by switching between self-states (parts) and losing time. It is possible to establish, with therapy, the ability to communicate with each other and work together harmoniously. Engendering cooperation and harmony has been a different process for Keith's and my Systems, but we have both succeeded. Recovering our memories and the traumatic material from our childhoods has been different as well, and so has processing that trauma in therapy. However, both Keith and I have had great success with EMDR—the only therapy that has ever helped either one of us—and are healing.

In saying this, I want to be clear that Keith and I only represent two people with DID. Each case of DID is different because brains are unique, and not every person with DID responds well to EMDR, either. There is a wide variety of life experiences among those with DID. My goal is not to represent everyone. My goal is to make a break with two common stereotypes in the media: the person with DID being a killer, and the person with DID being an incoherent mess who has no real life. These two portrayals are far too common —and are deeply hurtful and insulting. DID is more common than psychologists first believed, and people who have it deserve to not be eroticized or criminalized as "interesting" specimens. We are people, too.

I hope you have found *The Truth of a Kaleidoscope Mind* to be both an entertaining paranormal novel and educational about the reality of DID.

Patrick Bryce Wright

Acknowledgments

Several books and authors were mentioned in this novel because of their positive impact on my life: John Bradshaw, who wrote *Healing the Shame That Binds You, Bradshaw On: The Family,* and *Family Secrets*; Lundy Bancroft, who wrote *Why Does He Do That? Inside the Minds of Angry and Controlling Men*; and Merlin Stone, who wrote *When God Was a Woman.*

Also, I must thank my life partner, Keith J. Miller, for his assistance as a sounding board, reader, and editor, as well as his ceaseless support of me and my writing.

About the Author

© Patrick Bryce Wright

Patrick Bryce Wright, an unconventional English professor adorned with tattoos and piercings, whose passion for supernatural horror, fantasy, and science fiction fuels his impactful storytelling. Patrick proudly embraces his neurodivergence, third-gender identity, and survivor status, all of which enrich the narratives within his books.

As a vocal LGBTQIA+ activist, Patrick focuses on portraying diverse characters in his novels, aiming for sensitive depictions of the queer, d/Deaf, and dissociative identity disorder communities. Armed with degrees in English and Psychology, Patrick weaves intricate tales that reflect his academic background.

www.patrickbrycewright.com

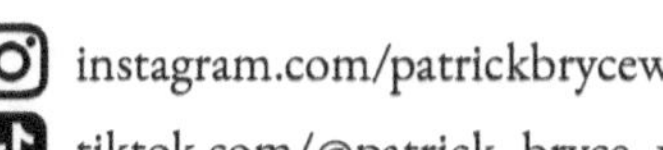

instagram.com/patrickbrycewright

tiktok.com/@patrick_bryce_wright

x.com/PBryceWright

youtube.com/PatrickBryceWright